LAND OF THE SHADOW

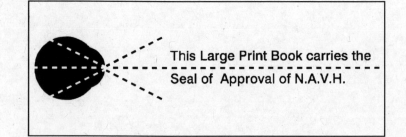

This Large Print Book carries the
Seal of Approval of N.A.V.H.

APPOMATTOX SAGA

LAND OF THE SHADOW

1861-1863
ADVENTURE AND ROMANCE THRIVE
DURING THE WAR BETWEEN THE STATES

GILBERT MORRIS

THORNDIKE PRESS
A part of Gale, Cengage Learning

GALE
CENGAGE Learning

Farmington Hills, Mich • San Francisco • New York • Waterville, Maine
Meriden, Conn • Mason, Ohio • Chicago

GALE
CENGAGE Learning®

LIBRARY OF CONGRESS CATALOGING-IN-PUBLICATION DATA

Morris, Gilbert.
    Land of the shadow : 1861–1863 adventure and romance thrive during the War Between the States / by Gilbert Morris. — Large print edition.
        pages ; cm. — (Thorndike Press large print Christian historical fiction) (Appomattox saga ; #4)
    ISBN-13: 978-1-4104-6640-2 (hardcover)
    ISBN-10: 1-4104-6640-X (hardcover)
    1. United States—History—Civil War, 1861–1865—Fiction. 2. Large type books. I. Title.
PS3563.O8742L36 2014
813'.54—dc23   2013047812

Published in 2014 by arrangement with Barbour Publishing, Inc.

Printed in Mexico
1 2 3 4 5 6 7 18 17 16 15 14

GENEALOGY OF THE ROCKLIN FAMILY

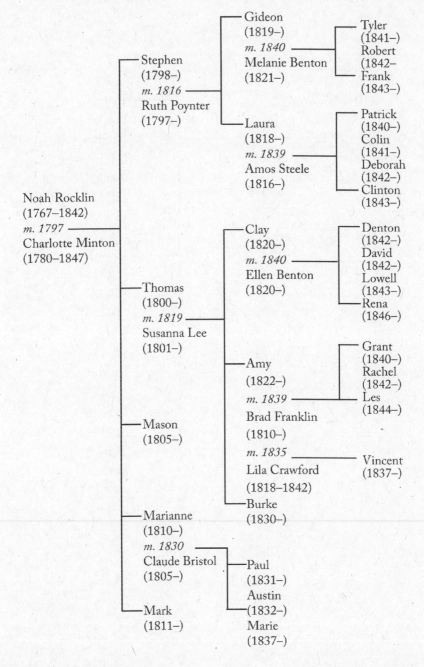

Noah Rocklin
(1767–1842)
m. 1797
Charlotte Minton
(1780–1847)

Stephen
(1798–)
m. 1816
Ruth Poynter
(1797–)

Gideon
(1819–)
m. 1840
Melanie Benton
(1821–)

Tyler
(1841–)
Robert
(1842–
Frank
(1843–)

Laura
(1818–)
m. 1839
Amos Steele
(1816–)

Patrick
(1840–)
Colin
(1841–)
Deborah
(1842–)
Clinton
(1843–)

Thomas
(1800–)
m. 1819
Susanna Lee
(1801–)

Clay
(1820–)
m. 1840
Ellen Benton
(1820–)

Denton
(1842–)
David
(1842–)
Lowell
(1843–)
Rena
(1846–)

Amy
(1822–)
m. 1839
Brad Franklin
(1810–)
m. 1835
Lila Crawford
(1818–1842)

Grant
(1840–)
Rachel
(1842–)
Les
(1844–)

Vincent
(1837–)

Burke
(1830–)

Mason
(1805–)

Marianne
(1810–)
m. 1830
Claude Bristol
(1805–)

Paul
(1831–)
Austin
(1832–)
Marie
(1837–)

Mark
(1811–)

GENEALOGY OF THE YANCY FAMILY

Buford Yancy
(1807–)
m. 1829 ————————

Mattie Satterfield
(1813–1851)

——— Royal
(1832–)
Melora
(1834–)
Zack
(1836–)
Cora
(1837–)
Lonnie
(1843–)
Bobby
(1844–)
Rose
(1845–)
Josh
(1847–)
Martha
(1849–)
——— Toby
(1851–)

To June Parsons

I like old things — old cars, old books, old houses.

Most of all, I like old friends.

The new friends might not make it.

Some are lost through geography — separation by space. Others find I do not wear so well, so they trade me in on a whole new model.

Now, as I grow older, I find myself clinging more tightly to that little band I have known and loved for years. And when I make my list of dear, dear friends who have not failed me or turned aside ("We few — we happy, happy few," as the poet says!),

I always find you, June!

EDITOR'S NOTE:

This book begins shortly after the family reunion that takes place in chapter 15 of book 3, *Where Honor Dwells.*

■■■■

PART ONE:
THE OUTSIDER —
NOVEMBER 1861

■■■■

CHAPTER 1
RETURN OF THE PRODIGAL

Paul Bristol was an expert in three distinct areas: painting, horses — and women.

It was the latter of these that enabled Bristol to understand exactly what had brought Luci DeSpain to the party at his parents' house one November evening. He had descended the beautifully constructed curving stairway expecting to find only his own family, but his father met him, saying, "The DeSpains are joining us tonight, Paul."

Instantly a tiny alarm went off inside Paul Bristol's head, a warning device that had enabled him, at the ripe old age of thirty-one, to still be single. He said nothing about this, however, and spent the evening never more than a few feet away from the beautiful and charming Luci. And somehow, between visiting with the DeSpains and dinner, he found himself alone with her in the long gallery, examining the family portraits. Luci, he knew, had seen all the portraits

13

before, but she stopped to examine each one, sometimes touching Paul's arm when one of them impressed her.

It was when the couple paused under a fine portrait of Noah Rocklin, Paul's grandfather on his mother's side, that the tiny alarm began to ring more insistently. Luci was petite and had to look up to Paul as she said, "What a fine-looking man, Paul. . . ." She had not seemed to move, yet somehow her body pressed against Paul, and as she looked up, her blue eyes were bright and her lips softly pursed, saying, "All you Rocklin men are such tall fellows!"

Ah, the chase was on. . . . Paul held back the smile of amusement that wanted to curve his lips and simply spoke his lines, as smoothly as any actor in a play: "And you DeSpain women are all beautiful." He needed no stage direction to know what came next, and so he took her in his arms and kissed her thoroughly. It was a long kiss, and Bristol was somewhat surprised at Luci's eager response. But only somewhat surprised.

As the kiss ended, he knew she would pull away and rebuke him soundly, all the while giving him the impression that she was not really angry.

"Paul — you mustn't do that!" Luci cried,

pushing him away. Paul almost applauded and said, "Bravo!" so well did the girl perform. Unfortunately for Luci, however, his attention had been drawn away from her by the image reflected in the full-length mirror just to Luci's left. There Paul saw a fine-looking couple embracing — but it brought back memories of other images he'd seen in that same mirror. The same man but different girls . . . several different girls, all playing their parts beautifully, all determined to convince Paul he could not live without them.

This has always been a good hunting ground, he thought sardonically. His gaze went back to Luci, who was watching him with a slight frown. He had missed his cue, and it would take some quick thinking to keep the girl from growing miffed. He smiled at her, a smile full of both apology and promise, and said, "I beg your pardon, Luci. But you don't know what a beautiful girl like you can do to a man!"

That ought to brighten her up, he thought and once again almost applauded when she lowered her lashes demurely, a slight smile playing at her beautifully shaped lips. "I do fear, Paul, that you've been spoiled by all those terrible women in Europe," Luci said, pursing her mouth into a pout. "I've heard

15

all about them, about how free they are with their favors." She looked up suddenly and met his eyes. "Do you think so?" she demanded.

Ah no, my dear, you won't catch me in any careless admissions, he thought, and he looked at her blankly. "Do I think you've heard about them?"

Luci laughed. She did it so well — with a fine, tinkling sound — that Paul suspected she practiced the thing. "No, silly! I mean, do you think the women over there are . . . I mean, do they . . . ?"

Paul enjoyed Luci's inability to ask straight out what was on her mind, and took full advantage of this opportunity to tease her. "Yes, I'm afraid they do," he remarked rather piously. "I must say that it's wonderful to be back in America with respectable ladies again — ladies such as yourself, my dear, who would never dream of employing such coquettish ways."

Luci paused for a moment, and her eyes narrowed just the slightest bit at the faint irony in Paul's tone. Surely he wasn't implying that she was the least bit like those loose women! What she wanted at that moment, more than anything else, was to go deeper into the "coquettish ways" of those women, but before she could think of a way to

16

broach the subject, Bristol forestalled her.

"I think I heard the dinner chime, Luci," he said, extending his elbow gallantly. She had no choice but to slip her hand through it and follow as he led her out of the gallery and down the hall. As the two of them took their places, side by side, at the long cherry table, Luci had the distinct sense she'd just been bested at her own game. But, never one to give up too easily, she put on a bright smile and exclaimed at the beautiful setting before her, remarking over the fine white tablecloth and the way the table all but sparkled with crystal glasses and gleaming silver. From the corner of her eye, she caught Paul's admiring expression. (She would not have felt quite so pleased by it, however, had she realized it stemmed not so much from his appreciation of her charm and beauty as from his appreciation of her ability to regroup so quickly.)

Paul's father spoke his usual rather oratorical blessing, and for the next hour the talk flowed around the table freely. There were only eight at the meal, including Paul's parents, his sister, Marie, and his brother, Austin — plus Luci and her parents. They were all old friends and knew everything there was to know about each other. Paul, having been in Europe for a good part of the last three years, found himself feeling like a foreigner. He listened to Luci's conversation and decided he'd be as surprised if she uttered a single brilliant and unusual speech as if his mare, Queenie, were to turn and speak to him on their morning ride!

Not that Luci was an ignorant person, far from it. But her world was bounded by invisible strands that circled Richmond. If an event didn't happen in Richmond, then — to Luci and her friends — it might as well take place on the moon!

Paul's lips thinned as he listened to the conversation so common in polite society. He could usually hold his own in such conversation by drawing on one of his three areas of expertise. However, the mere thought of doing so bored him to distraction. For all his well-developed social graces, only his experiences with fast horses had brought him much satisfaction. He was admired as an expert breeder and had made quite a bit of cash riding his own races. As for his other two areas of involvement, he had gained little money and only slight recognition as a painter . . . and his extensive success with women had made him slightly contemptuous of most females.

Perhaps most people secretly despise what

comes too easily, and Paul Bristol had experienced few rebuffs from the women of Richmond. The corps of mothers in that city — those with eligible daughters — had practically flung their female offspring at Bristol. As for the gaggle of perfumed, powdered, and polished young women, they themselves were more than willing to be flung.

There was, of course, a sociological factor in this eager sacrifice: What else was a young daughter of Southern aristocracy to do except marry well? Women in the lower classes might become schoolteachers, but the daughters of high society were taught as soon as they were able to function that the acquisition of a husband was their single hope of happiness.

Paul Bristol had the dubious distinction of being one of those young men who met every requirement of both hawkeyed mothers and dewy-eyed maidens. His family was good, for the Bristols were of that part of the aristocracy that — though not rich like the Hugers, Lees, and Wainscots of Virginia — owned fine plantations and had exactly the *proper* number of slaves. That is, enough to be impressive and do the work, but not so many that they got underfoot or made the family seem showy. Claude Bristol,

Paul's father, was ornamental and fairly useless, but his wife, the former Marianne Rocklin, was capable enough to keep the plantation from disaster. She saw to it that enough cotton was grown to pay for her husband's fine clothes, horses, and gambling losses — in addition, she made sure there was enough extra to enable her family to keep up the style of living demanded by the Southern aristocracy. This being the case, Paul Bristol easily met the requirements set by parents who sought suitable husbands for their daughters.

Paul himself provided an enticing opportunity for the young women. He was handsome, witty, and wicked — that, combined with his family and money, made Paul an irresistible combination guaranteed to flutter a young woman's heart. The trouble was, Paul had yet to find even one woman who stirred within him more than a passing interest. He glanced again at Luci DeSpain and sighed. Perhaps he was looking for something that didn't exist. . . .

The turkey had been devastated, and house slaves started carrying in freshly made pies — pecan, pumpkin, apple, and cherry. House Mary — so called to set her off from Field Mary — knew Paul well enough to bring him a wedge of cherry, his favorite. "You thinking this pie will get you a Christmas gift, House Mary?" Paul teased the servant. "Well, I think it might work." He grinned as she protested, then hewed off the tip of the wedge, placed it carefully in his mouth, and chewed slowly. His mother was watching him with a smile, and he winked at her.

"Mother, this piece of pie is worth the trip home from France!" Waving his fork in a salute, he added, "Nothing in Europe to beat it!"

Marianne Bristol's black hair showed traces of gray, but at the age of fifty-one she was still a strikingly beautiful woman. Her eyes were royal blue, and when she smiled, as she did now at her eldest son, dimples appeared on each side of her shapely mouth. "Tell us about the king and queen," she said. Paul smiled at his mother, studying her for a moment. She was wearing a green silk dress and a pair of jade earrings, and Paul thought she was one of the most beautiful women he'd ever seen — and perhaps one of ten women he'd ever known from the land of his birth who could discuss something besides cotton and new dresses.

But as Paul started to repeat the story of his visit at Windsor Castle, his brother, Austin, interrupted. "Paul, never mind all that

— what about recognition from England?" Austin was twenty-nine years old, short and strong with his father's brown hair and eyes. He was caught up in the war that had begun at Fort Sumter in April 1861. Now he was staring defiantly at Paul and added, "England will *have* to recognize the Confederacy! Everybody knows England exists on her looms — and she can't run her looms without cotton!"

"I expect you're right, Austin," Luci's father, Clarence DeSpain, agreed. "England can get along without the North, but not without King Cotton!" DeSpain was a tall, portly man, handsome in a florid way, and had been a secessionist for years.

"Well, sir," Paul said cautiously, "England does have many mills and has used American cotton for a long time."

"So they'll *have* to recognize us, won't they?" Austin insisted.

Paul didn't answer, preferring not to get involved in what he knew would be a less-than-satisfying discussion, but his father asked him directly, "Well, isn't your brother right, Paul? If we don't let England have our cotton, they'll go broke! Isn't that a fact?"

"I'm no expert on British economy," Paul protested, but when he saw that the others would not let him off, he shrugged. His mother was watching him carefully, and he saw something in her expression — a warning of some kind. As tactfully as he could, he began to speak of the situation as he'd seen it when in Europe, knowing all the time his views would find little approval from those who waited so expectantly to hear what he would say.

"I was busy painting while I was in Europe, but what I heard from those who seemed to know the situation isn't too encouraging for the South." He picked up his glass, drank a few swallows, then set the glass down and looked at the circle of faces. "What they say is that England has been having a devil of a time financially, and many of the mills have been forced to close. One fellow who worked for the government told me that there are at least half a million bales of cotton on hand right now — enough to do the British for a long time. He also said that the government has gotten very interested in Egyptian cotton."

"They grow cotton in Egypt?" Paul's sister, Marie, who was seated at his right hand, drew his attention. "I didn't know that."

"Well, they do, and it's long staple, better than our cotton."

"I don't believe it!" Austin said heatedly. Paul listened quietly as Austin and Clarence DeSpain spoke at great length on how England *would* buy American cotton. Neither offered any evidence but spoke what many in the South considered to be truth as solid as the sun rising in the east.

Marianne sat quietly, paying almost no heed to the arguments mouthed by DeSpain and her younger son. She had been somewhat embarrassed at first that her husband and son had had little interest in the war. Now, however, they seemed to grow more interested with each passing day — and to echo the sentiments expressed by so many in the South. Why, she had even heard such declarations once from the lips of Jefferson Davis, the president of the Confederate States of America, himself. So none of this surprised or concerned her.

Of more concern to Marianne was this youngest son of hers, Austin, who lounged across the table from her. She knew him better than he knew himself — for he was an openhearted young man, easy enough to read. And she was proud of him, for he had been a good son, hardworking and happy in making his life at their plantation, Hartsworth. He knew every foot of the plantation, knew the slaves, and was sensitive to the seasons — so much so that Wiley Otes, the overseer, paid him the highest compliment in his power: "Mister Austin, he *knows* when to plant cotton!"

Marianne considered her son thoughtfully. *Austin will marry one day, and he'll bring his bride to Hartsworth. And someday he'll be buried along with his people.* Marianne felt a sudden flush of joy, for she was a woman who loved stability and loathed change. This was one reason she never sought to change her husband or their situation. Though she had long known that her husband was weaker than she, rather than try to change anything, she simply became adept at working behind the scenes, taking care of business, making up for Claude's lacks without drawing attention to herself. She was a proud woman, this Marianne Bristol, and would accept pity from neither man nor woman — especially over her husband's weaknesses, which were legion.

But even Claude she could understand — and forgive. He had been unfaithful to her more than once, and little remained of the fervent love she'd had for him in her youth. He drank too much and cared little for the things that made a plantation profitable. Yet underneath the shallow veneer of manners and charm, Marianne still believed that

25

something of the man she'd fallen in love with remained.

If only he were as fine as he looks! The thought had come often to her, for Claude Bristol was indeed handsome, even at the age of fifty-six. Not tall, but erect, with a pair of sharp brown eyes and evidence of the classic lines of his French blood in his smooth, unlined face. His was not a strong face, but it certainly was an attractive one.

Marie, their only daughter, was a fine combination of the best of her parents. She carried Claude's fine looks, with curly brown hair and large, almost luminous brown eyes, and her mother's common sense and delight in living. Marianne let her gaze rest on Marie, suddenly grateful that her daughter had more substance than Luci DeSpain — indeed, more than any girl she'd ever known.

But Paul! What and who was he, this eldest son of hers? He had been gone for almost three years, but even before he had returned, bringing with him a slightly foreign air, Marianne had found no key to understanding him. He was turned now to face Clarence DeSpain, and slowly she analyzed her son's face. She felt pleasure at his good looks but was perplexed by what lay behind the smooth expression Paul always seemed to wear. She studied his wedge-shaped face, which tapered from a broad forehead and over smooth olive-tinted cheeks to a strong, almost defiant chin. A small scar — the result of a fall during a horse race — marked his chin. A thin black mustache traced the upper lip, and the lower lip was almost too full for a man. She studied the deep-set blue eyes, covered by a shelf of bone capped by black brows. Eyes that could grow tender — at least, that had been so when he was a young boy — or that could blaze with a fierce anger that made one want to step back.

I don't know him at all, Marianne thought. *He's like a stranger. And an unhappy stranger, at that! Even when he smiles, there's some sort of sadness in his eyes.* She tried to think back, to remember when she'd last seen Paul completely happy — but she could not recall such a time.

Marianne's gaze shifted to Luci, and the sight of the girl both pleased and troubled her. *She'd be a fine wife — beautiful and from a good family. And yet . . .* Though she couldn't explain how she knew it, Marianne was certain this wasn't enough for Paul. She frowned. *I wish Luci was interested in Austin.* The thought jumped into her brain, and she shook it away, feeling somehow that there was something disloyal about it. At the same time, she became aware that Mrs. DeSpain was speaking to Paul with a thinly veiled annoyance in her voice:

"But, Paul, surely you see that we *must* fight?" Lillian DeSpain was somewhat overweight and given to wearing dresses that were too young for her, and she was also outspoken at times. She had a round face with light blue eyes and spoke in pronounced tones, accenting her words with short motions of her hands. "What else can we do? The Yankees have put that dreadful embargo on agricultural products, so planters must do something or we'll all go to the poorhouse! And besides, after we gave the Yankees such a thrashing at Bull Run, why, I don't think we'll have to worry about our brave boys!"

"Exactly right, Mrs. DeSpain!" Austin nodded, his face beaming with excitement.

Marianne could not help herself. "Well then, you won't have to enlist, will you, Austin? If the war is really over, there's no need of it, is there?"

Paul grinned at his mother, allowing one eye to droop in a slight wink. She was a knowing woman, quick-witted and capable of a biting satire when she was so inclined. Austin flushed, then stammered, "Well . . .

I mean, after all — there'll be *some* more fighting, Mother! And I want to get in on it before the Yankees turn tail and head back to Washington!" He saw the smile on Paul's lips, and it angered him. He had been cautioned by his mother not to meddle in his brother's business, but he was a man who could keep nothing back. "Are *you* going to join up, Paul?"

"No, I'm not."

Paul's quick reply struck all of them forcefully. Ever since Fort Sumter had been fired on and the war had become a certainty, a fever had swept the South. Though it was strong everywhere, it was especially virulent in Virginia. Young men — and some not so young — were now stirred by the sound of bugles. Every town began to raise a company. It was exciting, this going off to war! Much more thrilling than clerking in a store or following a mule! And it would soon be over, in maybe six months at the most. It'd be a shame to miss it, to have to stand back while the other young fellows took all the good-looking girls!

Bull Run had proved the war was going to be a short affair, at least to the South. An article in the *Richmond Examiner* had spoken ecstatically of "the sprightly running of the Yankees." Indeed, there was some truth in this, for the North had gone to war in a picnic spirit. The Union soldiers had marched toward Bull Run with flowers inserted in the barrels of their muskets, and the congressmen and their wives and families had packed picnic lunches and gone to see their men put the Rebels to flight.

Somehow, though, it hadn't gone that way. The Rebels had been fierce; the battle bloody and ugly — and the Union troops had panicked, fleeing back to Washington. The same newspapers that had been screaming "On to Richmond!" began calling for peace at any cost.

Abraham Lincoln had been one of the few to see the thing clearly and had said to his wife, "The fat's in the fire now — and we'll just have to tough it out!" He had put General McClellan to work, and the small general turned to the task with a will. The North would not be so easily routed again.

A few Southern military men, such as Stonewall Jackson and Robert E. Lee, had tried to sound the alarm, but the South was euphoric. It held victory balls and wrote songs about the brave soldiers, while McClellan forged the Army of the Potomac into a formidable fighting force. Watching all of this, General Stonewall Jackson said bitterly, "It would have been better if we'd lost at Bull Run, for the South is overconfi-dent."

Now as Paul looked around those gathered at his family's table, he drew a deep breath. He had long ago, even while in England, decided that he would not fight for "the Cause." It was becoming quite evident that such a decision was going to make life pain-ful indeed. Still, he knew no way to explain — even to his parents and family — why he could not join in the rush to the colors.

He noted that both of the older DeSpains were staring at him, and he knew they typi-fied what the world might become: outspo-ken, certain of the rightness of their cause, and shocked by and intolerant of any who did not have the good sense to agree with them. Luci, he noted, was less shocked, but still there was disappointment in her face.

She'll do a little more shopping around for a husband now, Paul thought wryly. *And he'd better be wearing a uniform and be dedicated to killing Yankees!*

It was Marie who took over the conversa-tion, changing the subject at once. "Mother, that was a delightful meal," she said with a dimpled smile. "But I do believe it is time we moved into the parlor. I know Paul has some wonderful tintypes to show us, and I've barely been able to contain my excitement during the meal! I can't wait to see what the women in Europe are wearing!" She rose, giving the others no choice but to follow her out of the dining room into the parlor, where they spent the rest of the evening looking at the tintypes Paul had brought from France. The tension lessened, and even Austin seemed to forget that Paul was not going to wear Confederate gray.

Later, when their guests were gone, Paul found himself alone with Marie. He went to her, hugged her with affection, and said, "You're a smart girl, sister mine." The edges of his lips pulled upward in a slight smile. "I think they'd have had me shot for cowardice if you hadn't led them off to look at pictures."

Marie reached up and brushed a lock of his hair back from where it had fallen over his brow. She was a merry girl, but her face was serious as she said, "Paul, are you sure—"

"About not grabbing up a gun and killing off the Yankees?"

"It's not like that," Marie said quietly. "You can't make fun of what's going on. Look at how many of our men are already in the army. Even cousin Clay . . . and he doesn't even believe in the Cause!"

A gloomy light darkened Paul's eyes, and

he nodded. "I know, Marie. And I'm not making fun of Clay — or of anybody else. They feel it's what they've got to do. But I just don't see any sense in it."

Marie took his hand and held it. She and Paul had been very close once. She studied his hand, admiring the long, tapering fingers, which were so strong and flexible. Thinking of how it had been years ago, she looked up at him, saying, "You know, Paul, when I was a little girl, I thought you were the greatest person in the whole world. You — you weren't like my friends' brothers. Most of them didn't have any time for kid sisters. But you always did, didn't you?"

Paul nodded. "Yes, I did. You were such a curious little thing — always underfoot. No matter if you got stepped on or hurt, you never cried. I thought that was fine! And you're just the same now." A sudden bitterness swept over him, and he lowered his eyes. "Those were good days, but we can't go back to them."

"No, but we can have something else," Marie urged at once. She had said little to Paul since his return, but now she burst out, "Oh, Paul! What's *wrong* with you? You used to have such joy — but now you seem so — so *jaded*! Can't you tell me what it is?"

Paul Bristol stood there looking down into

his sister's face. He wanted to tell her how the years had passed so quickly and about the changes that had taken place inside of him. He tried, saying almost hoarsely, "Marie, I remember when we were kids, we always looked forward to something. Maybe nothing much . . . like a coon hunt — remember how we loved that?"

"I remember!"

"And when we grew up . . . or when I did, anyway, I looked forward to great things. But there was one thing in particular that I always knew: I was going to be an artist! Not just any artist, either. A great one! Even when people doubted me . . . even when Father made it clear painting just wasn't a manly thing to do . . . even then, I knew I was going to be a great artist." A bitter laugh broke from his lips, and he shook his head almost fiercely. "Well, that's not going to happen. I'm *not* going to be a great artist, Marie."

"Maybe you will —"

"No, I found that much out, at least, while I was in Europe. Artists are pretty rare around here, but they're thick as fleas over in France and Italy and England." Paul's voice dropped to a whisper. "I . . . I gave it all I had —" He broke off, and his face contorted. "All I had! And it's not enough!"

Marie ached for him. She longed to put her arms around him, to comfort him and to tell him it would be all right. She did say quietly, "We all have our disappointments, Paul. Look at Mother. She wants a strong husband, but she'll probably never have one."

Paul stared at his sister, surprised. This was the first time she'd ever put into words what both of them knew. The silence ran on, and finally Paul said, "I know, but she's got this place. She's got you and Austin. It may not be all she hoped for — but it's *something*!"

They stood there, shocked at what had exploded from a seemingly simple conversation. Marie yearned for some sort of wisdom but could find no comfort to offer her brother. Finally she asked, "What will you do?"

"Do?" Paul summoned a smile, and there was a mocking light in his eyes as he said, "Why, I guess I'll make the best of things. Do something about the war. Don't know what, but a man can't live in the South unless he proves he's a real patriot. I've sponged off Father and Mother for thirty-one years. Seems only fair that a rich man like Clarence DeSpain should have to take over for the next thirty."

"Don't talk like that, Paul!"

But Paul Bristol's jaw was set in a hard line. "I'll throw all of my paints and brushes away — get that nonsense out of my head. Marry Luci, of course. Have to give her father *something* for his money, don't I?"

Finally he stopped, and his eyes narrowed. "You know, sister, I might just enlist after all. It'd be a lot easier to take a bullet in the brain than to put up with such an empty life for the next thirty years!"

He wheeled, and as he left the room, Marie shook her head, saying, "Oh, Paul — !" But he was gone, leaving her with a dark sense of foreboding. She saw nothing hopeful in the future for her older brother, and grief for him had a sharp tooth that cut like a razor as he left the room.

Chapter 2
Cold Steel or Hot Lead?

The artistic side of Paul Bristol always responded to Gracefield, the home of the Rocklins. He pulled Queenie up sharply, holding the fiery mare in a firm grip, admiring the long sweeping drive lined with massive oaks that led to the house. In the spring, those oaks formed a leafy canopy. Now, however, they were bare — a ruined choir loft where few birds sang. But even the black, naked limbs lifted to the bleak sky had an austere beauty, looking symmetrical and somehow mournful.

"Come on, Queenie! Stop your fussing!"

The sleek black mare snorted and pawed the earth, then tried to unseat her rider with a lurching sideways motion. Bristol was taken unaware and, for one moment, was in danger of losing his seat — but he recovered quickly, a grin breaking across his face, and brought the mare up short. "You contrary female! Why don't you settle down and behave yourself?" But as he spurred the mare down the driveway, a thought flickered through his mind: *What about you, Mr. Bristol? You're the one who needs settling down, not Queenie!*

Shaking his shoulders as if to clear his mind of the unwelcome thought, Bristol pulled the mare down to a walk, turning his attention to the house that Noah Rocklin had built for his bride many years ago. A simple two-story house, Gracefield was given an impressive air by the white Corinthian columns across the front and on both sides. A balcony, set off by an ornate iron grill that was painted gleaming white, enclosed the house; tall, wide windows with blue shutters broke the gleaming white clapboard. The steeply pitched roof, which ran up to a center point, got a glance of approval from Bristol. He admired the three gables on each side, recalling how effective they were at giving light and air to the attic rooms. The high-rising chimneys, which were capped with curving covers of brick, released columns of white smoke that rose like incense on the morning air.

Bristol pulled Queenie up, came to the ground with an easy motion, and tossed the reins to a grinning black servant. "Highboy, you rascal! How are you?"

Highboy, a tall, strongly built man of thirty-eight, grinned and nodded. "Mist' Paul, you sho' been gone a long time!"

Bristol fished in his pocket, came out with a fistful of change. Handing it to Highboy, he said, "Happy birthday, Highboy."

"Why, thank you, suh!" Pocketing the money adroitly, Highboy lowered his voice and said, "Marse Paul . . . ?"

"Yes? What is it?"

"Well, suh, when you marries up wif Miss Luci, me and Lutie would make some mighty nice house servants." Highboy's warm brown eyes smiled, and he said, "Iffen you could buy us and our chilluns, we sho' would do a good job, Marse Paul."

Bristol was flattered and amused. "Miss Luci and I aren't engaged, Highboy."

"Oh no, suh!" Highboy said instantly. "But when you *is* married up wif her, I wants you to think 'bout Lutie and me." Feeling the impact of Bristol's gaze, the black man hesitated, then said quietly, "We thinks a heap of our folks here, Marse Paul, but things ain't so easy these days."

Instantly Paul thought of what he had heard about Clay Rocklin's difficulty with his wife, Ellen, and asked, "Is Miss Ellen giving you problems, Highboy?"

But the servant was too well versed in the

tenuous and fragile ties that bound slave and owner together to answer that question directly. He looked steadily at Bristol, saying only, "We be mighty happy if you buy us, Marse Paul. You knows how much we bof thinks of you."

"I'll think about it, Highboy," Bristol said with a nod. He was very fond of Highboy, for it was he who had taught Paul much of what he knew about horses. In fact, some of Bristol's best memories were tied in with the times he had spent at the stables with Highboy. "If I don't see Lutie, be sure to tell her I've missed her."

As Highboy led Queenie away, Bristol was troubled about what he had heard, for he admired his cousin Clay Rocklin. As he went up the broad steps, he thought of Clay's tragic life, remembering how he'd lost out in his courtship of the woman he loved, Melanie Benton, who married Clay's cousin Gideon. On the rebound, Clay had married Melanie's cousin, Ellen, but their marriage had been stormy from the beginning.

It must have been a pretty bad marriage, Bristol reflected as he reached the top of the stairs. *Bad enough for Clay to abandon her and the children for years.*

The enormous white door opened, and

Zander, the tall butler and manservant of Thomas Rocklin, greeted him. "Come in, Marse Paul. Lemme take yo' coat and gloves."

"You're looking well, Zander." Paul smiled, yielding the items. "How's Dorrie?"

"We both fine, suh." He hung the coat carefully on one of the brass hooks set in the wall of the spacious foyer. "Mistuh Thomas, he ain't well. I worried about him." The intelligent eyes of the butler studied Paul for a moment, and then a smile spread on the man's dark face. "My, my! You done been all over the world, Mistuh Paul! I bet yo' ma and pa glad to see you back. An' Miss Luci, too, I 'spec'?"

Paul Bristol returned the smile. "Well, it's nice to be back where everyone knows my business, Zander. Saves me a lot of thinking about what to do." He had almost forgotten how efficient and tightly knit was the system that existed in the South. The slaves knew practically everything about their owners, for the house servants picked up the details and passed them along to the field hands. Paul had been amused at how vitally interested the English were in the activities of the Royal Family, but now as he looked at Zander, he suddenly realized that nothing that the Rocklins or the Bristols or the

Franklins did was hidden from the eyes of these black pieces of property.

Pieces of property . . . The thought drew Paul's attention to Zander, and he studied the handsome features of the coal-black face thoughtfully. Though he could think of those thousands of faceless slaves all over the South as "property," he had always had problems thinking of the slaves he himself knew in that fashion. Zander and Highboy and the other black men and women who had been part of his world — how could they be "property"?

His mare, Queenie, she was property. How could anyone believe that this tall man who had given a life of faithful service to Thomas and Susanna Rocklin was of no more consequence than a horse? Paul shrugged his thoughts off impatiently. This was the question that was tearing the United States apart, and he wasn't going to answer it by himself. Even so, a rebellious streak ran through him, for — no matter how Southern he might be — he refused to believe that Zander was the same in kind as a dumb beast.

"The family, dey expectin' you, Mistuh Paul," Zander prodded. "Dey havin' breakfus' in de fambly dinin' room."

"All right, Zander." He paused and took

out some bills, peeled two of them off, and handed them to the butler. "Christmas gift, a little early." He smiled.

Zander stared at the bills, his eyes opening wide. "Why, dat's a mighty fine gif', Mistuh Paul!"

"I've missed three or four Christmases. And that's some of that new Confederate money." Bristol smiled. "Better spend it while it's still good."

"Yas, *suh*!"

Bristol moved out of the foyer and, as he passed the broad stairway that divided the lower sections of the house, thought of how Gracefield seemed to have been constructed for the purpose of holding formal balls. Fully half of the space on the first floor was designated for that purpose. Even now the maids were decorating the enormous ballroom for the ball that was to take place that evening. Turning to his left, Paul moved down the wide hallway and heard the sound of voices. He followed the sound through a large doorway into the small dining room, where he found the Rocklins gathered around the table.

"Paul!" Susanna Rocklin was sitting beside her husband, Thomas. As Thomas looked up, an expression of genuine pleasure crossed Susanna's face. "You did come after all! Come and sit beside me." At the age of sixty, Susanna was a most attractive woman. She had long been a favorite aunt of Paul's. He went to her at once, bent over, and kissed her cheek, saying, "You'd better keep an eye on this woman at the ball, Uncle Thomas. Some handsome devil will run off with her!"

"Good! Let him pay her bills!" Thomas Rocklin smiled faintly at Susanna, but the smile faded quickly. "Sit down, boy, sit down!"

He looks very bad, Paul thought. *There's a shadow on him, just as Mother said.* But he hid his reaction and began to pile his plate high with the battered eggs and sausage that Susanna handed him. Looking across the table, he nodded to Ellen, saying, "How are you, Ellen?" He had met his cousin Clay's wife only once, when the family had gathered earlier in the month at Lindwood for a photo session. She had been anything but pleasant then.

"I'm not well," Ellen snapped waspishly.

Paul did his best to keep his voice soothing as he answered her. "I'm sorry to hear that." He hadn't spoken to Clay at any length since his return from Europe, and he asked, "Didn't Mother tell me that Clay came home on leave?"

44

Ellen's brown eyes seemed to harden, and her lips tightened. "He's on leave, but he's never here. You'd think a man would want to be home with his wife and family after being in the war, wouldn't you?" Her voice rose shrilly, and she gripped the arms of the chair until her knuckles turned white. "But no, he's got *better* things to do!" She glared around the room, challenging them all. When no one spoke, she turned her bitter eyes back on Paul. "If you want to see Clay, you'll have to go over to where he stays, with that white trash Yancy bunch!"

Paul felt the oppressive silence that had fallen on the room, and a quick glance at Ellen's children showed him the pained embarrassment that both of them felt. Rena, at fifteen, was a sensitive young girl, and she dropped her head at once, her cheeks red. David masked his feelings better, for at nearly twenty he was more able to do such things. Though his features were almost a copy of his brother Dent's, David was the most thoughtful and steadiest of Clay Rocklin's children. He said quietly, "My father is in a venture with Buford Yancy, Paul. He thinks it's unwise to plant cotton, so he and Buford are going to plant corn and feed pigs out."

Paul nodded. "I'd say that's smart. We

45

can't eat cotton, and neither can the army. Are you going to do the same, Uncle Thomas?"

But Ellen was not interested in pigs and cotton. She glared at David, saying bitterly, "Clay's not over there to talk about growing corn, and you well know it, David! He's there chasing after Melora Yancy!"

"Oh, don't be silly, Ellen!" Susanna Rocklin held her head high, and temper flared in her fine eyes. She was furious that her daughter-in-law would say such a thing, especially in front of Rena! "If you can't speak more properly, I'll be glad to have your meals served in your room."

The suddenness of Susanna's attack brought a dead silence into the room. Ellen gasped and pushed her chair back from the table. "I see what I'm to be treated like!" she panted, her face contorted with anger. "You're all against me!"

David rose at once, took hold of Ellen's arm, and led her away from the table. "Come along, Mother. We'll finish our coffee in your room."

When the pair disappeared, Susanna looked across at Rena, saying, "Don't mind your mother, dear. She's upset."

"Yes, Grandma."

Paul saw the stricken expression on the

girl's face. "I brought you a present, Rena," he said quickly. "I meant to give it to you for Christmas, but it didn't get here in time. You still like to draw and paint?"

"Oh yes!"

"Well, if you'll go find Highboy and have him take the package out of my saddlebags, you'll find something you'll like — lots of brushes and paint and pencils."

Rena forgot her humiliation, her eyes lighting up. "Oh, will you give me a lesson, Paul?"

"Sure I will!"

Rena ran out at once, and Thomas said heavily, "That was kind of you, Paul." Rocklin had been a handsome man in his youth, but sickness had drained him of much of his vitality. He had been, Paul sensed, as humiliated by Ellen's behavior as the rest of them but was too tired to do more than say, "You'll have to excuse Ellen, Paul. I sometimes wonder if the events in her life haven't disturbed her emotionally."

"Yes, sir, that can happen." Paul felt uneasy, for the history of Ellen Rocklin was not only tragic, but sordid. She had been an immoral woman for years — behavior that had only seemed to grow worse when Clay rejected her. Even now, Paul had noted that she had the look of a loose woman about her.

Paul shook his head slightly. He had heard how Clay had returned just in time to save Gracefield from falling into the hands of creditors, but he had also heard that Clay was in love with Melora Yancy. Everyone in the Rocklin and Bristol clans knew that Ellen Rocklin didn't want Clay — hated him, in fact, and made no secret of it — and yet she was filled with a blind, unreasonable jealousy over Melora Yancy. As a result, Ellen did all she could to make Clay's life miserable, which greatly affected the rest of the family, as well.

Thomas took a drink of his coffee, then asked suddenly, "So you're giving away your paints and brushes, are you? That mean you're through with that sort of thing?"

"I suppose so, Uncle Thomas." Paul shrugged. "I'm just not good enough at it." He saw the look on his uncle's face and smiled. "I suppose you're thinking you could have told me that ten years ago, aren't you?"

Thomas brushed his thin hand across his lips, attempting to hide the smile that came there, but gave it up. "Well, it's a rather unmanly sort of way to spend your life, as I told you once."

"Nonsense, Tom!" Susanna snapped impatiently. "I wish *one* of our young men would do something besides grow cotton and fight duels and hunt!"

"Susanna!" Thomas Rocklin gasped, shocked by this heresy. "What a thing to say! I only hope that now that Paul's got this art business out of his system, he'll settle down and — and —"

"And marry Luci DeSpain and live happily ever after? Is that it, Uncle Thomas?"

Thomas thought of his son Clay, trapped in a loveless marriage, fighting for a cause he didn't believe in. "There are worse things, nephew," he said gently, and the pain in his eyes made Paul look away.

"Well, sir," Paul said quietly, "if I can't paint, I guess I can do that. Provided, of course, that this war doesn't bring the whole thing down around our heads." He thought of the split in their own family . . . on the South were Clay and Dent and the Franklin men — Brad and Grant . . . and then he thought of Mason Rocklin, Thomas's younger brother, who was an officer in the Union army. *We'll all be killing each other soon,* he thought. Suddenly the hopelessness of it all descended on him, and he rose, saying, "Well, it's a good time for a ball. Did you two plan it so I could court Luci

DeSpain?"

Susanna smiled at him. "No, but that's what balls are for."

"Just be careful about how you talk about the war, Paul," Thomas spoke up. "You're not joining the army, and that's bad enough at this time, but if you say the wrong thing, you'll have half the young fireballs in the room offering to trade shots with you!"

"I'll be careful, Uncle Thomas. The last thing I want is a duel!"

Luci DeSpain had never looked lovelier than she did that evening. She came into the room wearing a pale blue crinoline dress, which almost matched the color of her eyes, and which set off her figure in a spectacular fashion. The young men swarmed her at once.

Paul was standing with Clay Rocklin and Brad Franklin, who was married to Clay's only sister, Amy. Franklin was a major in the Richmond Grays, and he cut a fine figure as he stood there in his uniform. Clay was not wearing his uniform but looked very handsome in a brown wool suit.

"You'd better not let those young fellows have too much of a head start, Paul," Clay teased Bristol. Sipping the cider that Zander was passing around, his eyes went over the room. When Paul asked him about the army rather hesitantly, he shrugged and spoke mostly of his sons Dent and Lowell, and of Brad's son Grant.

"The Richmond Grays is one of the finest companies around," Clay said proudly, "and I like to think that's because of our sons' involvement." Brad Franklin smiled and nodded in agreement. Their sons were among the most respected soldiers in the Richmond Grays, a company filled mostly with young aristocrats from the area.

Just then Amy Franklin came up and laid her hand on her husband's arm. Amy, the only daughter of Thomas Rocklin, was not really a beautiful woman, but she made people think she was. She was tall and dark like her father, and her fine dark eyes were her best feature.

"Excuse me, gentlemen," she said, "but I need to steal the major away. I so seldom get the chance to dance with him, and I'm not letting this opportunity pass me by."

Clay and Paul laughed at the look on Franklin's face, but Brad quickly recovered. "If you'll excuse me, gentlemen," he said, "I never refuse the request of a beautiful woman." And with that he swept Amy out onto the dance floor.

Paul watched them for a few moments;

then he and Clay began talking again about the war. Paul had read what the papers had to say, but he was more interested in Clay Rocklin's views. He had heard so much about the man and discovered that his cousin was very different from the man he remembered. The two of them had been well acquainted, of course, and Paul remembered Clay as a wild young man, given to fits of temper and moodiness. But the man who stood beside him was as solid an individual as Paul had ever met. Clay was one of the "Black Rocklins," with raven hair and dark eyes. He was a big man, six feet two, and heavier than Paul remembered. There was an air of authority about him, and Paul had heard his father say, "Clay enlisted as a private, but he'll be an officer before this war is over. He's got whatever it is that makes men obey and follow."

Paul sensed that power as the two of them stood there talking, and once again he felt a queer sort of kinship with his cousin. Perhaps, he thought, it was because both of them had been aliens, wandering far from their homes. Clay had left in disgrace, had even become a slave trader, but eventually left that sordid profession in disgust. Paul had been away from the South for years, trying to find some sort of meaning for his life. Now the two of them seemed to be thrown together, and Paul was curious about Clay's views on the war.

"Do you think the South will actually win this war, Clay?" he asked. As Clay spoke, he discovered his cousin held little real hope for final victory in the South. He spoke of the huge armies of the North and how the smaller population of the South would soon be depleted. He soberly reflected on the might of Northern factories, one of which was owned by their uncle Stephen Rocklin.

"The only hope the South has," Clay concluded finally, "is that the North will get tired of the struggle. There's a peace party now in the North, and if we can hurt their armies badly enough and quickly enough, they might be able to bring enough pressure so that Lincoln will have to cave in."

Paul shook his head. "Well, I'd like to see the thing over at once. It's a bad war, and I think the South will suffer for it!"

They had not noticed that several young men had come to stand close, listening to their conversation. And it was one of these who took exception to Paul's remark. "If you like the North so much, why don't you go live there?" the man demanded roughly.

Paul blinked in surprise, becoming aware of the small group. He turned to find a tall, bulky man, who was dressed in a black suit, glaring at him. He had to think to come up with the fellow's name, but finally succeeded. Leighton Huger . . . and he was, Paul remembered, one of Luci's suitors.

Paul frowned. "Why, I didn't mean —"

"You've got a fine right to talk, Bristol!" Huger broke in, his eyes hot with anger. "Go on back and play with your little paintbrushes in France! I've heard those artists over there are womanish enough for a fellow like you!"

"Now, Leighton," Clay Rocklin said at once, "let's not have any trouble."

"Not with you, sir," Huger said at once. "We all know where you stand. You and your sons are a fine example to Virginia, but I have no patience with a coward who runs away and lets his native state fight to the death while he draws pretty little pictures!"

There was more to Huger's anger than the matter of politics, Paul understood at once. *He figures to show me up in front of Luci,* was the thought that came to him. But he was determined not to let that happen. "Look, Huger, I'm sorry if my remark offended you. I love the South and wouldn't do anything —"

"Love the South!" Leighton Huger's florid face glowed with anger. "You insult the

Cause, then stand there and say you love our Confederacy?"

"I didn't say I loved the Confederacy," Paul snapped, aware that the quarrel had attracted the attention of many, most of whom had turned to stare. "I said I loved the South!" But he knew it was hopeless, and when Huger grew abusive, he shrugged. "This is no place for talk like this. Not for a gentleman."

That was when Huger lifted his hand and slapped Paul in the face. A gasp went around the room, and Paul saw that Luci's eyes were gleaming with some emotion that he'd never seen in them before. But he didn't have the time to figure out what she was thinking — he had to deal with the situation at hand. Huger had left him no choice, not unless he wanted to leave Virginia. The code of his people was strong, and any man of his class who refused to stand up to such an offensive act as Huger's was forever branded.

"Shall it be cold steel or hot lead, Mr. Huger?" he inquired.

"You must choose, sir!"

"Very well. My man will call on you."

Paul left the room at once, furious and disgusted. He turned when he heard his name called. "Paul, let me be your friend in this matter." Clay had come to stand in front of him, his face creased with concern.

"That's generous of you, Clay." Paul nodded. He shook his head sadly. "What a stupid thing! Two grown men trying to kill each other over a harmless remark! Well, make the arrangements, Clay. And pray that we both miss!"

The duel took place at dawn, just as the sun reddened the sky. One of Huger's friends, a heavy young man who was so nervous he could hardly speak, stood with Clay as the two men examined the weapons — a fine set of dueling pistols that had belonged to Noah Rocklin. Clay loaded them carefully, then offered the pair of them to Huger. He took one indifferently, then watched as Paul Bristol took the other. Paul noticed that Huger's face was pale and that he had nothing to say.

He's about as scared as I am, Paul thought suddenly. As Clay gave them the instructions and he moved into position, he realized that he *was* afraid. He had never faced death, and the idea that in a few seconds his brain might be suddenly shut down and his heart stilled brought fear. Not of the pain that a bullet might bring, but of what might follow. He was not a godly man, but he had seen true faith in his own family, in a fighting man like Clay Rocklin.

He recalled the words from Shakespeare's play *Hamlet,* that it was not the fear of death itself that caused alarm, but "in that sleep of death, what dreams may come?" As he held the pistol at the ready and began to pace off the distance while Clay counted clearly, he was sad that he might leave the good things of earth — and fearful of what might come after death.

He heard the final count, whirled, and lowered his piece until it pointed at Huger. He pulled the trigger at once and heard Huger's pistol go off at almost the same instant.

And nothing happened!

He stood there, swaying slightly, and saw that Huger was doing the same. A great relief swept over him, and then Clay said, "Now your honor has been satisfied, and there will be no more action. The two of you should shake hands."

And then it was over, the two parties leaving the little mound as if they were guilty of some crime. When they were out of hearing of the other party, Paul stopped and pulled out his handkerchief. He mopped his brow, then stared at Clay. "I might as well tell you, Clay, I was scared spitless!"

"Sensible." Clay nodded. Then he said, "Makes a fellow think about what his life means, doesn't it, Paul? Seems like we don't really think about it much until it looks like we're going to lose it."

They moved down the path, and when they mounted their horses, Paul remarked a little critically, "It didn't seem to bother you much that I might get killed."

"Didn't bother me at all," Clay said cheerfully. "Because I knew that was impossible."

Paul looked at him in surprise. "How could you know we'd both miss?"

"Because I loaded the pistols."

Paul pulled Queenie up sharply and stared at his cousin. A light dawned, and he exclaimed, "You did something to those pistols, Clay!"

"Sure I did," Clay agreed. "Didn't want to see either you or Huger get killed. Be a waste."

"What did you load the pistols with?"

"I had Dorrie bake me some little pieces of bread, nice and round — just the size of pistol balls. Matter of fact, they *looked* exactly like the balls that were in Grandfather's set." Humor twinkled in Clay's eyes, and he said, "Had to be real careful that I got the right ones when I loaded the pistols."

For a moment, anger rose in Paul, and his face turned hard. Then a strange thing happened. He thought of how solemn he and Huger had been . . . and how it must have looked to Clay. . . . His lips began to twitch, and he suddenly grinned. "You scoundrel!" he cried. "I ought to shoot you with a real bullet!"

And then he began to laugh, and Clay joined him. Soon they both were roaring, and finally he gasped, "I can't — help thinking, Clay — how pompous — we were! And then we shot each other — with *toast!*"

"Don't tell anyone, not ever, Paul!" Clay warned, merriment still dancing in his eyes. "It would humiliate Huger."

"Huger!" Paul demanded. "What about *me?*"

"You've got more sense," Clay remarked. "Let's go get some hot chocolate. This foolishness has frozen me to the marrow!"

CHAPTER 3
AN OFFER FROM
THE PRESIDENT

When the Southern Confederacy chose Jefferson Davis as president, the choice polarized the newborn nation.

Half of the Southern people were disappointed, for the new chief magistrate was an austere man, not given to gestures designed to please the multitude (as were others who had sought the office). To this segment, Davis seemed a cold, unbending man who lacked warmth and charm.

But the other half of the population saw in Davis the noblest aristocrat whom the South had yet produced. As a senator from Mississippi, he had skillfully led that body in a masterful fashion; as a hero of the Mexican War, he had the military mind necessary to lead a nation at war.

To Varina Davis, his beautiful young wife, he was a man capable of gentleness and fervent love, but she was well aware that this side of her husband's nature was not easily seen by those who viewed him only as a soldier or a statesman. Mrs. Davis was small, dark, and very beautiful, and she felt that she had been selected by destiny to rule over the newborn nation. She was a vibrant woman, vivacious and witty, who saw far more clearly than her husband that the Confederacy was not one in spirit. How could it be, when they were fighting for states' rights and, by definition, that meant that the various elements of the Confederacy were at least as loyal to their native states as to the Confederacy itself? Already this had become a problem, for the governor of South Carolina refused to surrender the huge supplies gathered by that state to troops from other areas!

Varina Davis had one friend with whom she shared almost everything — a confidante in whom she put complete trust. It was to this beloved friend, Mary Chesnut, that the president's wife turned for assurance one bright and sunny day in early December.

"Mary," Varina said as the two of them sat knitting socks for the soldiers, "did you read what the *Examiner* wrote about President Davis this week?"

Mary Boykin Chesnut was originally from South Carolina. However, she had become a leader of Richmond society since coming to live there. Though not a beautiful woman, she had the sort of attractive manners that drew admirers from both sexes. Her dark hair was parted in the center and drawn back to form a bun, and her eyes were dark and penetrating.

"It wasn't as bad as what the Charleston *Mercury* said," Mrs. Chesnut remarked.

"It was frightful!" Mrs. Davis jabbed at the yarn spitefully, then tossed the unfinished task aside. She had made many speeches urging the women of Richmond to do their best for their boys in gray, but so far as Mary Chesnut knew, the president's wife had finished only four pair of socks since the war had started. Varina got up and paced the floor nervously, speaking of the unfair criticism her husband had received from the press. She had some justification for her anger at the criticism, for many felt that the South should be attacking the Northern forces, not sitting around basking in the glory of one battle won.

Finally Mrs. Chesnut tactfully changed the subject. "Has your husband been getting along with General Johnston better?"

"Oh my, no!" Mrs. Davis said emphatically. "That gentleman is as touchy as a man without a skin!"

"Well, Johnston feels that he was passed over when the president chose other men above him."

"He must accept my husband's estimate of the situation. After all, the president knows more about military matters than any of the generals. He told me that he would rather have been chosen general of the army than president."

This was true, and it was a fact that was destined to cause grave problems for the Confederacy. Jefferson Davis *did* see himself as an expert in military matters, which hindered him from ever completely trusting his generals to do the wise thing. He developed a habit of voiding the plans of campaigns, which only irritated and shocked Generals Beauregard and Joseph E. Johnston. Unfortunately, neither general ever seemed to learn that Jefferson Davis had a large ego that demanded constant attention. Johnston especially was so proud himself that he never bothered to placate the president. He considered himself the best military mind in the South and spent much time expounding on this publicly.

Mrs. Chesnut spoke about the feud between General Johnston and the president, adding, "Your husband prefers Albert Sidney Johnston, I believe."

"Yes! He says that he has one *real* general, at least."

"I wonder how General Lee feels about this," Mrs. Chesnut mused. "He never says a negative word about anything."

"Oh, my husband thinks there's no man like General Lee! But he can't spare him for active duty. Lee is such a thoughtful man, isn't he? He takes a great load from my poor husband's shoulders, but because of that, we could on no account allow him to go into the field."

Mary longed to reply that it was a terrible waste to keep one of the ablest generals in Richmond cooped up just to soothe President Davis's nerves, but she was wise enough to say only, "I suppose Lee's chance will come."

Ten minutes later the door opened and President Davis entered. His rather haggard features lit up at the sight of his wife, and he went to her at once, touching her shoulder and murmuring a few words. Then he turned to say, "Well, Mary, how is the sock situation in the Southern Confederacy? I'll venture you knit them in your sleep!" The president was fond of Mary and had great confidence in her husband, Colonel James Chesnut — so much so that he had sent him on the all-important mission of settling the surrender of Fort Sumter. The president sat down and, for half an hour, talked about books with Mrs. Chesnut, his face relaxing as he put aside the heavy weight of office.

Eventually, though, the conversation turned to the war, as all conversations ultimately did in Richmond. It was the president who brought up the subject of the power of the press. "That fellow Horace Greeley does us more harm than the Yankee Army," he snapped. "He's a fool, but people listen to him. The peace party might be fairly effective if the newspapers would stop hammering at the people to go to war!"

"Well, some of our own newspapers do us more harm than good," Mrs. Davis said. "I don't see why you put up with the lies they tell about you."

"I put up with it, my dear," Davis said with a trace of a smile, "because I'm the president and not the king. I hardly have the power to behead those who disagree with me."

"I wish you did!" Varina Davis snapped. "You could start with the editor of the *Mercury*. Getting rid of him would be something to be proud of!"

"Yes, I daresay you're right, but I can't call the man out and fight a duel with him." Davis had a lean, almost shrunken face, with deep-set eyes and a thin, ascetic mouth. He had been a most able senator, but he had not and never would master the art of choosing capable men and then letting them have full authority. He was in poor health, which may well have lain at the root of many of his poor decisions. But Davis was astute, and he well understood that hard, difficult days lay ahead for the South, despite the fact that since the first battle, both the North and the South had pulled back and experienced only minor engagements in Kentucky and Tennessee.

"You know," the president said, watching the two women thoughtfully. "I've been thinking of a plan to make our people more aware of the war." He laced his long fingers together, adding, "The Yankees are sending artists to the battles. They make sketches of the battle scenes, which the newspapers print. I think we must do something like that."

"Why, that's a splendid idea!" his wife exclaimed, her dark eyes glowing. "Think of how wonderful it would be if people could actually see pictures of our noble troops being led into battle!"

As the president and his wife spoke of the advantages of the use of drawing, Mary Chesnut was getting another idea. When the pair seemed to have agreed that something should be done, she said, "Mr. President, wouldn't it be possible to send someone to take actual pictures of the battles?"

Davis blinked in surprise, then exclaimed, "Why, I've seen some of those, Mary! Some fellow named Brady took one of those camera contraptions to Bull Run. Actually got daguerreotypes of the Washington crowd on their way back to Washington!" Davis rose at once and began pacing the floor, his face alight with excitement. "Yes, that would be just the thing! This fellow Brady . . . I met him once. He's got a studio in New York. Does wonderful work! I think he's taken a daguerreotype of all the living presidents. I've seen the one he made of Old Hickory. Marvelous!"

Mrs. Chesnut was pleased that her suggestion had taken hold so quickly. When the president began to ask, "Now let's see, where do we find a man who could do such a thing? Most of those fellows are in New York and Washington —," she broke in quietly:

"I have a suggestion, Mr. President."

Jefferson Davis came to sit beside her, and Mrs. Chesnut said, "There is a young man named Paul Bristol . . ."

"And this is Mr. Paul Bristol, the young man I was telling you about, Mr. President." Mary Chesnut smiled. "Mr. Bristol, President Jefferson Davis."

Bristol took the lean hand the president offered, saying, "It's a great pleasure, Mr. President."

"I'm happy to meet you, Mr. Bristol," Davis said with a smile. "I suppose you're wondering about being summoned here on such short notice?"

"Well . . ." Paul hesitated, not certain how to answer. When a messenger had brought the brief note from President Davis, he had been perplexed — and a little apprehensive. His father had been the same. "I wonder if he's heard about that affair you and Huger had?" Claude Bristol asked nervously when Paul showed him the note.

"Perhaps so," Paul had answered. "But I don't think it's about that. If Jefferson Davis summoned everyone who had doubts about the government, he wouldn't have time for anything else."

Paul had thought about the strangeness of it for two days, and when he'd finally entered the Chesnut home, where the note had instructed him to appear, he'd simply given up. *I guess he can't have me shot,* he thought as he entered the house and surrendered his hat and coat to the servant. *I can always tell him that Huger and I used toast instead of real bullets!*

When he met the president, he saw at once that he was not in trouble, for Davis was smiling warmly. "Here, sit down and let's let these ladies wait on us." Davis sat down on a horsehide chair, waving toward a matching chair that faced him. "Coffee, Mr. Bristol? Oh, I forgot, there isn't any. The Yankee blockade is getting to be a real inconvenience. But we do have some wine, don't we, Mrs. Chesnut?"

"Yes, we do, Mr. President." While Mrs. Chesnut moved to a large sideboard and poured two glasses of wine, the president spoke in an animated fashion about England, and Paul, at Davis's request, gave his opinion of the Confederacy's chances of recognition.

Finally Davis took the wine glass and proposed a toast: "To the South — may her future be as glorious as her past!" He drank his wine, then smiled as he saw that Paul had joined him. "You concur with that toast, I take it, Mr. Bristol?"

"Why, of course, Mr. President!"

Davis rarely smiled, but when he did, it changed his entire appearance, making him look much younger. Now as he considered Paul, his eyes had a definite glow of humor. "I'm happy that your little affair with Mr. Huger ended so pleasantly. Our country needs young men such as you." For one awful moment, Paul was afraid that Clay had betrayed him, that the president knew about the trick with the bullets and was about to laugh at him! But he relaxed when the president nodded and continued firmly, "You are both young men of courage. It would indeed have been a tragedy for the Cause to have lost either of you. But no more duels, I take it?"

"Oh no, sir!"

Davis sat there studying Paul carefully. He had heard this young man's history from Mrs. Chesnut and had planned out how to approach him. "Mr. Bristol, you are a little out of step with most young men of your age," he said finally. "I suppose that is because you are an artist and most men of art seem to be out of step with this world, at least to some extent. Of course, you've been in Europe, Mrs. Chesnut informs me, for the past few years, and that means you haven't been in the center of the storm as have the rest of us."

Bristol saw that a response was expected and said, "Why, that's about the way it is, Mr. President. I feel like an old man when I see these young fellows twenty years old getting ready for the war."

"Yes, I can imagine. You are — what? Thirty years old?"

"Thirty-one, sir."

"Well, that's young from *my* point of view," Davis said with a nod. "But war is a young man's affair." A sadness touched his deep-set eyes, and he said quietly, "We'll see boys and old men in uniform before it's over." He shrugged his shoulders, then seemed to grow more businesslike. "Mrs. Chesnut tells me you've had some experience with making pictures . . . with daguerreotypes? I'd like to hear about that, if you don't mind, Mr. Bristol."

Bewildered, but willing enough, Paul spoke of his days in Paris, where he'd studied under Louis-Jacques-Mandé Daguerre, inventor of the daguerreotype. "I was taking some drawing lessons from one of his students, and he invited me to go for a visit to Daguerre's studio. Well, it was quite a show, Mr. President!" Paul spoke excitedly, unaware that Mrs. Davis and Mrs. Chesnut had come to sit close by. "He's such a fine man! So unselfish — Monsieur

71

Daguerre, I mean. Why, he *gave* the secret of his process to the world when it would have made him a millionaire!"

"I didn't know that," the president said, impressed. "And did you master the process?"

"Oh, I wouldn't say that," Paul protested. "I learned a great deal from my friend: how to take the pictures, how to develop them, how to use the equipment . . . that sort of thing." Paul had been thinking rapidly and came to a conclusion. "Are you thinking of some sort of unit to photograph the battles, Mr. President?"

Davis nodded. "That's exactly right, Mr. Bristol. What do you think of the idea?"

Paul said thoughtfully, "It could be a two-edged sword, Mr. President."

Davis was surprised. "How do you mean?"

"You were in the Mexican War. Imagine if there had been pictures of the American dead. What effect would that have had on the country's support of the war?"

Davis grew thoughtful. "I see that I haven't thought this thing out thoroughly. That *would* be a problem. Of course . . . if the people saw pictures of the Yankee dead only . . . ?"

For the next hour the president, Paul, and the two women spoke of the project. Finally

Davis asked, "Mr. Bristol, would you be willing to undertake such a task?"

Paul had expected this but said honestly, "It would be a great challenge, sir, but I must tell you that there are men in the South who are much better qualified than I am."

His manner pleased Davis, who nodded briskly. "There will be room for them if this turns out well." He hesitated, then said, "This cannot be a military unit. I will have my secretary work out the details of financing the equipment, salary, and so forth. Are you free to begin at once?"

"Yes, sir."

"Fine!" The president rose, saying, "Oh, one more thing, Mr. Bristol. In view of the rather controversial nature of this thing, I would prefer that you send all of your plates to my office."

"I understand." Paul smiled. He knew that the selection of pictures for release would be made by the president and his wife, which didn't disturb him. After a few more moments, he had received his instructions from the president, and Mrs. Chesnut showed him to the door.

"I know this was your idea, Mrs. Chesnut," he said. "I'm sure you know it will make things a great deal easier on me."

Mary Boykin Chesnut did indeed know a great deal about Paul Bristol. Some of it came from Clay's daughter-in-law, Raimey, who was married to Dent. She was the daughter of one of the leading citizens of Richmond and so had known Mrs. Chesnut for some time. They often discussed each other's families.

"I hope this won't interfere with your other obligations, Mr. Bristol . . . such as Miss Luci DeSpain?" When Paul stared at her in amazement, Mrs. Chesnut laughed, saying, "I'm an incurable romantic, Mr. Bristol, like most of my sex. But I daresay you can manage an engagement *and* a new profession at the same time."

Paul said, "I'll bring my camera by and take your picture."

"Don't waste your time with old married women." Mrs. Chesnut smiled, then revealed her vanity by saying, "Well, bring your camera, Mr. Bristol, but give me notice so I can get my hair fixed!"

Later that same day, at suppertime, Paul gave his news to his family. "I'm going to work for the government," he announced when Marie kept after him about his interview with the president. He told the story, and their reactions were amusing. Marie began at once to clamor for a picture of

74

herself. His father and Austin were obviously relieved. *Now they have a good explanation for people who wonder why I'm not in uniform,* Paul thought. His mother, he saw, was not as happy over his new career as he'd expected.

"Does this mean you won't paint anymore?" she asked quietly.

"Just for my own pleasure — and yours," he said, putting his arm around her. "The camera does it better than I ever could."

"No, I don't think so. It's so — *mechanical!*"

"I don't think so . . . not altogether," Paul said pensively. "That fellow Brady, he's got a knack of getting the — the *quality* of a person in his photographs. I saw the photograph he made of Jenny Lind. Even if you didn't know who she was, you'd *like* the woman who smiles out at you. And that's what I'm going to do, Mother. I'm going to catch the essence of what I photograph."

"But — I thought President Davis wanted you to take pictures of battles, Paul!"

"Battles are men, and one picture of one man with his eyes dazed with the horror of war . . . that's more effective than a picture of a thousand men marching in neat little ranks."

Marianne Bristol reached up and put her

hand on Paul's cheek. "I'm afraid President Davis may have trouble with you!"

Paul kissed her, then laughed. "Well, it's his turn! I've given you and Father trouble for the first half of my life; now let President Jefferson Davis have a taste of it!"

CHAPTER 4
THE ADVENTURE BEGINS

New York was colder than Virginia, as Paul quickly discovered. December snow was still hard-packed on Broadway. The footing was precarious, and as Bristol disembarked from his carriage, his feet slid out from under him. He sprawled on the ground, and the cabby peered at him, grinned, and said, "Careful, gov'ner! Street's a bit slippery!"

Paul heaved himself upright, cast a baleful look at the man, and said, "Thanks for the warning." He paid his fare, taking some consolation in withholding the extra dollar he'd planned to give the driver for bringing him from the railway station. The cabby, in turn, tossed Bristol's suitcase down deliberately so that it hit the frozen sidewalk with a loud thumping noise. "Yer welcome, gov'ner!" He nodded disdainfully and touched the horse with his whip.

Picking up the suitcase, Bristol turned to face the building and was disconcerted. He had told the cabby to take him to Brady's Photographic Gallery, but he found himself standing in front of Thomson's Saloon. Then he lifted his gaze and saw that the three upper floors were labeled BRADY'S DAGUERREOTYPE GALLERY. In the glass window resided some specimens of Brady's fine daguerreotype work.

After climbing the stairs to the second floor, the first thing Paul saw was two large folded doors made of glazed glass etched with figures of flowers. Passing through them, he found himself in a reception room at least twenty-four feet wide and forty feet long. The floors were carpeted in a deep rose, and velvet drapes embroidered with gold threads hung to the floor. The ceiling was frescoed, and in the center was suspended a glittering glass chandelier from which prismatic drops sparkled like stars. Imported curtains with intricate needlework decorated the windows, and the way the deep rich wood of the furnishings imprisoned the glow of the chandelier immediately told Paul that the furniture was rosewood. A large reception desk was to his left, and the walls were covered with portraits of great men and women — American leaders, living and dead, who had sat for Brady and for history.

"Would it be possible to see Mr. Brady?" Paul inquired of a slender man wearing steel-rimmed glasses who was seated at the desk.

The man looked up from the ledger he was examining and smiled. "Why, I think so. It's uncommonly slack just now. He's up on the top floor. You can go up those stairs."

"Thank you."

Bristol climbed the stairs and found himself in a large room where sunlight poured through skylights covered with mesh. Several men were gathered around a stove — drinking coffee, it seemed — and one of them spotted Paul. Leaving the group, he came forward to ask, "May I help you, sir?"

"My name is Paul Bristol. I'm looking for Mr. Brady."

"I'm Mathew Brady."

Paul was surprised, for Brady was small and not at all impressive. He had sharp features, a pair of weak-looking eyes, and a mass of curly black hair. He wore a plain black suit covered with a white apron.

Paul had come to New York after discovering that the equipment and supplies he needed could only be purchased there. It had occurred to him on the train that he might get some sound advice on new techniques from some of the New York photographers, and he'd come to Brady's studio, not really expecting to get in to see the man. He knew Brady was very busy and tried at once to engage the smaller man's interest.

"I'm just back from France, Mr. Brady," he said quickly. "I was a pupil of Monsieur Daguerre."

He had chosen his introduction well. Brady's face lit up at once, and he said, "Ah! We must talk, Mr. Bristol. Yes, indeed. Come to my office."

For the next thirty minutes, Paul was rather hard put: Mathew Brady knew his trade and was vitally interested in any new developments in the world of photography. Though Paul did all he could to make his brief time under Daguerre seem much longer, he soon was out of his depth as Brady fired questions at him concerning techniques.

"Mr. Brady!" Bristol said at last, holding up his hands. "I must confess, I am not a professional photographer. Only a beginner."

Brady was disappointed. "Oh. I was hoping you might be interested in joining my staff." He saw that the young man was astonished at his proposal and laughed. "Well now, let me explain. I have a dream,

Mr. Bristol. I want to photograph this war we're in. . . ." Paul listened as Brady went on to speak of how he'd gone right to the top, to General McClellan and President Lincoln. "Both have sat for me, of course, and they agreed that it would be a good idea. General McClellan even suggested that he would like photographs of enemy installations if such a thing were possible."

Bristol made a note of that in case it was something that President Davis might find interesting! But he said only, "A tremendous undertaking, Mr. Brady. But you're the obvious choice for the job. Of course, you'll be needing a great deal of extra help, covering the entire war."

"Yes, which is why I was hoping you'd come with us."

Paul took a deep breath, then said carefully, "Actually, Mr. Brady, I intend to photograph the coming battles myself, but from . . . a different point of view than the one you propose."

Brady's eyes narrowed. "Where did you say you were from, Mr. Bristol?"

"Virginia."

Brady's expression changed, and suddenly a smile touched his lips. "I believe I understand." He studied the young man, and Paul thought, *He's going to turn me in for a spy!*

But Brady had no such intention. "Well, sir, as a Union man, I must be for my country, but as an artist, I must be happy that the conflict will be covered from, as you say, a 'different point of view.' What can I do for you?"

"I know you're very busy, but if you could have one of your assistants fill me in on new techniques and give me some advice about where to buy equipment and supplies —"

"Of course! The latter is easy enough. Go to Anthony's Supply House. It's on Broadway. Tell him I sent you and that I'd appreciate it if he gave you professional rates."

"Very kind of you, sir!"

Brady looked across the room. "James, come here, please." When a young man with a bushy crop of whiskers came to say, "Sir?" Brady nodded. "This is Mr. Bristol. James Tinney is my best assistant. James, take Mr. Bristol on a very thorough tour. Explain our new processes. Be very polite, for he's going to do some fine things with our battle scenes."

"Really, sir?"

"Yes, indeed!" Brady's eyes gleamed with humor. "He's going to photograph them from . . . a different point of view." Then Brady put out his hand, saying, "If you will, send me some of your plates, Mr. Bristol.

I'd like to see things from your perspective!"

"If I am able, I'll certainly do that, sir. And thank you very much!"

James Tinney proved to be a gift from heaven to Paul Bristol. He was one of those people who loved to *explain* things, and for the next three days he kept Bristol at his side. There was no aspect of the art that he failed to demonstrate or to permit his pupil to try. Thus Paul was able to do the actual work while Tinney looked on and gave instruction and encouragement. Of course, everything in Brady's was of superior quality. On one floor was the plate cleaning room and the electrotype room, and on another a spare operational room and chemical room.

Paul used what little spare time he had at Anthony's Supply House, laying in an enormous inventory of chemicals. In addition, he purchased a fine camera, complete with extra parts. *It's not like I can run down to the corner store and buy this material,* he consoled himself as the costs soared. *Whatever I use, I have to get right now!*

One week later — though Paul felt more as though he'd been in New York for months — he took the train for Richmond. He traveled in the boxcar to make sure no careless brakeman treated his precious cases roughly.

As the train rattled and clicked along, Bristol smiled as he thought of his last visit to Anthony's Supply House. When the clerk had presented the bill, a terrible temptation came to Bristol. He longed to say, "Will it be all right if I pay for this in Confederate money?" But he stifled that urge and paid in gold, the money having been advanced by President Davis's secretary.

Now I've got something to work with, Paul thought as the train rushed toward the heart of the Confederacy. *All I need is time to learn, some good help — and lots of luck!*

CHAPTER 5
A MOST UNUSUAL ASSISTANT

Paul Bristol's first month back home was hectic. Richmond had been a relatively small town a year earlier, but when it was decided to move the capitol of the Confederacy from Montgomery to Richmond, the city had mushroomed! Paul sought in vain for a place, almost any sort of place, to store his equipment and chemicals. But there was no place, or so it seemed. Desperate, he went to the president's office, but Davis was off on one of his periodic trips to view military units and fortifications. The secretary could not suggest anything, and finally Paul hired a wagon and hauled his camera and supplies to Hartsworth, where he commandeered a part of a barn for his studio.

But that was just the beginning. He had to build a lightproof room and places to store his equipment. Not being much of a carpenter, he would have been in trouble if his father and brother had not come to his aid. Not that they did much of the actual *work,* of course, but they put the hands to work. If it had been planting time, neither of them would have thought of taking the men out of the fields, but in January there was little field work to do.

It took a few weeks, and when the last board was nailed in place, Claude said, "Well, I think we've done a fine job! I certainly hope President Davis appreciates it!"

"Well, I don't know about the president, Father, but *I* appreciate it!" Paul smiled warmly and clapped his father on the shoulder. "You and I and Austin, we make a pretty good team, don't we?"

Claude Bristol turned suddenly to stare at Paul. The pressure of his son's hand on his shoulder gave him a queer feeling. It was, he realized, the first time he could remember Paul touching him since he was a boy. He nodded slowly, then said, "Remember how we used to go fishing at the river when you were just a little boy?"

"Of course I remember."

"Those . . . those were fine days, weren't they, Paul?" There was a sudden loneliness in his father's eyes that caught Paul off guard. He had not been close to his father for years, and it came as a revelation to him to discover that somehow his father *needed* him. He kept his hand in place, and the two of them stood very still. "Yes, Father, they were good days. Very good days. I've never forgotten them."

Then the moment was broken as Austin came running up to ask Paul when the picture taking would start. "I'll need about fifty pictures to keep the girls happy," he said with a nod, at which both Paul and his father laughed and told him to go soak his head.

"What's next?" Claude asked, looking around at the cases of supplies neatly stacked on shelves.

"Learn how to take pictures."

"Why, I thought you already knew how to do that!"

"It'll be a little different, what I plan to do. It's one thing to get a picture in a studio, but I can't imagine how to handle it in a wagon with cannon fire exploding all around."

Claude was startled. "I — I guess this photography thing is going to be a little different from what I had thought. Anything I can do to help?"

"You've done a lot, Father." Paul smiled. "Next thing is a What-Is-It wagon."

"A *what* kind of wagon?"

"That's what the soldiers called Brady's wagon at Bull Run. It's got to be tight as a jug, part of it has to be lightproof, and it's got to have shelves specially built to hold supplies in place so they won't bounce around or leak."

"Have you ever *seen* one of these contraptions?" Claude demanded.

"No . . . but as soon as we build it, we'll both have seen one!"

"All right. What else?"

"Got to hire an assistant. This isn't going to be a one-man job. Takes one man to make the exposures, and another man to get the plates ready for the camera and develop the exposed plates."

"Better put an ad in the paper."

"Already did that. There won't be too many applicants, though. Not many unemployed daguerreoists running around Richmond, would you say, Father?"

"Not only would I not say it; I can't even *pronounce* it." Claude grinned. "But if any applicants show up, I'll send them on to you."

The What-Is-It wagon was finished a week later, but not a single applicant had appeared. "What'll you do if you can't hire anyone?" Marie asked Paul at breakfast.

88

"Do without," he grunted. He was growing thin, and the twenty-hour days he'd been putting in were cutting his nerves raw. He'd simply ignored everyone's pleas that he slow down, for he felt that he had to get his technique perfected. Now he looked at his sister with bloodshot eyes and tried to smile. "I'm going to make a run. Don't open the door to the wagon, okay?"

When he left, Marie said, "Mother, he's not going to hold up. He's so tired he's almost falling down. Why don't you make him stop?"

Marianne smiled at her daughter. "The last time I 'made' Paul do something was when he was twelve years old." She looked thoughtfully out the window, catching sight of her son as he trudged toward the barn. "He was always this way — anything he did, he did it with all the strength he had."

The barn was warm, and Paul had mastered the technique of developing the plates in high temperatures. But he knew that battles would be fought in the snow, so he pulled the wagon outside and let the cold air bring the temperature down. Then he got back inside, closed the curtain, and began to work awkwardly. He was so tired that as he waited for the time to lapse between steps, he found himself dozing off.

His fingers grew stiff and numb with cold, and he dropped a bottle of vile-smelling hypo, the fumes filling the room and making him feel sick.

Then, just when he was involved in the last step, the curtain behind him suddenly opened! Paul yelped, "What the devil — !" He came out of the dark area and stopped abruptly, blinded by the sun. Squinting, he saw a figure standing before him, but he could only wait until his eyes grew accustomed to the light to see who it was.

"Don't you know better than to open the curtain in a darkroom?" he yelled. "Who are you, anyway?"

"My name is Frankie Aimes. I came to apply for the job as assistant photographer."

Paul had opened his mouth to berate the intruder, but changed his mind at once. At last he might get some help!

"Well . . ." Bristol squinted hard but could see only a blurred shape. "Let's go inside where it's warm and talk about it." He walked toward the barn, asking, "Do you have any experience?"

"Yes, I do."

Paul opened the door and marched into the barn. "Shut the blasted door," he commanded. "It's cold out there this —," and then he halted and his jaw dropped.

"Why, you're a . . . a girl!"

"Yes. The ad didn't specify anything about gender."

Paul had heard of people being speechless but had always considered it to be a figure of speech. Now he knew it was not. He stood there, his mouth open, and simply could not think of a single thing to say. Anger suddenly built up in him — the result of too much work, too little sleep, and the dashing of his hope that he'd found some help.

"I can't use a female," he said in disgust. "Never thought about one asking for the job. Sorry you made the trip for nothing," he added grudgingly. "I'll see you get a ride back to town if you don't have a way."

"I want the job, Mr. Bristol. I can do the work, and it doesn't seem that the job has been filled yet."

Paul glared at the girl, trying to keep a hold on his temper. She was a strange-looking sight. For one thing, she was wearing men's clothing — which was shocking to him, to say the least. She wore a pair of loose-fitting black trousers, and a pair of boots peeped out from under the cuffs. A thick red-and-black wool coat covered her upper body, and a black felt hat with a broad brim came down over her brow. She might have passed for a young man, but her face — though stronger than most women's — was clearly feminine. Fair skin with a very faint line of freckles across a short nose complemented her green eyes, which were large and wide set, and her thick eyelashes could only belong to a woman. Her hair, what showed from under the hat, seemed to be auburn and curly.

She endured his inspection silently, then held out her hands so suddenly that he blinked. "Feel the palms," she said quietly.

Paul took one of her hands and was startled when she squeezed his hand so hard that he flinched. "Those are calluses," she said. "I'm as strong as lots of men, Mr. Bristol." With that, she pulled her hand back abruptly and waited.

Paul had to smile at her methods. "I'm not looking for field hands, Miss . . . What's your name again? Frankie Aimes? Well, I'm impressed with your strength, but I need a little more than that in an assistant."

"I learned photography from Mr. Mathew Brady," the girl said suddenly, and when she saw the surprise in his face, her lips curved slightly in a smile. "I have a letter of introduction from Mr. Brady," she said, holding it out. As Paul took the letter and glanced over it, Frankie said, "I'll be glad to show you what I can do."

Paul snapped a question at her. "What is collodion?"

"Collodion is a mixture of bromide and iodide of potassium, or ammonia, or cadmium."

"What's it used for?"

"Copper plates are coated with it to make them ready to receive the image."

Paul shot out question after question and was highly surprised to discover that the blasted girl knew as much about photography as *he* did! Finally he shook his head. "Well, you *know* enough, Miss Aimes. But I still can't use you."

"I have another letter for you, Mr. Bristol."

Paul took the second letter, glanced at the signature, and gave the girl a startled glance. "You know my cousin — Gideon Rocklin?"

"Yes, sir. I worked for him, nursing his son Tyler when he was shot."

Paul read the brief letter, which simply stated that Frankie Aimes, who had been very helpful to the Rocklin family, wanted very much to have a career in photography. One sentence said, *"Miss Aimes is not involved in politics and takes no sides in this war. I believe you feel the same way, Paul, so if you could help her, I would appreciate it."*

Still, Bristol was not convinced. "It just wouldn't work," he said harshly, shoving the letter back at her. "Sorry you went to all the trouble for nothing."

Every young woman he knew would have turned and fled at such abrupt and ill-mannered treatment. It was what he expected, but the girl stood there patiently, saying, "You need an assistant who's able to help with the picture-taking process. And you'll be going to the battlefields, so you need someone who's able to rough it, to camp out and sleep on the ground and do without hot food and sleep."

"Well, that's right, but —"

"I don't mean to be proud, Mr. Bristol, but I reckon I can do those things better than . . ."

Paul stared at her, then finished her sentence. "Better than I can? Is that what you mean?"

The girl faltered slightly at his angry tone, then pulled her head up. "I didn't mean to say that, but I have lived outdoors all my life, and you haven't, have you, Mr. Bristol?" She glanced at Paul's hands, and he knew that she was reminding him that his own hands were smooth and uncalloused.

Once again he felt his anger rising; only this time it was because he suspected the girl was *right.* "Makes no difference," he snapped. "An unmarried man and an unmarried woman can't go all over the country in a wagon alone." A thought came to him, and he asked, "You're not married, are you?"

"No, I'm not."

Paul was irritated at the girl and asked angrily, "Don't you have a family? All I need is for your father to catch up with me and wave a shotgun in my face for ruining his daughter."

"You . . . don't have to worry about that, Mr. Bristol. Nobody's going to come looking for me."

For the first time, Paul caught a sense of fragility, of femininity, in the girl. She was so abrupt and strongly made that it was only a hint, but he dropped his abusive manner. "Miss Aimes, I just can't do it. It . . . it wouldn't look proper."

"You wouldn't harm me, would you, Mr. Bristol? And you wouldn't ask me to do anything that's wrong, would you?"

Her directness caught him off guard. He flushed but said, "No! Of course not!"

"Then you're afraid of what people would say about us?"

"Well, not exactly *afraid.*" Paul was growing very uncomfortable, and he turned away abruptly. "Have some coffee," he said to take the strain from the moment. "I keep it on the stove all the time." He poured two cups and added, "It's the last of the real coffee."

She took the coffee in both her hands, and his gentler manner caused her to smile at him. His eyebrows rose, for it was a surprisingly attractive smile. She sipped the coffee, and he was pleased that she didn't rattle on. *At least she can endure silence, which is more than I can say about most women.* He looked at her again. *But what will people say? What will Luci say?*

Then he gave an angry snort. *What business is it of theirs? As long as the girl does her work?* Standing suddenly, he said, "Miss Aimes, I think this might be a disaster. I can't be responsible for you. I intend to take this wagon as close to battle lines as I can drive it, and a shell doesn't know the difference between an enemy soldier and a mere photographer. Either of us could be killed or maimed."

"I know that."

Paul was suddenly impressed with her coolness. "Well, I might mention that you'll be right in the middle of thousands of soldiers. Not all of them are gentlemen. They'll try to force themselves on you."

"I know. But they won't have any luck."

Bristol smiled. He admired courage above all things, and the girl seemed to have plenty of that! As for her being a woman, well, Bristol had been subjected to beautiful women for years. And as he looked at Frankie Aimes in her rumpled clothing, he thought, *Well, the one thing I won't have to worry about is falling in love with her! She's too peculiar for my tastes.*

"All right, I'll give you a try," he said suddenly. "If you can do the work, you get the job."

Again the smile crossed her face, and this time it reached her green eyes. "I'll do my best to please you, Mr. Bristol."

And so it was that Frankie Aimes came to be Paul Bristol's assistant. But only after several minor wars, all over the same thing: *"Paul! You can't do it! Not a woman!"*

Two specific responses surprised him: His mother was dead set against it, while Luci laughed at the thing.

"Mother, don't you like the girl?" Paul asked when Marianne begged him to abandon the idea.

"Yes. I do like her," she said. Frankie had spent almost a week at Hartsworth, and Marianne had taken pains to get to know her. Now a slight frown crossed Marianne's face, and she said, "But you're not as strong as you think you are where women are concerned, my boy. You could fall in love with her — or worse, get involved with her *without* that. Then you'd either have to cast her off or marry her."

"Mother, please! Don't be . . . well, *ridiculous* is the word. She's how old? Seventeen or eighteen? And I'm thirty-one. Besides, have you taken a look at her? She's really not my type."

"Oh? And men are never attracted to women younger than they are?" Marianne loved this tall son of hers and said earnestly, "It will be a lonely, dangerous job. You two will be cut off from the world, you know. And when you're tired and weak and lonely, she'll be right there. Your 'type' or not, Paul, she is still a woman. And you are still a man. Don't do it!"

His mother's warning almost changed Paul's mind, but there was literally no one else to fill the position. *Besides,* Paul thought ruefully, *she's my mother. It's her job to worry about me!*

When he told Luci about his new assistant, she had stared at him, her lips growing tight. "A woman? You're going to take a woman with you?"

It was rough sledding, but when Paul took

98

Luci to the barn and introduced her to Frankie Aimes, all was well. Frankie had just come out of the What-Is-It wagon and was dripping with sweat and smelling of chemicals. She was wearing the oldest clothing she had, which was tattered and baggy. She had on a pair of steel spectacles, which she wore for close work at times — and she looked terrible.

Luci greeted her; then when she and Paul were alone, she laughed at her fears. "What a ragamuffin! Paul, I was jealous, but I see how foolish I was. But can you stand her? She's such . . . such a mess!"

"She can develop plates." Paul smiled, relieved. "That's all she has to do. Looking good isn't a job requirement."

Luci leaned against him and whispered, "You asked me to marry you last month, Paul. Do you still want me?"

"Yes!" He kissed her, and when she stepped back, she gave him an arch smile. "There, think of *that* while you're out taking your old pictures!"

When Luci left, Paul went back and helped Frankie clean up.

"Are you going to marry her, Mr. Bristol?" she asked, watching him carefully.

"Yes, I am."

Frankie lifted her green eyes and gave him

a sudden smile. "She's so beautiful. I hope you'll be very happy."

"Got to take lots of pictures first." Paul stood quietly, thinking of the days to come. "We'll leave tomorrow. There's a battle shaping up west of here. I think I'd like to have a try then to see what we can do."

"I'm ready," Frankie said, then thought again of Luci. "She sure is beautiful."

"Yes, she is, Frankie. Well, let's get loaded. We'll get away at first light."

"All right, Mr. Bristol."

■ ■ ■ ■

PART TWO:
THE VIVANDIER —
JANUARY 1861

■ ■ ■ ■

CHAPTER 6
A WOMAN GROWN

The first morning of 1861 came on the heels of a heavy snow that almost buried Flint, Michigan. All night long, flakes as large as quarters swirled out of the sky, covering the towns and the countryside with a thick white blanket of pristine snow.

Frankie Aimes forced open the front door of her house, shoving back the deep mound of snow piled against its base and stepping outside. She blinked at the brilliance of the landscape before her. Shutting the door quickly, she stood for one moment, taking delight in the smooth, unbroken expanse of white, glittering with diamondlike flashes. The rawness of the brown earth was clothed with a flawless layer of white, which looked like a blanket of cotton. Even the trees with their bare, naked arms had become graceful, sweeping forms under the white mantle.

"Well . . . this won't get the milking done." The young woman spoke aloud — a habit she had formed while working alone in the fields or hunting in the woods. She stepped into the eighteen-inch blanket of snow, sank at once to her knees in the fluffy drift, then forged her way across the yard to the barn. The air was biting cold, which brought a rosy flush to her cheeks.

She loved the cold weather! As she opened the barn door, having to clear the snow away in front of one of the doors first, she thought of how she might go fishing later in the day. She had learned long ago how to cut a hole through the ice covering the nearby pond and drop in her line, complete with a bait custom-designed to tantalize the fish below. "Fresh-caught fish for dinner," she said with a smile. "Now that's something to look forward to."

All five of the cows looked up as she entered the barn, and soon she was engaged in milking. Leaning her cheek against a silky rump, she smiled at Blaze, the black-and-white cat who took station a few feet away. "Want some breakfast?" She sent a stream of the frothy milk at him, and he took it in greedily, not minding the spatters that covered his face and front. Frankie laughed as the cat at once began taking a bath. "If you don't start cleaning up on the rats out here, I'm going to trade you in for a terrier who'll do the job," she threatened. But Blaze, as cats are wont to do, ignored her totally and went on licking his fur.

When the milking was finished, Frankie fed the horses, pigs, and chickens, then took a pail of the warm milk back to the house.

"Morning, Tim," she said, greeting the young man who was standing in front of the cookstove warming his hands. "Want some nice warm milk while I fix breakfast?"

"I guess so." Timothy Aimes, the only boy in the family, at the age of twenty was only three years older than Frankie. However, he looked much older. He was below medium height, and something in his face reflected that a childhood sickness had almost killed him. He had fragile features, with soft brown eyes and a vulnerable mouth. "You sit down and let me cook this morning," he said.

Frankie poured a glass of milk into a cup, then moved to hand it to her brother with a fond smile. "All right, you can spoil me. I'll read the paper out loud to you."

Tim grinned as he began collecting the eggs and bacon from the larder. "Good. We've only read it about ten times up until now." Still, he listened raptly as she read aloud from the editorial on the front page. His movements were slow, and his hands were thin and frail, not at all like the strong, rounded arms and firm hands of the girl who read the paper.

When he put the bowl of eggs and the platter of bacon on the table and poured the coffee into two mugs, he said, "Let's eat, Frankie. Those girls are going to sleep all day."

"They always do when Pa's away." She bowed her head while Tim asked the blessing, then plunged into her food with gusto, talking about the story in the paper. "Looks like there's going to be a war, doesn't it, Tim."

"I guess so." Tim picked at his food, shoving it around with a fork. "Looks as though 1861 is going to be a pretty bad year for this country. President Buchanan's never been a strong leader, and now he's a lame duck. He's so out of touch with things, it's pitiful, Frankie."

"What does that mean, Tim, all that about Fort Sumter?"

"When South Carolina seceded from the Union, she claimed all the Union forts in her territory. One of those was Fort Sumter. Now a Union officer, Major Anderson, has moved his troops into the fort. The hotheads in South Carolina consider that an act of aggression, so if the new president tries to send help or supplies to Anderson, they'll fire on them. And if that happens, the North will have to shoot back . . . and we'll be in the middle of a war."

Frankie and Tim sat at the table talking until the younger girls got up. This brother and sister were very close, partly because of their ages. Sarah and Jane, ages ten and twelve, were cut off from Frankie and Tim by a generation gap — but there was more than that to account for the elder siblings' closeness. There was their father, Silas Aimes. He had wanted a large family and longed for boys to help with the farm. His wife had been a happy woman, attractive with auburn hair and green eyes, and when their first child had been a son, Silas had been happy, assured that Tim would be the first boy of many to come.

But Silas's dream had died. The first deathblow came when Tim was stricken with some sort of fever that the doctors could neither name nor cure. Though the boy lived, he would never be strong. Sadly, he was an especially bright lad, which meant it didn't take long for him to realize he was a disappointment to his father. As a result, though his mother did her best to make up for his father's disdain, Tim gave up on his own hopes and dreams.

The final blow to Silas Aimes's dream came when Leah, his wife, presented him with three more children — all girls. With each new daughter, Silas grew more taciturn and bitter.

Like Tim, Frankie was quite bright and observant. She had grasped at a very early age the fact that her father was not happy with her. Confused and troubled, she labored to understand why this was. When she finally understood that it was because she was not a boy, it almost broke her heart. She was a loving, affectionate child, and as long as her mother had lived, there was some outlet. But Leah Aimes had died when Sarah was born, thus leaving a terrible void in the lives of both Frankie and Tim — another factor that drew them closer together.

As the years had passed, a pattern established itself, without being planned or discussed, in the Aimes household. Frankie, because she was hearty and strong, began to do the heavy work of the farm, while Tim had no choice but to take over the running of the household. By the time Frankie was fourteen, she could plow a furrow as straight as her father. By the time she was sixteen, she could put in a full day sawing wood or breaking new ground.

Of course, the reversal of roles between Tim and Frankie had some hidden costs. Tim grew more dependent and less decisive, and Frankie's assumption of a male's role went deeper than just doing a man's work. She entered puberty and passed through it without gaining any of the feminine graces or insights that come to girls with mothers. Frankie lived far out in the country, worked hard at all times, and passed from being a girl to being a woman — in form, but not in spirit.

Tim had seen some of this as he watched his sister grow, and now as he sat there watching her, he said suddenly, "Are you going to go to the dance over at Henderson in two weeks?"

Had he asked her if she were going to China, Frankie could not have been more surprised. "Why, I can't do that, Tim!"

"Why not? You need to have some fun once in a while." A bitterness touched his lips, and he added, "You sure don't get any around here!"

Frankie, for all that she was three years younger than her brother, had a strong maternal instinct. She got to her feet, went to the sink, set down her plate and cup, then came to stand beside him. Brushing his unkempt hair into place, she said, "I have lots of fun, Tim. This afternoon I'm going fishing on the pond."

Tim shook his head and turned to face her. "You never go to dances or do any of the things young girls do. How are you going to ever find a husband, Frankie? You've got to think ahead. Someday you've got to get married and have a home and children of your own."

Tim's words disturbed Frankie, and she threw up a defensive shield. Laughing lightly, she said, "I've got you, Tim. Taking care of one man is enough for me."

"It's not the same thing." Tim's thin face was haggard, and he shook his head. "*I'll* never do anything, but I want to see you have a good life, Frankie. Why, you . . . you've become little more than a hired hand around this place. Pa will work you to death if you don't get away." He cast a pleading glance at her. "Go to the dance."

Frankie spoke nervously. "I . . . don't have anything to wear . . . and I can't dance, anyway." Then her voice dropped to a whisper. "Besides, none of the young men want me, Tim."

It was the most revealing statement Frankie had ever made to her brother, and Tim wanted to put his arm around her and comfort her. Instead he said, "Frankie, you've got to make an effort. Buy a dress; learn to dance. You'd be pretty if you'd do what the other girls do. Men would notice you; I know they would."

But the years had ground something into Frankie that could not be changed by simply putting on a dress. Somewhere along the line she had packed away the dreams that most girls had and now was resigned to the fact that she always would be different. Instead of regretting her life, she took pride in her physical strength and her ability to keep up with most men. That was what fulfilled her and satisfied her, and it was enough. At least, that's what she told herself.

But no matter how content she believed she was, she could not stop the dull pain that would sometimes overwhelm her when she saw a young couple together, walking hand in hand, laughing into each other's eyes. Nor could she rid herself of the longings that would come to her unbidden — longings to be loved, cherished, and accepted as she was by one man who cared for her above all else — longings that could still keep her awake at night as tears coursed down her face and soaked into her hard pillow.

Only once had she let those longings come

to the surface. With Davey Trapper. She had met him while out hunting several years ago. His surprise at finding a young girl in the woods had been evident — as had his amazement at her ability with a rifle, for she was a far better shot than he. When Davey asked her to help him learn to shoot better, she could not find a valid reason to refuse such a simple request. And so they spent the afternoon hunting together, and by the end of the day, Frankie suddenly found herself with a friend — something she had never before experienced. She was careful, however, never to mention Davey to her father. She had no doubt that he would not approve.

Frankie and Davey went hunting together often. They would meet in the woods, then go tramping through the wilderness, talking and growing ever closer. Before long, Frankie found herself thinking about Davey more and more. His quick smile and laughing eyes were a balm to her heart in all its weariness. And she grew more and more certain that here, at last, was a man who loved her despite the fact that her dress and manners were different from those of other girls.

Certain, that is, until that day in the woods when her fragile confidence came crashing down around her. The memory still brought a blush of humiliation to Frankie's cheeks whenever she let herself think of it — which she seldom did. She had worked up the courage to tell Davey her feelings, but instead of smiling and taking her hands — as she had imagined he would do — he had stared at her, dumbfounded.

And then he had started to laugh.

"Oh, Frankie, that's some joke!" he'd hooted. "You almost sound serious!" One look at her stricken face had put an abrupt end to his laughter, and his eyes had widened in shock. "You . . . you *are* serious," he'd said in disbelief. Desperately hurt, Frankie had only been able to stand there, fighting to keep the tears that clamored at her eyes from sliding down her cheeks. An uncomfortable silence had fallen over the two. Finally Davey tried to stammer out an apology, to explain that she was a "right capable hunter and a good pal," but that he'd never really looked at her as a woman.

They had finished their hunt — Frankie never shirked her responsibilities to her family, and they needed meat — but the usual talk and laughter were glaringly absent . . . and Frankie's one friendship died a painful death. That was the last day she ever saw Davey.

And it was the last time she had trusted her heart.

Now she smiled at her brother and said, "It's too late for me, Tim. I'll be fine the way I am."

Suddenly the girls bounded into the room, loudly demanding breakfast. They had been protected by both Frankie and Tim from the pressures that had made their lives so hard. Now, though, as Frankie looked at her young sisters, she thought, *They'll learn pretty soon that Pa has no use for girls. I wish they didn't have to!*

The cold weather was to hold on for the rest of the month, but ferment heated up the political climate in both the South and the North. It was Jefferson Davis, then a senator from Mississippi, who had broken the news to President Buchanan that Major Anderson was at Fort Sumter, adding, "And now, Mr. President, you are surrounded with blood and dishonor on all sides!"

Buchanan wanted only to keep clear of the problem of Fort Sumter, so he did nothing, waiting for Lincoln to assume the burden. On January 5, 1861, General Scott sent the *Star of the West,* a merchant vessel, with 250 troops to reinforce Major Anderson at Sumter. But on January 9 the ship was driven off by cannon fire from a South

Carolina battery and had to make her way back home with the troops. All that Scott had accomplished was to pour oil on the fire. Robert Barnwell Rhett, the fire-eating editor of the Charleston *Mercury,* wrote that "powder had been burnt over the degrees of our state, and the firing on the *Star of the West* is the opening ball of the Revolution. South Carolina is honored to be the first thus to resist the Yankee tyranny. She has not hesitated to strike the first blow in the face of her insulter."

Frankie read about the struggles in the paper, how the Southern states began to coalesce, with Mississippi voting eighty-four to fifteen in favor of secession. Then on January 10, Florida joined Mississippi and South Carolina. A day later, Alabama left the Union. Other states were certain to follow.

Frankie had left to go hunting on that same morning, hoping to bring back a deer. She rose at dawn, saddled her mare, and rode ten miles deep into the hills, where she bagged a fine six-pointer a little after noon. By the time she had loaded the buck and made her way home, the shadows were beginning to lengthen. As she rode up to the house, her father stepped outside and came to inspect the kill.

Silas Aimes was a big man, standing slightly over six feet and weighing over two hundred pounds. Years of hard work had hardened his muscles and turned his features heavy. He was only fifty, but his gray hair and lined face made him look several years older. He glanced at the deer, then at Frankie. "Get him with one shot?"

"Wasn't too hard." Frankie shrugged. "He came up twenty feet away." She started to lead the horse away from the house, saying, "I'll have time to dress him out before dark, Pa . . . ," but then paused, for another man had stepped outside the house and walked to the edge of the porch.

Silas glanced toward the visitor, then stepped over to take the reins of Frankie's mare. "I'll do that. You go get cleaned up. Tim's got supper started." He hesitated, then added, "Mr. Buck's going to take supper with us."

"Howdy, Miss Frankie." Alvin Buck owned the farm that joined theirs — a large farm that covered over seven hundred acres, including the timber. He was forty-six years old, and a widower with five children. "You always bring back your deer, don't you, now?"

Frankie nodded. "Do my best, Mr. Buck. But I miss once in a while." She moved up on the porch and entered the house, followed closely by her father's visitor. "Smells good, Tim," she said with a smile. "I'm starved." She went upstairs, washed in cold water, changed clothes, then ran a comb through her stubborn curls without looking in the mirror. When she went downstairs, she found the girls helping Tim with the meal.

"Sit down here and rest up, Frankie," Buck said, nodding toward the seat next to him. "I brought the latest papers along from town. Thought you might like to read up on how the war's going." Buck was a short man, no more than five feet nine inches tall, and very thick. His huge limbs filled his trousers and shirtsleeves so tightly that they looked like fat sausages. He had a round, florid face with small dark eyes and an incongruous rim of hair around his bullet-like head. He was wearing, Frankie noted, what seemed to be new clothes, but she seldom saw him dressed in anything but overalls, so she could not be sure.

She sat there growing drowsy before the open fire, listening as Alvin Buck read items from the paper and commented on them from time to time. Frankie answered in monosyllables and was almost asleep when her father came in. "Supper ready?" he asked.

"Soon as you wash up," Tim said. When this task was done, they sat down to eat, Silas at the head of the table, with Tim at the other end and Sarah and Jane at his right, which placed Frankie and Buck on his left. Most of the conversation concerned farming matters, with some speculation on what the South — and the new president — would do.

Frankie listened as the men talked, commenting mostly to Tim on how good the food was. Once she felt Alvin Buck's knee touch hers, but she moved at once, hardly noticing.

After supper Silas said, "Sarah, you and Jane do the dishes and clean up."

"Oh, I'll do that, Pa," Frankie said, but her father shook his head. "Let the young-uns do it. They don't do enough work as it is."

The evening was a long one for Frankie. She sat with the others, taking little part in the talk, until, about eight o'clock, Tim set the girls at the table. "Time for your schooling," he said firmly.

"Pa, I'd better go put Julie in the barn. She might drop her calf tonight, and I don't want her to do it out in the cold," Frankie said.

"I'll just go along with you," Buck said quickly. "Got to be on my way home, but I'll help you with the cow."

Frankie looked up with surprise but said only, "Well, it's not much of a job, but come along if you want."

She put on her heavy coat, and the two of them left the house. "Won't snow again for a few days," Buck observed. "Hope we have an early spring. I'm going to break fifty acres of new ground. Need to get an early start."

A pale moon illuminated the barnyard, and Frankie had only to speak to the cow, who followed her into the barn. When she had put some feed in the box, she turned to go but found her way blocked by Buck's stocky form.

"Been a'wantin' to talk to you," he said. His small eyes were bright and eager in the lamplight, and there was something about his manner that made Frankie grow still and alert. "You know, it's been pretty hard on me and the kids, losing my wife like I did a couple of years ago," Buck went on. "Got so much land it takes all a man can do to get the crops in. 'Course, my boys are big enough to do a man's work, but Ellie's too young to keep house much, especially with the baby hardly out of diapers."

A brown rat that had sought the heat of the barn suddenly poked his head out from between two boards, and Frankie frowned. "Rats been bad this winter over here. You bothered much with 'em, Mr. Buck?"

"What? Oh, well, we keep a dog and some cats," Buck said. "Sure wish you'd call me by my first name, Frankie."

Again a slight warning went off inside the girl, and she shook her head. "Pa would thrash me if I did. He taught me to call people Mister and Missus."

"That was when you was a little girl, but you're a grown woman now, Frankie." Buck grinned suddenly and added, "And a right purty one, too!"

Frankie had never been good at handling compliments, mainly because she hadn't had much experience receiving them, so she tried to change the subject. "Well, guess I'd better get back —"

But Alvin moved closer and suddenly reached out and seized Frankie by the arm. "You're a woman, sure enough, and I been thinking how wasted you are. Not married, I mean."

Panic shot through Frankie — and shame, for there was a light in Buck's small eyes that was not right. She tried to break away, but he was a powerful man, and he only laughed deep in his chest. "You ain't never had no doin's with men, have you, Frankie? Wal, that's good . . . but a man like me can teach you all you need to know!"

With that, Buck jerked Frankie into his arms and, before she could react, kissed her full on the lips. Revulsion swept over her and her skin crawled, for there was something feral about the man. With surprising force, she fought clear of his embrace.

"Don't you *ever* do that!" she spat out, furious. "I'll tell my pa!"

"Go right ahead," Buck said with a nod and a pleased expression on his face. "He won't be mad. I done talked to him. Only proper thing to do — see a gal's pa before asking her to marry."

"Marry!" Frankie shook her head and spun around to flee from the barn, dodging Buck as he reached for her again.

"You're just scared," he called after her. "Which is what a gal's supposed to be, but you'll like me better after we git hitched!"

Frankie ran to the house but could not bear to go inside and face her father, so she turned to the left and, for the next half hour, walked along a narrow trail that led to the nearby river. Anger and shame rose within her, and she wanted to scream and beat her fists against the bark of one of the huge oaks that lined the path.

When she got to the river, she walked along the bank, able to see by the moonlight, staring morosely at the glittering black water as it flowed silently along. The sibilant sound of the wave at the brink of the stream seemed to soothe her nerves, and finally she turned back to the house.

Pa won't let him come around, she thought, drawing a deep breath. *He wouldn't want to lose me.* But when she stepped inside the house, one look at her father's face told her she was wrong.

"Guess Alvin told you — about marrying up with you."

Her stomach tightened into a knot, and she struggled to keep her voice steady. "I — I can't do it, Pa!"

"I guess you will, girl." Silas's voice was hard, much the way it was when Frankie had heard him speaking to stubborn animals. She knew, all too well, that if the warning note in his voice was not enough, he would beat them.

"You've got to get married sometime, Frankie," her father said. "Only natural thing for a woman to do. And I won't have you runnin' off with some worthless boy.

Now Alvin's a little older than you might like, but he's a steady man."

"Just let me stay here, Pa," Frankie pleaded. "I'll work lots harder!"

Her father continued as though she had not spoken. "And there's this we got to consider: Alvin's farm joins mine. If you marry him, one day his place will be yours. Then we'll have one of the biggest and best farms in this part of Michigan."

"I just . . . can't do it, Pa!"

Silas laid his eyes on her, and she saw with a sinking heart that there was no softness in them. "I say you will, and that's the end to it." He moved away from her, but when he got to the door leading to his bedroom, he turned to add, "Alvin's in a hurry. Guess it might as well be soon. You and him can go to town first of next week and see the justice of the peace."

Frankie had not cried in front of her father for years, but now tears ran unbidden down her cheeks as she stared at him dumbly. Some faint trace of compassion stirred inside Silas Aimes as he studied the girl, then said, "Well, it won't be so bad, Frankie. You'll get used to it."

Then he turned and left her alone — more alone than she'd ever been in her entire life.

CHAPTER 7
THE RUNAWAY

The third step from the bottom squeaked loudly, so Frankie carefully skipped it and was able to make the journey from the second floor silently. Her father was a heavy sleeper, but she took no chances. She wore wool trousers, as usual, and her heavy coat over a man's shirt. The suitcase she carried was old and patched, and it bulged at the seams, for she had stuffed into it all it would possibly hold.

The house was still, for at two in the morning everyone would be sound asleep. She herself had not slept at all, and now as she moved across the wooden floor, her nerves were frayed — so much so that when a voice spoke off to her left, she uttered a desperate cry despite herself.

"Frankie."

Whirling around, Frankie saw by the light of the single lamp that Tim was sitting in a chair by the fireplace. "Tim!" she gasped and looked upstairs suddenly, afraid that her father might have heard.

Tim got up and came to stand in front of her. "I knew you were going away."

"How did you know that?" Frankie whispered.

"Because I saw you couldn't do anything else. Every night I looked in the attic, because that's where the only suitcase we have is. It wasn't there last night, so I knew you'd be leaving."

Frankie shook her head, desperation in her eyes. "I have to go, Tim. I *have* to!"

"Sure, I know." Tim reached into his pocket and pulled something out, then held it toward the girl. "You'll need some money."

"Why, this is the money you're saving to buy that guitar you wanted, Tim!"

"I'll get it someday. Go on, take the money."

Frankie put the thin packet of bills into her pants pocket, then reached out and hugged her brother. She clung to him fiercely, and a great sadness came over her. "It'll be bad for you when I'm gone," she whispered. "You won't have anybody to talk to."

Tim stepped back, and in the yellow light, his thin face seemed even frailer than usual.

"I'll miss you. Write to me, but send it to Johnson's Store. I'll pick it up there."

"And you'll write me back?"

"Sure I will. And when you get settled, I may come and visit with you." They both knew this would never happen, but the pretense made the leaving easier. "You have food for the trip? You know it'll take you near all day to get to town, and you'll need something to eat on the way." She nodded, touched at his concern for her.

Tim took a deep breath, then said, "Pa will be after you, Frankie. First thing he'll do is check the trains out of Henderson."

"Oh! I hadn't thought of that!"

"The train leaves at one fifteen. On foot it will be tight. But if you take your mare, you can make it. Pa may find out you got on the train, but he won't go any further once he knows you're out of town."

"What about the horse?"

"Leave her at the blacksmith shop. Have you written a note to Pa?"

"N–no."

"Here, sit down and write it now. Tell him you're leaving and won't be back for a long time. And tell him about the mare."

Frankie wrote a brief note, saying only that she could not bear the thought of marrying someone she did not love and that

126

she would make out on her own. She wrote about the mare, then tried to put in some sort of personal word — some fond farewell — to her father. But nothing came. Finally she signed it, then put it on the table. "Let him find it here, Tim. I don't want him to know you helped me. And try to make Sarah and Jane understand. . . . Tell them I love them!"

"Better get going," Tim said gently. He walked with her to the door, and she turned to kiss him. It was an awkward kiss, for they had not been outwardly demonstrative. "God will take care of you, Frankie," Tim said quietly. "And I want you to listen when He speaks to you."

Frankie knew that her brother was a man who believed deeply in God — he'd gotten that from their mother — and as she whispered her final good-bye, she wished with all her heart that she had some of that same faith.

Quickly she saddled the horse and tied the suitcase behind the saddle with some twine. She swung into the saddle and walked the mare out of the horse lot, holding her breath until she made the dogleg turn in the road. As the house was lost to view, her courage almost failed her. But then she thought of Alvin Buck and lifted her head. "Come on, girl, let's go!"

She kept the mare at a fast walk. She knew some of their neighbors would be starting to get up for their morning chores before too long and was grateful that she saw none of them. Not to speak to, at least. Old Mrs. Crane came out on the porch and waved at her, but Frankie merely returned the salute and moved on. The ride was long. She got to Henderson an hour before the train was due, so she had plenty of time to take the mare by the blacksmith shop, taking care to conceal the suitcase in some bushes before-hand.

The blacksmith boarded horses regularly and agreed to keep the mare until her father came for her. Frankie slipped the saddle off and rubbed the animal's velvet nose in a final gesture. She loved the mare and knew wherever she went she'd never again have one she loved so well. Then she turned and walked away, her back straight and her face stiff, not even turning when the horse whickered after her.

Retrieving her suitcase, she walked to the station, devoutly hoping that she'd encounter nobody she knew. She bought a ticket for Detroit — for no other reason than the fact that her mother had a sister who lived there, her aunt Clara. It had been years since her aunt had written. She might have moved, or even have died, but it was all that Frankie could think of to do.

The train came huffing in, blowing clouds of steam that frightened Frankie. Picking up her suitcase, she moved to the step. The conductor looked at her ticket and nodded. "Get aboard, folks," he called loudly as Frankie climbed the short steps. She turned to her left and entered the car — the first one she'd ever seen. It had two rows of wicker seats, each seat wide enough for two people, with an aisle between. There were no more than ten or twelve people seated, most of whom were reading or looking out the window. One passenger, a huge, black-bearded man, stared at Frankie curiously as she moved down the aisle and took her seat. Soon the train lurched backward, then forward. As it picked up speed, the whistle screamed, and the station seemed to move backward.

Frankie sat stiffly on the seat, watching the country flow by. Then the conductor stepped inside and came to her. "Ticket?" He took her ticket, punched it, and handed it back. He paused, his blue eyes curious. "Long ride to Detroit. We'll stop long enough at Haysville to eat. I'll make sure we don't go off and leave you if you want to buy something."

"Thank you," Frankie said gratefully, smiling. The conductor moved on, and she leaned back and relaxed. For the next hour she watched the scenery, then grew sleepy. The *click-clack* of the wheels and the heat from the coal stove at the front of the car combined to make her drowsy. Putting her head back, she closed her eyes and began to plan what she would do when she got to Detroit. She drifted off to sleep, awaking sometime later with that strange and bewildering sensation that sometimes comes upon awakening in a new place. For one sickening, frightening moment, she had no idea where she was. Her head jerked forward, and she restrained the cry that came to her lips as she remembered what she had done.

"Not far to Haysville," a man's voice said. Frankie jumped at the sound and turned to see that the big man who had watched her enter the car had stopped beside her seat. He smiled and added, "I'm hungry as a bear. Like to have something to eat?"

"No, I'm not hungry." Actually, she *was* hungry and had planned to get a sandwich, but something warned her that she must not go with this man.

"Aw, come on," he coaxed. "Nice little

café there, and the train can't leave for an hour. Has to make connection with the northbound."

When Frankie shook her head, the man's eyes narrowed. He sat down suddenly in the seat across from her and studied her carefully. "Going to Detroit? So am I. Maybe we know the same people there."

Frankie ignored him, or tried to, but he was loud and kept himself directly in front of her. Finally the conductor stuck his head in the car, crying out, "Haysville! One-hour stop. Café is half a block to your left!"

"C'mon, no sense sittin' on this train for an hour." The big man took Frankie's arm and pulled her to her feet.

At that moment a woman's voice said, "Let her go, trash!"

The big man swiveled his head to see a very small older woman, dressed in black, who had come to stand beside him. "What did you say?" he blustered.

"Are you deaf as well as ugly and stupid? I said to let that girl go."

"You'd better shut your trap, Grandma!" The big man kept his grip on Frankie's arm and leered at the woman. "Get on your broomstick and stay outta my business!"

All of the passengers were now watching the scene, and one of them stepped out of

131

his seat. He was a tall man with a tanned face and a pair of level gray eyes. He walked down the aisle and asked in a rather gentle voice, "Can I help you ladies?"

The elderly woman nodded primly. "Yes, thank you, sir. Would you please take out that pistol I see beneath your coat and point it at this white trash?"

Frankie saw that the old woman was speaking the truth. There *was* a gun under the tall man's coat. The rough man suddenly released her arm and stood there staring at the gray-eyed stranger. He could not take his eyes off of the other man's gun and said hastily, "Now . . . wait a minute!"

"Shut your mouth," the tall man remarked almost pleasantly. Then he turned to the two women, and a smile touched his thin lips. "You two ladies just go on now and have your lunch."

"Thank you, sir." The old woman nodded, pleased, the sunlight from the windows making her silver hair shine. She gave the man an open look, her bright black eyes warm and appreciative. "You're from the South, I believe?"

"Yes, ma'am. From the sovereign state of Alabama."

"Well, Alabama should be most proud of you. You have shown great honor today."

"I couldn't do any less, dear lady," the man replied with a warm smile. "As for you —," he said, then nodded at the big man, and the two of them moved off.

"Now let's get something to eat!" the woman said briskly, taking Frankie's hand, pausing only to look around at the staring passengers. Frankie suppressed a grin as the woman lifted her voice and remarked, "All right, the show's over!" at which all of the passengers left the car with alacrity. "Now," the woman said, a satisfied tone in her voice, "let's find that café."

Fifteen minutes later Frankie had discovered that Deborah Simms Satterfield was a widow, that she had been born and reared in Georgia, and that she had an insatiable curiosity. The first thing she asked when they had ordered their meal was: "Why in the world are you wearing that outlandish garb, my dear?"

Before they had returned to the car, Frankie felt that she had been drained dry. Mrs. Satterfield would have made an excellent detective, for she had gotten the entire story from her young charge, then had at once invited her to stay in her home for a few days. When Frankie had awkwardly protested, Mrs. Satterfield scoffed, "Nonsense! Of *course* you're going home with

133

me! Why, you might be *arrested* if you walked the streets in that outfit!" Then she'd smiled and put a kinder note in her voice. "Mr. Satterfield had the poor judgment to die two years ago. I rattle around in that huge house he built for us. I have my two sisters with me, but it'll be good to have someone young to talk to." Then she nodded sharply, adding, "And I think I can find something a little more feminine than that — that — *thing* you're wearing!"

During Frankie's visit with Mrs. Satterfield, she grew very fond of the old woman. She was not surprised when, after only three days, the widow asked her to live with her. But the restraint of the life in the Satterfield home was killing to the young girl, for the three widows lived in a Victorian past. The sisters, Violet and Maybelle, like Mrs. Satterfield, wore black, and all three were tied to the routine of their limited lives. There was little money and little color or excitement in the household. So Frankie gently explained that she must move on.

"I knew you'd say that." Mrs. Satterfield nodded. "This place would bore a mummy to death! If it weren't for Maybelle and Violet, I'd sell it and move back to Georgia!"

Frankie said, "That might not be a good

place to be right now."

"Because of the war? Yes, you're right."

"Do you think the South can win?"

"Win? Of course they can't win!" She thumped the table with her tiny fist, her eyes bright. "Southerners have a wagonload of courage and a thimbleful of sense! And they're stubborn as mules! They'll die to the last man before they'll admit they're wrong!" And then she grew quiet, adding in a small voice, "But I wish I could go be with them when they make their stand!"

One day Frankie tried to please the three sisters by putting on a dress, one that had belonged to a daughter of Violet. But the next morning she was back to her trousers and man's shirt. "I just feel all trapped in a dress," she explained with a shrug. "I've worn men's clothes so long. Had to, what with working and hunting and riding."

"Well, you won't attract a man in that outfit," Mrs. Satterfield sniffed. "But then — you don't especially want to attract a man, do you, Frankie?"

"No."

The old woman considered her young friend but did not argue except to say, "Someday you will. Then nobody will have to beg you to put on a dress."

For a week Frankie read the ads in the

papers, hoping to find some sort of work. But there was nothing for young women such as herself. She walked along the streets, thinking maybe she'd see a need she might fill, but all she knew was farming and caring for animals. It came to her that she might get on as a hired hand with a farmer, and that became her goal.

Then one morning, Mrs. Satterfield brought her a paper with an ad circled. "Why don't you look into this, Frankie?"

Taking the paper, Frankie read the following advertisement:

BOOK AGENTS WANTED IN NEW YORK STATE

L. P. Crown and Company, publishers, requires young agents to canvass for New Pictorial, Standard, Historical, and Religious Works. The company publishes a large number of most valuable books, which are very popular and of such a moral and religious influence that a good agent may safely engage in their circulation. The agents will confer a public BENEFIT and receive a FAIR COMPENSATION for their labor.

To persons of enterprise and tact this business offers an opportunity for profitable employment seldom to be met with.

There is not a town in North America where a right, honest, and well-disposed person can fail selling from fifty to two hundred volumes, depending on the population.

Persons wishing to engage in the venture may apply at the Bradley Building, Room 222. References are required.

"Why, I'm not a salesman!" Frankie said at once.

"You're honest and well disposed, aren't you?" Mrs. Satterfield snapped. "That's what they want."

"But . . . they want *men*!"

"Doesn't say a word about gender. It says 'agent.' I should think that could be either a man or a woman."

Frankie read the ad again and began to grow interested. "I do love to read," she confessed. "But could I *sell* anything?"

Mrs. Satterfield smiled suddenly. "Child, you can! You just wear that rig you've got on. Why, I'll wager they've never seen anything like you in New York! They'll let you in the house just to find out what you are. And when you smile and blink those long lashes of yours, they'll buy books like they were made out of gold!"

It took a great deal of persuasion, but the

next morning at nine o'clock, Frankie took a deep breath and pushed open the door to room 222 of the Bradley Building. It was a very small room that contained only one desk, four chairs, and one man.

The man was seated in front of a window, his back to the desk. He was smoking a cigar and staring out at the traffic in the street. When Frankie entered, he didn't even turn around. He just said, "Fill out the form on the desk."

Frankie looked down and saw a stack of forms and, without saying a word, sat down and filled one of them out. Her three references were Deborah, Violet, and Maybelle. Under "Business History" she wrote, "Farm work."

"I'm finished," she said. At the sound of her voice, the man swiveled around and stared at her. He was a small man, and his checked suit was crisp and businesslike. He must have been about sixty, though it was difficult to tell, for his face had a kind of ageless look to it. He had a pair of brown eyes, a small round mouth, and a large nose. "Oi! What's this?" he demanded. "I thought you was a person seeking a job."

Frankie took the advertisement out of her pocket and put it on the desk. "I am looking for a job. This one," she said, nodding.

138

A look of astonishment touched the man's face, and then he chuckled. "Well, now I've seen it all! You want to sell the books? No, no, no. Only young men can do that."

"Why?"

" 'Why?' " Frankie's simple question caused his large eyebrows to fly up, giving him an expression of astonishment. "She asks me why?" He looked up as though carrying on a conversation with someone on the ceiling. "Because no young woman can do it, *that's* why."

"Did you ever let one try?"

The man's eyes widened for a moment; then a curious light came into them. "So what's your name, young woman?" He waited for it, then nodded. "I'm heppy to meet you, Miss Aimes. My name is Solomon Levy. And no, I didn't let no young ladies try to sell no books." He seemed interested in what he saw and asked, "Why do you want to sell my books?"

Frankie smiled, and her green eyes glinted with humor. "I want to confer a public benefit and receive a fair compensation for my labor, like it says right here," she concluded, tapping the advertisement.

Levy smiled and nodded. "You're a clever young lady. You got a husband? No? And a family, you've got? No? Ah, that's too bad."

139

He put the cigar between his teeth and sucked on it industriously, sending billows of purple smoke toward the ceiling. He studied the patterns of the smoke, sitting still for so long that Frankie feared he had forgotten about her.

"All right," Levy said, bringing his round face to bear on her.

"All right . . . *what*?" Frankie asked, startled by his suddenness.

"All right, we see if you can sell my books."

"I get the job?"

"No, you get a chance to see if you can do the job," Levy corrected her. "I pay your expenses to New York. You sell the books, you get the job."

"Oh, thank you, Mr. Levy!"

"Don't thank me," he protested. "It's hard for young men, being an agent. Long hours and lots of walking."

Frankie laughed in delight. "Well, walking and long hours are my speciality. I . . . don't know too much about books, though."

"That I will teach you myself." He rummaged through some literature, then tossed some of it to her. "Go home and learn how to say all this. Practice looking sincere. Come back tomorrow and try to sell me a book."

Frankie went back to Mrs. Satterfield's house, and the old woman drilled her until nearly midnight. The next morning when Solomon Levy came to open his office, he found Frankie waiting. Smiling, he said, "You going to sell me a book?"

"Yes, sir, I sure am!" Frankie followed him inside, and when he sat down, she held up a book. With a bright smile, she poured out the approach that had been written in one of the sales booklets. When she finished, she said, "Now you see, don't you, Mr. Levy, that you simply can't *afford* to do without these wonderful books! Why, a man in your position *owes* it to the community to keep up his education. . . ."

Levy took his cigar from his lips, rolled his eyes to the ceiling, and demanded, "Who is this girl? Why is she selling me these books?" Then he looked at Frankie and smiled, and it was a strangely gentle smile. "All right, I'll buy the books."

They talked about the details, how Frankie would be paid, and finally Levy grew serious. "My other agents are all young men, Miss Aimes. I must say this to you — there will be no wrongdoing."

Frankie divined his meaning at once. "Oh no, Mr. Levy!"

"I am very serious about this." Levy

studied the young woman and asked, "Are you a Christian, Frankie?"

The question came as a total surprise. "N-no, I'm not."

"Well, *I* am!"

Frankie stared at him with such astonishment that Levy laughed deep in his chest. "Oh, I'm Jewish; anyone can see that! But I'm a Christian Jew." Levy spoke quietly for the next ten minutes, telling her how he'd been brought up as an orthodox Jew, then had drifted into an immoral life. He spoke of how he'd made a great deal of money, yet confessed that he'd had no joy at all. And then he told her how he'd met a man — a Christian — who, after several years, had won him to Jesus Christ.

"So I am now a Christian." Levy smiled, and Frankie could see the joy in his eyes. "My agents, however, are not. And they will try you, as young men try young women. And you must promise me now that you will be virtuous when that temptation comes."

"I'm a good girl, Mr. Levy," Frankie said quietly. "My brother is a good Christian, as was my mother before she died." Dropping her eyes, she whispered, "I hope someday I'll be a Christian, too."

Solomon Levy stared at the girl, compassion in his warm brown eyes. "You are not far from the kingdom, child," he said. "If you have troubles with the young men, or any problems at all, come to me. Will you do that?"

"Yes! I will!"

Sol Levy nodded. The night before, he had been troubled with grave reservations about hiring a young woman, but now he felt a real peace about it. *Maybe I'm put here especially for this one,* he thought. He smiled gently at Frankie. "We'll leave for New York in three days. Study the books — and ask the good Lord to be with you."

"I will, Mr. Levy."

As she left the office and stepped into the street, a strange feeling came over Frankie. *It's going to be all right!* was the thought that came, and somehow she felt that all that had just happened was somehow *right.*

For three days she worked hard, and when she left Deborah Satterfield's home, the widow hugged her and said, "Good-bye, Frankie. Don't forget to write. You can always come back here."

Frankie left Detroit that night in the company of Mr. Solomon Levy and five young men. She was well aware that she would have to prove herself to her employer — and she was equally aware that the young men would put her to the test — but she was happy. As the train pulled out of the station, its whistle screaming, Frankie said a little prayer: *God, I don't know where I'm going, but I guess You do. Don't let me disappoint Mr. Levy — and make whatever You want out of me!*

CHAPTER 8
THE VIVANDIER

"She's just a stuck-up hick, Jack! And I'm sick of hearing Old Man Levy always talking about how great she is."

The two nattily dressed young men were sitting in the lobby of the Crescent Hotel in Melton, a small town in upstate New York. The speaker, Harry Deal, glared upward toward where Sol Levy's room was located. "Those two been in their 'meeting' for over an hour." Suspicion gleamed in his pale blue eyes, and he swiveled his head to stare at his companion. "Say, Jack, I think there's something funny about them."

"The old man and Frankie?"

"That's who we're talking about, ain't it?" Harry lowered his voice and motioned upward toward the second floor. "You notice he don't never have *us* in his room for no long *private* meetings, don'cha?" A knowing grin appeared on his thick lips, which were almost hidden under a bushy

mustache. "You ever wonder if them two
—"

"Aw, come on, Harry!" Jack protested.
"The old man's at least sixty years old! And
he's been fair enough to us."

"Fair! He gives Frankie all the good territory! No wonder she's sold more books
since we come to New York than any of the
rest of us! Not only that, but he's always
taking her out to eat and givin' her special
lessons." Harry stared upward again and
shook his head. "Something ain't right
about that pair, Jack. And don't give me that
sixty-year-old bit, neither! Lots of old guys
go after the girlies!"

Jack Ferrago grinned suddenly at the
angry face of his companion. "You know
what, Harry? I think you're just sore because
Frankie gave you the brush-off."

This seemed to enrage Harry, who snorted
indignantly, "What you talking about? That
freak give *Harry Deal* a brush-off? Not on
your tintype, buster! Sure, I felt a little sorry
for the kid when Levy dragged her into the
firm," he added righteously. "The way she
dressed in those baggy old clothes was pitiful! Nothing but a field hand, Jack, you
remember! So I tried to help her out, kind
of show her the ropes."

"You never went out of your way to help

me or any of the rest of us guys when we first started, Harry," Jack jibed with a wicked grin. "And don't I remember that she dumped a plate of dumplings over your head once at supper? Said you were pinching her leg?"

"It was a blasted lie! I — I dropped my fork and was trying to pick it up when that crazy girl up and done that!"

"Oh sure! Any man could mistake Frankie's leg for a fork," Jack said with a grin. "You're just sore, Harry. The old man's square and so is the kid. She just outworks and outsells you; that's why you're always putting her down."

"You'll see, Jack," Harry growled. "I'm glad this tour is over. I'm telling the old man that I ain't working with that freak no more! It's her or me, and that's it."

"Well, it's been nice working with you, Harry," the other man said with a shrug. "Hope you get another job without too much trouble." He got to his feet and picked up his suitcase. "Come on, let's get something to eat before the train comes in."

Harry gave one last malevolent glare upward, then snatched up his own suitcase and stalked out of the lobby. His parting shot to Jack was: "Notice the old man and Frankie are staying over another night?

147

Don't that mean something?"

"It means that Fredrickson and Johnson won't be in with their final sales until tonight, and that'll be too late for Mr. Levy and Frankie to catch a train. Now shut your face, Harry. I'm sick of your whining!"

Harry shot another angry look upward, but his gaze was off by about seventy feet. Levy's room was that far down the hall from the spot the young man had been glaring at. Inside the room, Sol was sitting at a large table that was covered with papers, humming to himself as he sorted through the pile. Periodically he would pick up a pen, dip it in an inkwell, then make an entry in a large black book that lay open. Finally he drew a line carefully and began to total the figures, totally immersed in the task.

Frankie looked up from the chair where she was reading the book Levy had given her. She started to say something but stopped and waited for him to finish. The clothes she wore now, though still men's garments, fit her better than the rough outfit she'd worn when applying for work. Her light brown wool trousers were held up by maroon suspenders, and her white cotton shirt was covered by a loose-fitting vest with small blue checks. Her hair was still clipped short but now was clean and lay in curly ringlets around her head. Her hands, though still hard from years of hard work, were clean, and her nails were neatly trimmed.

I'm sorry this job is over, she was thinking as she studied Levy's face. The past few months had been an exciting time. She remembered suddenly how she'd been petrified with fear the first time she'd stepped up to a strange house and knocked on the door to sell books. It had been in upstate New York, and she had almost turned and fled in a panic. Fortunately, the woman who answered the door was a cheerful lady of sixty, a well-to-do widow who was puzzled, then fascinated, by the young girl who stood before her in the strange garb. She'd invited Frankie in and, being a rather voluble individual, had done quite a bit of talking — enough to give Frankie time to regain her composure. Frankie smiled as she thought of how she'd run at once to find Sol Levy, crying out, "I did it! She bought the whole set, Mr. Levy!"

Frankie set her book down, then idly rose and moved to the window, which was open to let in fresh air. The day had been warm and humid, and the air in the room was almost stifling. Frankie perched on the windowsill and watched the activity in the street. The town was a small one, like all the others she'd been in since coming to New York. But she hadn't spent much time in the actual towns.

"Country people are easier to sell to," Sol had informed her at once. "And a country girl like you, why, they'll like you right off."

He had been right, Frankie had discovered. The men on the team had stuck to the towns, but Frankie had rented a horse and headed for the country lying in the hills. The people there were like those she knew, and in almost every case she could win a hearing by saying, "I've got a mare just like the one in your pasture back on the farm in Michigan." She knew farming and animals, and the rural people she met trusted her in a way they would not have trusted a man like Harry Deal.

She also discovered that she actually liked the work, and this showed in her clear green eyes, which glowed with excitement as she made her pitch. She always insisted on having the children present if possible, so that she could show them the beautiful pictures in the large Bible and the other books. She had realized at once that the children could sell more books than she ever would. Often all she did was turn the presentation over to them.

Still, she had never forced a sale, not even

once. If the prospect didn't want the books, Frankie would be just as cheerful as if they had bought the entire stock. More than once she had said gently to a poor family who wanted to overbuy: "You might like to wait for a time on some of these. Why don't you just take this one and see how you like it?" Several times when a rough-handed mountain woman would handle a book, usually a Bible, with tender longing, then would hand it back with a regretful sigh, Frankie had said, "You keep the Bible, ma'am. Compliments of the publisher."

She had mentioned one of these instances to Sol, who had said, "You were right, Frankie; the publisher pays!" Frankie smiled at the recollection.

Suddenly Levy spoke up, causing Frankie to turn from where she stood. "Well now! It looks like the winner is you!"

"Winner?" she asked. "Winner of what, Mr. Levy?"

"Winner of the prize for most books sold on the New York tour," he answered with a broad grin. "Come and see." He held the book out, and Frankie leaned over his shoulder to see the columns he had totaled up. At the top of each list was the name of an agent. As she scanned the totals, Frankie took a sudden sharp breath.

"You beat them all! And in your first season!" Sol nodded, beaming at her. "I'll bet those boys will be sick when they hear about this!"

Frankie stood up, but the smile faded. "It — it really wasn't fair, Mr. Levy," she said. "The only reason I sold more than they did was because you helped me more. Besides, lots of people let me in just because I was different, you know?" She hesitated, then looked at him, her eyes wide. "Why don't you just divide the bonus up among all of us?"

Sol stared at Frankie, then nodded slowly. "If you say so. But I'll tell the other agents it was your idea." He closed the book and began to put the papers into some sort of order. As he worked, he spoke of the past few months, mostly about how well Frankie had done. Finally he stood up, saying, "Let's go eat. We got to stay over until Fredrickson and Johnson come with their final sales over in Bentonville."

"All right."

The two of them left the hotel and walked down the board walkway toward the small café where they'd eaten a few times. Several people glanced at them curiously, for they made a strange-looking pair: the short, rotund Jew dressed in a black suit with a round derby on his head and the tall, athletic, unusually dressed young woman. As they entered the café, they were greeted by the owner, Al Sharp, who said, "Got a table right here, folks. Roast beef is good tonight."

Frankie, who had never eaten in a café in her life before joining Levy's crew, had developed some taste. She had sampled some pretty bad food at different restaurants all over upper New York, and when their meal came, she waited until Sol asked a blessing, then sampled the roast beef critically. "This *is* good." She smiled. "Not like that shoe leather we had in Elmira."

Sol ate hungrily, for he was a man who loved to eat, but he could eat and talk and think at the same time, so he was aware that Frankie was not as cheerful as usual. He kept her entertained until after the dessert was out of the way; then as they sipped the strong black coffee the waitress brought, he said abruptly, "Tonight you're a little sad, Frankie. Wot's the trouble?"

"Oh . . . nothing!" Frankie looked up quickly, drawn out of her thoughts by the question.

"Now you think old Sol don't know about you? After all these months?" A fond smile touched his lips as he said, "You don't know

153

I can read minds?"

"Oh, don't be silly!"

"Silly? I'll show you, den, what it is that's taken all your sparkle." He leaned forward and whispered, "Right now, Frankie, you are thinking: *I wonder what in the world I'll do with myself now that the job is over.*" He laughed aloud then, for the girl had blinked with astonishment, her jaw dropping. "Oi!" he cackled, pleased that he had surprised her. "Maybe I go into vaudeville."

Frankie smiled, confessing, "I guess I don't hide my feelings very well, do I? But it's been such a wonderful time that I . . . I hate to see it end!"

Levy leaned back and studied the girl. He had grown very fond of her. His own wife had died twenty years earlier, and they'd had no children. He'd lived alone, throwing himself into his work, but was actually a lonely man. Being a Jew had not helped, for there was much feeling against his race, even in America. He knew hundreds of people all over the country but was close to few of them. He stayed on the road constantly, for there was a restlessness in him that could not be content.

This young woman had been a challenge to him — and he loved challenges, this short, fat Jew! And he had won! For Frankie

154

had been a jewel that he had polished with loving care. The agents resented her, for he had spent much time with her, not only teaching her about the book business, but just talking. He had introduced her to a better sort of literature than she had known, and he had listened. He was a good listener, and though Frankie never said much about her past, he sensed the tragedy that had driven her alone into the world.

And he had been vaguely troubled these last weeks, as the end of the tour rushed to meet them. He had been selling books for years, but something in his profession didn't satisfy him. An idea had been slowly forming in his fertile mind, and now as he sat across from Frankie, he knew that he was going to take a bold step — one that might well be disastrous.

"I'm a little sad myself, Frankie," he said slowly.

"Why, what's the matter, Mr. Levy?" Frankie was surprised, for in the time she'd known him, the man was always cheerful. But she saw now that he was indeed not smiling in his usual fashion, and there was a sober light in his brown eyes.

"It's this terrible war," Levy answered, shaking his head. "All the killing that's going to come . . . I feel so bad about it!" He held his hands palms upward in a helpless gesture. "But what's an old Jew like me to do? I can't fight like the young men."

"Maybe it won't come, this war."

"Child, it's here already! The North is raising an enormous army, and the South is armed to the teeth! Any day now the Union army is going to move south, and when they do, there'll be war." He looked at her, then asked, "Do you have any relatives — brothers, perhaps — who are of age to fight?"

"Only one brother, but he's almost an invalid."

"Ah, well, that may be best." Sol Levy sat there quietly, then said, "I have asked God to tell me what to do, and I think He has told me something." He smiled abruptly, seeing Frankie's shocked expression. "Oh, I'm not going crazy or hearing voices, child! But I've learned to wait on God since I've become a Christian. And now I have waited, and I know what I must do. And it concerns you, Frankie."

"Me!"

"Yes. I think God has put me in your way, to be a father to you for a time, to watch over you."

Frankie felt a warm glow as she heard this, and she whispered, "You . . . you've been the only real father I've ever known!"

"Ah . . ." Sol was pleased, and his eyes glowed as he regarded Frankie. "That makes things much easier! Now here is what I must do. I must become a sutler."

"A sutler?" Frankie asked. "What's that?"

"A person who sells supplies to the soldiers: tobacco and paper and even whiskey. But in this case, I will take many books — not to sell, but to give to the soldiers." Sol grew excited as he spoke, making gestures with his fat hands. "Books and tracts for the soldiers — all Christian books, telling about the Savior, Jesus Christ! I am not a preacher, Frankie, but I can pass along the Good News about my Lord in this way. Men who face death," he said more soberly, "they will be hungry for the gospel, and I will see that they have it!"

"But what does that have to do with me?" Frankie asked.

"Why, you will help me, child!" Sol said, his eyebrows going up. "It is why God sent you to me, I think. We will take the books and the tracts to the camps and to the hospitals."

"But, Mr. Levy . . . I'm not a Christian!"

The old man looked at her, wisdom in his warm brown eyes. "Ah, that doesn't matter — as far as the men are concerned. It's the message, not the messenger, that saves

157

people. And I believe that your time is coming, child."

"My time?"

"Yes. Every man and every woman — every person on this planet, in fact — has a time. A time to choose for God, for His Son, Jesus. Jesus said one time, 'No man can come to me, except the Father which hath sent me draw him.' Oi! God knows how to draw a man!" Levy smiled. "If He can draw an old Jew like me, He can do the same thing for a young girl like Frankie Aimes!"

Frankie sat very still, and the old man put his hand on hers. "Will you do it, child?"

Frankie felt again the same inexplicable sense of assurance that had come to her months ago, a peace that she had never been able to explain. It washed over her now, and she smiled at the man who was watching her so anxiously.

"Yes, Mr. Levy, I'll help you."

"Good — I am so happy!" Sol beamed and patted her hand; then a thought came to him. "I have been doing a little study on this, and I find out that I will be a sutler, but you will be called something else. There is a French word used for women who sell supplies to the soldiers. I think it sounds nice."

Frankie asked curiously, "What will I be,

Mr. Levy?"

"You will be a *vivandier*!"

Frankie pronounced it carefully, imitating Levy as closely as possible: "*Vee-vahn-dee-ay?* Like that?" She repeated it again, then laughed, her eyes bright and her lips curving in a delighted way. "I'm a vivandier! Oh, Sol!" she cried, using his first name for the first time. "I'm so glad we're not going to be separated!"

The old Jew nodded and whispered, "I, too, am most glad, child!"

"Well, Frankie, so what do you think of Washington?"

Frankie and Sol had entered the city and driven along the main thoroughfare, which was four miles long and 160 feet wide. To get there, however, Sol had driven through Center Market — where brothels and gambling houses operated openly — and through Swampoodle, Negro Hill, and other alley domains. They had traveled along the Old City Canal, a fetid bayou filled with floating dead cats — and all kinds of putridity — and reeking with pestilential odors. Cattle, sheep, swine, and geese ran everywhere.

Now as they were leaving the city, Frankie made a face at her companion. "It stinks!"

"Yes, it does," Sol agreed. "I hope the camp will smell better." He looked back under the canvas at the heavily loaded wagon and remarked, "We'll have to get permission to set up our shop. I hope the bribe I'll have to pay won't be too steep."

"Bribe? What's that?" Frankie asked.

"All business in government has to be paid for." Sol shrugged. "Every sutler will have to buy a license, but that's only the beginning. There'll be other palms to grease before we can do business."

"Why, that's *terrible*!"

"It's the way of the world, Frankie. If we want to help the soldiers, we'll just have to pay for the privilege."

By the time they reached the camp, a large area filled with parade grounds and acres of tents, the sun was high in the sky. The corporal who stopped them and asked for a pass listened as Sol explained their mission, then said, "You'll have to go to regimental headquarters." He gave them instructions, adding, "Ask for either Colonel Bradford or Major Rocklin."

As they drove along, they were overwhelmed at the tremendous activity in the camp. Sergeants were yelling at their squads; horses raced by with couriers; and caissons rumbled along, forcing Sol off the narrow road. Somehow they found their way to a large tent with a narrow pennant waving over it. "I guess that's it," Sol said. "Come along and we'll see about a permit."

Frankie scrambled down, and the two of them approached the large round tent. "We'd like to see the commanding officer, Corporal," Sol said to the soldier standing there.

The man peered at the two suspiciously, then shrugged. "I'll have to ask." He disappeared into the tent but came back almost at once. "Major Rocklin says you can come in."

"Thank you." Sol fished in his pocket and came out with a slender pamphlet and handed it to the soldier. "For you."

"Why — thanks!"

The pair entered the tent and were met by a tall officer with dark hair and eyes. "I'm Major Gideon Rocklin," he said. "What can I do for you?"

"We need a sutler's permit, Major," Sol said.

"I can arrange that." He moved to sit down at a portable desk, selected a single sheet of paper, and dipped a pen into an inkwell. "Your name?"

"I'm Solomon Levy, and this is Miss Frankie Aimes."

Rocklin paused and looked up with interest. His eyes rested on Frankie, and he hesitated before saying, "Miss Aimes is your . . . ?"

"She's my employee, Major." Levy added quickly that he was actually a bookseller and wanted to use his office as a sutler to distribute Christian books. He saw at once that this pleased the tall soldier. Levy continued, "I am a Jew, as you see, but a Christian, as well. And Miss Aimes has been my best agent for some time."

"I'm glad to have you in the regiment, sir. And you, too, Miss Aimes," Rocklin said. He filled out the form, then stood, handed it to Levy, and remarked, "The sutler situation is terrible. Some of them sell shoddy goods at outrageous prices to the men. I'm happy to finally meet one who'll be different."

"You are a Christian, Major?"

"Yes, indeed!" Gideon smiled. "And you'll find others." He turned his gaze on Frankie and asked, "You do know that soldiers are a rough lot, Miss Aimes?"

Frankie understood at once what the major implied. "Yes, sir. But Mr. Levy will watch out for me."

"Fine! Fine!" Then Rocklin frowned, saying, "You can set up your shop. I'll have someone take you to a proper place, but I'm afraid you won't have much time."

Sol gave the officer a keen stare. "I take it the army is moving out soon."

The major nodded soberly. "Very soon, Mr. Levy. I can't say when, of course, but don't count on more than a few days."

"We'll do what we can until then. And thank you, Major."

He walked outside with them and spoke to the soldier standing guard. "Corporal, take these two over to the west side of the camp, close to the big trees." He turned to say, "There's an evangelistic meeting to-night. You might like to attend it. A fine preacher, Rev. Steele, will be doing the preaching."

"Thank you. We'll be there, sir."

"He's my brother-in-law, so I can recommend him. Glad to have you in the regiment — both of you."

"A fine man!" Sol exclaimed as the two climbed into the wagon. "And a Christian! We'll have no problems now, will we, Frankie?"

"What about when the army leaves?" Frankie asked.

"Why, the sutlers will go along, of course. We'll stay well behind the troops, but every night we'll be able to provide supplies and tracts to the soldiers."

They set up shop under a large pin oak and at once began doing a tremendous business. Most of the soldiers wanted whiskey, which Levy had refused to stock, but there was a brisk sale of everything in the wagon, especially tobacco and paper for writing letters. Their "store" was composed of boards placed over barrels, and both of them were busy until a bugle drew the men back to their tents.

Frankie cooked a supper of ham and beans over a small fire, and the two friends ate hungrily. As they talked over the meal, Sol said, "I hope there are no Confederate spies around here." He took a swallow of the scalding coffee, adding, "Every private I talked to knows where the army's heading."

"I know." Frankie nodded. "Some place called Centerville. They all say the Confederates are waiting there. Where is that place, Sol?"

"Close to a little town . . . what was the name of it?" He tried to remember but couldn't, so he got up and came back to the fire with a map. Spreading it out, he squinted. "I can't see with these old eyes, Frankie. You look; it's close to a little river or creek . . . but I forget the name of that, too."

"Here it is — Centerville," Frankie announced, putting her finger on the map.

"So? And what about that little town and the river?"

Frankie peered closer, then looked up at Sol.

"Manassas. The town is Manassas. And the creek is called Bull Run."

CHAPTER 9
A SPECIAL PATIENT

The blue-clad Union soldiers who went out to fight at Bull Run with flowers stuck in the barrels of their muskets returned to Washington bleeding and in total disarray. The city was in a panic, expecting to be invaded by the victorious Confederate Army at any moment, and President Lincoln and his cabinet made plans to evacuate and find shelter in another site.

But the Confederates were almost as stunned by their victory as the Federals were by their defeat, and they were unable to take advantage of the Union rout. Stonewall Jackson begged to be allowed to press on to Washington but was ordered not to move. The victors returned to Richmond to receive a triumphant reception, while the shattered Union forces brought their dead and wounded by the thousands to the hospitals hastily set up in the capital.

Solomon Levy and Frankie Aimes narrowly escaped being trampled by the mob that stampeded back to Washington. They had been moving along in a leisurely fashion a few miles behind the last of the Union troops, and when the rush for safety began — led by the congressmen and their families who'd gone out in a picnic mood to view the battle — Levy had taken one look at the wild-eyed drivers beating their horses on to greater speed and said abruptly, "Something's wrong, Frankie!"

His fears were confirmed when a stream of soldiers came stumbling along, some of them shouting, "Black Horse Cavalry!"

Levy turned the horses around at once and drove back to the capital. He hurried to the camp, and all day and all night, soldiers with dazed eyes came stumbling in. Some of them had minor wounds, and Solomon and Frankie put a bandage on the hand of a young private from Illinois. He could barely speak at first, but as they bandaged his wound and gave him plenty of cool water, he calmed down enough to tell what had happened.

"We come at them fellers with all we had," he mumbled. "But they kept on comin' at us. Just kept right on comin'." A shiver passed through him, and he whispered, "My best friend, Scotty . . . he got shot right off.

Got hit in the stomach, and he was on the ground screamin' and beggin' me to help him, but the sergeant drove us on into the charge."

When he stopped, Frankie said, "Maybe he'll be brought back to the hospital."

"No, I went back . . . and he was dead. His . . . eyes were open . . . but he was dead!" Tears began to roll down his cheeks. "I didn't think it would be like that!"

The young private spoke what the entire nation thought, for neither side had been prepared for the violence that had wiped out so many young lives. The South began to celebrate, but the North gave up overnight on the idea that the war would last only six months. General McDowell was blamed — somewhat unfairly — for the defeat, and Lincoln called on General George McClellan to pull the army together. McClellan began at once, and he had the flair and the drive to do the job. His first job was to give the army confidence, and he did exactly that. He was everywhere, riding on his big black charger, going from unit to unit, giving stirring speeches, telling the men that they were the Army of the Potomac and that they were victors and not losers. He gave them leaves and better food and marched them in stirring parades. He put order into an army that had had little, and he created hope where there had been none.

Sol Levy and Frankie would be there through all those months that the Army of the Potomac rose like a phoenix from its own ashes. And as the first of the battered, bleeding troops poured into Washington during those terrible, dark days after Bull Run, Sol said, "Frankie, this is very bad, but we've come with hope, you and I. Let's put ourselves into a different sort of battle — a battle for God!"

They did so, moving among the men, giving out books and tracts, selling their goods at prices that made no money for Levy, and giving much of them to those who had no money at all.

At first Frankie was shy and did not get more than a few feet from Sol's side. She slept in the wagon while Sol slept in a tent, and the two of them went almost every night to one of the religious services that were held at the camp. In the beginning, the soldiers merely stared at Frankie — most of them, at least. Some bolder spirits attempted to get closer only to discover that the young woman was simply not available. But what puzzled them even more than Frankie's aloofness was that she never got angry with those who tested her.

In the minds of most soldiers, even of most men, there were two kinds of women: good and bad. The good women stayed at home, kept house, and reared children. The bad women could be found in the numerous brothels and dance halls that were scattered all over Washington. The entire regiment speculated as to which exactly Frankie was — good or bad. They discussed her often — how she lived with an old man, wore men's clothing, and talked with men freely — but they could not figure her out. Finally, as the days and weeks passed, the men came to accept her for what she was: sincere, honest, good-humored, and decent.

Three weeks after Bull Run, Major Rocklin came by to speak to Sol and Frankie, and he mentioned the men's reaction to Sol's assistant. He'd been telling Levy how grateful he was for the good work the pair of them were doing, and he turned to smile at Frankie. "The men had quite a time trying to put a label on you, Miss Aimes," he said. "But I think you've shown them what you really are. Have any of them been ungentlemanly?"

"Quite a few, Major," Frankie said with a shy smile. "But they come around. I think they miss their wives and sisters."

"Of course, some of them are away from home for the first time." Gideon nodded. "I've seen you at our services, too."

"It's wonderful to be able to serve the Lord," Sol said happily. "Your brother-in-law is a fine preacher!"

"I'll tell him you said so." Rocklin gave the two of them a speculative look, then said, "I know you two work hard, but if you have a chance, I wish you'd go by and pass out some tracts, and maybe even some tobacco, to our boys in the hospital. They get pretty lonesome. I'll be happy to pay for the items —"

"No! No!" Sol protested. "It will be our privilege, Frankie's and mine. Will they let us in?"

"Let you in!" Rocklin grinned. "The question is, will they let you out! I visit as often as I can, and they practically hang on to me just to have someone to talk to!"

That afternoon Sol and Frankie loaded themselves down with tracts, tobacco, and sweets, then went into the city. They found the regimental hospital of the Washington Blues easily, for it was a huge old mansion that had been converted to house the wounded men. They also discovered that Major Rocklin had been exactly right: The men were so happy to see them that they stayed until very late.

Frankie moved from bed to bed, shyly approaching the men. She was horrified by some of the terrible wounds but managed not to show it. It was not difficult to talk to the men, for most of them were starved for someone to listen. And they were frightened. For the most part, they were very young, not much older than Frankie herself. Even if they'd ever had any inclinations about romance, they had little now. Most of them had more important things to worry about, such as gangrene, which killed as many men in the long run as were slain instantly on the battlefield.

The third young soldier she talked to revealed this almost universal fear. His name was Jimmy Seeger. He was nineteen years old — and had a stump instead of a right arm. When Frankie sat down and asked him if he needed tobacco or paper, he shook his head. "Don't smoke and can't write," he said with a faint smile. Then he looked down at his ruined arm and said bitterly, "Even if I'd ever learned how . . . I couldn't write now."

Frankie said quickly, "I'll write a letter for you, Private."

"Would you, miss?" Seeger was delighted and dictated a short, highly stilted letter to his mother. When it was written, he asked to see it. "My, look at all them words!" he breathed. Then he lay back and grew still. Frankie was not sure how to talk to him, but she did the best she could. Finally it came out. The boy was convinced that he was going to die. "Every day they come and get one of our fellers, take him out, and bury him," he said, biting his lip. "It's that there gangrene that kills 'em." He blinked his eyes and said, "It's going to finish me off, too, I reckon."

"Oh no! You mustn't say that!" Frankie began to encourage him as best she could. But when he asked, "Are you a Christian, miss?" she could only shake her head. When the boy's face fell, she felt terrible — and then she had a quick thought. "I have a friend who's a fine Christian," she said. "I'll go get him!"

Ten minutes later Frankie stood back, watching and listening as Sol Levy sat beside Jimmy Seeger. Levy spoke quietly but earnestly for some time, reading scriptures from time to time from the Bible he always carried. Some of the verses Frankie remembered faintly, for they had been favorites of her mother's. She bowed her head as the old man prayed fervently for a complete healing for the soldier, and when he was finished, she saw tears in Seeger's eyes.

But Levy was not finished, not at all. He said, "Now, my boy, you must look to God, not only to keep you from dying, but to save you from hell. And that's exactly what Jesus Christ came to do. He died for you and for this old Jew, and I don't want to go to heaven and not find you there!"

"I–I'd sure like to know I was going to heaven, sir!" Jimmy whispered. "But I ain't been very good. Matter of fact, I've done some pretty bad things."

"Good!" Sol Levy exclaimed, and when the boy's face grew shocked, he said, "You're a sinner, Jimmy? Then that makes you a friend of Jesus!"

"It does?" he asked in surprise.

"Yes, because the Bible says in Saint John 15 that Jesus is the friend of sinners. And all of us are sinners, Jimmy. It says so in Romans 3:23: 'All have sinned, and come short of the glory of God.' But it says in that same book, 'But God commendeth his love toward us, in that, while we were yet sinners, Christ died for us.' The only question is, Do you want to have the Lord Jesus Christ in your heart? Do you really want to be saved from hell and to be clean from sin?"

Jimmy swallowed hard and nodded. "Yes, sir, I sure do!" he whispered.

"Then God is ready to save you, and you are ready to be saved!" Levy said. "What do you do, my boy, when you want something from someone?"

"Why, I ask for it."

"Exactly! And in Romans chapter 10 and verse 13, the Bible says, 'For whosoever shall call upon the name of the Lord shall be saved.' And so I want to pray for you, Jimmy, and as I pray, you just ask God for what you want. Will you do that?"

"Y–yes, sir."

Frankie felt strange as she stood there, her own heart pounding. Something like fear came to her as she listened — it was as though God was right at her side. Suddenly she bowed her head and closed her eyes. She began to tremble and felt her eyes burning. She heard Jimmy pray, asking God to save him, and then she heard him say, "I done it! I asked Jesus to save me, and He done it!"

For the next few minutes, Levy spoke with the wounded boy and then rose, saying, "We'll be back to see you tomorrow, Jimmy. And we'll bring you some books that will help you in your Christian life."

"Oh — I can't read!"

Sol hesitated, then nodded. "This young lady will read some to you, won't you, Miss Aimes?" Without waiting for a reply, he turned and the two of them left the hospital. As they got into the wagon and started back to the camp, Sol was practically ecstatic. "Wasn't that wonderful, Frankie! That dear lad! And now he's saved!"

Frankie said little, for the experience had shaken her. She went to bed early and, the next afternoon, joined Sol on another visit to the hospital. They went at once to Jimmy, who greeted them with a big smile. "I been telling all my friends about how I got saved," he announced. "And I told them they could listen while Miss Aimes reads to me."

"Splendid!" Sol beamed and left at once to visit other men. Frankie felt like an impostor, but the men were all watching her, so she sat down and introduced herself. She learned their names and saw to it that they all had something from the bag of goodies she'd brought. Finally she took out the book that Sol had given her, marked at the place, and began to read. The men listened quietly, and she read for almost an hour. Then she closed the book and asked, "Would one of you like to keep the book? Then you can read it to Jimmy anytime."

One of the men agreed at once, and Frankie handed it to him.

"Will you come back?" a tall, bearded man named Dowley asked. "Sure would like to get a letter written to my wife."

"Yes, I'll come tomorrow."

That was the beginning, and there was no end. For weeks and even months, Sol and Frankie spent every waking hour with the men, either at the camp or at the hospitals. And they went to more than one hospital, for Washington was filled with them. They also attended the services held in the out-of-doors, and as Frankie heard the gospel preached, she became more and more aware that there was an emptiness in her — a longing that it seemed nothing could fill.

And so the days went by, with the army growing ever stronger. New recruits came in to be trained in the art of war, and both North and South waited for the next alarm that would call the men in uniform to the clash of battle. It would come, they all knew. Often as Sol watched the troops drill or march by in long columns, he would shake his head sadly and say, "Some of them will not be here next year, Frankie. Oh, that they were all saved!"

"Miss Aimes, this is my son, Private Tyler

Rocklin. And this is Miss Frankie Aimes, the best vivandier in the whole Union army."

Frankie had moved along the line of beds at the regimental hospital late one afternoon and had not paid any heed to the tall officer who stood beside one of the beds. But when she heard her name, she turned at once to find Major Rocklin smiling at her.

"Hello, Miss Aimes," the young soldier on the cot greeted her. "And what in the world did my father say you are?"

"Oh, just a fancy word for a lady sutler." Frankie shrugged. The young man looked very strong, but his left leg was heavily bandaged and there was an unhealthy pallor in his face. "You must have come in today, Private Rocklin," Frankie ventured.

Major Rocklin spoke up. "Yes, he came in early this morning." Frankie saw that the man was worried, although he tried not to show it. "He got damaged a little in a fracas with the Confederate cavalry."

"Shot by a cavalryman!" the wounded man groaned. "I'm disgraced!"

"Don't worry about it, son," his father said quickly. "You'll be up and around soon. Maybe you can get a crack at that bunch the next time." He tried to smile, but when he saw that the young man's face was tense and pale, he said hurriedly, "Well, your mother will be here as soon as she gets home, Tyler." He bent over and patted the younger man's uninjured leg. "I'm proud of you, son!" Then he straightened up and gave Frankie a nod, indicating that he wanted her to follow him. She did, and when they were outside in the hall, Rocklin said, "My wife's away for an overnight visit. These people are pretty busy, so I'm going to ask a favor of you."

"You want me to sit with him tonight, Major?"

A look of relief came to Rocklin's face at the offer. "I'd feel better about it if you would. Just for a while, until he goes to sleep."

"I'll be glad to, Major Rocklin," Frankie said promptly. Then she asked, "What do the doctors say?"

"Well, they don't like the looks of the wound. A shell went off, and the leg was badly damaged, especially the knee. And these wounds are tricky, as you know. Always a danger of their going bad."

"I'll be happy to help all I can. You've been very kind to Mr. Levy and me."

Rocklin nodded. "I'll come tomorrow, but I'd like someone with him tonight."

When the major left, Frankie went back and found the young man moving around uncomfortably. "Is the pain bad?" she asked.

"Bad enough!" Tyler gasped. "I never could sleep on my back, but that's the only way I can lie down now."

Frankie had had some experience with this sort of thing. The men with certain wounds could only lie in one position, and this produced such discomfort some of them almost wept. She studied the young man, then said tentatively, "I'm not a nurse, but do you think if I could prop your leg up you could lie on your side?"

He stared at her, his lips tight, then said, "It's worth a try. Don't pay any attention to me if I holler."

Frankie went to the male nurse in charge and asked for extra pillows, which he found for her. She carried them back and dropped them on the floor. "It'll probably hurt when you roll over," she said, but Tyler only nodded, so she pulled the sheet back, then put her hands under his bandaged leg. "I'll hold your leg as steady as I can. . . ." As the young man pushed himself over, she held his leg carefully, and when he was over, she quickly put two of the pillows under the wounded limb and eased it down.

"Is that any better?" she asked, moving to the head of the bed.

"I'll say!" Tyler whispered. His face was

pale, but there was a relaxed look to his mouth, and he lay there with his eyes closed for a moment, then said, "Never thought lying on my side could feel so good!"

He grew still, and Frankie leaned forward to see his face. He had gone to sleep at once, and she smiled and straightened up. Carefully she pulled the chair close to his bed and then sat there watching him sleep. For over an hour he slept, and twice she had to hold the leg to keep it from moving. The male nurse came by and saw what she was doing. "That's a good idea. First time he's slept since he's been here." He grinned at her, adding, "You'd make a good nurse, miss!"

Frankie had planned to go back to the camp with Sol, but when he came, she saw that young Rocklin's fever was going up. "Sol, do you think I might stay here with him tonight? He's in a lot of pain, and I think if I could get some cool water and cloths, I could get his fever down. It's what I did with my sisters."

"I'll see." Sol moved away, then came back at once. "We'll both stay," he said quietly. "The doctor said it was all right."

They spent most of the night working with Tyler, bathing him with cool water, keeping his leg elevated from time to time. They took turns dozing in the chair, until Sol finally left to lie down on a couch in the outer room. Frankie sat there dozing until finally morning came.

"Well . . . I didn't expect you to do this, Miss Aimes!"

Frankie came out of a half-sleep with a jolt of alarm, then looked up to see Gideon Rocklin standing over her. She got to her feet, her neck aching. "He's had a restless night."

"Hello, Dad. . . ." Tyler was awake and looked very weak.

"Hello, son. How do you feel?"

"Better than if my nurse hadn't been here." He told his father how Frankie had found a way for him to change positions, then tried to grin. "Lots of the fellows here didn't get such good care. Guess it pays to have your father running the show."

Rocklin turned to Frankie, saying, "Go get some rest, Miss Aimes. I appreciate all you've done."

Frankie smiled tiredly. "I hope you get better today, Private," she said, and then she went to find Sol.

He was asleep on the couch and got up slowly, his old bones aching. "How's the boy doing?" he asked, trying to straighten his neck.

"Not very well, I'm afraid," Frankie said. "I think his leg is hurt pretty bad."

The two of them rode back to camp, and soon business was under full steam. It was a long day, made even more so by the nearly sleepless night they both had experienced. Sol gave up and went to bed at noon, so Frankie had to manage the sutler business by herself. That evening, Major Rocklin came by to give them a report.

"How's your boy, Major?" Sol asked at once.

"Not doing well, I'm afraid." Rocklin's face looked craggy, and he shook his head in a discouraging motion. "He's had a fever, and the leg hurts all the time."

"I'm sorry, but we will pray that God will do a healing work," Sol said quietly.

"I appreciate that. Just wanted to stop and tell you how grateful I am to you two. It means a great deal to me and to his mother."

"Is your wife back, Major?" Frankie asked.

"Yes, but she's not too well herself. There's an epidemic going around, and I hope she's not got that." He straightened his broad shoulders, saying, "Thanks again for taking care of him."

"He's worried," Frankie said after the major walked away. "He's afraid his son might get gangrene and lose the leg — or die."

"You can't blame him." Sol nodded. "We'll have to go back and see the young fellow."

They did go back the next day and found that the patient was little improved. He tried to smile, but the fever was eating away at him, and his leg was very painful. He tried to talk but was obviously very ill.

Frankie went back to the camp depressed, and all the next day she thought about the young soldier. She was still thinking about him when Major Rocklin rode up and dismounted. "Is Tyler any better, Major?"

"Not really. Doesn't seem to be able to get any strength." Rocklin stood there, a strong figure in his blue uniform, and seemed unable to speak.

"What is it, Major Rocklin?" Frankie asked.

"I've been talking to the doctors — to my family doctor, too. He came out and took a look at Tyler. They all say the same thing — that he might be better off at home."

"Are you taking him there?"

"Well, we want to, but my wife is not well. She just can't seem to shake off that thing that's got her down. But I've *got* to see that my boy gets every chance. So —" He took a deep breath and asked, "Would you come to my house in town and take care of him, Miss Aimes?"

"Why, I'm no nurse!"

"You're enough of a nurse for us," Rocklin said. "Tyler told me how much you helped him. If you could come, just until I can find somebody else . . ."

Frankie stood there watching his face, and then she said, "I'll come if Mr. Levy says I can."

"Good! I believe he'll be agreeable." They went at once to find Sol, who immediately gave his consent.

"Go along, Frankie!" He nodded, and at Major Rocklin's urging, Frankie got her clothes. "Can you ride a horse to the hospital?" he asked.

"Can I ride? It's what I do best!" Frankie said with a smile. The two of them rode to the hospital, where Major Rocklin made arrangements to have Tyler brought out to the ambulance. A private drove the black vehicle to the Rocklin home, and he and the major carried the patient inside on a stretcher.

"Take care of him, Frankie," the major said quietly when they had Tyler in bed. "My wife is asleep, so the house is yours."

He left then, and Frankie moved to stand close to Tyler. He woke up out of the drugged sleep. His eyes were cloudy as he focused on her.

"Where am I?" he muttered thickly.

"Home," Frankie whispered.

CHAPTER 10
FRANKIE LOSES A FRIEND

Frankie met Major Rocklin's wife the next day when she took her breakfast into the large bedroom. She knocked on the door and, when a faint reply came, pushed it open and entered. She found Melanie Rocklin in bed, her face pale. "Oh, you must be Miss Aimes," Melanie said at once.

"Yes, ma'am." Frankie nodded. "Major Rocklin said you've been poorly, so I thought I'd fix you a little something to eat."

Melanie smiled, and as pale and wan as she was, Frankie thought she was one of the most beautiful women she'd ever seen. "Oh, don't get up, Mrs. Rocklin," she protested when the woman started to sit up. "I put it on a tray so you could have breakfast in bed." Before the sick woman could protest, Frankie had placed the bed tray in position, saying, "I just made some light food, an egg and toast. And tea is always good when you don't feel well."

"Oh, this is so nice, Miss Aimes!" Melanie said. "I *am* a little hungry this morning."

"Just call me Frankie, Mrs. Rocklin." Frankie nodded. "When you finish, I'll help you into that nice overstuffed chair and change the sheets on your bed."

"That will be nice," Melanie said. She buttered a piece of toast, then put some strawberry jam on it, asking, "How is Tyler this morning?"

"Well, he had some fever, but I got it down about midnight. His leg seemed to be hurting pretty badly, so I gave him some of the medicine the doctor sent from the hospital. Then he slept pretty well."

"I feel so terrible." Melanie shook her head. "He needs me, and here I am wallowing around in bed!"

"You'll be better soon; then you can take care of him." Frankie moved around the room, picking up clothing. "I'll wash these things, Mrs. Rocklin."

"Oh, we have a woman who does the laundry," Melanie protested. "Just put it by the back door." She smiled and added, "I daresay you have more than enough to do already, my dear." She took a sip of the hot tea and smiled. "My, that tastes wonderful. Now come and sit down for a while, Frankie. My husband has told me a little

188

about you and Mr. Levy, but you know how men are! They give you headlines, but we women want the fine print, don't we? Now tell me how you got to be a lady sutler."

When Major Rocklin hurried up the front steps and entered the house that evening, he had a concerned look on his face. His duties had required all his time that day, and though he'd let none of his concern show on his face, he was very worried about Tyler. He'd waited anxiously until he could finally get away from the camp, then mounted his horse and ridden home.

"How is Tyler?" he demanded as Frankie came out of the kitchen to meet him. "Did the doctor come by?"

Frankie was wearing a pair of light gray trousers and a pale yellow shirt. Her auburn hair ringed her face, and she looked very competent. "He's better, a little bit, Major. The doctor came this afternoon. He changed the dressing and showed me how to do it, too."

"What did he say, Frankie?" Rocklin shot the question at her.

"He said if we can keep the fever down and keep the wound clean and see that Tyler eats, the chances are good for a full recovery." Frankie nodded emphatically.

"He's a good doctor, isn't he? You can tell he tells the truth."

"Yes, he is." Rocklin took a deep breath as much of the concern that had been plaguing him melted away. He smiled ruefully at Frankie. "My apologies, Frankie, for sounding so brusque when I came in. Things were infernally busy today, and all I could think of was Tyler and the fact that I couldn't be home . . . and what I would do if I came home to the news that . . . that he —" His voice broke, and Frankie was deeply touched by the man's evident love for his son.

What would it be like to have a father who loved you so much? she wondered.

"Well . . ." Rocklin recovered his voice. "Thank God for the good news! Now how are you getting on, and how is Mrs. Rocklin?"

Frankie smiled reassuringly. "She's pretty weak, but she ate this morning, and a little tonight. I think she must be over the worst of her illness. I expect she'd like to see you." Frankie added, with a twinkle in her eye, "She's the prettiest lady — and so *nice!*"

Gideon laughed, saying, "Well, *I* think so, Frankie."

He turned at once toward the bedroom he shared with his wife, and Frankie went

190

to the kitchen, where she got a basin of hot water and some towels. Then she went to Tyler's room, announcing at once, "Your father just came in. Let me fix you up a little so you won't scare him to death."

"Do I look that bad, Frankie?" Tyler managed a small grin. "It'll take more than a nurse to pretty me up!" Frankie picked up a comb and brush and began to smooth his black hair. When she caught a snag, he yelped, "Hey! That hurts!"

"Oh, don't be such a baby!" Frankie said. "Tomorrow I'm going to wash your hair and cut it, too. You're woolly as a bear."

"How would you know how woolly a bear is?" Tyler growled.

"I've killed four of them," Frankie shot back.

"Aw, you never did that!"

Frankie smiled, pausing to concentrate on her task. Tyler's matted hair was hard to manage, so she began to hold to the thick locks with one hand, pulling the comb through with the other. "Sure I did," she finally responded. "And I faced down another one that just about got me." As she worked on Tyler, getting him cleaned up, she told the story of how she'd met a female grizzly bent on guarding her pair of cubs — and how she'd nearly been their lunch. It made an exciting story, and Tyler listened with intense interest.

"I've never even *seen* a grizzly bear, Frankie," he observed, "let alone had to face one down. You must be pretty good with a gun."

"Had to be," she said, smiling. "When there's a family to feed and you've got only so much money for powder, you can't afford to miss." She stepped back, studying her handiwork with some degree of approval. "That'll do until I can wash it," she announced. "Now let me have that nightshirt."

Tyler flushed, his square face showing some embarrassment. He began to struggle to pull the garment off, but Frankie saw his face grow tense with pain as the movement strained his wounded leg.

"Hold on, Tyler." She pulled a sheet over his lower body, then stepped forward, saying, "Let me help you with that." She was very strong, Tyler saw right off as she moved him easily into a sitting position and eased the nightshirt off. He pulled the sheet up, saying, "A sick man shouldn't worry about modesty, I guess."

Frankie grinned at him. "Don't worry about it, Private. I've taken care of a sick brother most of my life. You won't shock me. Now why don't you wash while I get you a fresh nightshirt."

When Gideon entered the room five minutes later, he found Tyler looking much better than he had the previous night. His freshly combed hair and clean clothing vastly improved his appearance. His eyes were clearer, too, which was a good sign. "Why, you look fit to soldier!" Gideon remarked with a smile and moved over to sit down next to the bed. Frankie was gathering up the towels and the basin, and he asked, "He been a good patient, Frankie?"

"Contrary as a mule," she shot back. "You tell him if he doesn't shave himself, I'm going to do it for him!"

Rocklin laughed, and as the girl left, he turned back to his son. "If I were you, I'd mind that girl. She's liable to do what she says."

"Where'd you find her?" Tyler asked. "She sure is a funny sort of girl."

Rocklin gave a brief history, telling what little he knew of Frankie, and ended by saying, "I think she's had a pretty hard time, Tyler. Pretty tough to live like she does." He shrugged his shoulders, adding, "You know how soldiers are as far as women are concerned. I was pretty skeptical at first whether she'd be a help or a problem. Some of these women who call themselves sutlers are no better than camp followers. But this one is a fine girl, maybe because of Sol Levy."

Tyler sat there listening and finally said, "Well, she's a strong young woman. Handles me like I was stuffed with feathers! And did you know she's killed four bears and outwitted a mama grizzly bent on protecting her cubs?"

Gideon laughed, exclaiming, "No, but it doesn't surprise me." He sat there talking with Tyler, and finally the boy expressed a fear that had been in him.

"I . . . worry some about this leg, Dad," he said, looking down at the bandages.

"Dr. Smith said you're doing well."

"You know how quickly these things can go bad," Tyler said slowly. He was a blocky young man, built much like his grandfather. His dark brown eyes usually danced with devilment, but now they were filled with apprehension. "And if the knee is torn up too bad, I–I'll be a cripple."

"The doctors were pretty sure that wouldn't happen," Gideon said quickly, wanting to give Tyler some assurance. What he didn't mention was that all of the doctors had agreed that, even at best, the knee would heal slowly — which meant Tyler would be out of the army. He smiled at his son. "First, we've got to get this wound healed up. Then you can begin exercising that leg a little at a time. It'll take awhile, but I'm thanking God that you didn't lose the leg and that you weren't killed."

"Sure, Dad," Tyler agreed with a nod. "I am, too. But it's going to be hard lying here with nothing to do."

"Coax Frankie to entertain you." Gideon smiled. "She's very good with the men in the hospital."

"She can't stay here forever, though."

Gideon had no answer for that, for he felt that he had already asked too much of the girl. Later, however, when he sought out Frankie, who was cleaning up the kitchen, he cautiously began to explore the possibility of keeping her on.

"I know Mr. Levy must need you, Frankie," he said. "You two stay busy all the time."

"He told me to stay as long as you needed me, Major Rocklin," Frankie answered. She looked up from the sink, and the amber glow from the light overhead brought a reddish glint to her short curly hair. She had, Rocklin noticed, strong, square hands.

"I've got to hire someone to take care of

Tyler for a while, and my wife needs looking after, too. I know it's asking a great deal, but you've done so well that I'd like to keep you on." He mentioned a salary, then added, "It would be doing us all a great service if you could stay here for a time."

"Why, I'll be happy to stay, Major," Frankie said. "Personally, I think I'm better at plowing behind a mule than I am at housework, but I'll do my best. I'll stay as long as Sol says it's all right."

"Fine!" Rocklin said, greatly relieved. He got to his feet at once. "That's a great relief to me, and to my wife, too. I'll just go tell her that you'll be staying on. I'll let you break the news to Tyler."

When Frankie told Tyler that she'd agreed to stay, he looked as relieved as his father had. "I'm glad to hear that! Hate to go to all the trouble of breaking a new nurse in!"

Frankie sniffed, saying, "I'm not going to put up with your bossy ways, Private Rocklin. Now I'm going to try to get you cleaned up." A humorous light touched her green eyes, and she added, "I entered a pig in the contest at the county fair once. Got him cleaned up fine enough to win first place, too."

Tyler stared at her. "I'm not a pig!"

"I should say not! You're not in as good a

shape as my pig was! You certainly won't win first place! But I'll do the best I can. Person has to use whatever's at hand."

She left the room, and Tyler called out as she passed through the door, "Hey, I can always go back to the hospital, where I'll get a little respect!" When the door closed behind her, he chuckled and ran his hand through his hair. "I am a pretty sorry sight, I guess," he muttered. Then he raked his fingernails across his jaw, thinking, *Guess a shave wouldn't hurt, either. . . .*

In the weeks that followed, Gideon Rocklin offered fervent thanks that God had sent Miss Frankie Aimes his way. Melanie seemed to improve for a time, but then a setback that even Dr. Smith could not explain laid her low, keeping her bedfast for many days. As for Tyler, his progress was erratic at best. His leg healed very slowly, and sudden fevers would assail him, leaving him weak and pale.

During the trying days of his family's illnesses, Gideon was forced to spend long hours at camp, working with the Army of the Potomac, which was composed of still-shattered men in desperate need of confidence in themselves or their cause. General George McClellan worked at putting the army back together night and day, and he had sent for Gideon early on. The two men had spent a pleasant half hour reminiscing about their days in service in the Mexican War. It amazed Gideon that the general remembered him, but McClellan was a remarkable man in many ways. Primarily he was a man of organization, able to pull loose threads together. As their talk had drawn to a close, he had said, "Major, I'm depending on you to pull your regiment into a strong unit. The president wants to strike at the enemy as soon as possible, and I propose to do exactly that!"

"General Scott believes we must first control the Mississippi and the coast — that we must strangle the South."

McClellan had waved his hand airily. "Oh, I admire General Scott, of course, but his plan would take far too long. We must strike the South where it lives: Richmond."

"Well, it will take a strong army, General McClellan. We'll be on their ground, and our supply lines will be very long. You know Jeb Stuart and what he can do."

But McClellan would acknowledge no danger of failure, and Rocklin had committed himself to getting the regiment up to full strength. Throwing himself into that task forced him to rely greatly on Frankie to care for his family, which she did with great efficiency.

Sol Levy came often, visiting with Tyler and keeping Frankie posted on his activities. He came at odd times, sometimes early in the morning, and once in a while in the evenings. Late one afternoon in October, Frankie answered a knock at the door and found the old man standing there. He looked very tired, and, startled, Frankie pulled him inside, scolding him for going around in such cold weather without a heavier coat.

"Can't have you getting sick," she fussed, making him sit down and pull his soaked shoes off beside the wood cookstove. She fixed him a hot meal of eggs, ham, and biscuits and molasses. Finally she sat down and drank coffee with him.

He ate slowly, and Frankie watched him, a worried frown creasing her brow. She noted that he had lost weight, and his eyes seemed sunken back more deeply into his skull. He appeared to be in good spirits, but he spoke far more slowly than was his habit, and he looked exhausted.

"Tell me about the boy," he said, sipping his coffee as Frankie gave him the details of Tyler's recovery. Sol listened and nodded. "He will be all right. I have prayed much for him. Now I will tell you about the work. . . ."

He spoke with pride of how many thousands of tracts and books he had passed on to the soldiers, and Frankie understood that his work as a sutler meant nothing to him. He was very proud of how he'd learned to speak with the men about their soul, though he laughed ruefully as he added, "Some of them get offended, but I think even they know I love them." He leaned forward, resting his arms on the table, saying with wonder, "I *do* love them, Frankie! And that's a miracle, because until I found Jesus, I never really loved anyone except myself."

"I can't believe that, Sol." Frankie put her hand on his and squeezed it. "You've shown such love to me!"

"Only because God put it there." Levy lifted his faded eyes and studied the face of the young woman. He wanted to say so much more to her, to warn her that life was short and every day without God was not only dangerous but a tragic loss. But he had learned when to speak and when to keep quiet, so he only smiled at her, saying, "You will find out someday, daughter, that the thing most people call 'love' isn't really love at all. Only the love that flows from God through us . . . only *that* love is real and

200

lasts forever."

He left shortly afterward, and when Frankie went in to give Tyler his medicine, he saw at once that she was not as cheerful as usual. "What's the matter, Frankie?" he asked. "All this nursing getting you down?"

"Oh no," she sighed. "It's just that I worry about my friend, Mr. Levy." She poured the dark brown medicine from a bottle into a spoon, then said to him as he opened his mouth, "You're just like a baby bird opening his mouth for a worm!"

Tyler made a terrible face, then grinned. "I'd just as soon eat worms as that stuff!" He shifted in his bed, then said, "Sit down and talk to me, Frankie. I'm so tired of myself I could scream." When she was seated, he said, "Tell me about yourself. I've told you everything I ever did in my whole life, but I don't know anything about you."

Frankie began to speak of Sol Levy and how he'd come to her at a time in her life when she desperately needed somebody. The room was quiet, and without intending to, she spoke about her past and her family. She even told Tyler how much her father had wanted sons, and how her brother, Timothy, had been a disappointment to him. She shared stories of her childhood days, talking of hunting, fishing, and riding —

unwittingly painting a poignant picture of a young girl learning to work and play like a boy.

Tyler listened quietly, thinking as Frankie spoke: *Poor girl! Why, she never had a childhood! That old reprobate of a father ought to be horsewhipped, and I wouldn't mind taking on the job!* He began to understand why Frankie wore men's clothing and seemed somewhat mannish in her ways. *She's got to learn to be a woman,* he decided. *Can't go through life wearing britches and acting like a man.*

He tried to touch on this when she was finished and got up to leave. "Frankie, haven't you ever wanted to buy a frilly dress and go to dances?"

Frankie gave him an odd look but merely said, "I guess I'm too old for all that, Tyler. I'll just have to be what I am." She left the room, and the young man lay there, growing drowsy from the effects of the medicine Frankie had given him. He tried to think of some way he could help but could come up with nothing. Just before he dropped off, he gave an impatient snort and mumbled, "Well, blast it! What can I do?"

Melanie Rocklin recovered from her setback as rapidly as she had come down with it —

within three days she was up and about. She was so happy to be able to take care of Tyler and do her work that Gideon and Dr. Smith took her to task for overdoing it, but Melanie was a woman who hated inactivity.

"God has healed me, and He doesn't intend for me to stay in that bed and be waited on," she told them with a bright smile. "It's His present to me, and I intend to enjoy it!"

Before long, she had decided that nothing would do but to have a party to celebrate her recovery — and Tyler's, as well, for by the middle of November, he had passed through the crisis. Dr. Smith gave his opinion to the family that the wounds were healed. "No chance of gangrene now," he said, smiling.

Gideon and Melanie rejoiced, and Tyler was relieved. "What about this knee, Dr. Smith?" he asked. "Can I start using it?"

"Yes, but have a little sense, young man. The knee is one of the most complicated and fragile mechanisms of your body. It needs a slow period of light exercise, plus rest. Miss Aimes, I'm going to give you the exercises our young friend should do and trust you to run herd on him." A smile touched the doctor's thin lips. "And you'd best go cut yourself a switch to use on this young fellow if he gets too ambitious."

"I think Mrs. Rocklin will have to use the switch," Frankie said. "I've got to get back to work."

"Oh?" Dr. Smith lifted his eyebrows. "Well, I want to tell you what a fine job you've done, Miss Frankie. I'm sure the Rocklins will miss you. They've all told me how fond they've become of you, so don't be surprised if they object to your leaving."

They did protest, Tyler most of all. He moaned, "I'm spoiled, Frankie! Mother won't bring me hot chocolate every night like you do!"

But Frankie only shook her head when both Gideon and Melanie asked her to stay on. "You don't really need me now, and I'm worried about Mr. Levy. He hasn't been well this winter."

"No, he hasn't," Gideon agreed. "You ought to make him take time off and rest up."

"Just what I'm going to do!"

When Gideon took Frankie back to camp, he spoke of his gratitude. "Money won't pay for what you did, Frankie," he said. "Don't know how we'd have made it without you." He paid her a bonus, but it was his words and the knowledge of a job well done that pleased Frankie the most. She shook the major's hand and gave him a warm smile, then went in search of Sol.

When she finally found him, Frankie was shocked at the sight of her friend. He was in his tent, too weak to get out of bed. "Sol! How long have you been sick?" she demanded.

"Oh, I've just been a little under the weather," he whispered. "Be all right soon, now that you're here."

"You're not staying in this tent another day!" Frankie announced. "You're going into the hospital!"

Frankie marched into regimental headquarters and asked to see the major. He came out immediately and asked, "What's wrong? Is it Mr. Levy?"

"Yes, sir. He's real sick. He's got to be cared for, and I was wondering if you could get him a bed in the hospital here. That way I could take care of him and still keep the store open."

"Why, of course!" Rocklin nodded. "It may bend regulations a little, but I think the army owes that man a great deal. Sergeant, go with this young lady. Get an ambulance and take Mr. Levy to the hospital. I'll give you a note for Major Turner. See to it that Miss Aimes here gets whatever she needs to take care of Mr. Levy." He turned back to Frankie. "Don't worry, Frankie. We'll see that he gets good care. Come and see me if you need anything at all."

"Thank you, Major!"

Sol Levy found himself helpless in the hands of his employee. He tried to protest, but by noon he was in a bed, all washed and shaved, with an army doctor poking at him. Major Turner, the chief surgeon, was a muscular man of fifty with a thick mane of white hair. He was a rough sort, but said in a straightforward fashion, "Mr. Levy, you're old enough that you should have come in sooner, but I think we'll be able to fix you up."

But when he spoke to Frankie alone, there was a somber look on his face. "He's a pretty sick man, Miss Frankie. His age is against him, of course, and he's pretty frail."

"But . . . he'll be all right, won't he, Doctor?"

Turner hesitated. "I never make guarantees. Been wrong too many times. We'll do our best, but . . . well, if he gets pneumonia —"

Frankie was frightened by Major Turner's warning. She began at once spending much time with Sol, taking only as much time selling merchandise to the men as was necessary. For two days Sol seemed to hold his own, but Frankie noticed on the third day that he was having trouble breathing. When Major Turner came through, she asked him to look at Sol, and he complied. He was cheerful enough while speaking to Sol but took Frankie outside at once. "It's not good, I'm afraid," he said slowly. "His lungs are filling with fluid."

"Pneumonia?" Frankie whispered.

"I'm afraid it is."

"Can't you do *anything*?"

Turner gave the girl a compassionate look. "There's not much we doctors can do: set a bone, stitch up a cut. Most of the time it's the body that does the healing." The surgeon knew a little about the young woman who stood before him, her face filled with fear, for Major Rocklin had told him some of her story. He hesitated, then said, "I'll be honest with you, Miss Frankie. He doesn't have much of a chance."

"He's going to die?"

"We all have to do that eventually." Turner hated this part of his job, but he was a fine doctor and knew he had to be honest: Levy would die unless a miracle took place. He himself was not a Christian, so he could only say, "He's a fine man. He's done a lot for the men. But if he has any family close by, you'd better tell them to come at once."

Frankie knew then that the doctor had given up hope, and when he left, she had to fight back the terrible grief that swept over her. She waited until she could smile, then went back to sit beside Sol. He was asleep, but he woke up later and peered at her. As sick as he was, he saw at once that she was disturbed and knew what was troubling her.

"The doctors can only do so much, daughter," he whispered. His voice was weak, and it rattled in his chest. He lifted his hand, and she grabbed it blindly. It was so thin it felt like a bird's claw, all bones and skin.

Sol lay quietly all afternoon, and when he drifted off to sleep, Frankie went outside. She was standing in the cold, tears running down her face, not even noticing that the men who passed were watching her. She tried to pray, but nothing came. Finally she went back inside.

Sol slept fitfully for most of the night, but at dawn he roused up. His eyes were clear, and he once again reached for Frankie's hand. Nodding, he smiled at her, saying, "I don't want you to grieve over me, Frankie. Will you promise me that?"

Frankie could not speak. She shook her head, then dropped to her knees, throwing her arms around the old man's frail form.

"I — I can't help it!" she moaned. "You've done so much for me, and I never did anything for you!"

"Ah, you are wrong! Very wrong!" Sol seemed to grow stronger, and he pulled her tearstained face up so that he could see her eyes. "God gave you to this old man for a daughter, just for a little while." He touched her cheek, and his eyes traced her face. "I must go now . . . to my Savior. But I don't have to go alone, for you are here with me."

They held on to one another, and for a while Sol Levy spoke quietly. He told her again how he had been so happy since finding Jesus. Then he seemed to fade away.

Frankie was alarmed and begged, "Don't go! Sol, please! Don't leave me!"

But Sol smiled — an easy, gentle smile. "It's only . . . for a little while . . . daughter. You will find Jesus. God has told me that! Praise His name forever!"

Five minutes later he opened his eyes and whispered, "You have been . . . a blessing . . . my daughter."

Thus saying, he took one shallow breath, and then Solomon Levy went to join the God of his fathers.

CHAPTER 11
A TASTE OF BLACKMAIL

By early December Tyler was walking with crutches — and driving his mother crazy.

"Gideon," Melanie finally said one night when her husband was home for one of his rare weekend leaves, "what are we going to do about Tyler?" She was sitting on the side of her bed, brushing her long blond hair as he undressed.

"Do about him?" Gideon asked, throwing a puzzled glance toward her. "Why, he's improving faster than any of us thought he might." He pulled a flannel nightshirt over his head and turned the lamp wick down, then quickly got under the covers.

Melanie had only enough time to put her comb down before the light was dimmed, but as she turned to slip under the covers, she persisted. "Oh, he's well enough physically, but you know how active he's always been. Gid, he's read every book in the house, and he follows me around all day long." Gideon's arms went around her, and she felt as always when he embraced her . . . like a young girl. She had heard of women who endured the intimacies of marriage with distaste, but she had never been able to understand how that could be. She loved Gideon's caresses, but now she drew back, saying, "Tyler misses Frankie a lot. She was such good company for him. He can't go back in the army for a long time, can he?"

Gideon was stroking Melanie's long hair, not thinking so much of his son as he was of how nice his wife smelled and how soft, yet firm, she was. "Hmm? Oh — no, not for quite a while, Mellie. That knee's got to have lots of rest."

Melanie reached out and imprisoned his hand, which was tracing the smoothness of her neck. Holding it tightly, she said, "We simply must find something for Tyler to do, or he'll go crazy. And drive the rest of us crazy right along with him! Maybe he could go to work at your father's factory."

Gideon smiled tenderly. "I'll talk to him about it," he assured her, holding her small hands in his big ones. His eyes regarded her warmly, and the love Melanie saw reflected in their depths touched her so deeply she felt a wave of emotion wash over her. How good God had been to let them come together!

"You know," Gid went on, his voice soft, a crooked smile on his face, "I'll be gone for quite a while when the army moves against Richmond. Sure hate to think of all the handsome chaps who'll be left to guard Washington. . . . Maybe I'd better hire some sort of duenna to keep an eye on you."

"You idiot!" she laughed and moved against him.

Only three days later, Tyler left the house for the first time since being brought there by the ambulance. He had Amos hitch up the family carriage and help him make his way down the sidewalk, which was icy and dangerous.

"Miz Rocklin gonna skin bof of us!" the tall black man complained as he hoisted the young man into the closed vehicle. He leaned in and arranged a blanket around Tyler's knees, grumbling steadily. "Fust time you cotches her gone, you gits dis crazy idea to go rummaging around. It ain't right! No, it ain't!"

Tyler grinned at the man, saying, "I won't tell if you won't, Amos. Now let's get going!" He sat back, enjoying the cold air, which was refreshing after the long weeks in the confines of the house. All around him the trees were heavy with ice and glittered like diamonds as the breeze shook them. Christmas was two weeks away, and he saw signs of the coming holiday in a few decorations already appearing in windows and on the fronts of houses lining the streets.

He moved his knee carefully, noting that it was less painful than it had been two days ago when Dr. Smith had tested it. *"Stay off it for another week. Then we'll see,"* he'd said. But Tyler had endured being cooped up in the house for as long as he could. When his mother had left to go to the church and roll bandages for the troops, he knew that he was going to have a holiday, even if it killed him. Amos had argued and fussed, but Tyler had bribed him with a gold coin, and now as the carriage rolled along, Tyler's eyes drank in all that was around him with a new appreciation. Life seemed fairer than ever.

Tyler had never been sick before, and the long convalescence had been hard on him. As long as Frankie had been there to read to him, to play chess and checkers, or just to talk, it had been bearable. But after she left, he had been thrown back on his own resources, and he had to admit that he had found himself a poor companion.

He sat back, enjoying the ride, and when the carriage turned off the main road toward the camp, he grew eager. Sitting up, he took in the long rows of tents that made up the camp. "Take me to the Washington Blues' regimental headquarters, Amos," he called out. The servant knew that place well, having brought his mistress there often. When they reached the area, Tyler called out, "Over there, where those wagons are." When the carriage stopped, he threw the blanket back and carefully let himself out of the coach.

Amos said sharply, "Now will you wait jes' a minute till I can get there!" He reached up and helped Tyler down, then fished his crutches out. "Now where at you goin'?" he huffed when Tyler started out.

"Not too far," he answered. "You can come along, but if I nod at you, I want you to skedaddle!"

Amos stared at his young master, frowned, and shook his head. "You up to somethin', Mistuh Tyler! I kin tell!"

Tyler only laughed at him and swung himself across the frozen ground toward an open area where three large canvas-covered wagons were set up about twenty feet apart, each with an adjacent tent. Tyler called out, and a man stuck his head out of the flap of one of the tents, asking, "Want to buy something, soldier?"

"Looking for Frankie Aimes."

"Last tent down."

"Thanks." Tyler swung along, calling out when he got close to the third tent, "Hi! Any vivandiers in there?"

At once the flap opened and Frankie emerged. Her face lit up when she saw who was calling, and she ran to meet him. "Tyler! What in the world are you doing way out here?" She was wearing a pair of blue wool trousers with a shirt to match, and on her head was perched a blue forage cap. Her eyes were brighter than he remembered, and her hair redder.

"You look different," he said, grinning. "First time I've ever seen you in uniform."

"Come in where it's warm," Frankie said. "You, too, Amos." She ducked inside the tent, and soon the three of them were drinking scalding coffee that she'd brewed on the small woodstove that warmed the tent. She gave them both some pie and plied Tyler with questions.

After the pie, Tyler sent a subtle signal to Amos, who rose from the wooden box he was sitting on and said, "I gonna look around for my friend Washington. He one of de cooks fo' Major Gideon."

As soon as the black man left, Tyler said quietly, "I was sorry to hear about Mr. Levy, Frankie. He was a fine man, and I know losing him was hard on you."

Frankie dropped her eyes, fingered a button on her shirt, then looked up at him. "It's still hard, Tyler. He was so kind to me!" She gave her head a shake and, pulling her shoulders together, came up with a small smile. "I'll see him again — that's the last thing he said to me, Tyler." Then she began to ask him how he was doing, and Tyler knew she wasn't ready to talk about her loss any further. He gave her his report on his knee, told her about his mother and his relatives, and regaled her with the antics of the cat, Lothar, who had been a favorite with Frankie.

He also told her about the Southern branch of the Rocklin family, for Frankie had grown very interested in them during her stay with Tyler's family. After telling her about his uncle Clay and his family, he asked, "Did I ever tell you about my uncle Paul?" When Frankie shook her head, Tyler said, "I only met him once, but he's really something. Artist type, studied in Europe. Came back all against the Rebellion."

"Don't guess his family likes that much, do they?"

"No, it's been pretty tough on them, but he fell for a Southern belle, and he's gone to work for the government, taking pictures of the battles." Tyler shook his head, a thoughtful look in his brown eyes. "That's a funny way to fight a war — taking pictures."

"Will he marry the girl?"

"Oh, I don't know, Frankie." Tyler shrugged. "I suppose so. Her family has money, and she's supposed to be a raving beauty. Now tell me about your family."

Frankie pulled out some letters from Timothy and notes from her sisters and read parts of them to Tyler. When she finished, he asked hesitantly, "Nothing from your father?"

"No. I . . . I don't think there'll be anything." Frankie changed the subject, and for the next hour the two drank coffee and finished off the pie. Just as the last slice was disappearing, a voice called out, "Any wayward soldiers in there with you, Miss Aimes?"

"It's my father!" Tyler said and got to his feet, grabbing his crutches. He followed Frankie outside and saw his father with another man, a civilian. Amos eyed Tyler from a position at the wagon.

"You scoundrel!" Tyler called out to the

servant. "Why, you're nothing but a — a —"

"He did his duty," Major Rocklin cut in with a grin. "Told me he wasn't taking any punishment from your mother over this trip."

Tyler looked crestfallen but faced his father, setting his jaw firmly. "I *had* to get out of the house," he said. "I need the exercise."

"Nice how you came straight to see your father." Gideon tried to sound severe, but Tyler could see the smile that threatened to break out on his father's face.

"I was coming to see you before I left," he said lamely.

Gideon did smile then, and he shook his head indulgently. He glanced at the man standing beside him. "Mr. Pinkerton, this is my son, Private Tyler Rocklin. And this is Miss Frankie Aimes, one of our fine sutlers. Tyler, Frankie, meet Mr. Allan Pinkerton."

"The detective?" Tyler asked, giving the man a startled look. He offered his hand. "An honor to meet you, sir!"

Though only of medium height, Pinkerton was powerfully built. He had a round, pleasant face and brown hair. His searching blue-gray eyes took in the young man, then shifted to Frankie. "Pleasure to meet both

218

of you," he said.

Tyler had read a story about the famous detective in the newspaper and had been impressed by it. Pinkerton had been a police officer before opening his own detective agency, and he had been called on by General McClellan to put his talents at the service of the government. So far, he had been instrumental in capturing several spies — including the most famous of all, Rose O'Neal Greenhow.

"I'm sending you home, Tyler," Major Rocklin said firmly. "Your mother would skin me alive if I didn't. And since Mr. Pinkerton has to go back to town, you can give him a lift."

"Why, of course!"

Tyler said a hasty good-bye to Frankie, adding urgently, "I came to invite you to our Christmas party. Mother says if you don't come, she'll have Father arrest you and put you in the stockade. It's on the twenty-fourth."

"I'd like that," Frankie said, smiling.

Pinkerton walked with Tyler to the wagon, and when he saw the black man start to get down from the driver's seat to help young Rocklin on, he said, "I'll do it." With surprising strength for a small man, he almost lifted Tyler into the coach, then got in himself. Leaning out the window, he said, "I'll be back next Wednesday, Major. I'd appreciate it if you'd have your estimates ready."

"I'll have them." Rocklin nodded. "See you tomorrow, son."

As the coach pulled away and turned around for the trip back to the city, Pinkerton pulled out a cigar, bit the end of it off, and lit it. "Your father is very proud of you, sir." He smiled at Tyler as the smoke ascended. "And I know you're proud of him."

Tyler shrugged. "He's a good man — and a fine soldier, but it looks like I'm out of it. The war will be over before this knee heals up."

"Wouldn't be too sure of that," Pinkerton replied. "Anyway, there are other things you can do while you're waiting. They need men to run the War Department. Your father could get you into something along that line."

"I'd be bored to tears!"

Pinkerton studied the young man, a critical light in his eyes. "You like adventure, eh? Well, most young men do."

"Not very likely to have any, not with this knee."

Pinkerton said nothing more about Tyler's prospects but began to tell of a case he'd worked on once. When he got out in downtown Washington, he said, "Don't get discouraged, Private. Something will turn up. Let me know if I can help."

Tyler was quiet and thoughtful on the rest of the drive home. The next day he asked his father about Pinkerton's business with the army.

"Well, it's not to be talked about," his father said, "but he's organized a Secret Service. General McClellan has great confidence in him. As I understand it, Pinkerton will handle the spies and their reports."

Tyler's face had grown serious as he listened. "He's a pretty smart man — and tough, too. I could see that."

"He's got to be," Gideon replied. "He's got a tough job!"

By December 24, Tyler had exchanged his crutches for a cane. When he admitted Frankie at the door early that evening, she noted the change at once. "Oh, you're walking so much better, Tyler!" she exclaimed.

"Yes, and ready to get better still!" He smiled, surveying the young woman who was smiling at him. He was not surprised that Frankie had arrived for the party wearing her usual garb instead of a dress. He'd told her the occasion would be informal, but he knew any other young woman would have come dressed to the teeth. Still, he had to admit that she looked very well. With a grin, he said, "Come on in. We've got to sample the eggnog."

The party was not large; it was small enough for all the guests to assemble in the large parlor. Frankie had met most of those present: Tyler's grandparents, Stephen and Ruth Rocklin, and Tyler's younger brothers, Robert and Frank, she had met several times while taking care of Tyler. She'd met Major Rocklin's sister, Laura, and had heard her husband, Amos Steele, preach many times. One of their sons, Clinton, she hadn't met before, and their two other sons were not able to be there.

"And this is my daughter, Deborah, Miss Aimes. And this is Private Noel Kojak, her fiancé." Laura Steele smiled as she introduced the couple to Frankie, adding, "We're very fortunate to have Noel here for Christmas."

"Tyler told me about how you helped him escape from a Confederate hospital, Miss Steele," Frankie said. "I couldn't have done a thing like that!"

Deborah Steele was a beautiful young woman, and Frankie noted that she had as much poise as any man. "I think you could,

Miss Aimes," she said, smiling. "Uncle Gideon has been telling us how you jumped in and took care of Tyler. I think you must be very resourceful."

Noel said, "I only hope your future husband has better sense than to get himself put in a Confederate hospital under guard." Frankie considered the young soldier. He was not handsome, but his steady gray eyes and regular features gave him a pleasant appearance. He looked rather shyly at Frankie, adding, "I'm glad you're here tonight, Miss Aimes. We're all grateful for the way you helped Tyler and Mrs. Rocklin."

"Watch out, Frankie!" Tyler had come to stand beside Frankie, his eyes gleaming with humor. "That fellow is deceiving! He's a writer, you know, and if you're not careful, he'll put you in one of his stories!"

They stood there chatting, and Frankie slowly relaxed. She had been rather terrified of coming, for she knew her manners were rough. But Tyler stayed beside her, making it easy for her. He sat next to her while they talked and made it a point at dinner to sit at the big table at her right.

The meal was stupendous: turkey, dressing, ham, vegetables, baked breads, apple pie, all cooked exquisitely. Frankie soon was able to relax and eat without worrying too much over her manners. She listened as the talk and laughter flowed around the table, deciding that this was a happy family — totally unlike her own.

Amos Steele glanced at her at one point during the meal and said, "I know how much you miss Sol Levy, Miss Aimes. The rest of us feel his loss, too. He was wonderful with the men! I think he must have won at least fifty of them to the Lord!" His words brought a warmth to Frankie, and she was pleased when Major Rocklin joined in the conversation, speaking of the work her friend had done.

After the meal, there was a little ceremony in the parlor. Gideon read the Christmas story from the Bible, and Rev. Steele spoke briefly about the meaning of the birth of Jesus. Then everyone bowed their heads while one of the family members prayed.

It was over about ten o'clock, and Tyler limped out to the carriage with Frankie. When she was bundled up inside, he looked at her, saying with some hesitation, "I'm glad you came, Frankie. My family took you in . . . I could tell. I mean the others, of course, the Steeles and Noel. My parents already think you're very special."

"It was wonderful," Frankie said, a smile lighting her face. "I won't forget it." Then she said, "Good night, Tyler!" and the coach pulled off.

Tyler stood there staring after the carriage as it disappeared. He frowned and muttered aloud, "Have I done the right thing?" He shook his head doubtfully, then took a deep breath.

"It'll be all right," he said with a nod. "She'll see how it is. . . ." Then, with another shake of his head, he limped back inside.

"I suppose you're wondering why I wanted to see you, Miss Aimes?"

Frankie was sitting nervously on one of the three straight-backed chairs in the office to which a corporal had led her. He'd given her a message from Major Rocklin, which said briefly, "Mr. Allan Pinkerton would like to talk to you. The corporal who brings this note will take you to his office."

Frankie looked at the detective, nodded, and waited for his answer.

"Well, I suppose you know what it is that I do?" Pinkerton was standing beside a window and gave her a sudden smile. "Nobody is supposed to know about the Secret Service. And, of course, everybody *does*. You've heard of it, I would suppose?"

"Why, yes, sir." Frankie nodded. "The

men talk about you a lot."

"Ah, well, there it is!" Pinkerton frowned and came to stand beside the pine desk. "Impossible to keep a thing this large a secret. Quite impossible." He pulled out a cigar, lit it, and, when it was drawing to his satisfaction, looked at her keenly. "Miss Aimes, I need your help."

Surprise showed clearly on Frankie's face. At once she shook her head. "Why, I can't think what I could do for a man like you!"

"No? Let me tell you, then. The war is stepping up, Miss Aimes, and soon there is going to be a great battle. The North has to move an enormous amount of supplies and a great many troops to the South. Now the South doesn't really have to move much. It's their home ground, and they know it like a man knows his own backyard. When the attack comes, our generals and our officers will be at a great disadvantage. They won't know the territory, and they won't know the strength of the enemy."

He paused for a long moment, then said evenly, "My job is to see that General McClellan *does* know those things. And I'll use anything or anyone I can to help our army achieve a victory."

Frankie saw that the small man was entirely serious, but she was totally bewildered.

"But . . . Mr. Pinkerton, I've never even *been* in the South! I couldn't help —"

Pinkerton interrupted her, saying, "You are a great friend of Private Tyler Rocklin, Miss Aimes?"

"Why . . . yes."

"Well, he came to me recently with a very interesting proposal. A proposal that requires your help if it is to succeed." Pinkerton drew on his cigar, then suddenly sat down in the chair behind the desk. "He said that he has a relative who has just contracted to take pictures of upcoming battles for the Confederate government. I think he's mentioned this to you?"

"Yes. Paul Bristol is his name, isn't it?"

"That's the man. Private Rocklin has been thinking about a plan involving this situation. Though his days as a soldier are over — for a time, at least — Rocklin wants to serve his country."

"What does he want to do?"

"He wants you to go to Richmond and work for this man Bristol." Pinkerton was watching the young woman's face carefully and saw a flicker come to her green eyes. "Yes, you will be an agent working for the government of the United States." He grew excited then, adding, "It's *perfect*! Photographers go everywhere, and both sides leave them alone. Our Mathew Brady has proven this. So you will travel as an assistant to Bristol, and you will collect information, which you will pass on to Tyler Rocklin."

"To *Tyler*?"

"Oh yes! He will be there in Virginia, too. Under cover, of course. He wants to help our cause, and he was certain that you'd want to do the same."

Frankie shook her head. "I — I couldn't do it, Mr. Pinkerton. I couldn't be a spy!"

The next fifteen minutes were among the worst that Frankie had ever known. She tried desperately to convince the man across from her that she could not do what he asked, but he refused to give in. Finally she grew angry. "I won't do it!" she cried, rising out of her chair.

She had reached the door when Pinkerton said calmly, "That's very unfortunate. It's going to be hard on your brother, Timothy."

Frankie whirled and stared at Pinkerton. "What does my brother have to do with this?"

"Haven't you heard about the new conscription act?"

"What's that?"

"A new law, Miss Aimes. Able-bodied men will be conscripted, that is, taken into the army. We need more soldiers, and we aren't getting enough volunteers. Congress just passed the act, and your brother is the right age."

Frankie stared at Pinkerton. "Tim can't be a soldier! He's been sick all his life! Forcing him to be a soldier would probably kill him!"

Pinkerton's blue-gray eyes were cold. "Be that as it may, I believe he'll be conscripted, Miss Aimes. Unless, of course, you agree to help your country. If you volunteered, I believe I have enough influence to get your brother exempted."

Frankie had never felt such rage as washed over her at that moment, but with a jolt she realized it was hopeless. Everything in her hated the idea of being a spy, but the thought of poor Timothy being thrown into the rough life of a soldier . . . *He wouldn't live a week!* she thought desperately.

"Well, Miss Aimes? Which will it be? You or your brother?"

Squaring her shoulders and lifting her chin, Frankie gave Pinkerton a level look. "I'll do it . . . what you say." Her voice was even and cold. "But it won't work. I don't know a thing about taking pictures. And Bristol would never hire a girl, anyway."

Pinkerton smiled. "Oh, I think we can handle those two problems. Mathew Brady has agreed to train you in the science of taking pictures. And Tyler has told me how much Major Rocklin appreciates your kindness to him. He'll tell his father that you want a job and ask him to write his cousin Paul a letter of recommendation concerning one Frankie Aimes, aspiring photographer."

Frankie shook her head, feeling as though she was drowning. "But . . . I'm from the North! He won't hire a Yankee!"

"Ah, another excellent point. Which is exactly why the letter will state that you have no political affiliations, that all you want to do is take pictures. It will suffice, believe me!"

Then Allan Pinkerton smiled, his eyes shining. "Welcome to the Secret Service, Miss Aimes!"

Chapter 12
Frankie Learns a Trade

Allan Pinkerton was two men, Frankie quickly decided. He was capable of crushing anyone who stood in his way, and yet he could show great kindness to those who cooperated with him. Frankie tried to put this in a letter to Timothy but was hampered by knowing that she must not say too much. It occurred to her that Pinkerton might have her letters intercepted, so she said nothing at all about becoming an agent for the Federal Secret Service.

Dear Timothy,

I'm writing to tell you that I will not be working as a sutler for the army any longer. Since Mr. Levy died, I have not been able to do as well, so I have decided to accept a new job. I am being trained by Mr. Mathew Brady to make pictures, and when I am ready, I will travel over the country taking all sorts of pictures.

I was so nervous when I first went to Brady's gallery, because he is a famous man. But he was so nice to me that I quickly felt at ease. He showed me all over the studio — which is very large! — and introduced me to all of his employees. One of them, a young man named James Tinney, will train me since Mr. Brady is too busy to take much time for lowly pupils!

It may be that I will have to leave here suddenly to begin the work, so don't be worried if my letters don't come as often. I'll write when I can and will keep on sending money for the girls. You can write me in care of Brady's studio in New York for now.

Love, Frankie

She put the letter inside an envelope, sealed it with wax, then addressed it. She glanced around the small room that Pinkerton had found for her, thinking, *It won't take me long to become a liar in this job!* The reality of what was happening to her was far different from what she had stated to Timothy. Pinkerton had taken the reins firmly in hand, giving her little to say about anything. He had found a room for her and assigned her to one of his chief agents: a tall man named Nick Biddle, who spent considerable time with both Frankie and Tyler.

With a sigh, Frankie rose from the small table, slipped into her heavy coat, and left the room. As she made her way down Broadway, she thought of how difficult it had been for her to adjust to Tyler after her meeting with Pinkerton. He had arrived at her tent the day after the meeting and was enthusiastic, to say the least. His eyes had been glowing, and although his leg still gave him problems, he could not keep still. He had spoken with excitement of all that they might do, finally saying, "I can't be a soldier, Frankie, but I can do this, and it might mean more to my country than being a private!"

He had been so eager, his face so filled with the desire to serve! But Frankie was still fighting the anger she'd felt at the pressure put on her by Pinkerton. She had assumed that Tyler was somehow involved in Pinkerton's threat against Timothy — how else could Pinkerton have known she even *had* a brother except from Tyler?

But as Tyler had spoken, she'd studied him carefully, and her certainty began to ebb. *Maybe he didn't have anything to do with it,* she thought and finally decided to test him. Cautiously she said, "It'll be hard for me to be so far away from my family, especially Timothy." Tyler had nodded and voiced his regret. Then Frankie had said casually, "I've been worried about the new conscription law, Tyler."

Tyler had stared at her with blank surprise. "Why, you're not thinking about your brother, are you? I thought he was an invalid."

"Oh, he is, but he's able to be out of bed and to work around the house. What if they just take him and put him in the army?"

"Frankie, there's no danger of that," Tyler had responded at once. "I've talked to my father about it, and he says they're only going to take able-bodied men."

As he had rushed to explain the way the law worked, Frankie realized he was concerned for her, that he didn't want her worrying about her brother. There was such an innocence and honesty in Tyler's broad face that relief had washed over Frankie as she decided, *He doesn't know about Pinkerton's threat!*

Now as Frankie entered Brady's Daguerreotype Gallery, she felt again that sense of relief. It would have been very difficult to work with Tyler feeling the resentment she'd felt earlier. She was still bitter at being forced to do something she didn't

234

agree with, but at least she knew that Tyler was in no way responsible.

James Tinney met her as she entered the laboratory, smiling as he said, "Good morning, Miss Aimes. Ready for another lesson?"

"Yes, Mr. Tinney."

"Oh, call me James," the young man said. "Come along. I think you're ready for something new."

As Tinney led Frankie to a large table covered with photographic equipment, she wondered how much he knew about her mission. Brady knew, for Pinkerton had spoken of it when introducing Frankie to the photographer. "This young lady," he'd said, "will be working for the Secret Service on the other side of the line, Mr. Brady. She'll need to know a great deal about taking pictures." Brady, an ardent patriot, had found the plan fascinating and had pledged to do everything he could to help.

Frankie was certain that neither Tinney nor any of the other employees had any idea of her real task. As far as they were concerned, she was just a young woman who had somehow gotten Mr. Brady to agree to teach her the skills of photography.

Tinney turned, and his bushy beard fascinated Frankie. It covered his entire lower face so that only his ruddy lips appeared. *I*

235

wonder if he keeps that brush just to cover a weak chin? she wondered, but decided that the young man felt the whiskers made him look older. He was no more than twenty, Brady had confided in her, and yet he was one of his best men.

"Now you've learned quite a bit about working with daguerreotypes — and I must say you've picked the elements up very quickly! — but I want to show you something this morning that's going to make all that outdated before you know it!"

"You mean daguerreotypes won't be used any longer?"

"Oh, they'll be around for a while." Tinney shrugged, looked around cautiously, then added in a lower voice, "Mr. Brady got his start with daguerreotypes, so he clings to them. But the future of photography lies in wet plates."

"Wet plates?" Frankie asked in a puzzled tone. "Sounds like dishes being washed!"

Tinney laughed and went on to explain, which he loved to do! "Back in 1851, Miss Frankie, photography took a giant step forward. An English sculptor named Frederick Scott Archer came up with a new method of preserving an image. You know what collodion is? A sticky liquid made by dissolving nitrated cotton in a mixture of alcohol and ether. It's used as an agent to make the light-sensitive image adhere to a glass plate."

As Tinney spoke, showing Frankie various elements of the process, she concentrated on every word, knowing that the success of Pinkerton's scheme depended on her ability to perform.

"You see," Tinney concluded, "the ether and alcohol evaporate quickly, leaving behind a smooth, transparent film on the glass. This glass is sensitized by dipping it into a bath of silver nitrate solution. The sensitivity is lost when the plate dries. Then all you do is develop it in a solution of ferrous sulfate with acetic acid. Then you simply 'fix' the image by dipping it into a solution of potassium cyanide."

Frankie asked, "And you make a picture from the plate?"

"As many as you like!" Tinney beamed. "That's the great advantage of the wet-plate process, Miss Frankie. You can make an unlimited number of prints from a wet plate."

"So the daguerreotype is doomed?"

"Oh, don't let Mr. Brady hear you say that!" Tinney burst out quickly. Then he added in a low tone, "But you're right. You see, Miss Frankie, photography a few years ago was just a fascinating new art. Now it's big business." A sly smile came to his red lips as he added, "Men like P. T. Barnum use huge pictures to catch attention, and if Brady makes a large print, why, Guerney makes them larger, and then Lawrence tops them both! But Mr. Brady topped them all," he added. "He made hanging portraits of Morse, Field, and Franklin on a transparency measuring fifty by twenty-five feet, lighted by six hundred candles, just outside the gallery last summer!"

"He photographs lots of important people, doesn't he?"

"Oh my word, you've no idea! But you'll see some of them before you finish our training."

Tinney's words were prophetic, for three days later Brady's gallery had a distinguished client — indeed, the *most* distinguished visitor it was possible to have!

"Look, Miss Frankie!" Tinney whispered excitedly. "It's the president!"

They were on the second floor, where portraits were made, for Tinney had decided that his pupil needed some training in the taking of formal portraits. Frankie watched as Mr. Brady entered, accompanied by a major and President Abraham Lincoln. She had seen many pictures of Lincoln, but seeing him in person was quite a different matter! Expecting to be asked to leave, she saw Mr. Brady's eyes fall on her, and at once he leaned forward and whispered something to the president. Lincoln nodded, then turned to look at Frankie. He said something to Brady, who at once called out, "Miss Aimes, come here, please."

Frankie was so nervous as she approached the men that she was afraid she'd trip over her own feet. When she stood in front of the president, he smiled suddenly, saying, "I'm most grateful for your help in serving the Union, Miss Aimes. Mr. Pinkerton has told me all about it." He put his hand out suddenly, and when Frankie took it, Lincoln said, "It's a difficult and dangerous task, and I pray that you'll be kept safe."

"Th–thank you, Mr. President!" Frankie whispered. She looked up into Lincoln's face and thought, *How sad his eyes are — and how kind!* His hand was so large that her own was lost in it, and she knew that she'd never forget the moment. Not ever.

Then Brady gently ended the scene by saying, "Now, Mr. President, I'd like to get a full-length portrait."

Frankie moved away, but as she came to stand beside Tinney, she could still hear their conversation. "I'm six feet four," the president said, and a smile touched his full lips as he added dryly, "I saw a picture not long ago of a landscape. It had been made in several segments and pasted together. Guess you can use that method on me."

"Not necessary at all, Mr. President," Brady assured him. He began adjusting the camera, and Lincoln, at his signal, asked, "Shall I hold my arms like this?"

"Just be natural, sir."

Lincoln smiled again, humor in his deep-set eyes. "Just what I wanted to avoid," he remarked. As Brady hovered around, he said, "Major Flowers, there was a fine custom-built sawmill in my home county in Illinois. The owner was very proud of it. One day a farmer brought in a big walnut log, and while the owner was cutting it, there was a tremendous crash. Somebody had driven an iron spike into that tree, and the wood had grown over it. Well, the owner began investigating the cause of the accident, and the farmer came over and demanded, 'You ain't spoiled my plank, have you?' The owner yelled, 'Blast your plank! Look what it's done to my mill!' "

Lincoln winked at the officer, adding, "Mr. Brady's worried about the picture, but he ought to be worried about what I might do to his camera!" Brady and the officer laughed, and Lincoln kept up a lively conversation until the sitting was over and Brady came back with the plates.

"Which one do you like the best, Mr. President?" Brady asked.

Lincoln stared at them, then shook his head. "They look as alike as three peas," he remarked. "I will leave the choice to you, sir." He picked up his coat and put it on, then placed his tall stovepipe hat atop his head. As he left the room, he had to pass close to Frankie, and seeing her, he halted abruptly. "My best wishes to you, Miss Aimes," he said gently, and there was a kind look on his homely face.

After he left, Tinney stared at Frankie. "I didn't know you were so important," he said.

Tiny tips of gold came to the hard buds of the trees as spring broke the iron grip that winter had held on the land. Snow melted, creating rivers that ran across brown fields that had seemed dead but were beginning to put up tender shoots of emerald.

The Army of the Potomac — tired of drills and the long, monotonous months of winter — emerged as a first-rate fighting force, molded and inspired by "Little Mac," as the soldiers affectionately called General

241

McClellan. He had managed somehow to wipe away the shameful memories of their flight from Bull Run, and now they were poised, aimed at the South, and ready to march — a quarter of a million men organized into army corps, divisions, brigades, and regiments, with artillery, cavalry, engineers, a signal corps, and a transportation unit of wagon trains. All the while, Allan Pinkerton had driven the intelligence corps hard, gathering information about the enemy's operations and intentions.

Frankie said good-bye to Mathew Brady late one afternoon, and the photographer seemed anxious. He took her hand in both of his, saying, "Now, my dear Miss Aimes, you must be very careful. Very careful indeed." His kind brown eyes glowed, and he tried to make a joke out of the danger he was well aware that the young woman was about to plunge into. "Mr. Tinney and I have spent too much time teaching you my art to see it go to waste, so you come back to us safe and in good health."

"I will, Mr. Brady," Frankie replied. "I won't ever forget these days."

She left on that note and later in the day met with Allan Pinkerton and Tyler at the detective's office. Pinkerton spoke rapidly, stressing the need for accurate information about troop movements. Once he pounded his fist into his palm, saying emphatically, "General McClellan depends utterly on my information. And I will depend on you two and others like you. Don't fail me!"

Tyler spoke up, excitement in his voice and eyes. "Don't worry, sir; we'll get the best reports in the whole service for you!"

Pinkerton liked the young man, and the young woman, as well. He had regretted having to force the girl into service, but planned to make it up to her. "Fine! Fine!" he said, nodding. "Now I don't think it wise to keep anything in writing. If nothing's on paper, there's no way you can be convicted if you're captured. Miss Aimes, keep all the figures in your head. You have a fine memory, a fact that Mr. Brady has commented on often. Give the figures to Tyler verbally, and he'll give them to his contact the same way."

Tyler said thoughtfully, "I'm not sure that's wise, Mr. Pinkerton. Every time something gets told, there's a chance for error. I think it would be better if Frankie and I worked up some sort of a code — something that looks innocent but can be interpreted by you. That way the figures wouldn't get changed by repetition."

Pinkerton stared hard at the young man.

"Well, that would be much better from *my* standpoint, but more dangerous for you."

"Oh, Frankie and I can come up with something, can't we, Frankie?"

Frankie had been thinking as the two men spoke. "I think we might do it by an order for photographic supplies," she said slowly. "We could give each army unit a chemical name."

"I don't understand," Pinkerton said.

"Well, let's say we agree that potassium stands for a regiment. If I put down on an order blank 'three pounds of potassium,' that will mean three regiments."

"Why, that would be absolutely safe!" Pinkerton exclaimed. "And how would you indicate where these regiments are?"

"How about if we give the latitude and longitude as an order number? Three pounds of potassium, number 2459, would mean three regiments at where the 24 and 59 lines cross on a map."

Pinkerton clapped enthusiastically. "That will do it! And since Rocklin here will be posing as a traveling peddler, no one would ever suspect a simple order form of holding a message! Miss Aimes, I take my hat off to you!"

They spent an hour working out the code, and when it was time to part, Pinkerton detained Frankie as Tyler left to get the wagon. He seemed upset and embarrassed, and finally he said, "Well, Miss Aimes, I have been unfair to you." He smiled briefly at the young woman's look of surprise. "Everyone says I'm too busy with my job to understand the needs of people, but I'd like to think that there's another side of me. I *do* care about people, and I care about you. I forced you into this job, and it's too late to back out now. But I'll make you a promise. You do this one job for me, and when it's over, you're free to go your way."

"And my brother?"

Pinkerton shook his head. "He won't ever be conscripted, Miss Aimes. I bluffed you on that one. So even if you walked away from this job right now, your brother is safe." He watched the young woman's face, knowing he had just left himself vulnerable — a thing he did not do often. For one moment he feared she was about to call his hand, but he was wrong.

"I'll go with Tyler," Frankie said at last. "I can't let him down. But it makes a difference, what you just said, Mr. Pinkerton. I — I think better of you now."

Pinkerton was a hard man, but he showed a rare flush of pleasure as he took the young woman's hand. "I'm glad you do, Frankie.

I . . . have worried about you, for this is a dangerous mission. God bless you and bring you back safely."

Frankie left Pinkerton's office and walked rapidly to where Tyler was seated on the wagon. He was to drive her to the railroad station, then drive the wagon south to Virginia. It was Sol Levy's wagon, or had been, but he had left it to Frankie. Pinkerton had come up with the idea of sending Tyler into the South posing as a peddler, but thought it best for Frankie to take the train. *"The two of you must not be seen together any more than necessary,"* he had warned them.

Now it was time for the mission to begin, and as Frankie rode along, she felt that there was something unreal about it all. She said as much to Tyler, who agreed. "It's like something out of a dime novel," he said, nodding, his face serious. "But it'll be real enough when we get to Virginia."

They spoke of the arrangements for meeting until they got close to the station, and then Frankie said, "I'll walk from here on, Tyler. There'll be Southerners on the train, and we don't need to be seen together."

When he pulled the horses up, he suddenly reached out and put his arm around her waist. Frankie was so startled that she could not speak.

"I'm sorry I got you into this, Frankie," Tyler said slowly. "Now that we're almost into it, I see how unfair I was, dragging you into a dangerous thing like this. I should have done it alone."

Frankie was very nervous, acutely aware of his arm around her. "It–it's all right," she said quickly. "I was against it at first, but it's something we have to do."

Tyler didn't respond. He was too startled to do so, for he had been made aware of a strange fact. He was so accustomed to thinking of Frankie as a good companion, or a nurse, or a fellow conspirator, that the feel of her slim waist beneath his hand somehow shocked him. Looking into her face, he saw nothing masculine at all in the wide green eyes, the smooth skin, and the clean sweep of her jaw. He sat there, suddenly aware that this was not a fellow soldier, but a young and lovely woman. He stared at her, noticing for the first time how well shaped and somehow enticing her lips were . . . and, without thinking, he pulled her close and kissed her.

For one moment he was intoxicated by the feel of his lips against hers, the warmth of her breath on his face — and then he was shoved away almost frantically. Caught off guard, he scrambled to avoid falling from the wagon seat. He looked at Frankie, confused, and was startled by the desperate look in her eyes.

"Don't you *ever* do that to me!" she whispered hotly, then jumped to the ground, snatched her suitcase from the seat, and whirled to leave. She paused long enough to say shortly, "I'll get word to you when there's a report," and then she was gone, striding up the street toward the station. Indignation showed clearly in the set of her stiff back, and Tyler knew he had made a sad mistake.

"Well, old boy," he said aloud, "you certainly know how to turn on the charm, don't you?" He jiggled the reins, and the horses moved forward. As he headed for the outskirts of Washington, he thought about what had just happened. He was a little shocked at himself, wondering at first what could have possessed him to kiss Frankie, and then wondering why he'd never considered doing so before.

He realized that he'd always had a sense, despite the masculine clothing and manners, that Frankie Aimes was a tender and warm woman — and he was suddenly aware that this very fact somehow frightened her. She did all she could to give the image of being strong and capable, someone who didn't need anyone else. And yet . . . Tyler knew better. He'd seen her with Sol Levy, and with his family, and with himself.

He addressed the horses, saying, "Well, boys, I guess I've discovered a secret already — only this is Frankie's secret. Funny thing is, I'm not even sure she knows she has it. See, she doesn't want a man — or, more to the point, she doesn't *want* to want a man. She doesn't want to open herself up to anyone, or seem like she needs anyone to take care of her — that's for sure. Guess that's why she dresses like a man and tries to act like one, so we'll just leave her alone." He mused on that, then finally shook his head.

"Too bad trappings don't make a bit of difference. Like it or not, Frankie Aimes is very definitely a woman. But it doesn't seem too likely she'll ever let that part of herself out!"

■ ■ ■ ■

Part Three:
The Impostor —
March 1862

■ ■ ■ ■

CHAPTER 13
A STRANGE PAIR

From his earliest days, Claude Bristol was better at gambling than he was at raising cotton. He had appeared in Richmond from nowhere, and with the help of an aristocratic charm — and a rather small mare that could travel a quarter of a mile faster than any other horse in the county — he had successfully established himself in the second level of Virginia aristocracy.

Not the first level. That, of course, belonged to the Lees, the Randolphs, the Hugers, and a dozen other families. Still, Bristol was a handsome man, and his French ancestry had provided him with enough wile and sense to obtain Hartsworth — a fine plantation — and with enough romance to sweep Marianne Rocklin off her feet for the first and the last time in her life.

Marianne had always had much good sense and, as a rule, fine judgment. It was quite unfortunate, then, that in this one instance she failed to see that the young Frenchman who had won her heart was much better as a suitor than he would ever be as a husband. Her parents, on the other hand, had not been so deceived and had taken every opportunity to warn their daughter against the man. But Marianne was possessed of the one trait that identified a Rocklin faster than lightning: mule-headed stubbornness. And so she stuck to her guns, went against the wishes of her parents, and married the young man. And she lived to regret it.

Even so, it was a silent regret. If there was one thing that Marianne was not, it was a whiner. Her father, the late Noah Rocklin, had brought her up with the firm rule that people had to live with their errors. More than once she had heard him remark, "Whining about matters that we ourselves have helped to create . . . well, that simply is not the act of a lady or a gentleman."

Now, at the age of fifty-two, the mistress of Hartsworth had managed to overcome the disappointment of having chosen a weak man. She had Hartsworth, she had three children who had not yet disgraced the family — though Paul had been a sore trial — and she had God. Most of all she had God. Long ago she had given her heart to serve

Him, and she had found His love to be sufficient, even when her marriage had demonstrated a sad lack of either love or fidelity.

On a blustery Sunday in March of 1862, Marianne rose early, went about her work, then got into the carriage with her daughter, Marie, and drove to church. They went alone, for Claude never attended, and Austin, the youngest son, was sporadic in his churchgoing.

They arrived late but entered and took their places — the same pew that the child Marianne had sat on when she had attended with her parents. The church was cold despite the two woodstoves that burned, for most of the heat ascended to the top of the high-pitched ceiling. Looking upward, Marianne thought as she always did, *I wish I could sit up there. At least my feet would stay warm!*

She listened critically to the minister, Rev. Dan Parks, and as they left the church, she took his hand, saying, "Your theology was sound today, Brother Parks."

Dan Parks was a sturdy young man who had made his share of mistakes since coming to pastor the church, but he had a quiet wit. And it gleamed in his eyes as he nodded, saying, "I've got just enough theology to be dangerous, Mrs. Bristol. But I always feel safe with you sitting out there in the congregation."

"Safe?"

"Yes. I have the absolute certainty that if I fall into error in one of my sermons, you'll leap to your feet and demand that the service be dismissed until the pastor has time to clear his doctrine up a little!"

Marianne liked Rev. Parks very much. She and her sister-in-law, Susanna, the wife of her brother Thomas, had been responsible for keeping Parks in the church when his impolitic pronouncements moved the leaders to decide to run him off. Now she said, "The Bible says, 'Let your women keep silence in the churches,' Brother Parks." Her dark blue eyes gleamed with humor as she asked, "Do you think I would go against the scripture?"

Parks shook his head. "I never try to think about what a woman will do, because I'm always wrong. But I do think you'd find a scripture to back you up if you had to."

"It *was* a good message," Marianne said warmly. "You are one of the few ministers I know who hears from God. Too many get their sermons from other men. It's good to know that my pastor has an audience with the Almighty!"

Later, as Marianne and her daughter rode home, Marie spoke of her cousin Clay Rocklin with some hesitation.

"And they say cousin Clay is in love with Melora Yancy. That's not right, is it, Mama?"

Marianne defended her nephew instantly. "I brought you up better than to listen to gossip, Marie. Clay has had a hard life, and he did great wrong to his family. But if ever a man tried to make up for his mistakes, it was Clay Rocklin. As for Melora, well, she is a fine girl. All the talk about the two of them comes from a bunch of gossips who've got tongues long enough that they could sit in the parlor and lick the skillet in the kitchen! If there is anything I cannot abide, it is people who try to make their own pitiful lives seem better by gossiping about others. The good Lord gave us enough to concentrate on in our own lives, so for heaven's sake, let's leave other people's lives alone!"

Marie was surprised at her mother's sudden outburst. "Why, *I* don't believe there's anything wrong between Clay and Melora, Mama!" She sat there quietly, thinking suddenly of her parents. She was a bright girl and for years had known that they were not happy. It had broken her heart when she had first discovered that her father was a weak man who was unfaithful and prone to the sins of the flesh. If anyone had a right to complain or gossip, it was Marianne Bristol, but Marie had never heard her mother speak a word of criticism about her father. She shook her head slightly, wishing that things could have been better for her mother. Then she asked, "What do you think about Paul, Mama? When will he and his assistant start for the front?"

"Didn't you know? They're leaving tomorrow."

Marie looked surprised. "Paul didn't tell me he was going."

"He's been working very hard. I suppose he just forgot to mention it."

"Is he going to the Valley where Jackson is fighting?"

"No, that's too far. He said this first trip would be sort of a trial run. He has to try out his camera and What-Is-It wagon under actual conditions."

They were within sight of the Big House now, and Marie suddenly said, "Look, there's Paul now, Mama. Let's go see what he's doing."

"No, he's busy. You can see him when he comes in to eat dinner."

"Mama . . . ," Marie asked tentatively, "don't you think there's something . . .

funny about that girl he hired?"

Marianne looked at her daughter at once. "What's funny about her?"

"Oh, Mama!" Marie said, tossing her head. "Everyone is talking about it." She saw her mother winding up to deliver another sermon on gossiping and held up her hand quickly. "Now don't start preaching at me again! And you might as well get used to people talking about Paul and Frankie, because they're going to do it!"

Marianne didn't speak until she pulled up in front of the tall white house. Then she said, "I suppose so. She *is* a strange young woman, Marie, but Paul said he didn't have any choice. Come on, now," she said abruptly, "we're going to be late with dinner."

Blossom, the cook and second-in-command to Marianne Bristol, already had the meal cooked, however, so all that the mistress of Hartsworth had to do was summon the pair working outside. Claude Bristol and Austin were in the library arguing about horses when Marianne called them to the dining room. When the four of them sat down, Claude asked, "What about Paul and his young woman? Aren't they going to eat?"

Even as he spoke, they heard the front

door close, and Austin called, "Better hurry up, you two. You know how mad Blossom gets when people are late for her meals."

Paul sat down across from Austin, and Frankie took the seat next to him, opposite Marie. He smiled at his mother, saying, "Not a long grace, Mother. Frankie and I have a long way to go."

They all bowed their heads, and right on the heels of the "Amen" from Marianne, Claude asked, "You're not starting at this time of day? It'll be dark in a few hours."

"We're only going to the camps outside Richmond, Father," Paul replied. "From what I've heard, they've really started to throw up some stout works."

"The soldiers don't like it — all the digging," Austin said. He stuffed a biscuit into his mouth.

Paul slathered a flaky biscuit with yellow butter, tasted it, then called out, "Blossom, these biscuits are *good*!" He waited until Blossom's voice came faintly: "Yassuh, Mistuh Paul!" Then he responded to Austin's comment. "When the Yankees get here, those fortifications will come in handy."

"Oh, nonsense!" Austin retorted. "The Yankees will never get to Richmond!" He began to explain in a dogmatic fashion how impossible it was for a Yankee army to whip the Confederate Army, informing everyone that any Southern soldier could whip six Yankees. Austin was a husky man of thirty and was very strong. And he was, much like his older brother, the despair of the mothers with marriageable daughters in the vicinity. He had been engaged twice but somehow had never made it to the altar. He was faithful in doing his work at Hartsworth but was more interested in hunting and social life in Richmond than anything else.

Finally Marianne asked, "Didn't my nephew say that you were some sort of sutler at one time, Miss Aimes?"

"Yes, Mrs. Bristol. I worked for a man named Sol Levy." Frankie spoke carefully, hoping no one noticed how tense she was. Knowing there were weak spots in her story, she explained vaguely, "After he died, I didn't have anything to do, but I'd always been interested in photography. I was quite fortunate that Mr. Brady took me on. Then when I heard from Major Rocklin what Mr. Paul was doing, I asked him to help me get a job here."

"But don't you feel a little out of place?" Claude asked, not unkindly. "I mean, *I'd* feel that way if I were in the North."

"I — don't really feel strongly about the war," Frankie said, uncomfortably aware that they all were watching her. "I don't care for slavery myself, but I think the South has a right to run its own business." It was the answer that she and Tyler had decided was best, and she breathed a sigh of relief when she saw by the reactions around the table that it was a success.

"Why, that's the way many Southerners feel. General Lee, for one," Marie said with a nod.

"What did you think of the Yankee Army, Miss Aimes?" Marianne asked. "Everybody in the South seems to think since we whipped them at Bull Run, it'll be easy to do it again."

Frankie shook her head. "I don't know much about that, Mrs. Bristol. I just worked for Mr. Levy. We sold tobacco and supplies to the soldiers and passed out tracts and Bibles. But there's a lot of them. Soldiers, I mean. After Bull Run, they were pretty well whipped and discouraged, but I guess General McClellan has pulled them together."

"They won't give up," Paul said with certainty. "This is not going to be a short war."

After the meal was over, Paul looked at his family. "Well, we'll be leaving for Richmond. I think we'll be back pretty soon.

We'll take lots of wet plates, then bring them all back and try to figure out what we did wrong."

After the good-byes were said and Frankie and Paul had taken their leave, the other members of the family sat at the table discussing the pair. Marianne listened more than she spoke, but as she saw the black, hearselike wagon roll out from the barn and head down the road to Richmond, she thought, *What a strange pair! But Paul's always been on the outside of what most consider normal, somehow. He never quite fit in anywhere. And now he's hooked up with this girl, who doesn't fit either.*

"I hope they don't get too close to the bullets and shells," Claude murmured.

But his wife said, "There are some things more dangerous than minié balls and cannons, I think."

"Wish we had Blossom here to do the cooking," Paul said regretfully. He dumped the armload of dead branches he'd gathered from the woods on the ground and then began feeding them into the fire. "I hope you can cook better than I can, Frankie," he said with a shrug. "Otherwise we're in big trouble."

Frankie had pulled the cooking gear out

of the compartment reserved for groceries and utensils and was cutting strips of beef from a large chunk of meat. She looked up and smiled, saying, "I like to cook, Mr. Bristol. Especially over a campfire."

Bristol sat down and watched her, noting how efficiently she worked. He had been so involved with the details of photography that he had thought little of such mundane things as food, but as the smell of hot coffee and cooking meat came to him, he said, "I'm glad you got the food. I'm hungry as a bear. Can I help?"

"Not with the cooking. That's my job."

Bristol grinned. "I won't argue with that." He leaned back against a tree, soaking up the warmth of the fire. It had been an easy day — easier than many would be, he knew, for he was soft and out of shape. The little fire made a beacon under the heavy timber, and he was pleased with the feeling of security. Soon he drifted off to sleep, coming awake with a start when Frankie said, "Come and get it!"

"What!" Bristol jerked up and pushed his hat back, confused for a moment, then relaxed against the tree. He reached out to take the plate Frankie handed him, sniffing appreciatively. It was piled high with fried potatoes, roast beef with gravy, and biscuits.

He ate hungrily, asking only, "How'd you make the gravy?"

"Oh, I brought it from the house in a jar. The biscuits are Blossom's, but I'll make some fresh ones tomorrow. I brought my sourdough starter."

"You're sure a fine cook, Frankie!"

She put her plate down and filled a mug with coffee, handed it to Bristol, then poured one for herself. "Wait until you taste my black bug soup," she said, nodding.

"Your *what* kind of soup?"

"Black bug," Frankie said, a glint of humor in her eyes. "I cut up the cooked beef, add vegetables and spices, then put it over the fire to simmer."

"What about the black bugs?" Bristol demanded.

"Oh, every once in a while a big black bug dives into it. Makes kind of a sizzle. But they make the stew tasty."

"You keep a lid on the pot, you hear me?" Paul ordered. "I'm not eating any bugs!"

"Why, I heard that people in France eat snails. Did you eat any while you were over there?"

"Well, yes, but —"

Frankie said emphatically, "I'd rather eat a bug than one of those slimy old snails anytime!"

Bristol grinned at her across the fire. "I guess it all depends on how you're brought up." He finished his meal and sat back, taking a sip of the coffee. He grimaced slightly, for real coffee was no longer available, thanks to the blockades. The "coffee" Paul drank was actually a brew made from roasted and ground acorns. Still, it was hot and black.

An owl was hooting deep in the woods, and he listened carefully. "Always thought that was a sad sound, the hoot of an owl."

Frankie nodded but said nothing. The silence ran on, and Bristol watched her, noting that she seemed totally aware of her surroundings. The flames made a flickering yellow play on her smooth face, throwing her features into stark relief. Her eyes were dark and shadowed, but her cheekbones seemed high and sculpted, as though cut out of some sort of smooth stone. She had a calmness about her that most women lacked . . . and Paul suddenly realized he was puzzled by her — had been from the first. Now he wondered how the experiment would turn out. For that was what this trip was, though he had not told her so. It was a test to see how she would do. If it went badly, he would just let her go. And he had been

266

convinced that was exactly what would happen.

Now, however, as she sat quietly, listening
to the sibilant whisper of the wind and letting her eyes go from point to point seeking
some movement in the darkness of the
woods, he was not so sure. She was certainly
efficient, not only in photography, but in
the business of driving the wagon and setting up camp. Besides, it would be a relief
to have a good cook, for he hated the job.

Still, he was uncertain. There were too
many factors involved that could not be
planned, and the possibility of subjecting a
woman to some of them made him frown in
displeasure. He stirred, pulled his coat col-
lar up, and said, "Cold tonight. I hope it
warms up tomorrow." It was not what he
had planned to say, and he was irritated
with himself. *If it was a man here with me,*
he thought with some frustration, *I wouldn't
have to manufacture conversation.*

He asked in an offhand tone, "Do you like
the South?"

Frankie had her mug half lifted to her lips.
She paused and looked across the fire. "Oh,
it's all right. I guess the summers will be
hotter than I'm used to."

"I mean the people, not the weather."

"I like your family." A glow came to

Frankie's cheeks, and she added, "You're lucky, having a family like that!"

Paul moved uneasily. He let the silence run on, then shrugged. "Well, they're not so lucky to have me."

"Don't say that!"

He looked up sharply, surprised at the force in her words. "Why not?" he demanded. "It's true enough. I haven't brought them any happiness."

"That's not true. Your mother loves you very much, and so do the others."

"My mother would love Judas Iscariot," Bristol replied with a shrug. "But yes, they do love me. Even so, I think it's the kind of love families have for an outcast child . . . more pity than real love." He saw the slight negative motion she made with her head and asked, "You don't believe that?"

"No, I think love doesn't have anything to do with what a person *does*. It's what he *is* that matters."

"That's an interesting theory, but it doesn't really hold true. Just look around you, Frankie. You see people all the time practically screaming about how they love each other, but most of the time it doesn't last. A man loses his teeth and his hair, and suddenly the woman wonders what has happened to the fine-looking chap she fell in love with."

Frankie was not ready for such a debate, but something in her denied what Bristol was saying. She'd had almost no experience with the kind of love she'd referred to, neither had she read a great deal about such things. . . . Still, she was filled with some sort of strange certainty that real love had to be more than Bristol made out.

"In the hospital in Washington, Mr. Levy and I used to go take gifts to the soldiers who'd been wounded. Some of them were in terrible shape . . . just awful!" The memory brought a sudden tension into the girl's smooth lips. She halted as the owl called again, then continued speaking. "One of the patients was a young sergeant . . . only eighteen years old. He'd lost both hands and one eye, and his face was terribly scarred. He . . . showed me his wedding picture. It had been taken only a month before he left for the army."

Frankie picked up a stick and began poking at the glowing coals, her eyes half closed as she sat looking in the fire. "He was so afraid! He told me lots of times he wished he'd been killed instead of all cut up. He loved his wife so much, and he was afraid she'd turn from him. He'd been such a handsome fellow! I — I was afraid, too," she whispered. "But she came into the hospital one afternoon. I was there and I saw it!" Frankie's eyes glistened, and she smiled tremulously. "She was such a pretty girl . . . and she went right up to him and kissed his cheek, then kissed his stumps —"

Her voice cracked with emotion, and she paused for a moment, then looked at Paul, meeting his eyes with confidence as she continued: "When he started to say how he wasn't the same man she'd married, she smiled at him and kissed him again. And she said, 'I didn't marry your hands, Bobby; I married *you*!' "

Bristol had listened to her carefully, and now he said quietly, "That's a wonderful story, Frankie."

She saw the doubt in his eyes. "But you don't think most people are like that, do you, Mr. Bristol?"

Paul met her eyes and was forced to tell the truth. "I'm glad you believe people are good, Frankie. I hope you always do, but I'm too old and have seen too much, I guess, to think like that."

Frankie wanted to argue with him but saw that it was no use. They sat watching the fire in silence for a while, until Bristol turned the talk to technical matters. Finally he got to his feet, saying, "I guess we can go to bed. We'll have a long day tomorrow." He hesitated, then said, "Sure you want the tent? Be more snug in the wagon." The matter of sleeping arrangements had troubled him, but Frankie had been quite practical: "If you'll get me a little tent," she'd said, "I'll make out fine. And we can fix you a nice bed in the wagon. It's the way Mr. Levy and I did it."

"No, I like sleeping in a tent. I'll clean the dishes, then turn in."

Bristol nodded, then climbed into the wagon. He pulled off his boots, then shucked off his shirt and breeches. The air was sharp, but he burrowed under the warm blankets and dropped off to sleep at once.

After cleaning the dishes and mugs, then scrubbing the frying pan, Frankie sat in front of the dying fire. She thought of her family and wished she could see them. Even her father. How long would it be before she saw them again? Then her thoughts turned to Tyler and to the kiss he'd given her. A disturbed wrinkle creased her brow. She liked Tyler very much, but something in his kiss had made her uneasy, and she could not get it out of her mind.

The future was as uncertain as the wind, and though she did not fear the dangers of battle, an uneasiness began to fill her. She had come on this mission first because she'd had no choice, but even when an opportunity to avoid it came, somehow she had persisted.

What am I doing here? she wondered, not for the first time. She looked up and saw the stars glinting far overhead like a handful of diamonds scattered by a mighty hand. She thought of Sol Levy and wished she could have his warm voice to encourage her — but that voice was stilled forever, and the thought saddened her.

Finally she banked the fire and went into the tent. She removed her boots, took off her clothing, and slipped into a heavy nightshirt, one that had belonged to Sol. Then she wrapped herself in the heavy wool blankets and drifted off to sleep.

The last sound she heard was the owl hooting, calling mournfully from somewhere deep in the dark woods.

CHAPTER 14
BLOSSOM'S WARNING

"This place looks like it's been hit by an earthquake!"

Frankie took a moment to adjust the legs of the tripod holding the bulky camera before answering. It was high noon, and they had waited for maximum light conditions so they could record a series of trenches faced by odd-looking devices made of large saplings. The saplings were sharpened on the tips and bound together at the center with all the points radiating outward. Carefully Frankie opened the lens, counted off twenty seconds, then closed the lens. Only then did she answer.

"It's not very pretty, is it?"

Paul shook his head, studying the miles of ditches with raw dirt piled high and wooden palisades pointing outward away from the city. He felt depressed. "Looks pretty grubby, and it's going to get worse."

Frankie removed the plates from the

camera and moved to the What-Is-It wagon. Mounting the low step they had built on the rear, she lifted the black curtain and disappeared inside. Paul watched the cloth stir as she went through the process of developing and fixing the plates. When she emerged, he went on. Scowling at the trenches, he said, "I don't think pictures of holes in the ground are what President Davis had in mind to inspire the Confederacy. He wants a cavalry charge with sabers flashing in the sun and guidons snapping in the breeze."

"Well, he won't get *that*!" Frankie wiped her hands carefully on a towel and came to stand beside the camera again. "To get a really good picture, we have to have the subject remain absolutely still for as long as twenty seconds. Be hard to get a charging regiment of the Black Horse Cavalry led by Jeb Stuart to be still that long, wouldn't it?"

Paul grinned suddenly, struck by her droll observation. He had discovered that despite her rather reserved manner, she had a pixieish wit. He had even suspected her of laughing at him at times behind her solemn greenish eyes, though he could not prove it. "No, I suppose not," he said, still grinning. "But we're going to have to get *somebody* to stand still. Got to have more than piles of dirt and sharpened sticks to show."

A cloud passed over Frankie's face as a thought came to her. "We'll have subjects who'll be still enough," she said evenly.

At first Bristol didn't understand her, and then it came to him. "The dead? Well, it'll have to be Federal dead. I can't imagine the president approving pictures of dead Confederate soldiers." He gave a characteristic shrug, then said, "Let's pack up and head for home. I'm tired, and I know you are, too."

"Don't go home on my account, Mr. Bristol," Frankie said quickly. "I feel fine."

Bristol gave her a sour look. "Wait until you're old like I am; then you'll see how it is."

"You're not old!" Frankie spoke without thought and at once was embarrassed. To cover her confusion, she said, "I'd like to stay in Richmond for a couple of days. Would that be all right?"

"I guess so. Someone from Hartsworth comes into town pretty often. They can bring you back."

They loaded the wagon, and as they passed through town, Paul stopped in front of the Spotswood Hotel. "Payday," he announced, taking some cash out of his pocket. Handing it to her, he said, "This is a pretty rough place, you know. Lots of soldiers come here. You sure you'll be all right?"

Frankie smiled as she took the money and stuck it in her pocket. "I'll be fine. And I'll hitch a ride back to Hartsworth with someone." A shy smile touched her lips. "It's been a good time, Mr. Bristol."

Paul slapped her on the shoulder as he would have done with a youthful male companion, smiled, and said, "You've been a great help. Couldn't have done it without you." He noted that she drew away from his touch, and this made him frown slightly. But he just said, "See you at home, Frankie. Have a good time."

She watched him drive away, then turned at once and went to the café across the street. After a quick meal of greasy pork and boiled potatoes, she left the café, asking the owner about a livery stable. Following his directions, she walked down the street for three blocks, turned right, and saw a sign that said SIMMONS LIVERY STABLE. A short, bulky man came at once to her, saying, "I'm Harvey Simmons. C'n I help you?"

"I want to rent a horse for two days."

"Well, I ain't got a gentle horse, miss," Simmons said, shaking his head. He had a pair of quick, dark eyes and was taking her

276

in carefully. *A born gossip,* Frankie thought. *He'll remember me, so I'd better be careful.*

"Oh, I can ride a spirited horse."

"Can you, now? Well, in that case I can accommodate you." He scratched his cheek, which sported a three-day growth of iron-gray stubble. "Don't mean to be nosy, but is they anybody in town who can vouch for you? Can't let a stranger ride out with a valuable animal. No offense, miss."

"None taken. I'm Frankie Aimes, Mr. Paul Bristol's assistant."

The words changed the man at once. "Sho' now, miss, that's good enough. Come along and I'll put a saddle on for you." As Simmons saddled the horse — a roan mare with long legs and a nervous disposition — he talked constantly, trying to find out as much about his customer as he possibly could.

Frankie said only enough to satisfy a fraction of Simmons's avid curiosity. Then when the mare was ready, she stepped into the saddle and rode out, keeping a tight rein on the prancing horse.

"So . . . that's the female ever'body's been buzzin' about!" Simmons said aloud. "Blast my eyes, but she's a daisy! Wearin' pants and riding astride like a man!" His beady little eyes grew sharp, and he nodded with a knowing expression. "Runnin' around all over the country alone with a man! Well, she ain't no better'n she should be, I'd say!" He was the type of man who always told what he knew, and when he knew nothing, he invented his own facts. He left the station, spotted two men leaning against the wall of a dry goods store, and called out, "Hey, Ed! You and Jim, let's go have one. I gotta tell you 'bout my new customer. . . ."

Frankie was aware that Simmons would give good coverage of her visit, but there was nothing she could do about it. Rather than worry, she concentrated on enjoying the mare. Once it was settled between them who was going to decide on the pace and the route, they got along very well.

It was a sparkling day, with winter pushed back by the warm winds of spring. The sky was a blue parchment, with puffs of cotton clouds, and the birds were back, their tiny chorus of song filling the air.

As she rode, Frankie realized that she was tired, more so than she'd wanted to admit to Bristol. But the fresh, crisp air drove the lethargy away as she rode at a steady trot that ate up the miles. Two hours later she arrived in Lake City, the small town she and Tyler had settled on as a rendezvous point. It was composed of one street, which ran parallel to the bank of a fine little lake that shimmered in the late afternoon sunlight. A few people were strolling along the walks in front of the shops and stores, but nobody paid more than casual attention to Frankie.

She was afraid that Tyler might be out scouting, then spotted the familiar wagon in front of what seemed to be a combination hotel and café. She noticed a sign on the side of the wagon that read MILLER'S ROLLING MERCANTILE. BARGAINS IN SOFT AND HARD GOODS! JAMES MILLER, OWNER. She dismounted stiffly, tied the mare firmly to the hitching post, then stepped up on the walk and glanced at the sign over the door: ELITE HOTEL. Stepping inside, she saw a desk, behind which were room keys hung on hooks mounted on the wall. To her left a door opened into the restaurant, and, moving inside, she caught the attention of a thin man wearing a white apron. He came toward her, eyeing her clothing suspiciously before saying, "What can I do for you?"

"I need a room and something to eat," Frankie said.

The man seemed undecided, and Frankie had no idea of how to ask any differently. She was pretty sure he was trying to figure out exactly what sort of girl she was — and having little success. *People want to put folks in boxes,* she thought. *They figure if I'm a good woman, I wouldn't be wearing pants. That's what he's worrying about.*

Then the man shrugged. "Be three dollars for the room," he said. "Supper's in an hour."

He walked to the desk, turned a book around, and read her writing as she signed it. He plucked a key off the hook, saying, "Number 112, right up those stairs."

Frankie picked up her small bag and, as she mounted the stairs, felt his eyes follow her. It gave her a queer feeling. She was accustomed to men staring at her — and women, too, for that matter — but this was different. She had a quick vision of herself in a courtroom of officers, with the man saying as he testified, *"Why, yes, I know her. Name's Frankie Aimes. Stayed in my place one night. I thought she looked suspicious, but didn't have no idea she was a spy."*

Frankie walked down the hall, opened the door to her room, then stepped in and threw her bag on the bed. Locking the door decisively, she took off her clothes and washed as well as she could using the basin on the washstand. Then she dressed in clean trousers and a white cotton shirt and combed her hair out. As she worked on it, she sat at the window and watched the street below. There was no sign of Tyler, so she decided that he was in his room in this very hotel.

She put the brush away, then lay down on the bed to rest before supper. But she misjudged her fatigue and awoke with a start in a dark room. Quickly she came off the bed, lit a lamp, and pulled the small pocket watch out. "Seven thirty!" she exclaimed and hurried out, locking the room carefully as she left. Descending the stairs, she had to step aside to let two rough-looking men pass. They gave her bold looks, and one said, "Why, hello, sweetheart!" She paid them no heed, ignoring the crude remarks and laughter that followed her as she came to the first floor and entered the café.

She saw Tyler at once, sitting at a table with another man, but never looked in his direction. When she took a table, a young woman came to say, "We got beef and chicken, potatoes, and apple pie."

"I'll have the chicken and potatoes." Frankie sat with her back to Tyler and his companion, but she could hear them talking. There were only four other customers in the café, and slowly the tension left her. Tyler was telling his companion how he'd been doing well in the country. "People are short of everything since the blockade," Frankie heard him say. When the man he sat with asked if he ever had any trouble bringing his merchandise through the Union lines, he laughed, saying, "Oh, I have to pay a little *tax* on my stores, but then I make it back twice over."

Frankie rose and returned to her room, knowing that Tyler had seen her. Thirty minutes later, she heard a faint tapping at her door.

"Frankie, it's good to see you!" Tyler exclaimed when she let him in. His eyes gleamed with excitement. He was wearing a plaid, rather outlandish suit, and she noticed that he was using his cane less than before. "Any trouble getting away?" he asked at once.

"No. I have to be back tomorrow, though." Frankie found that she was very glad to see him and said, "Sit down and tell me everything." She perched on the bed while Tyler sat in the single chair. He told her how simple it had been to get through on the road leading to Virginia. "I got stopped by Union and Rebel soldiers, but they weren't hard to satisfy. I made them presents of tobacco, and they waved me right on. I guess they figure a peddler doesn't have any country." He brushed his hair back from his forehead in a familiar gesture, then said, "Now you talk. How did Paul take having a girl come to ask for a job?"

Frankie recounted her meeting with Bristol, ending with, "He didn't want me, Tyler, but the letter from your father changed his mind. Does it bother you, deceiving your father about me?"

"Well . . . yes, to be honest, it does. But Dad would understand. I'd like to tell him, but we can't let anybody in on this."

"I — I feel mean about it." Frankie bit her lower lip, and when she lifted her eyes to meet his, he saw that she was troubled. "They all trust me . . . all the Bristols. And I'm nothing but a spy."

"Aw, don't think about it like that," Tyler said quickly. "We're soldiers, even though we don't wear uniforms. When I carried a rifle, I did it because I wanted to see the Union preserved. What I'm doing now is for the same reason."

Frankie was tempted to tell him how Pinkerton had forced her to agree to serve, for she was certain that Tyler knew nothing about it. But that was over now, so she said only, "I suppose you're right, but it hurts to think I'm betraying people who've been so good to me."

Tyler saw that there was nothing he could do to change her feelings, but he was not at all certain he wanted to. There was something touching about her as she sat there, a kind of grief pulling the gladness from her eyes. He chose to take her thoughts away from that aspect of their service by saying, "Well, what have you got for Pinkerton?"

"Jackson has gone to the Valley, which everyone knows," Frankie said. "But Paul and I have been taking pictures of the area around Richmond, and I think the officers need to know how hard it will be to get inside. The whole army is digging trenches. . . ."

They talked together for an hour, and finally Tyler said, "You're right, Frankie. I'll get word back to Pinkerton at once. But I don't think I need to put anything in writing."

"When will the attack come, Tyler?"

"I don't know. Father told me the president and General McClellan don't agree. Dad is on General Scott's staff — and though everyone knows Scott is out and McClellan is in, everything still goes through the old man. Dad says that the president wants to attack by land, right down the Valley. But McClellan wants to move the army by water."

"Who will decide?"

"Oh, Lincoln will have to give way to Little Mac." Tyler shrugged. "Can't have the president making military decisions like that, can you? No general worth his stuff would stand for it."

"I don't know about that," Frankie mused. "I think Mr. Lincoln would do whatever he thought he had to do to win this war."

"He's still new at his job. Let's hope Little Mac lives up to his boast to win the war quickly. If he does, the war will be over in a few weeks and we can all go home." He leaned forward to study Frankie, asking curiously, "What will you do then, Frankie . . . when the war is over?"

"Oh, I don't know. Sell books, I guess."

"Why, you can't do that the rest of your life! You'll get married someday."

His statement somehow fractured the warm intimacy of the moment. Frankie at once got to her feet, saying, "I'm played out, Tyler. Where will we meet when I have something else to pass on?"

Tyler rose, leaning on his cane. "Can't we talk a little longer?" he asked, disappointed. "It may be quite awhile before we get another chance."

Frankie wouldn't meet his eyes. "Not tonight. I'm too tired."

Tyler knew he had to leave, so they agreed on methods of contact. "Send a letter to John Smith here in Lake City, General Delivery," he said. "Mention that you've seen an old friend of mine, and name the time and place. I'll be there whenever you say. You know, like 'I saw Olan Richards at the Crescent Hotel last Thursday at noon.' I'll be there the next Thursday at twelve o'clock."

"All right."

For a moment he hesitated, then said, "Last time we parted, you got pretty mad at me." When Frankie only nodded, he continued, "You know, it seems to me that a young woman would be more likely to get mad if a young fellow *doesn't* try to get a kiss."

Frankie shook her head abruptly. "I — I don't want to think of you like that, Tyler. You're my friend. That's what I want . . . for us to be good friends and nothing more." She saw an argument coming and stepped to the door. Opening it, she looked outside and said, "Quick, now, you'd better go before someone sees you!"

Tyler gave up and stepped outside. "Be careful, Frankie," he whispered. "If you get found out, try to get away and meet me here. I'll get you back to the Union lines."

"All right — you be careful, too, Tyler."

The door closed, and Frankie leaned against it. *Why did he have to bring up that kiss?* she thought resentfully. *I just want a friend, that's all. I don't need anything else from Tyler . . . or from anyone.* For a fleeting moment, she saw the image of Paul Bristol's face . . . but pushed it away fiercely.

Still, she knew the matter with Tyler was not settled, and the thought of future confrontations disturbed her. She went to bed at once but tossed for some time before she went to sleep. The next morning she rose at dawn and was on the road back to Richmond as the sun fired the tops of the trees.

"You left your young woman in Richmond, Paul?" Luci DeSpain had come to Hartsworth for the purpose of bringing Clay Rocklin's daughter for a visit. At least, that was her stated purpose. The two women had arrived a few hours before Paul Bristol drove in, and he and Luci had come to sit in the parlor after supper.

"She's not *my* young woman, Luci," Paul said with just a trifle more force than was required.

Luci knew she was looking well. She'd chosen her dress carefully, aware that the beautiful green silk with white lace at the bodice gave her a delicate air. Her jade earrings caught the light as her head moved, and her lips were lightly rouged. "Well, I certainly hope not!" she said, smiling playfully. "But you needn't get so defensive. It was just a figure of speech."

Paul drank the last of the wine from his glass, then shrugged. "I'd guess that there have been worse figures of speech about the crazy Paul Bristol and his female helper."

Luci put her hand on his arm, urging him to look at her. "There *has* been some talk, of course. It's inevitable, you know, when a man travels all over the countryside alone with a young woman. People *do* notice."

"Do you resent Frankie?"

Luci DeSpain was far too clever to give a direct answer to such a question. If she said yes, she would be recognizing the girl as a threat. So she shook her head quickly, saying, "Of course not! But I *do* worry about you. Such talk isn't good for your reputation."

Paul grinned unexpectedly. "I haven't had any of that for quite a few years, Luci." He got to his feet, saying, "I'm so tired I can barely keep my eyes open. Photography is hard work."

"Tell me all about what you did," Luci commanded. She leaned back, making sure to sit in such a way that her figure showed to best advantage, and listened as Paul related the events of the past week. She cared little about the details of the work itself, but was highly interested in the accommodations.

"You mean you weren't able to get hotel rooms in the city?" she asked.

"Oh, I suppose we could have this time," Paul admitted. "But when it's really time to take pictures, there won't be anything around like hotels. The battles will be in the woods somewhere, and I'll want to be as close to the front as I can."

"You like comfort as well as any man I ever saw," Luci said with a nod. "Your idea of roughing it has always been staying in the Empire Suite at the Spotswood Hotel!"

"You've got that right." Paul smiled ruefully. "Never saw much fun in sleeping outside and trying to cook over a smoky fire in the drizzling rain. But at least the winter's over. All I'll have to worry about is being eaten alive by mosquitoes."

"You could have taken a cot, couldn't you?" Luci asked idly.

"No room in the wagon for that. But I had a pretty good bed fixed up inside." He understood suddenly where Luci was headed and added casually, "We carry a tent for Frankie. Just a small one, but it keeps the rain off." He was amused at how Luci refused to ask questions about Frankie, but finally said, "Frankie worked out all right. She learned her trade well from Brady. And she's a better woodsman than I am. And a *lot* better cook!"

Luci noted the admiring tone in Paul's voice and the light in his eyes as he discussed his assistant. A flash of irritation shot through her, but she quelled it when he got to his feet, then reached down and pulled her from the couch.

Paul smiled at her, breathing in the scent of lilac that surrounded her. He put his arms around her, and she swayed toward him willingly and looked up, her lips parted. When he lowered his head, she met his kiss, pressing against him. He savored the taste of her yielding lips for a long moment. He had known women — too many of them — and there was a hunger in Luci that matched his own. And that startled him at times.

Finally it was Bristol who stepped back. "You're sweet, Luci!"

She smiled. *Let his little assistant match that!* she thought, but said only, "Am I, Paul?"

"You know you are." He shook his head. "Women always know how to stir a man," he acknowledged with a smile, reaching up to touch her face gently. "Good night, my dear. I'll see you at breakfast."

Luci watched as he left the room, a slight frown on her face. Paul had said all the right things about his little assistant, and yet . . . there was something in the way he spoke of Frankie, and in the look on his face, that set off warning bells in Luci's head.

She frowned. Perhaps she should find out more about this girl. . . .

Paul slept late the next morning, soaking up the comfort of the feather bed. Finally, around eleven, he went down and found only Blossom in the kitchen. "I'm hungry!" he announced.

"If you gonna sleep all day, you kin wait another hour fo' dinner!" was the only response he got. Blossom ruled the kitchen with an iron hand, and Paul knew it. He got a biscuit from the pie safe, sat down, and nibbled appreciatively. "Miss Aimes and I missed your cooking," he said as he chewed. "Your biscuits are the best in Virginia!"

Blossom was not much over five feet tall, but she weighed enough to be six feet. She was not fat, just strong and firm. Now she laid a baleful eye on Paul and shook her head. "Nevuh you mind 'bout how good my biscuits is! You ain't gettin' no breakfus, so you might as well git!"

Bristol laughed out loud. "And people say I'm able to handle women! I never could get anything by you, could I, Blossom? Even when I was a little boy, you always saw right through me. Better than my parents."

"Dey wuz nevuh able to see whut a rascal you wuz." Blossom nodded. She was well over sixty, but only a few strands of her dark hair had gone gray, and her eyes were as sharp as when Paul was a child. "Yo' daddy spoilt you, das whut he done! Yo' mama and me, we bof tried to tell 'im you needed a stick, but dat man wouldn't listen!"

"I always came to you when I was in trouble, didn't I?"

Blossom's eyes softened. "Yas, Mistuh Paul, you did do that." A faint longing came into her eyes, and she said, "I wisht you wuz a little boy again. I can't help you now."

Paul came to put his arm around her. "Yes, you can, Blossom. I always knew I could come to you. And I still do." He squeezed her firm shoulders, then said, "Even if I've made too big a mess of my life for you to do anything about it now."

"But de Lawd kin do somethin'!" Blossom nodded vigorously. "I prayed fo' God to keep you the mornin' you come into the world, and I ain't missed a day since!" She gave Paul a direct look, adding, "And I gonna see the good Lawd answer all them prayers!"

Paul was greatly moved. This was a part of Hartsworth that he had missed. With an affectionate smile he said, "When Miss Luci and I get married, why don't you come and take care of me, Blossom?"

She gave him an enigmatic stare, then shook her head. "Go on with you. Dat young woman done come back; go see dat she comes and eats dinner."

"Miss Frankie? She's back?" He walked to the window and stared at the stable containing the lab and saw a thin spiral of smoke rising from the chimney. He turned to ask, "Blossom, what do you think of her?"

"She ain't proud, like some I could name," Blossom muttered. "Doan know whut fo' she wear men's clothes, though. Doan she nevuh put on a dress?"

"I don't think so."

Blossom stood there silently, kneading the dough. Finally she looked up and said, "Wal, men's clothes or not, dat gal is quality, Marse Paul."

Bristol knew this was the highest compliment the slave ever paid a white person. "I don't know what to make of her," he admitted frankly. "She works as hard as any man and never complains. But sometimes . . . sometimes it's almost like a scared little girl is looking at me from behind her eyes." He shook his head. "What in the world will become of her, Blossom?"

"You watch yo'self, Marse Paul," Blossom warned quietly. "You knows women, but dis heah gal, she different. Doan you be foolin' with her!"

Bristol flushed, the direct words of the old woman stirring memories he would prefer to forget. "Don't worry," he said quickly. "She's safe enough from me. I never think of her as a woman at all, just as a helper." He flushed as Blossom held her steady gaze on him. "Well . . . almost never, anyway."

Blossom studied the man, and all the affection that had built up for him since she had first held him as a baby welled up within her. She had seen him throw his life away, and it had hurt her as much as if one of her own had gone to ruin. It was one of those strange instances of love that slaves sometimes had for their masters that no abolitionist was capable of understanding. She longed to hold him, to protect him as she had done when he'd come to her as a child with his hurts, but he was past that sort of help.

Finally she did something she hadn't done for years. Wiping her hands on her apron, she came to him and took his hand, holding it tenderly between her own. Looking up into his face, she whispered, "Dis gal is jes' a baby, Marse Paul. If you cause any hurt to her, you won't nevuh be no man again!"

Paul had learned long ago of the deep wisdom this woman seemed to have within her. His eyes searched her face intently; then he said soberly, "All right, Blossom. I'll remember what you say."

He left the kitchen and made his way to the laboratory. When he found Frankie mixing chemicals, he greeted her casually, "Hello. I see you got back." She looked at him, a light coming to her eyes and a quick smile crossing her face, a smile that somehow had such a vulnerable quality that Paul knew he would never be around Frankie Aimes again without hearing Blossom's soft voice: *"If you cause any hurt to her, you won't nevuh be no man again!"*

Chapter 15
"What Is a Woman, Anyway?"

One thought, above all others, occupied the minds of those in the South. Nothing, not even the war, could stir as much excitement as this single realization: Spring was here!

Descendants of the Civil War–era Rocklins and Bristols would never be able to experience — or even grasp — the importance of this fact in the lives of their ancestors. Plantations such as Gracefield and Hartsworth were miniature empires, part and parcel of a feudal society that was no less rigid than that of the Middle Ages in Europe. At the tip of the social pyramid were the wealthy planters, such as Wade Hampton and the Lees. Below these aristocrats was a layer of professional men, such as lawyers and doctors. Next came the shopkeepers and owners of small businesses. Beneath them were the poor whites.

Yet all of this society rested on that which made up the bottom of the pyramid: black slaves — owners of nothing, not even their own bodies.

Later Americans, except for a few *isolatoes* who fled the cities and towns to disappear into the wilderness, would have no sense of the isolation of the plantation. The roads leading from town to town became quagmires during the winters, making travel at best unpleasant and difficult, at worst, virtually impossible. Cut off from the large cities and even the towns, the plantation of the antebellum South was an island surrounded, not by water, but by wilderness.

So it was with Hartsworth, which was a microcosm: a small world in itself that mirrored the larger world outside. The inhabitants of this world grew their own food, mined their own salt, grew their own cotton and wool — out of which they made their own clothing, constructed their houses from their own timber, and for the most part made their own tools.

Perhaps it was due to such isolation, especially in the dreary winters when even a trip to town was a major expedition, that spring came as a gift from heaven each year. For with spring the roads would grow firm; the biting weather would grow warm and gentle.

And the parties could begin!

Marie Bristol had cornered her father in February, when icicles still hung like daggers from the eaves of the house and the biting wind reddened the nose of anyone who stepped outside.

"Daddy, I want to start getting ready for a ball."

Bristol had stared at Marie blankly, then had laughed. "Well, of course, why not? The temperature's twenty below and a buggy goes up to the hubs in frozen mud. Why not have a ball?"

"Oh, not now!" Marie had assured him. "But I want us to have the very *first* ball in the county this year."

Her father had agreed, but not before he teased his daughter about her unmarried state at the ancient age of twenty-five. "I guess we'd better do just that if you're going to snare Bates Streeter. After all," he had said with a shrug, "got to get you off my hands somehow!"

Marie had made a face at him, for they both knew she had had several good offers already. "I'll take care of the party arrangements, Daddy," she had said. "All you have to do is pay for it!"

Bristol hadn't given it another thought — until he came into the house after a two-day visit to Richmond and found the house swarming with activity. He dodged past several of the male slaves who were moving furniture, craned his neck to see over a group of the female house servants, and finally caught sight of his wife and daughter.

"What's going on?" he demanded, coming up to stand beside them.

"Why, we're getting ready for the ball, Daddy," Marie said. "You didn't forget, did you? And I've got to have some money to get some new decorations."

Bristol shook his head. "Haven't you heard there's a war on?"

"Oh, Daddy, don't be obstinate! The ball is *for* the soldiers." Marie didn't wink at her mother, but Bristol had the feeling that she was laughing at him. However, since he was himself addicted to parties and balls, he protested only enough to save face. "Well, I suppose we'll have to go through with it, but I'm keeping a close eye on the expenses!"

Luci arrived the following day, bringing with her Rena Rocklin, the fifteen-year-old daughter of Clay and Ellen Rocklin.

"Clay begged me to bring Rena over for a visit," she explained to Paul. "Poor child needs to have *some* social life, doesn't she?" She had found Paul at the Big House and had pulled him aside to explain her mission. She was wearing a light green dress with a short yellow jacket and looked very pretty. She glanced toward Rena, who was being entertained by Marie, then added, "I thought it would be nice for her to spend some time away from Gracefield."

"Is Ellen giving her a hard time?" Paul asked, then held up his hand. "Never mind; you don't even need to answer that. Ellen gives everyone a hard time from what I hear."

"She *is* difficult," Luci said, shrugging. "But then, we mustn't be too hard on her. It must be quite an adjustment for her to have to live at Gracefield now and not have the money to be independent."

"Some of that 'independence' was ill used anyway," Paul said dryly. "But there's no profit talking about that. I always liked Clay, and Marie and Mother both say that Rena is a fine girl."

"Oh, she is," Luci agreed, then asked abruptly, "How's your little friend getting along? Miss Frankie, I mean."

"Why, well enough, I suppose."

"I've decided to help the poor thing," Luci said.

"Help her?" Paul was puzzled. "Help her how, Luci?"

"Oh, Paul!" Luci said with a shake of her

head. "I declare, you men are all blind as bats! You apparently can't see what a *mess* the poor girl is!"

"She seems to be fairly happy."

"Happy? How could she be happy when she doesn't know the first thing about being a lady?" Luci nodded, and there was a light in her eyes that Bristol couldn't quite identify. "I'm going to take the poor girl in hand and teach her how to be a woman, which she evidently hasn't ever learned. But don't worry your head about it; I'll take care of everything."

Paul was inexplicably disturbed about this idea of Luci's, but she shooed him away, saying, "Now don't you dare run off taking your old pictures before the ball. You'll be the handsomest man there, and I want to show you off."

"You make me sound like some kind of a cute puppy or a fuzzy kitten," he objected. "But don't worry; we won't go to the field. Not unless we get word a battle's started." He looked at Rena. "I want Rena to meet Frankie. Let me take her down there; then you and I can have some time together."

Five minutes later he was saying, "Frankie, you've heard about my cousin Clay Rocklin, I believe. This is his daughter, Rena. And,

Rena, this is my assistant, Miss Frankie Aimes."

Frankie smiled at once, for she had indeed heard a great deal about the girl's father. "I'm glad to meet you, Rena. Did you come for the ball?"

"Yes, Miss Aimes."

"Oh, you can't call me that!" Frankie said at once. "I'm not all that much older than you are. Just call me Frankie." The girl, she saw, was very pretty but terribly shy. "Why don't you let me make your picture, Rena?" she asked quickly. "Then you can watch me develop. We can make a nice copy for your parents, and that would be a nice present."

A shy smile broke over Rena's lips, and she said, "Oh, that would be fun!"

"Fine!" Paul said. "Make a good picture of her, Frankie. But that shouldn't be too hard, since you have such a lovely subject." He smiled, and there was a gentleness in his features as he moved to place his hand on Rena's shoulder. "We may enter it in a contest, especially if beautiful young ladies are candidates. And I'll bet we win!"

Rena flushed with pleasure, and when Paul had turned and left, she shook her head, saying, "I couldn't win a contest, but it was nice of him to say so."

Frankie cocked her head and studied the

girl. "Well now, when I was working in Mathew Brady's studio in New York, Miss Jenny Lind came in one day for a picture. She's a beautiful woman, but she doesn't have your coloring, Rena. Too bad we can't make a color photograph."

"You really saw her? Jenny Lind?"

"Sure did," she said with a grin. "And lots of other famous people. They all come to Mr. Brady. Come on and we'll take some pictures, and I'll tell you about some of them."

Two hours later, the two young women were holding a tintype, peering at it in delight. "Oh, I don't look that good!" Rena protested, fascinated by the image that looked back at her.

"The camera can lie, Rena," Frankie admitted. "We can take out some wrinkles and warts, when it's needed. But that wasn't necessary on this one." She was delighted with the portrait; it was truly fine. She'd managed to catch Rena with her lips slightly parted and her eyes open wide with wonder. The picture reflected the innocence and freshness of the girl, and more than any other picture she'd made, Frankie prized this one.

"My father will like it so much!" Rena breathed. "He's been after me to have a likeness made for a long time."

Frankie noticed that the girl didn't mention her mother, but said only, "Let's find a silver frame and make it into a birthday gift. When's your father's birthday?" When Rena informed her it was in September, she laughed, saying, "That's close enough!"

From that moment Rena was never far from Frankie's side. She was starved for the company of young people, being the "baby" at Gracefield, and Frankie was not "grown-up" in her ways. The young girl determined to stay overnight to be sure she didn't miss any of the excitement. Though several overnight guests were coming to stay for the ball, and the house would be crowded, Rena managed to get a small attic room for herself and Frankie.

Frankie enjoyed the girl. She had not been around young people since leaving her sisters, and somehow there was a vulnerable quality in Rena that gave Frankie a protective feeling. She took Rena riding across the fields and rabbit hunting in the woods. Once Frankie said to Paul, "Rena seems lonesome, Mr. Bristol. I know I'm taking up too much time with her —"

"Don't worry about that, Frankie," Paul broke in reassuringly. "Spend all the time with her you can." He hesitated, then added, "She's in a pretty bad spot. I guess you know the story of her parents?"

"A little. Rena never mentions her mother, but she talks about her father all the time. She's lost since he joined the army."

"Clay doesn't really believe in the Cause any more than I do. I think he believes in his family. And he knows that no matter how the war comes out, he's got to throw himself into the thing to keep his family unified."

They were sitting on a pair of boxes in the laboratory, and as they got up and started for the house, Bristol said, "By the way, Miss Luci said she wanted to get to know you better. I think that would be a good idea."

Frankie glanced at him quickly. Luci had made several overtures to her, but somehow she'd not been able to respond. There was something about her that Frankie just didn't trust. "She's — been very nice," she said quickly. "I guess we're so different, I feel ugly and awkward around her."

"You shouldn't feel that way," Paul insisted. "Why, you're graceful as a deer!" Frankie looked at him in surprise, and their eyes met and locked for a moment. A sudden warmth filled Paul as he looked into those green eyes — a warmth that shook him deeply. With an impatient gesture, he turned away. "Luci wants to help you, so give her a chance, all right?" he said brusquely.

"If you say so, Mr. Bristol," Frankie said tonelessly.

Paul whirled to face her, started to say something, then turned again and stalked out of the barn. Frankie watched him go, confused and hurt by his abrupt behavior — and disturbed by the look she had seen, for just a fraction of a second, in his dark eyes.

Later that afternoon, Luci came to Frankie, who was teaching Rena how to make a horsehair rope. "What are you two up to?" she asked. When Frankie confessed what they were making, Luci laughed. "My stars! What a thing to do!"

"It's fun, Luci," Rena said quickly. "They're lots more flexible than the other kind."

"I'm sure they are, dear," Luci said dryly. "But what about the ball tomorrow? I'll bet neither one of you has given a thought to what you're going to wear."

"I'm not sure Papa will let me come," Rena said.

"Nonsense! He will if you ask him properly. When I was younger than you, I could get anything I wanted out of my father!"

"How'd you do it?" Rena asked curiously.

"Oh, I'd sit on his lap and stroke his hair and tell him how handsome he was." Luci smiled placidly. "Men aren't hard to handle if you know the right things to say and do."

Rena grimaced. "I don't think that would work on my father. What I do is just ask him, and he either says yes or no."

"Well, you let me talk to him, honey," Luci said easily. "And I'll bet we can find you a dress that'll be just right." She turned to Frankie. "And what about you, Miss Frankie? What sort of dress will you be wearing?"

Frankie sensed that the girl was well aware that she had no dress but said at once, "I don't own a dress, but that doesn't matter because I'm not going to the ball."

"Oh dear, that is too bad!" Luci shook her head. "Didn't Paul ask you to go? He told me he thought you ought to attend."

Frankie looked at the woman, startled. "He said that?"

"Oh yes. I think he'd be very disappointed if you didn't come. Of course, as he said, he can't *force* you to come, even if you are his employee. . . ."

Frankie was caught off guard. "I–I'd want

to do whatever Mr. Bristol wanted."

Luci watched her with interest, noting the flush that was tinting Frankie's smooth cheeks. She forced herself to smile. "Of course, I *knew* you'd agree when the matter was presented to you in the right way. Now about a dress — let me see. . . ." She looked carefully at Frankie, then nodded. "I think I have one that will look just fine on you. About the shoes, we may have to see. My foot is so small, you see? Well, we'll worry about that after we get the dress fitted. Now I think I'd better take you and Rena to Richmond with me. I've still got a few things to pick up. We'll get one of the slaves to drive us in —"

"Oh, I can drive us," Frankie offered. "You want to go today?"

"Yes, we'd better. Come along, then, and I'll talk to Rena's father and get a buggy to go in."

When they entered the house, Luci led the way into the parlor, where they found the master and mistress of Hartsworth with Rena's parents, Clay and Ellen Rocklin, who had just arrived. When Frankie was introduced, she was shocked by the resemblance that Clay bore to his cousin Gideon. He was taller and thinner, and much better looking, but the Rocklin lines were clearly evident. Looking at Clay, Frankie could well believe he was the handsomest of all the Rocklins. He stood up to greet her and, at six feet two inches, looked lean and fit. He had olive skin, raven hair, and piercing black eyes. His features were classic: straight nose, wide mouth, deep-set eyes under black brows, and a cleft in his determined chin.

"So you are the young woman who saved young Tyler's life?" he remarked at once, smiling down on Frankie. "I received a long letter from my cousin Gideon and his wife, Melanie. Gid warned if I didn't treat you right that he would come to Virginia himself and give me a thrashing."

"Oh," Frankie exclaimed, embarrassed and pleased at the same time. "I didn't do all that much for Tyler, Mr. Rocklin!"

"That's not what the boy's mother said," Clay contradicted. "According to Melanie's version, you not only saved Tyler's life, but her life, as well."

"Odd that Melanie didn't write and tell *me* about all this," a cold, cynical voice broke in. Frankie turned to face the woman standing there, who gave her a rather condescending smile. "Since no one is going to introduce us, I'll do the honors myself, Miss Aimes. I am Ellen Rocklin."

"I'm sorry, Ellen," Clay said evenly. "I was

so pleased to meet Tyler's nurse that I forgot my manners."

"I'm sure your old *friend* told you everything." Ellen Rocklin had a strong face, one that had been attractive but now was heavily lined, showing signs of her less-than-respectable lifestyle. She had been one of those women — lush and full-bodied — whom men are drawn to. Now she had become somewhat overweight. She was wearing a dress that would have fit her well when she weighed less, but which only served now to make her look like a sausage in a tight skin. Her eyes were sharp and predatory; her lips sensuous and a little cruel, and painted with too much rouge.

Frankie had heard about Ellen Rocklin, and looking at the face of the woman, she now believed that much, if not all, of it was true. Still, she smiled and said, "I'm glad to know you both. Major Rocklin thinks so much of you. Of all the family, as a matter of fact."

"Major Rocklin will shoot my husband dead if he comes on him in battle," Ellen said and seemed to savor the thought. "*That's* how much that Yankee thinks of us!"

"Well, Ellen, I guess we don't need to talk about the war," Clay said quickly. "What about that ball? You have a dress picked out, Rena?"

Luci laughed at the expression on Rena's face. "See? I told you your father would want to show you off! Now you get some money from him, and I'll take you and Miss Aimes to town right now."

"A sergeant in the Confederate Army makes sixteen dollars a month," Clay said with a grin. "Can you get a dress for that?" But he pulled some money from his pocket, handed it to Rena, and said, "Get a pretty one, now."

"I will, Father!" Rena promised, hugging him, a look of pure joy on her face.

"Can I get you anything from Richmond, Mrs. Rocklin?" Luci asked politely.

"Me? What in the world could I possibly need? Nobody is going to pay any attention to an old woman at a ball!"

The harshness of her words silenced the group for a moment. Then Clay looked at Luci and smiled wearily. "Thank you for your offer, Luci. But you three had better get going to town before it gets much later." Luci gladly led the young women off at once.

"Come to my room, Clay," Ellen snapped. She said no more, letting Clay make the proper remarks. But as soon as he had reached the room, she turned on him, saying, "You love it, don't you? Getting letters from your precious Melanie!"

"Oh, for pity's sake, Ellen," Clay said wearily. "I've only got a few days' leave. Let's not spoil it by —"

"And maybe you think I don't know how you sneaked around and went to see your white-trash girlfriend yesterday?" Ellen's fury rolled over her face. "Make you proud of yourself, Clay Rocklin? Leaving your lawful wife to go be with that hussy?"

Clay stood there as her curses and vile flow of language rolled over him. He had learned that there was no reasoning with Ellen. Time only seemed to have sharpened her tongue, and she lashed him now with all the poison of her tormented mind.

She's not responsible, Clay kept reminding himself as she raved on and on. *She's a sick woman, in mind and spirit. She needs kindness, not anger and bitterness.*

Finally Ellen screamed, "Go on! Get out! Go to her, that whey-faced Melora! Oh God, if I had a gun, I'd kill her! And you, too, Clay!"

He left the room, aware that though he had faced bullets in battle, none of them had made his hands tremble and his knees grow weak as this scene had. He left the house, going like a sickened animal into the deep woods to seek healing. Only by prayer could he survive the virulent attacks that Ellen threw at him. He knew that if it had not been for God's grace, he would have lost the battle and fled Ellen long ago. But he had run away from his responsibilities once before, deserting his family, and had paid dearly for it. Now he knew, as he cried out to God for patience and wisdom, that he would never do it again, not even if Ellen crucified him!

"Luci is nice, isn't she, Frankie?" Rena's young voice was filled with admiration. The two girls were sharing an ancient cherry-wood bed in the attic, and they were both tired after a long day. Luci had dragged them into every store in Richmond, or so it had seemed to Frankie.

"Yes, she sure is," Frankie answered, keeping her voice level. She had been filled with doubts about the ball from the first and now was even more frightened at the thought of going. "I wish I didn't have to go to that old party!"

"Not go!" Rena was aghast. "But why not?"

After a moment's pause, Frankie began to tell Rena about her background. She knew the girl had been wondering about her, and she wanted her to understand. Finally she said, "I'm just not good at things like that — things like dancing and flirting. I'm good at hunting and shooting and farming."

Rena had indeed been puzzled by Frankie but had said nothing. Now that the older girl had brought the matter up, she felt it was all right to ask, "Frankie, aren't you ever going to get married?"

"No."

"But — what else *is* there for a woman?" Rena asked.

"Well, what is a woman, anyway?" Frankie's voice was low, but Rena caught the tone: anger and bewilderment. Old memories surged over Frankie — and old fears. "I just want to be myself, that's all! Why do I need anyone else, man or woman?"

Rena was silent, feeling very sorry for the older girl. She had not had a happy childhood and had seen firsthand the tragedy of a marriage where there was no love. For as long as Rena could remember, her mother had been careless, paying little heed to her children. And Rena had learned that her mother had been bad, too, though she never mentioned it to a soul. Then when her father had returned after abandoning them all, the girl had longed to see a real marriage between her parents, to have what other children had: a father and a mother who loved each other.

But that had not happened. At first Rena had blamed her father. She'd hated him for leaving them . . . for leaving her when she was only a baby. But in the short time since he'd returned, she had learned to love him as she did few others. And she knew her father would have made things right with her mother if he could have, if her mother would let him. Rena sighed. If anyone should lose faith in love, it was she . . . but she was still convinced, despite the failures she'd grown up with, that there *was* love in the world.

"A woman needs a husband, Frankie," she whispered. "And a man needs a wife. That's the way the Bible says it ought to be."

Frankie could not argue with Rena, but neither could she erase the images of Davey laughing at her and Alvin Buck leering at her. She forced her fears deep down and said, "I know, Rena. I'm just scared of making a fool of myself at the ball. Don't pay any attention to me. Now you're going to look *beautiful* in that dress of yours!"

The next day was a torment for Frankie. All

day long the carriages rolled up to the front door of the house and guests disembarked from them, disappearing into the house. The sounds of music began early, and it was Paul who came to find her still in the laboratory. He was dressed in a fine black suit with a ruffled white shirt and looked totally handsome, but there was a worried frown on his face as he said with agitation, "Frankie, you've got to get ready! Luci's looked everywhere for you!"

Frankie swallowed and said, "Mr. Bristol, I — I don't want to go."

"Not go? Of course you're going, Frankie!" Bristol had convinced himself that for her own good, the young woman had to be made to act like a lady. Now he smiled and tried to ease her fears. "You'll have a fine time. Come along; I'm looking forward to having a dance with you."

Frankie was paralyzed at the thought but allowed him to lead her to the house. "Now you go to the side entrance. Luci's waiting for you, to help you with your hair and dress. Go on, now!"

Frankie moved obediently and, when she got to Luci's room, was at once pounced on. "Where have you *been*?" Luci scolded her. "We only have twenty minutes. Now get those awful clothes off!"

Frankie undressed, her mind blank with terror. She put on the undergarments Luci had laid out, then stood like a statue while Luci pulled first the petticoats over her head, then the dress. "Now sit down and let me fix your hair," she ordered.

Twenty minutes later, Luci stepped back, cocked her head, and said, "All right, you look fine. Now for some makeup."

"Oh, I don't want —" But Frankie's protests were overwhelmed by Luci's firm voice.

"Of course you do!" she said with a smile that somehow didn't quite reach her eyes. "You want to look your very best for Mr. Bristol . . . and the others, don't you?"

Frankie sat there, confused, and Luci took the opportunity to attend to business — all the while noting with irritation how just the mention of pleasing Paul Bristol could sway the girl.

Finally Luci stepped back, a satisfied expression on her face. "Now I'm going to finish dressing. You'd better wait here, Frankie. Let me go down first, and when you hear the musicians playing 'Dixie,' you come right down, all right?"

Frankie frowned, but Luci didn't even give her a chance to object. "All right," she finally said to Luci's back as she left the room.

Luci examined herself in the mirror, a smile of pure satisfaction crossing her face. Her dress was a stunning pink that complemented both her coloring and her figure. "Let's see you resist this, Mr. Bristol," she said with a low chuckle and then went downstairs. At the bottom of the stairs, she was met by Paul.

"You look beautiful, Luci!" he said, his eyes bright with admiration.

"Do you really think so?" Luci said, a well-practiced note of uncertainty in her voice. "I'm glad, Paul. I want to be beautiful for you!"

Her hand on his arm, they entered the room, moving around and stopping to speak to their friends. Whenever they paused beside someone, Luci would pull one of the young women aside, careful not to catch Paul's attention as she did so and whisper in the girl's ear. The reaction was almost universal: an exclamation something like, "Not *really,* Luci!" and then a giggle of delight. With that, the girl would move on to do her own whispering.

Finally, after twenty minutes, Paul looked around the room. "Where's Frankie? I've been looking for her."

"Oh, she insisted on doing her own dressing and makeup," Luci said with a note of regret in her voice. "I'm sure she'll be down when she's ready. Now come dance with me."

Across the room Clay and Ellen were watching the dancing couples. Ellen was wearing a new dress, which was pretty but much too youthful for her. She commented on the dancers acidly, bitterness dripping from her words. Finally Clay got relief by saying, "Look, there's Rena!" He rose from his chair and went to meet his daughter.

"Look at you!" he said with pride in his fine eyes. "Not a baby anymore, but a beautiful young woman!"

Rena was wearing a lovely blue taffeta dress that was trimmed with white. Her hair was arranged in beautiful curls, with little wisps dancing around her face, and her eyes were like stars as she said, "Oh, Daddy! I feel so — so — !"

"And you look the same way," Clay laughed. "Come on! Let's see if those expensive dancing lessons I paid for were worth it."

Paul watched the two glide across the floor to a waltz tune. "They look nice, don't they?" he said to Luci, and she nodded.

"Clay's very handsome. What a shame

he's tied to that woman!"

Just then the waltz ended, and someone cried, "Let's have 'Dixie'!"

The lively strains of the song began, and as it played on, Paul heard someone giggle and say, "Oh my! Look at that!"

Curious, he turned just in time to see Frankie enter the room — and he wanted to run to her and hustle her out of sight!

"Great day!" he exclaimed before he could stop himself. "Luci . . . she looks . . . *hideous*!"

Almost choking on a giggle, Luci quickly laid a sympathetic hand on Paul's sleeve. "I tried to get her to let me help, but she insisted on doing it all herself." Luci put just the right amount of regret in her voice, but a light of triumph glowed in her eyes. Oh, this was perfect! She had planned this moment from the time she had tried to get Paul to send the girl away and he had refused. *Now let him see what a pitiful thing she is!* she thought, and she looked around to see that almost everyone in the room was staring at the girl.

Frankie had not even looked at herself in the mirror. She had followed Paul's instructions and trusted Luci, so she had no idea of the picture she presented. The dress that Luci had given her was too large for her and was a terrible shade of purple that made Frankie's clear skin look almost gray. The effect was terrible, and the makeup was worse. Luci had painted Frankie's face with layers of rouge, giving her the appearance of a woman of the streets. Her beautiful hair had been pulled back into a tight bun that made her face tight, and the huge cheap imitation gems that hung from her ears made her look like a clown.

When she first entered the room, Frankie had been paralyzed with fear. She had stopped abruptly, searching the room desperately for Paul's face . . . and then became aware that people were staring at her.

And then . . . then she heard the laughter, the giggling of the women and the guffaws of the men. Heat rushed to her face, and a shocked, sick feeling hit her and washed over her in waves.

They're — laughing at me! The thought came like a bolt of lightning, and she suddenly began to tremble. Her eyes swept the room, but she did not see the looks of compassion in the eyes of Clay Rocklin or of Rena. What she did see, with sudden focus, was the wretched look on Paul Bristol's face. She did not know, sadly, that it stemmed out of his miserable disappointment on her behalf. Instead, she interpreted it as shame *because* of her. Paul was ashamed of her!

As the laughter grew louder, Frankie suddenly uttered a cry of pain, then whirled and ran out of the room. She reached the outside door, opened it, then ran into the night. The moon was clear, throwing silver beams over the fields and trees, but the distraught girl didn't see the beauty of it all. She heard someone calling her name, but the shame that filled her like agony drove her to run faster. She reached a grove of pecan trees, standing tall like sentinels in the silvery night, and fell at the foot of one of them. Her breath was coming in short gasps, and as she pressed her face against the rough bark, hot tears ran down her cheeks.

She began to shake violently. And then the sobs came, racking her body in hard waves. Sobs that released the pain, grief, and shame that she had kept buried inside since the first moment she had realized she was not what her father wanted . . . or what Davey wanted . . . or what Paul wanted. Slowly she sank down to the ground as the tears that she had had under control since she was a little girl fell onto the earth.

A tall, rangy hound came from the house, his nose quivering. He advanced to within ten feet of the weeping girl, studied her curiously — then opined that it was not hounddog business by returning to continue his nap under the porch.

CHAPTER 16
ROAD TO SHILOH

Paul got up an hour before dawn, dressed, and went downstairs. Hearing a sound in the kitchen, he entered and found his mother standing at the cookstove pouring a cup of coffee. She turned to him, said, "Good morning," and then picked up the heavy coffeepot. "I'll fix you some breakfast."

"Don't want any. Just coffee." As he sat down, she brought the mug of coffee and sat down across from him. Taking a cautious sip, he watched with bleary eyes as his mother drank her coffee but said nothing. Still, he figured she noticed how unsteady his hands were. That, combined with his glum expression and bloodshot eyes, would be enough to tell her he had had too much to drink at the ball.

Indeed, Marianne was aware of all those things, just as she had been aware of Frankie last night when she entered the ballroom, and aware of the laughter. Now she fixed Paul with an intent stare and said, "Paul, what in the world possessed you to let Frankie come to the ball in such a terrible state?"

"Now, Mother, don't you start on me!" Paul's voice was tense, and he glared at her angrily. "It wasn't my fault. All Luci and I wanted to do was to help the ridiculous girl."

"Oh, I see," Marianne said, raising her eyebrows. *Well, I'd be willing to bet that the only help Luci gave that poor child was to dress her up in that awful rig and paint her like a clown,* she thought. Marianne was well aware that Luci did not like Paul having Frankie around. Now she was fairly certain young Miss DeSpain had chosen this way to humiliate a woman she perceived as some kind of threat.

Marianne took another sip of coffee, longing to point out the obvious to her son, but she knew better. She had learned long ago about dealing with Paul. He was, for all his outward polish, extremely sensitive — especially to criticism from her. So she sipped her coffee and let the moment go . . . for now.

Paul himself had been so disturbed by the incident at the ball that he had slept very badly. His mother's silence now only increased his desire to justify himself. He set his coffee cup down with a bang and said, "I should have been more careful! But Luci said Frankie wouldn't let her help with the dress and getting ready. Who would have thought she'd make such a mess out of it?"

"Well . . . from what I've heard of Frankie's life, she hasn't had the chance to learn the things other girls pick up, Paul. Actually, if anyone is to blame, it's me. I should have made sure I was there to help her."

Paul got up and paced the floor nervously. "I had a blazing row with Luci after it happened. I ran outside to find Frankie, to try to talk to her." He gave a frustrated snort. "Couldn't find a trace of her anywhere. It was like she up and disappeared! When I came back to the house, Luci lit into me for leaving the party. I was pretty shaken up, so I just got mad and walked out."

"A lot of people noticed that you were gone," Marianne said. "I'm sorry the party was spoiled."

"I don't care about the stupid ball, Mother," Paul said forcefully. He stopped and put his hands on a chair, leaning on it. "I'm worried what this has done to Frankie!" At his mother's surprised expression, he hurried to explain. "I mean, it's going to be hard to work with that girl now. I wouldn't be surprised if she packed up and left. Matter of fact, she may have done it already!"

"No, I checked last night. She came in after everyone else was in bed." Marianne shook her head. "She's pretty tough, Paul."

"Well — that was a brutal thing last night," he muttered. "I wanted to take a whip to the whole bunch of jackals. How they could treat her that way . . ." His voice trailed off, and he straightened up. "I'm going to work. When Frankie gets up, will you talk to her?"

"You're the one to do that, son."

He stared at her, certain there was some special meaning behind her words and trying to understand it. With a sigh, he finally said, "Yes, I suppose you're right." He walked to the door but turned and gave her a grimace. "Do you think you'll ever get me raised, Mother?"

Marianne rose and went to him, laying her hand tenderly against his cheek. "Oh yes. God gave Blossom and me a promise about you the day you were born. Your time will come, Paul. I'm sure of it."

He stood there looking down at his mother, thinking of all the years he had caused her pain and grief. "How do you do it?" he murmured. "All these years, and you never give up!"

"Love is like that, son," Marianne said quietly. "It never changes, and it never gives up. When I get upset with you and want to give up, I remember that God has never given up on me! And then I know that it will be all right."

"Frankie said something like that once. I told her I didn't believe it. But . . . when I think about how you've never thrown me off, it makes me think both of you are right." He suddenly leaned down and kissed her cheek, then left the kitchen. Stumbling through the darkness, he went at once to the laboratory, built a fire, and threw himself into his work.

When Frankie opened her eyes that morning, she prayed the night before had been a dream. But she knew in her heart it had not.

She had crept into the attic room after one o'clock, relieved to find that Rena was not there. She'd stayed in the woods for hours after running away from the party, coming in only after all the carriages had left and the lights in the house had gone out. Stripping off the hateful dress, she had thrown it with disgust to the floor, then washed her face with soap and cold water until every trace of rouge was gone. A powerful desire to run away had come over her, and she had had to struggle to force herself to put on a nightshirt and crawl into the bed.

She had been exhausted, weak from weeping, and emotionally drained. Even so, sleep had evaded her as time and again she relived that terrible moment when the whole assembly had turned to stare at her — and laughed! Burying her face in the pillow, she had willed herself to think of something else, with no success.

For what had seemed like hours, she struggled as anger rose like a burning flood in her. *It was her! Luci! She did it on purpose. I hate her!* She had been angry before, plenty of times, but never in her life had she known she possessed the depth of fury that had risen in her at that realization. Tossing in the feather bed, she'd wanted to scream out, to beat the floor with her fists. Strangely enough, though, there was no anger in her toward Paul Bristol. After all, he had been the one who insisted she attend the ball. He had been the one she'd been trying to please. . . .

No, it was all Luci's fault. Paul wanted me at

the ball. He didn't have anything to do with humiliating me! In fact, she'd felt almost certain that it had been his voice calling her name repeatedly as she lay in the pecan grove.

Tormented again and again by the memory of the event, she had thought she was going insane. Then, finally, relief had come — but in a most unexpected form. She had been lying on her back, fists clenched so tightly that they ached, tears of mortification trickling down her cheeks, when she suddenly thought of Sol Levy. She remembered asking him once how he stood the jeers and taunts that came from some who hated Jews. He had given her a gentle smile, then said, *"Frankie, that's their problem, not mine. I can't do anything about the way they feel, but I can let Jesus Christ do something about my feelings!"*

Until that moment, Frankie had not understood that statement, but as she lay there, she realized a little of what the old man had meant. She was no more able to control her feelings than a ship could control its movement when tossed by a fierce storm. If help came — if she ever would be able to rid herself of the bitter hatred that had settled in her heart for Luci DeSpain — it would not be her doing. God would have to do it! Knowing this, she had tried to pray and finally had drifted off to sleep.

Now as she awakened in the darkness, she felt the anger and shame of the night before rising in her. With a sound of disgust, she threw back her covers, rose, and dressed. Better to be up and busy than lying in a bed letting such things build up. She put on a pair of gray wool trousers and a warm shirt with blue checks, then pulled on warm wool socks and short boots. The act of putting on her own clothes gave her a good feeling, and she left the room and moved down the stairs. But as she walked down the hall toward the outer door, Marianne Bristol came out the kitchen door and spoke to her.

"I've got some biscuits made," she said. "Come on and help me eat them."

Frankie didn't want to talk to anyone but could not refuse. Soon the two were at the table, eating and drinking coffee. Marianne spoke of the new calf that had come, of the war, of spring . . . but she said nothing of the events of the past evening.

Frankie slowly relaxed and managed to eat a little. Smiling at Paul's mother, she said, "I think we'll be leaving pretty soon, Mrs. Bristol. I guess your son told you about it?"

"No, he didn't. Where will you be going?"

"Well, Mr. Bristol says that since General Grant's taken Fort Donelson, he's sure to push on south. General Albert Sidney Johnston's waiting for him, and there's going to be a big battle somewhere around in Tennessee."

"There's going to be a battle here, from what Clay says," Marianne said. "All our spies say that McClellan's on his way to attack Richmond."

"Yes, ma'am, that's what everyone says. I don't see what Mr. Bristol wants to go running to Tennessee for, but I reckon that's what he'll do."

The two women sat there talking about the war, and finally Frankie felt secure enough to speak of the party. "I–I'm sorry I made such a mess of things last night, Mrs. Bristol."

Marianne saw that the girl's fists were white as she clenched them around her coffee mug, and she longed to comfort her. "It was terrible for you, Frankie," she said. "Nothing is worse than being humiliated, is it? I'd rather be deathly sick for a month than to be terribly embarrassed. Once when I was a little younger than you, I was in a wedding. Oh, I was so proud! Mama got me a new outfit, and it was beautiful! All pink taffeta!"

"What happened?" Frankie asked when the woman stopped speaking, her eyes thoughtful as the memory came.

"Oh, it was frightful! I had on a pair of pantaloons that came down to my ankles and just peeped out from under my skirt. It was my job to walk down the staircase, carrying flowers. The bride was to come right behind me, of course. Well, I practiced walking down that staircase for *weeks*! And when I heard the music and started down in front of the bride, it was the most exciting and proudest moment of my life!" Marianne's eyes glowed as she spoke, and her lips curved in a smile.

"But I hadn't taken two steps when the string holding up those pantaloons came untied. I felt them slipping down, but it was too late! They went down around my ankles, and I went flying, head over heels! My head hit every stair, I think, and all the guests got a good view of my new underclothes!"

"How awful!"

"Oh, it was, my dear." Marianne nodded. "As I went somersaulting down those stairs, I prayed that I'd die, but no such luck. I hit the last step and sprawled out with my face up, and all I could see was Mary Jane

Jennings, the bride. She was up at the top of the stairs, and she was crying! I didn't blame her, of course. Here was the moment she'd lived for all her life, ruined!"

"Oh, Mrs. Bristol!" Frankie whispered, tears glinting in her green eyes. "What did you do?"

"Do? Well, I got up, and I was crying, of course. All I wanted to do was get away from there. I started running, blind from my tears, but I didn't get far! My father came down the stairs quick as a flash. He caught me, hugged me, and whispered in my ear, 'Daughter, you'll take harder falls than this one in the years to come. But you're the daughter of Noah Rocklin! So you're going to go back up those stairs, and you're going to come down them like a queen!' "

"Oh, how wonderful!" Frankie's eyes grew large, and she asked, "Did you do it?"

"Do it? Of course I did! I *am* the daughter of Noah Rocklin." Marianne nodded emphatically. "My father looked around at the guests and said, 'We'll have a thirty-minute intermission right now. Go get something to drink, and when you come back here, be ready to see my daughter float down those blasted stairs like an angel!' "

"What a wonderful story! How you must

have loved your father!"

"I still do," Marianne said quietly. Her eyes were misty as she added, "Christians never say good-bye, Frankie! My father and I will be seeing each other again soon, no matter what happens." She sipped her coffee, and her voice grew soft. She knew that a traumatic experience such as Frankie had gone through could leave very painful emotional scars on a young woman. And she had the feeling that this particular young woman didn't need any more scars! She prayed for wisdom, then said, "I'm sorry you had to go through that embarrassing business about the dress last night."

Frankie flushed, the color rising to her clear cheeks. She raised a hand to one burning cheek — a gesture that made her seem even younger than she was — then said, "I . . . shouldn't have gone."

Frankie was sitting on a pine deacon's bench made by one of the slaves. At her words, Marianne rose and moved around the table. Sitting down beside the young woman, she put her arm around her and looked into her eyes. "I wish my father were here," she said. "He'd say, 'Frankie, you've had a nasty fall, but I want you to get up and run at the problem. Don't let it control you! You're young and strong and have a great life ahead of you. Just don't you quit!' " Marianne saw the tears rise to the girl's clear eyes and, without planning to, put her other arm around Frankie and drew her close.

Frankie fell against Paul's mother. She had thought that she was cried out, but Marianne's kindness, and the motherly feel of her arms holding her close, was more than the girl could take. She clung to Marianne, burying her face on her breast, and let the tears flow yet again. A broad maternal smile came to the lips of the older woman, and she held the girl, rocking her back and forth as she would have done with a small child.

Finally Frankie drew back, saying, "Oh, Mrs. Bristol, I'm so sorry! I'm not usually such a crybaby."

"Tears have to be shed," Marianne said. "They turn bitter if you don't get rid of them. Nothing like a good cry to clean a woman out."

The two women sat there at the table for a long time, Frankie speaking of herself more freely than she ever had to any other person. Marianne Bristol was a good listener, and when the girl finished, she said, "You'll forget last night. Or maybe you won't . . . but soon it will be like an old scar, like this one on my hand. I cut myself when I was twelve years old. When it happened, it hurt dreadfully, but it doesn't hurt a bit now. Last night will be like that, my dear, if you let God do a little healing."

"I–I'll try, Mrs. Bristol."

"Why don't you call me Marianne? I'd like that very much."

"All right." Frankie rose and pulled a handkerchief from her pocket. She dabbed at her eyes and managed to come up with a smile. "I never really knew my mother," she said. "But if I had, I'm sure this is what it would have been like."

"I'd be so proud if you'd think of me in that way, Frankie!"

The two smiled warmly at each other; then Frankie turned and left. *If I could only be like her,* she thought as she went to the laboratory. Then a darker thought came: *If she knew I was a spy, I wonder if she'd be so kind.* She could not bear the thought of hurting Marianne, so she tried to push the thought away.

When she entered the lab, Paul looked up, and a strange light came to his eyes. He set the flask of amber liquid he'd been holding down on a table and came to her. "I'm sorry about last night," he said at once, taking her hands in his. His eyes looked tired, and his hair was rumpled. "I had a terrible fight with Luci about it. Where'd you go when you ran out? I looked everywhere for you!"

"I just wanted to be alone, Mr. Bristol," she said, acutely aware of the strength of his hands around hers. "And it's all right. I . . . was pretty hurt, but your mother . . . she helped me a lot just now."

"She's good at that," Paul said, suddenly aware that he felt as awkward as he could ever remember feeling. Frankie always seemed so sturdy and confident, yet as she stood before him now she seemed to be almost fragile. He wanted to hug her, to hold and comfort her. *Just like I would Marie,* he told himself, ignoring the small voice that called him a liar. But he knew Frankie would not stand for such action from him, so he just said, "Well, next time we'll do it better." A smile touched his lips, and he added, "Tell you what, next time I'll take on the job of getting you ready. It'll be like . . . well, like you were my daughter."

Frankie looked at him, startled and not at all pleased. "No!" she exclaimed, then when he looked at her in surprise, went on, "You're — you're too young to be my father!"

"Well, maybe an older brother," Bristol corrected, taken aback by her adamant assertion. Then, not wanting to drag the moment on, he said, "I've decided to leave for Tennessee."

"You mean right away?"

"Day after tomorrow," he said, nodding. "Grant's not going to wait long. He's got the men and the arms to fight, and that man's a fighter! I hear General Johnston's begging Davis for every man he can spare, but with McClellan coming toward Richmond, there just aren't any extra troops. I figure we'll have to hurry to get to Tennessee before the thing starts."

"All right. We'll need some more supplies, Mr. Bristol."

A frown came to Paul's face. "Look, you can't go on calling me that. It makes me sound . . . old —" He broke off for a moment at the unpleasant realization that he *was* old compared to Frankie, then pushed that thought away. "Everyone calls my father Mr. Bristol," he finished offhandedly. "Can't have you confusing them by calling me the same thing. My name is Paul."

"All right — Paul." The use of his first name gave Frankie a queer sensation, and she smiled shyly. "It sounds funny when I call you that. Like calling President Davis 'Jeff.' "

Bristol laughed, saying, "Better not try

that if you ever meet him, Frankie. He's pretty formal."

"Oh, I wouldn't do that. When I met President Lincoln, I didn't call him 'Abe.' " She saw him staring at her, astonishment on his face. "Didn't I ever tell you? He came to have Mr. Brady take his picture. I got to meet him, though. He has the hugest hands, Paul!" He noted with pleasure how easily his name came to her. "And the kindest eyes!"

"Not like what we see in the Richmond papers? A gorilla ready to kill us all?"

"Oh no! He's so . . . so very sad! He told funny stories and made everyone laugh, but his heart is breaking. I could tell."

Bristol thought about her words, then shook his head. "It's all so crazy. A man like that — and I'm supposed to hate him. And there's Clay and Dent and the Franklins — Brad, Grant, and Vince . . . most of our family's men from the South going to fight Gideon and Tyler and our own kin whose only fault is that they live in the North." A gloom came to him, and he shook it off, saying, "It's more than I can figure out. So I guess it's good that all I have to do is take pictures. Let's make a list of everything we need, Frankie. We'll have to load the wagon up to the sideboards!"

With that, they got to work, each one reflecting on what a pleasure it was to work with — to *be* with — the other . . . and then each one chastising him- or herself for having such unbusinesslike thoughts!

The sun was shining when Paul and Frankie left Virginia — a bright yellow April sun that poured its warmth over the land. They had left early, having said all their good-byes the evening before. All day they traveled west, making good time on the dry roads. They made camp very late, off the road beside a small stream. By the time Paul had unharnessed the team, set them out to graze, and put up the tent, Frankie had built a fire and was cooking supper. "Sit down, Paul," she said cheerfully. "Supper's almost ready."

Bristol lay down, propping himself up on his elbow, watching her as she took the bacon out of the pan and began frying eggs. "Made good time today," he said. "Hope the weather holds up." They chatted comfortably until she had finished cooking; then the two of them ate hungrily. Paul shoveled the eggs down, saying, "I've decided to head for the Tennessee River as soon as we're out of Virginia. I think we can get the wagon on a flat-bottomed barge. Unless the river's low, we can go through Chattanooga. The river cuts south for a bit, but we can ride it all the way back up to Shiloh in Tennessee, provided it doesn't get too dangerous."

"You mean we might run into Federal troops?"

"Sure. When Forts Donelson and Henry were taken, that gave the Yankees control of the Cumberland and the Tennessee. We'll have to get off the barge somewhere south of the Mississippi border and find the Confederate Army."

When they had finished the bacon and eggs, Frankie said, "Got a surprise for you." She rose and went to the wagon, then came back with a flat box. "Your mother said these were your favorite."

Bristol took the box, opened it, then looked up with pleasure. "Fried apple pies!" He fished one of the small pies out, took a huge bite, and mumbled, "Delicious! Did Mother make them?"

"No, I did, but she showed me how."

Paul had been lifting the pie to his mouth but paused and looked at her suspiciously. "You say *you* made these pies? I don't believe it! Nobody ever made them this good, except Blossom and Mother!"

"They're easy to make," Frankie said, pleasure filling her. She watched him for a moment, then arched an eyebrow. "Are you going to eat them all?"

"Oh! Here —," Paul said sheepishly, handing her the box. Then a devilish grin broke out on his face. "You can't have more than two or three, though," he warned. "You'll find I'm totally selfish — and even belligerent — when it comes to fried apple pie."

Never one to ignore a challenge, Frankie grinned at him impishly. "Is that so?" she asked casually, reaching out. "Well then, I guess I'd better just . . ." — she grasped the box — *"take what I can!"* She jumped up and ran for the wagon. In a flash, Paul was after her, and she screamed in laughter when he grabbed her from behind, lifting her from the ground. With a tug, he got the box away from her, then stood there, holding the box high with one hand and using his free arm to pin Frankie against his side. She struggled briefly, then gave it up, weak from laughter.

"You win, you big bully!" she said, looking up at him, and then her breath caught in her throat. Paul was staring at her as though he had never seen her before — or as though he were seeing her for the first time. Her eyes widened at the expression on his face, and for one panic-filled moment she thought he was going to kiss her.

Exactly what he had planned to do would remain a mystery, though, for it was at that precise moment that one of the pies chose to slip from the box and fall, landing squarely on Paul's head.

"Oh!" Frankie exclaimed, then could not help herself — she dissolved into laughter.

"What the — !" Paul yelled in surprise, letting her go. Then he, too, began to laugh as pie crust and filling slipped down his forehead. Still laughing, they returned to the campfire, and Paul went down to the stream to clean up. By the time he returned, Frankie had another pot of coffee brewed.

They sat there eating the pies — Paul ate four, Frankie one — and then drank coffee in thick mugs. The wind moved overhead, causing a dance in the branches of the water oaks they sat under. Now and then the rumble of a wagon from the road came to them, or the tattoo of a galloping horse — but it all seemed far away.

Paul found himself watching Frankie, admiring her skills and efficiency — and the way the firelight glowed on her face. "You like this, don't you, Frankie?" he asked, smiling. "Camping out, I mean."

"Well, I guess I've spent about as much time sleeping outside as I have inside. Yes, I like it. I miss hunting most, I guess. Did I ever tell you about my dogs?"

"No. Coon hounds?" He listened as she

spoke with affection of her dogs. He was tired, but warm and comfortable, and now and then he nibbled at a pie. When she ceased speaking, he said, "Look at the sky. . . . I never saw such stars!"

"I love it when the stars glitter like this." Frankie put her cup down on the ground and lay on her back, throwing her arms up over her head, studying the sky. The sudden movement threw her graceful figure into prominence — and the curves of her body startled Bristol. The feelings that had surged through him when he'd held her close during their pie struggle returned with a vengeance, and he thought at once of Blossom's warning. He looked away hastily and said, "Guess I'll go to bed. Long trip tomorrow, and I'm sore from sitting down so long."

"Good night, Paul," she said, still staring at the stars.

He stood up and started for the wagon, then turned to ask, "Frankie, you're all right, aren't you? I mean . . . you're not thinking about the ball anymore?"

"I'm fine." Frankie rolled over on her side, rested her cheek on her hand, and smiled at him. Her teeth were very white, and her curly hair framed her face. "Don't think about it anymore. I should never have gone. From now on, I'll hunt coons and run around with whiskery photographers."

Paul was relieved. The girl seemed to have gotten over the dreadful scene. "I'll shave in the morning," he said. "Good night, Frankie."

For the next few days they drove the horses at as fast a rate as they dared. They camped out, grateful for the fine weather conditions. As the days passed, they grew more comfortable with each other — though Paul was careful to avoid any real physical contact with Frankie — and by the time they reached the Tennessee River, they were so acquainted with each other's ways that they could sit for hours without speaking, neither one needing to make useless talk.

They managed to find passage on a flat-bottomed scow, and Paul paid the fare with gold instead of Confederate money, which pleased the captain of the small craft, a short, chunky man named Lomax. Paul watched as Lomax's men loaded the wagon and then unharnessed the team. There was a small store close by, so he walked with Frankie to buy feed for the animals. When they returned, Lomax grunted, "I'm ready if you folks are."

The scow moved slowly down the river, but they traveled at night and so made good time. Since the scow had no accommodation for passengers, Paul gave Frankie orders to sleep in the wagon while he bunked underneath in his blankets. Lomax turned out to be addicted to poker and would not rest until he got Bristol into a game. The result was that Paul won their fare back and probably would have won the barge, as well, but he refused to play any more.

Lomax was sullen for the rest of the trip. When they got to the Mississippi border, he said, "This is far as I go. The Yankees are upriver." So they unloaded their wagon and team and headed out on land.

That night they stopped at a farmhouse, and the farmer agreed to let them camp on his property. "Better not be headin' north," he warned them. "Army is there, over at Corinth, I heard. And the Yankees got more soldiers than a hound dog's got fleas, so they say." He peered at the two carefully. "Be you Yankees or Confederates?" he asked suddenly.

"Confederate," Paul said at once. "We've got to find General Johnston's army right away."

"Well, you kin sleep out in the pasture, and in the mornin' you'd better skedaddle down the road to Corinth. You won't have no trouble findin' the army, I don't reckon."

They slept until four in the morning, had a cold breakfast, and by dawn were on their way to Corinth. At three that afternoon, they were stopped by a patrol of Confederate cavalry. The lieutenant, a stripling of no more than nineteen, looked at their papers — especially the one signed by President Davis — and grinned. "Come to take pictures of the Bluebellies gettin' whipped? Come on, I'll take you to headquarters. Got enough generals there to stock a store."

He wheeled his horse, and Paul whipped the horses up to follow. "Well, this is the place, Frankie. Are you scared?"

"No. We'll be all right. Your mother's praying for us, didn't you know?"

Bristol grinned at her. "Well now, how did I forget a thing like that?" He laughed softly, shook his head, then cried out, "Git up, you lazy mules. We got some pictures to take!"

CHAPTER 17
A SMALL CASUALTY

The old adage "Too many cooks spoil the broth" found firm proof of its truth at Corinth, Mississippi, in early April of 1862. A revised version could read, "Too many commanders spoil the battle."

General Albert Sidney Johnston was the supreme commander of the Army of Mississippi in the West, but he had received too much help from General Beauregard, the hero of Bull Run. Beauregard considered himself a military genius and had carved the army into four corps, each with two or more divisions. The officers he appointed as corps commanders were distinguished men, though not necessarily in the military field. Brigadier General John C. Breckinridge, who headed a corps of 7,200, had been vice president of the United States under Buchanan . . . but he had never led troops in battle. Major General Leonidas Polk was outstanding as an Episcopal bishop, but lacked the experience to make full use of his West Point training as he commanded a 9,400-man corps. Major General William J. Hardee, whose corps had 6,700 men, was a capable officer and tactician who had served as commander of cadets at West Point.

The fourth commander was a puzzling figure. Major General Braxton Bragg, Johnston's adjutant and commander of the Second Corps, which boasted 16,200 men, was a West Pointer who had served with distinction in the Mexican War. Bragg was forceful in the extreme, highly confident — and deeply flawed. His foul temper, belligerence, and chronic inflexibility had become legend in both armies. Grant liked to tell a joke about the time Bragg did temporary duty as both company commander and quartermaster. As company commander, he demanded certain supplies; as quartermaster, he refused. He continued an angry exchange of memorandums to himself in these two roles and finally referred the matter to his post commander. That officer cried, "My God, Mr. Bragg, you have quarreled with every officer in the army, and now you are quarreling with yourself!"

On the evening of April 2, word arrived in Corinth from General Beauregard that the Confederate Army must strike their foes.

"Now is the moment to advance and strike the enemy at Pittsburg Landing."

The whole thing was a matter of numbers, as General Albert Sidney Johnston well knew. Grant was advancing with 30,000 men, approximately the same number as Johnston commanded. However, another Union force — the Army of the Ohio under Major General Don Carlos Buell — was marching from Nashville to join Grant with fifty thousand men. Once the two were united, the Confederates would be outnumbered two to one.

Johnston devised a simple plan of attack: The Confederate Army would move ahead in a simple order of advance in compact columns. But once again, Beauregard gave too much help. He concocted a more difficult scheme, suitable only for experienced units, in which three corps would attack in three successive lines, each spread across a three-mile front.

The weakness of Beauregard's plan was made apparent even as the troops tried to march to Pittsburg Landing, where Grant was camped. Merely managing the heavy traffic on the two roads to Pittsburg Landing required an intricate march pattern for infantry, cavalry, artillery, and supply wagons. The roads converged seven miles from the landing at a crossroads known as Mickey's, so called after a house that stood there. The army was to rendezvous at Mickey's, then move up and form battle lines.

Hardee was late, so there could be no attack on the fourth. Late on that night a cold rain began to fall. It came down in torrents all night. The roads turned to mud, guns and wagons sank to their hubs, units became separated, commands intermixed.

Noon passed on the fifth, and still the army was tangled in a hopeless morass. Johnston looked at his watch and exclaimed, "This is perfectly puerile! This is not war!" Finally the way was cleared, the tangle somewhat resolved, and the attack was postponed another day — to Sunday, April 6.

Now forty thousand Confederates were poised within two miles of the Federal camps. To have any chance at all of taking the enemy by surprise, the troops would have to hold strict silence. But the raw young soldiers popped away at deer in the woods and whooped and fired their muskets to see if their powder was dry. Bugles sounded, drums rolled, and men yelled. Officers frantically went about trying to hush the men, but to no avail.

Beauregard was noted for his mercurial

mood changes. That night in a meeting of the staff officers, he cried in desperation, "Now they will be entrenched to the eyes! We must call off the attack and return to Corinth!"

General Albert Sidney Johnston listened calmly to the nervous Beauregard, then said, "Gentlemen, we shall attack at daylight tomorrow. I would fight them if they were a million."

Meanwhile, the Federal Army had plentiful evidence of the enemy but had chosen to discount it. General Grant, the conqueror of Donelson and Henry, seemed to have fallen into some sort of depression. He remained in Tennessee at Crump's Landing, and his enemies would later say he went to Savannah every evening to get drunk. On Saturday, the day before the battle began, he telegraphed a message to his commanding officer, stating: "I have scarcely the faintest idea of an attack being made upon us, but will be prepared should such a thing take place." Later that afternoon, he said to a group of his officers, "There will be no fight here at Pittsburg Landing. We will have to go to Corinth where the Rebels are fortified."

General Sherman, left in charge at Pittsburg Landing by Grant, was no more discerning than his commander. When told that the Confederates were massing less than two miles away, he scoffed, "Oh, tut, tut! You militia officers get scared too easily!"

On the night of April 5, the stage was set for a massive Southern victory. The Confederates were poised to throw a tremendous attack against Union troops that had not even bothered to dig entrenchments or put out pickets. If the Confederates carried the day — as it seemed they surely would — the entire face of the war would be changed.

"Take one fer my gal back in Alabama!"

"Hey, missy, how about gettin' a picture of *me*? These ugly warthogs will shore break yore camera!"

Bristol and Frankie had no lack of subjects for their pictures on the afternoon of the fifth. The raw troops, most of them dressed in homespun and carrying whatever weapons they had brought from their homes, crowded around, curious as a band of raccoons. Most of them were amazed to find a young woman working with the photographer and were not shy about offering to show her the camp. They were respectful enough, though, and wanted only to be included in the pictures that Paul and

Frankie were taking.

The two photographers had arrived in Corinth late the night before and had caught up with the army that morning. Both of them were shocked and a little dazed at the confusion they encountered. There seemed to be no order, and despite the still-soggy ground, there was an almost festive air about the entire affair. Some soldiers were singing songs; others cooked over small fires as they laughed and told jokes.

"They act like they're going to a church social," Paul said to Frankie as they set up their camera at the edge of the encampment. "The battle must have been called off. Nobody as lighthearted as these fellows could be facing death tomorrow!"

Frankie shook her head. "I talked with one of the sergeants, Paul. He told me the battle will start at dawn for sure." She gazed around at the men who were seemingly as happy as larks. "I've seen men come back from battle — but they weren't like this. I don't understand it."

"This is the chance of a lifetime, Frankie!" Paul's dark eyes glowed with excitement. "We'll get as many shots as we can of these young fellows now . . . catch the happy-go-lucky atmosphere in camp. Smiling faces, happy grins — men playing ball like that bunch over there. It's never been done before."

Frankie looked around and saw at once what Paul meant. The two went to work, taking picture after picture of the youthful soldiers. Then they turned their camera on soldiers who weren't so youthful, and both noticed that these older men were more serious. Frankie asked one of the men, a grizzled veteran of Bull Run, about the lighthearted spirits of the men. "Well, miss, it's usually like that. Most of them are scared green but dassn't admit it in front of their friends. Wait until they've seen the elephant. Then you'll see some faces that have looked at hell. This time tomorrow, you'll be hard put to find a smilin' face."

Finally the light grew too dim for taking pictures, and the weary photographers cleaned up their equipment and made their small fire. They ate a little but found they were too keyed up for much appetite. Afterward they sat close to the fire, watching the other fires that dotted the landscape like the red eyes of demons.

"I'm pretty scared, Paul," Frankie confessed.

He smiled grimly, his white teeth gleaming against his mustache. "So am I," he said. "And we won't even be running straight into the guns of those fellows over there. I'll tell you something, Frankie — I don't think I could do it."

"Yes, you could. You'd do it if you had to, just like Clay and Dent."

"Sure about that, are you?"

"Yes."

"Glad that one of us is," he said, his eyes dark and uncertain.

They spoke quietly, speaking almost in whispers as if someone might be eavesdropping. Finally Frankie laughed. "Why are we whispering? Those Yankees can't hear us two miles away!"

Paul joined in, laughing at their foolishness. Then he grew serious, his eyes intent on Frankie's face. "When the battle starts, you stay back of the lines."

"I'll stay as far back as this wagon stays!" she retorted, a stubborn set to her jaw.

"You'll do what I tell you to do!" Paul said, suddenly angry.

Frankie crossed her arms over her chest and stuck out her chin. "As long as you don't tell me to do something silly, like not do my job." Nerves on edge, Bristol got to his feet. Frankie stood at once to face him, breaking in before he could speak. "You wouldn't tell a man to stay back, would you?"

"That's not the point, Frankie — !"

"Yes, it is!" she hissed, her voice low and angry. "I hired on to do a job, and right now that job means staying with you and with this wagon! I'm as good as any man at taking pictures."

"That's not the problem, and you know it!" Bristol argued hotly. He bit back his next words and deliberately forced himself to calm down. Looking into her mutinous face, he said, "You may not like it, Frankie, but the fact is that you're a woman. You can put on breeches and chew tobacco or do anything else to make yourself think you're a man . . . but that's your problem, not mine. My problem is that you *are* a woman, and I'm not going to let you get killed!"

"You could be killed, too! It's not like the bullets will know the difference between a man or a woman. We knew it would be dangerous before we came, and now you're trying to change the rules!"

Frustrated, Paul put his hands on his hips and leaned forward until his face almost touched Frankie's. "I'm not going to argue about it," he said through gritted teeth. "You're *not* going to stay with the wagon, and that's final."

"Are you going to tie me to a tree?" Frankie challenged. "Because that's what you'll have to do, Paul!" Her eyes were enormous as they reflected the light of the flickering fire and shot as many sparks as the burning wood, making her look fierce — and incredibly attractive.

For a moment Paul was taken aback. His eyes blinked, and he stared at her in surprise. *I'll bet she has no idea how beautiful she is,* he thought irrelevantly. He took in the set expression of her full lips, the tense attitude of her trim figure — and, with a sigh, gave it up. "Frankie," he groaned, "be reasonable! How could I ever forgive myself if something happened to you?"

Frankie saw that he was weakening, and her face and voice softened. "It wouldn't be your fault. We're both doing a job. If I get killed, you're no more responsible than a general is if one of his soldiers gets killed." He shook his head in disagreement, and she stepped forward and put her hand on his arm. Looking up, she pleaded, "Paul, don't worry about me! You just take care of yourself. If . . . if you were killed, I'd be —" She broke off, as though suddenly aware that she was saying something she shouldn't. She saw that he was staring at her with an expression of surprise. She dropped her hand hastily and stepped back. "Well," she finished lamely, "I'd be grieved. After all, you've been a good boss. But we still have to do our jobs. Both of us."

Bristol was not happy, but he had no choice. *Never should have brought her in the first place,* he thought. But he said, "Well, I hope Mother is praying for us."

Frankie's face broke into a smile. "She is, Paul! I know she is." Then she turned back to the fire. "Let's have more coffee. And are there any of those fried pies left?"

"Just one. I'll split it with you."

"My, you *are* getting generous!" Frankie's smile widened. She was glad that the argument was over, and as the two sat down side by side, she poured the coffee while Paul dug the surviving apple pie out of the battered box. "Wish you were a dozen," he said, eyeing it mournfully. Carefully he broke it in two, then handed one half to Frankie. He stared at his, then shook his head. "The last one," he muttered. "When it's gone, there'll be no more."

"Oh, I'll cook you a wagonload of the things when we get back to Hartsworth!"

"Will you? Promise?"

"Promise," Frankie said with a laugh. She nibbled at her morsel of pie, watching as Paul wolfed his down. When he had finished and was licking his fingers carefully, she reached out and handed her half to him. "Here, eat mine. I don't like them as much as you do."

His eyes lit up. "Really? I told you, I have no generosity or honor about fried pies." He took her pie, ate it, and licked the crumbs from his hands. Frankie shook her head, smiling indulgently.

They sat there for a while, listening to the fire crackle, and then a man from one of the fires began singing in a fine tenor voice.

When the daylight fades on the tented field
And the campfire cheerfully burns,
Then the soldier's thought like a carrier
    dove
To his own loved home returns.
Like a carrier dove, a carrier dove,
And gleams beyond the foam,
So a light springs up in the soldier's heart
As he thinks of the girls at home.

Now the silver rays of the setting sun
Through the lofty sycamores creep,
And the fires burn low and the sentries
    watch
O'er the armed host asleep,
The sentries watch, the sentries watch,
Till morning gilds the dome —
And the rattling drums shall the sleepers
    rouse
From the dreams of the girls at home.

The voice faded, and Frankie looked at Paul, who was watching the fire with hooded eyes.

"I guess you're thinking of Luci, aren't you?" she asked flatly, then rose and walked to the tent without another word, closing the flap behind her.

Paul watched her leave, startled. He had been thinking of the battle the next day and so could only stare at the tent in confusion. *Now what in blazes was that all about?* he wondered, then went to his bunk and lay down.

In the days that followed the battle of Shiloh, Paul learned a lot about the details of the fight. One of his military friends pointed out that the battle was neatly divided into two periods, with the Confederates winning on the first day, April 6, and the Union winning on the second day. To help Paul understand what had happened, the man drew two maps showing the movements of those days.

Paul's friend used small black rectangles to show the Union corps, white ones for the Confederates. It was all very easy and simple to follow as drawn on those two maps. On the map for the first day, Paul could almost see the driving Confederates as they stormed toward the startled Union troops, and how Johnston's corps commanders drove the bewildered Federals almost into the Tennessee River. Only darkness had saved the Federal Army that day . . . that, and a spot of ground that came to be called the "Hornet's Nest," where a small force of Union troops stopped the Rebel drive dead in its tracks. Looking at the map, Paul noted the peach orchard on the flank of the Hornet's Nest, where General Albert Johnston had led a furious bayonet assault on the Union stronghold — and was killed.

Paul glanced at the map that illustrated the fighting of the second day. It was simple enough to trace the change of fortune in the battle. Grant had returned to his army just in time to shore it up, and when the Federal Army had pushed ahead, the Confederates had to retreat back to Corinth.

But those bits of paper that told so much after the fact meant nothing *during* the battle — not to the soldiers who fought, and not to Paul and Frankie. For as the battle raged back and forth, most of the untested troops knew only their own little fragment of the huge battleground. Men fought and died, and their blood incarnadined the pond near the Hornet's Nest

— a pond that came to be called the "Bloody Pond."

Paul kept as close as he could to the fighting, and some of his best pictures were of wounded men staggering away from the furnace of battle, their eyes wide with fear, their mouths open as though they could not get enough air.

All day Bristol and Frankie worked, taking picture after picture — many of which were ruined when they had to move the wagon over rough ground and some of the glass plates were smashed. At noon they pulled the wagon under some trees. A field hospital was set up a hundred yards away, and Paul's face was grim as he said, "We'll get some pictures here." He asked the surgeon's permission — which he gave with a grim nod — and for two hours he and Frankie labored. Often one or both of them would cringe when the air filled with the screams of the wounded, the sound of the surgeon's saw grating on bone, and the cries for water or for a mother or sweetheart.

Paul photographed the pile of amputated legs and arms behind the surgeon's tent, then vomited until he was weak. He was glad that Frankie was in the wagon, developing plates, for he would have hated for her to see the carnage — or to see him showing such weakness.

Finally, blessedly, night came, and the armies lay panting, exhausted and waiting for morning. Paul and Frankie were too worn out to build a fire and could not have eaten if they had.

"It'll be bad tomorrow," Bristol said quietly. They were sitting in front of the wagon, watching the flash of distant cannon and waiting for the reports. "One of the staff officers said that Buell has joined with Grant. They'll outnumber our boys two to one. We'll have to be ready to move back at the first sign of a rout."

Frankie only nodded, staring into the darkness wearily, wondering if she would ever be able to forget the things she had seen that day.

At dawn they rose, and Paul managed to get what he considered the most powerful pictures of all. He drove forward to where a Union charge had penetrated the Confederate lines and found dead men strewed over a field. They lay in eloquent positions, as though they had fallen from a high place, their arms often raised, frozen in an unwitting attitude of prayer. Some of the soldiers had fallen with their muskets in their hands, and often a dead Federal would be found in the embrace of an equally dead Confederate

— frozen in a fight that ended the world for both of them.

Paul took the shots, and by the time Frankie had developed them, they grew aware that something was wrong. Paul frowned, watching the action around them intently. "We're being driven back!" he shouted suddenly, galvanized into action. "Get in the wagon!"

They mounted the seat and Bristol reversed the wagon, but it was too late. Figures in blue were breaking out of the woods, coming toward them, and the musket fire rose to a crescendo. It sounded to Frankie like a giant breaking thousands of small sticks. She clung to the seat as Bristol whipped the horses into a gallop, and they were almost clear when she felt something strike her in the back. She thought it was a branch from a tree, but then the pain hit her. Startled, unbelieving, she looked down to see a hole high in her shirt front and blood staining the fabric the most brilliant crimson she'd ever seen.

She tried to speak, but there was no air — someone seemed to be cutting it off. As she slid to the floor, she heard Paul cry out, but he sounded as though he were far away instead of beside her on the seat.

"Frankie!"

Then the floor of the wagon rose up and hit her on the forehead, and she slipped into a cold, black hole that closed around her.

By the time Paul got the team stopped and pulled Frankie up to a sitting position, he saw that the Union attack had been halted by a countercharge of Confederate cavalry. Frantically he jumped to the ground, pulled Frankie's limp form from the seat, and carried her to the shade of an oak tree. The horses were bucking, so he had to lay her gently down, then run for them. He grabbed their reins, tied them to a sapling, then dashed back to Frankie. His heart grew sick as he saw that the entire front of her shirt was soaked with blood. His first thought was to get her to a doctor; then he realized that might take too long. She could well bleed to death.

He knelt beside her, ripped the buttons off her shirt, and pulled it away to view the small hole high over her right breast. Pulling her forward, he saw that the bullet had entered her back and so had gone completely through. He was no doctor, but he knew that it was good that the bullet had gone clear through her flesh. And he saw that it had passed through very high, angling upward. "Don't think it hit a lung!" he said with a gust of relief.

Paul laid her gently back against the tree, his heart pounding. She had lost so much blood. . . . He at once ripped off his cotton shirt and used part of it to make two bandages, then tore the rest into strips. He placed the pads over the wounds and tied them in place, then looked around. A grim expression crossed his face. Sooner or later the Federals would come.

"Got to get her out of here!" he muttered. Knowing he had no choice, he picked her up and carried her to the wagon. It was difficult, but he managed to get into the wagon and put her into the bunk he slept in. He tied her fast so that she could not fall out, then jumped out and untied the team. Leaping to the seat, he drove away from the battlefield and half an hour later was on the road that was already filling up with wounded men staggering back toward Corinth.

The sounds of the battle came to him, muted by distance, but an hour later they were very faint. He stopped the wagon twice to go back and check on the wounded girl. She was pale and unconscious, but he noted with relief that the bleeding seemed to be stopped.

Finally he found a small stream that

crossed the road, and he turned the team to follow it. The ground was level, and soon he was out of sight of the main road. He pulled up under some chestnut trees, jumped down, tied the horses, and got Frankie out of the wagon.

As he was laying her down, her eyes opened. "How do you feel, Frankie?" Paul asked, trying to keep his voice calm.

A weak smile crossed her face. "Not — very good . . . ," she whispered, then closed her eyes and was unconscious again. Paul was filled with fear, for he thought she was either dead or dying. He leaped to the wagon, pulled blankets out, and made a bed. As he gently placed her on it, she stirred and licked her lips, which he saw were very dry. He got a cup, then scooped some of the water from the creek and tasted it. It was cool and sweet. Going to sit beside her, he lifted her head and held the cup to her lips.

Frankie's eyelids fluttered, and she began to drink. When she was through, she whispered, "That was so good!"

All that afternoon and into the night, Bristol nursed the wounded girl. As he removed the blood-soaked bandages and replaced them with fresh dressing, he found himself praying — something he hadn't done since he was a small boy. All night long he kept close watch, and he felt his heart tighten when Frankie developed a fever. Her skin grew so hot that he was alarmed, and finally he resorted to the remedy his mother had used on him when he was a child. He got a bucket of cool creek water and soaked a sheet in it. Then he carried Frankie to the wagon and removed her heavy boots and clothing. When he placed the wet sheet over her fevered body, she began to shiver and opened her eyes.

"What's wrong with me, Paul?" she whispered, delirium and fear in her eyes.

"Hush, now." His voice was low and soothing, his eyes gentle. "You've been wounded and have a fever, but you'll be all right." He saw her eyes focus on him, and as he watched, he saw the fear leave. His throat tightened painfully at her trust in him, and it was a few moments before he could speak. "I'll take care of you, Frankie," he vowed. "And remember, Mother's praying for you."

It took two hours, but by dawn the fever was broken. Exhausted, Paul pulled a blanket over Frankie and went and slumped down on a box beside her. She was sleeping a normal sleep, and he lay down on the bare wood of the wagon floor and dropped off to sleep as if he'd been drugged.

"Paul?"

At the sound of Frankie's voice, he awoke instantly and got stiffly to his feet. Leaning over her, he asked, "How do you feel?"

"Can I have some water, please?"

Paul got some fresh water and watched as she drank it. She gave him the cup back, and he frowned at how frail she looked. Dark circles gave her green eyes a sunken look, and she winced with pain when she moved. She reached up and touched the bandage on her chest, then let her hand fall. "I feel better. Last night I was burning up, wasn't I?"

"Yes. The fever was pretty high." He reached out and pushed her hair back from her forehead. "You gave me a pretty bad scare, Frankie. But you'll be all right now. I think we'll move away from here — if you can stand the ride. Federals probably will be headed this way pretty soon, and I'd hate to see us wind up in a Yankee prison."

Frankie closed her eyes, then said, "Yes, let's go."

Paul got out of the back of the wagon, then climbed into the seat. He drove steadily all morning, stopping often to check Frankie's condition and give her plenty of water. He made some soup at noon and was pleased that it seemed to do her good. Encouraged, he ate ravenously. That night he camped just outside a small town, and Frankie asked if she could go outside. "It's so stuffy in here. Let me sleep on the ground."

He fixed her a bed beneath the wagon, put her in it, then made a fire and heated more soup. She ate some and drank a lot of water. "I can't seem to get enough," she said, giving him the cup.

"It's that way with a wound, so I hear." He cleaned the dishes, then went to feed the horses. Coming back, he sat down close to her, saying, "I want to get you home, but it's a long way. We'll have to take it easy. I'll send a wire to my folks and tell them we're all right but won't be home for a while. Want me to send anyone a wire?"

"No, there's no need for that," she said but wouldn't meet Paul's eyes. She seemed preoccupied, though not depressed or in great pain.

"Are you all right, Frankie?" he asked, concerned.

She looked up at him, and he saw by the flickering firelight that her face was relaxed. "Yes, I'm all right. But something happened to me." She was propped up in a sitting position, back braced against one of the wheels, and she reached up and brushed her hair away from her face. "Last night when the fever was so high, I kept having a dream."

"A bad dream?"

She smiled then and shook her head. "No, a good one. I dreamed about Sol Levy. It wasn't like any dream I've ever had, Paul. You didn't know him, but he was the most wonderful man!" She spoke quietly, telling Paul about the man who had done so much for her. Then she said in a voice of wonder, "I heard him talk to so many soldiers about becoming Christians. It was all he cared about, really, to see men get saved. And when my fever was so high I thought I was going to burn up, I seemed to see him and to hear him talking."

"What did he say?" Paul asked, leaning forward with intense interest.

"He said, 'It's time for you, daughter.' He always called me that, and he always said that the time would come for me to be saved. I never believed it, though. Not until I had the dream."

Paul watched her curiously. Her face had a restful look to it, despite the strain of the sickness. She seemed somehow — different. He could not put his finger on it, but felt it had something to do with the wall that she'd kept around herself ever since he'd known her. It had been an almost palpable barrier, so that no matter how she smiled, he'd never felt close to her. Now that barrier was gone, and he wondered at the change in her.

"Sol said it was time for me to call on God," she continued. "To ask Jesus to save me." She closed her eyes, thinking about it, then opened them and smiled. "And I did. It wasn't hard, not like I always thought it would be. I just sort of . . . gave up. I was so tired and sick, and there was nothing I could do. So I asked God to forgive me in the name of Jesus, and as soon as I did that, Paul, I knew I wasn't going to die." She looked at him then, and her eyes seemed to glow. "And ever since then, I . . . I've had this wonderful peace! It's like I'm free, somehow . . . and I'm not afraid anymore."

"Afraid? Of whom?"

"Of myself, of who and what I am . . . and of . . . others . . ." Her voice trailed off wearily. She wanted to go on, to explain to him that the Lord had come in and taken away her deepest fear — the fear of loving, and being loved by, a man — but she was just too tired. *Later . . . ,* she thought. *I'll tell him later.*

Paul stared at her, not able to speak for a

moment. Something had happened to the girl, no question about that. *Probably just the strain.* But he could not shake off the feeling that it went much deeper than that. Finally he said, "I'm glad for you, Frankie. And my mother will be very glad, indeed."

He could see from her face how weary she was, so he made her lie down. As she dropped off to sleep, she reached up toward him. When he took her hand, she held it to her cheek and closed her eyes. "Don't leave me, Paul," she muttered with a sigh.

For a long time he sat there holding her hand, studying her face, and wondering what would happen to her. She was so different. Finally he laid her hand under her blanket, then went to roll up in his own blankets. He was bone tired, but thought of the past two days, his mind so hazy he could hardly piece the events together. It was a long way to Virginia, but they would make it. They would get home, back to his mother and father, back to Marie, back to . . .

Luci DeSpain. Paul frowned. Luci would be there, of course, waiting to talk about their wedding. But he would have to see to Frankie, too — make sure she'd be taken care of. And he'd have to give the pictures to the War Department, to the president. And he'd have to decide what he was going to do next. Suddenly the future seemed to rise up, with a thousand tasks ready to press down on him. He closed his eyes, and finally sleep came. He forgot the bloody battlefield and dreamed of Hartsworth . . . and a woman with laughing green eyes.

The darkness closed in on the two sleepers, and the stars looked down, glittering like jewels. The woods were silent, and except for the sound of the small stream, a holy quietness fell over the little glade.

■ ■ ■ ■

PART FOUR:
THE AWAKENING —
MAY 1862

■ ■ ■ ■

CHAPTER 18
A WOMAN'S JEALOUSY

Luci DeSpain arrived at Hartsworth just after one o'clock in the afternoon. She had heard from her father that Paul Bristol had returned from Tennessee and at once had rousted out one of the slaves to drive her to the Bristol plantation. When she arrived, she was met at the front door by one of the maids, who said, "Miz Bristol up takin' care of Miss Frankie, in de blue room."

Luci ascended the stairs and knocked at the door. When Marianne's voice called out, "Come in," she stepped inside. There she saw Paul's young assistant sitting on a straight-backed chair with Marianne standing beside her, a bandage in her hand.

"Why, Luci," Marianne said with obvious surprise. "Paul's gone to your place to see you."

Luci had been angry since hearing that Bristol was back — he had not come to her at once. Now she swallowed the bitter words that had been rising to her lips and managed to smile. "Oh, I guess I missed him," she said lamely. Then she stared at the young woman sitting on the chair. "I hope you're better, Miss Aimes. Paul wrote me about your wound."

Frankie looked up at Marianne with a smile. "I'm fine, Miss DeSpain," she said easily. "My nurse won't let me do much, though."

Luci had expected the girl to look pale and washed out, but there was no sign of sickness in the rosy cheeks and clear eyes she saw before her. Frankie was wearing a petticoat, and the wound high up on her chest was clearly healing well.

"She's a healthy girl," Marianne said with a smile, noting Luci's stare at the small puckered wound. "And Paul's a good nurse. He drove back from Shiloh very slowly and was careful to change the bandages. Look, the scar on the back is even smaller than the one in front."

Luci came to peer at the wound on Frankie's back, which was, indeed, healing well. "I didn't know Paul was a nurse," she remarked. "I suppose the doctors took good care of you?"

"Oh, they didn't have time for a little thing like this," Frankie said at once. "Men were dying everywhere. Paul had to do it all." Her face glowed, and she smiled at Paul's mother. "He said once all he did was try to think of what you would do, and then try to do the same."

Marianne laughed, then said, "Well, let me see about this." She studied the wound. "I think we'd better keep a light bandage on for a day or two." Skillfully she secured the bandages, wrapping a thin strip of cotton cloth over the girl's shoulder, then around her chest. "If that bullet had been much lower," she remarked, "it would have hit the lung. But the worst evidence you'll have now are two small scars, front and back." She stepped back and said without thinking, "But they'll only show with ball gowns and party dresses that are cut low —"

All three women were aware of the sudden silence, and all three were thinking of the last party dress Frankie had worn. Luci flushed, but it was Frankie who eased the moment. "Oh, I don't go to many parties," she said, "but when I do, I'll put one of those beauty marks on the scar."

The stiffness went out of the atmosphere, and Luci said quickly, "Well, I'm glad to see you're recovering so well." She hesitated, then asked, "I imagine you've had enough of battlefields. You won't go back with Paul when he leaves for another assignment, will you?"

Frankie looked at the girl, aware that the question was not as simple as it seemed — and her eyes widened with sudden comprehension. Luci DeSpain was jealous! Though Frankie was far from adept in the manners of courtship — she had never taken any interest in such things — she was very quick at reading people. Now she saw the slight tension at the corners of Luci's lips and the resentful glint in her eyes . . . and was disturbed. She didn't want to make trouble for Paul.

Choosing her words carefully, Frankie said, "Oh, I don't think we'll be leaving, Miss DeSpain. McClellan's on his way here. Paul says we can get all the pictures of battles right around Richmond."

"I'm glad to hear that," Luci said. Then she looked at Marianne. "I'll wait for Paul if I may. I assume he'll come back here when he finds out I'm not at home."

"Of course, Luci. Would you like to sit down and visit with Frankie for a while?" There was a mischievous streak in Marianne that sometimes surfaced. She well knew that Luci would rather do *anything* other than sit and talk with this young woman, but she

382

just couldn't keep herself from asking.

To Luci's credit, she did manage to keep a pleasant smile on her face as she said quickly, "Oh no! I'd just be in the way. I'll just go get Blossom to fix me some tea."

Luci turned, and as she left the room, Frankie rose and picked up the blue robe that Marianne had provided for her. Slipping into it, she said, "I can't get over it . . . how different I feel about Luci now." She moved carefully as she fastened the buttons, her eyes thoughtful. "After the ball, I hated her worse than I ever hated anybody, I think. But now that's all gone."

"It may come back," Marianne warned. "You've let Jesus Christ come into your heart, Frankie, but there are some difficult times ahead." She smiled pensively, adding, "I thought when I became a Christian that I'd never have any problems with anger or bitterness, but I soon found out differently." Her eyes twinkled as she looked at the younger woman. "If a person likes chocolate cake *before* they're saved, they'll like chocolate cake *after* they're saved."

Frankie frowned. "But — I don't hate her like I did!"

"No, and that's a sign that God is doing a work in your heart. But if you find one day that some of that ugly feeling has crept back, don't panic. You're like a baby, Frankie. We all are when we first come into the kingdom. And every day you'll be growing, learning how to please and worship God. But I've seen so many who slipped back into bad feelings or habits after they were saved, and they thought they'd lost God. The truth is, we don't lose God when we fail, no more than we lose our parents because we fail them."

Frankie looked up quickly at that. "You're thinking about Paul, aren't you?"

"Yes, I always think about him."

"He was so gentle with me, like I was a baby. I was just about as helpless as one! I tried to get him to drive faster, but he said it might hurt me." She looked out the window, the memory putting a thoughtful expression into her eyes. "I couldn't even hold my head up to drink, Marianne. He had to do it. I've never been sick, and . . . it shamed me, somehow. But he did everything so kindly that I didn't mind after a while."

"Paul's always prided himself on being a man's man," Marianne said. "But he's always had a tender heart. Oh, he tries to cover it up — he's like my father in that. Why, I remember a time when Paul was a boy, oh, no more than seven or eight, I think. One of his dogs died, and he tried to keep the tears back, but I saw them. When he knew I'd seen, he grew very gruff. 'Got something in my eye!' he said." She smiled tenderly. "But I knew better."

"Men don't cry, do they?"

"Not often, and it's not good that they don't!" Marianne sniffed, and a disdainful look swept over her face. "Look at the Bible. King David cried, and Prince Jonathan, and they were the two greatest soldiers of Israel. If they can cry, I can't see why our men should be ashamed to do so. I suppose it all comes from our English blood . . . keep a stiff upper lip, never let anyone see you show emotion . . . what nonsense!"

"Well, I showed plenty of emotion when I got shot and while I was sick. I guess Paul thinks I'm a crybaby. And I wouldn't blame him."

Marianne gave her a level look. "He thinks you're quite a woman. He told me that most women would have gone to pieces if they had to go through what you did, but you bore it all with calm and courage."

A flush came to Frankie's cheeks, and she said, "Miss DeSpain doesn't like it, my going around the country with Paul. She doesn't think it looks right." She turned to Marianne, her lips drawn tight. "Do you think it's wrong?"

"No!" Marianne wanted to say more but held the words back. After a few moments, she said, "I only hope she doesn't start in on Paul again. He's polite and likes to let her have her way, but Luci will soon find out something about Paul Bristol. When he *does* set his foot down, he can make the heavens ring!"

Marianne's hope that Luci would not speak of her displeasure about Frankie to Paul was to go unfulfilled.

When Paul came into the house an hour later, she went to him at once, and he put his arms around her and kissed her. She held him tightly, saying, "Oh, Paul, I've been worried sick!"

He kissed her again, then teased her, "I'm fine, but I figure it only does a woman good to worry about her man. Now come on down to the laboratory. I'll show you some of the plates."

Ten minutes later the two of them were studying the plates. Paul had laid them out on a table, and at once Luci exclaimed, "Oh, how clear these are!"

"I had to throw quite a few away, but we got a pretty good selection." He watched her as she picked up the plates to study them closely. She was a beautiful girl, well able to stir a man's blood . . . but Paul was hesitant to broach the subject he knew she most wanted to discuss: their wedding.

"Oh — how awful!" Paul looked at her, startled from his thoughts by her dismayed exclamation. She was staring at the picture of the pile of arms and legs outside the surgeon's tent. It had been one of the clearest plates of all — so clear that a wedding ring was plainly visible on one of the hands.

The sight of it brought back the memory of the men's screams, and he repressed a shudder. "Awful, isn't it?"

Turning to face him, Luci put the print down, saying, "Why in the world did you take a picture of *that*?"

"It was there, Luci," he said with a shrug. "A product of this war. People need to know what it's costing us."

Luci was horrified. "President Davis didn't send you to get pictures like this, Paul! He wanted you to take pictures that would make people feel *good* about the war, make them support it!"

"Well, we got some of those, too. Here, look at these." Paul showed her the pictures that he and Frankie had made the night before the battle. "See how happy they are? Smiling and laughing —" He broke off, his voice growing hard. "Now a lot of them are in shallow graves . . . or in hospitals, missing arms and legs."

"You can't show these awful things to President Davis!" Luci cried. "He knows what war is like. He's *been* a soldier. He needs someone to help him pull the people together. Do you think these . . . these *things* will make men want to fight, or women want to send their husbands and sweethearts to war?"

Paul refused to argue, for he'd known that the pictures showing the reality of war — the raw horrors — would not be accepted by many people. "Well, I'm just the photographer, Luci. Someone else will decide which pictures to release."

Luci looked at him quickly, then felt pleased, for it seemed she had won the argument. She took his arm as the two of them walked out of the lab. The sun was warm, and Paul said, "Let's go down to the pond and see the ducks." They took the well-worn path across the pasture, arriving at a large pond surrounded by tall pines. It was cool in the shade, and Paul said, "Look, there they are! I was afraid the turtles might have gotten them."

Luci was delighted with the flotilla of yellow ducklings that came toward them at once. "Oh, how darling!" she cried. "I love baby animals!"

They watched the ducks for a time; then Luci turned to Paul, a shadow crossing her face. "I heard about Ellen Rocklin's accident, Paul. How terrible for her, to be crippled for life! Have you spoken to Clay since the shooting?" Paul shook his head, recalling his father's explanation about the "accident" that had brought Ellen to her present state. *"She was seeing this fellow Simon Duvall,"* he had said, his eyes showing his disapproval. *"And there was a shooting. Duvall's bullet wasn't meant for Ellen, but it hit her in the back. The doctors said it was too close to the spine to get it out. So she lived, but she'll never walk again."*

It was Paul's sister who had given him the rest of the story. *"Everybody said Clay would leave Ellen when she was paralyzed, but I knew he wouldn't. He was converted, you know, and even though he loves Melora Yancy, he'll stay with Ellen, as awful as she treats him, as long as she lives!"*

Now he looked at Luci, who was the picture of grace and health, and felt pity for Ellen and the life she faced.

"No," he said, "I haven't spoken to either of them. But I know this has not been an easy time for either Clay or Ellen."

Luci watched Paul's face, noting the emotions that crossed his handsome features, then stepped toward him, saying, "I've been lonely without you, Paul. You won't be going away again, will you? Not soon, anyway."

"No. The battle will be here around Richmond." He studied the ducks as they turned upside down, then added, "It may be the South's last battle."

"Oh, Paul, don't talk like that! We can't lose!" Luci, like many Southerners, had a blind spot about the war. They simply refused to consider the possibility of losing. To talk to them about the North's superior numbers or the South's pitiful factory system was a waste of time. *"One Confederate can whip five Yankees!"* Paul had heard it over and over, with only a slight variation. Sometimes it was *ten* Yankees.

"Luci, if we do lose, life won't be the same around here," he said. "And even if we win, I don't have anything to offer you. I can't claim any part of Hartsworth. Austin and Marie, they've stayed and worked for the place while I was out making smears on canvas."

Luci shook her head. "Your mother doesn't think like that. She told me the plantation would be divided equally between her three children."

"I wouldn't take it," Paul said adamantly.

"And you ought to think about this seriously, Luci. You're used to fine things, and I don't think I'll ever be able to provide that for you."

Luci insisted that she would share whatever he had, but Paul knew that she had no idea what it meant to do without. *I don't either,* he thought cynically. *Never made a dollar in my life on my own.*

Luci waved away his words but then asked cautiously, "Paul, you won't be taking Frankie along with you, will you?" At his look of surprise, she spoke more quickly. "I mean, well, surely she's not able to do much, is she? With her wound and all?"

"She'll be all right." Paul shook his head, saying, "I was just about crazy with worry for a while, Luci! If she'd died, it would have been my fault."

"Nonsense!" Luci snapped. "You didn't *force* her to go!"

"No, but she was in my care." Taking a deep breath, he shook his head, still not over the anguish he'd felt when he realized she'd been shot. "It was bad, Luci, very bad! No doctor, and Frankie shot all the way through."

Luci stared at him, her lips tight. "You must be a pretty good nurse. I didn't know you were so expert in bullet wounds."

Paul didn't see the hard light in Luci's eyes. "I didn't know it, either. I've doctored a few dogs and horses that were injured, but that's a little different from nursing a young woman with a bullet wound."

Luci thought suddenly of Frankie Aimes's rounded, smooth shoulders, and a streak of jealousy ran along her nerves. "It's a good thing she's not a modest person," she said, a hard edge in her tone.

"Modest?" Paul was bewildered. "What does that mean?"

"I think it's obvious, Paul." Luci shrugged. "I was there this afternoon while your mother was changing the bandage. Don't try to tell me she was fully dressed when you changed her bandages!"

Bristol could not believe what he was hearing. "Why, I don't think I ever thought about it, Luci. She was so sick, and I was so frantic, it never occurred to me —" He broke off, frowning. "Frankie's about as modest as a woman can be."

"How can you say that?" she demanded hotly. "Why, the girl has done nothing but hang around men, Paul! She says so herself, doesn't she? No woman could stay around soldiers as she's done without losing her delicacy."

Bristol stared at Luci, his eyes narrowing.

"Don't you trust me, Luci?"

"Would you trust me if I was running around the country with a young man, alone and subjected to all sorts of — temptations?"

"Yes, I'd trust you," he said, his voice growing hard. "I don't know much about love, but isn't marriage built on trust? Don't the man and woman vow to be faithful to each other? Well, I'm asking you to be faithful, to have faith in me. Because if you don't, then we might as well know that now."

Afraid she had gone too far, Luci put on her most winning smile and reached up to touch Paul's cheek. "Oh, let's not quarrel, dear! You don't think I could be *jealous* of that poor thing, do you?" She laughed. "I might be jealous if you ran around the country alone with Violet Cunningham, but not poor Frankie." She pulled his head down and kissed him, then stood back, smiling. "Now Mrs. Davis has asked me to come for a tea at her house tomorrow. The president will be there, and General Lee. You can ask them to let you take their pictures."

"Yes, that would be a good time," Paul agreed. He seemed to forget all about the argument, but it was only a temporary lull in the battle for Luci. As she smiled and clung to him, she made an inner vow that Paul Bristol had made his last tour with Frankie Aimes!

CHAPTER 19
ELLEN'S REVENGE

"Want to go see some hogs, daughter?"

"Hogs?" Rena looked up from her book to her father, who had come into his small house. He had moved into it when he had returned from his wanderings, choosing not to move into the Big House with Ellen. It was a small summerhouse, old and weathered, but he'd fixed it up with cast-off furniture and bookshelves. Rena, who loved books, spent more time at the summerhouse than she did at home — which irritated Ellen a great deal.

"Yes, hogs . . . bacon on the hoof. Want to see some?" Clay grinned at Rena's puzzled look and explained, "Buford sent word that our first crop of young pigs is about ready to sell. Wants me to come and look at them."

"You don't know anything about hogs, Daddy!"

Clay grinned. "I sure don't, but they're going to be worth a lot more than bales of cotton left sitting on the wharf. Well, do you want to come or not?"

"Yes!" Rena said at once. When she went outside, she saw that her father had saddled her little mare along with his own horse. She gave him a sideways glance. "Pretty sure I'd go with you, weren't you?"

"I know you could never resist a ride with a good-looking man."

"My, you *are* conceited!" Rena sniffed but privately agreed. She thought that her father was the best-looking man in Virginia, or anywhere else, for that matter. She loved him with a single-minded devotion.

Clay knew this about his daughter, and he was as proud of that fact as of anything on earth. As he watched her ride beside him, he thought, *She's growing up so fast! Soon she'll be thinking of marriage, and I'll lose her.* The thought saddened him, but he snapped out of it. *Better to enjoy today than fear tomorrow!* He listened, smiling as she told him about one of the stories she was writing.

They followed the main road for five miles, then turned off and made their way along a dusty road that wound through first-growth timber. It was cool under the shade of the big trees, and Clay felt a peace that was rare for him. Even so, he was worried about his boys and said so. "Dent will be going back on active duty pretty soon," he said. "And Lowell will be in action. We all will, I guess."

"Daddy, I'm afraid," Rena said. She turned to him, and for one moment he was startled. She looked very much as Ellen had years ago, when he had first met her. Rena had the same dark eyes and brown hair. *But she's not like Ellen,* he thought with relief. *She's like Mother and Grandmother.*

"We all are, I guess, Rena. Not for ourselves so much as for others." As they rode along, he tried to cheer her up and succeeded. He had the power to give her assurance, and it troubled him to think that when he was gone back on duty — very soon, now — she would be left pretty well on her own. David was still home, and his mother. But Rena could not confide in either of them. Clay thought of all the men who had to leave children and wives, and he knew that all over the country men were worrying about sons and daughters. That was one of the high costs of war.

They reached the Yancy cabin before noon, and as the youngsters came running out to meet them, Clay said, "I hope you remember their names. I get some of them mixed up." Then Melora came out to meet

397

him, and he found himself — as always when first seeing her — a little stunned.

Melora Yancy was as tall and slender as a mountain spruce, or she seemed to be. She had green eyes and the blackest hair possible and was one of those people who never seemed to age. It was difficult for those meeting her for the first time to believe that she was twenty-seven instead of nineteen or twenty.

"Hello, Mister Clay," she said, a smile on her wide lips. She glanced at Rena and winked. "You know, of all the times your father's come here, I can't remember once when it wasn't mealtime."

"I'm no fool." Clay grinned. "Where's Buford?"

"Out with those pesky pigs," Melora said tartly. "I believe he thinks more of them than he does of his children."

"Oh, not really, Melora?" Rena stared. She admired Melora tremendously, wanting to be and look like her more than anyone else in the world.

"Well, I got a bad cold last week," Melora said, smiling impishly, "and Pa never even noticed. But you let one of those blasted swine so much as cough, and he'll be down there quick as a shot pouring medicine down its throat!" Glancing at the children, who had ringed the two visitors, she said, "Rose, you and Martha watch that corn bread so it doesn't burn. I'm going to take Mister Clay and Rena to see those beautiful animals." She ignored the cry of protest, saying, "You can all see Mister Clay at dinner. Come along, Rena. I want to hear about your new stories."

The three made their way along the trail leading away from the house, Clay walking behind the two women. He watched Melora, noting how much — and how little — she had changed since he'd first met her when she was a child. Then she had been a small girl he was kind to, whom he bought books for . . . someone who believed in him. Then when he'd come back to try to pick up the threads of his life, he'd been startled to discover that the little girl was gone, replaced in that mysterious way of nature by a startlingly beautiful young woman.

Before long, they knew they loved each other, but he was a married man, in name and under the law. The fact that his wife made life as difficult for him as possible was not a factor, for his goal was to honor God in his role as a father and husband, and as a son to his parents. That meant staying with and caring for his wife, despite the anger and bitterness that constantly spilled out of her. It meant that he could not make promises to Melora, except that he would continue to be her friend, as he always had been. He had tried to get her to marry Jeremiah Irons, a pastor whom both Clay and Melora had counted a dear friend, but Irons had died in the war. Clay frowned, troubled. *Lord, I don't understand. Wouldn't it have been better if Jeremiah had lived? He would have made Melora a good husband. . . .* He shook his head, praying that God would care for the woman who walked in front of him.

Before long they heard the grunting and shrill yelps of the pigs and soon arrived at the hog pens. Buford Yancy saw the three walking out of the woods and came at once to offer his hand to Clay. "Make you feel proud to own such a mess of fine hogs, Clay?" Yancy, a widower in his early fifties, was six feet tall and lean as a lizard. He had greenish eyes and tow-colored hair and was strong and agile in the way of mountain men. He looked at Clay Rocklin, approval and admiration evident in his eyes. "Glad you made it back. How are my boys, Bob and Lonnie?"

"Best soldiers in the regiment, except for Lowell, of course!"

Yancy spit an amber stream of tobacco

juice to one side, then grinned and waved at the hogs. "There they be. Ain't they purty?"

Clay looked doubtfully at the pigs, then shook his head. "I guess so, Yancy. I'm not much of an authority on pigs. We going to sell them?"

"Not right off. I saved enough grain to feed 'em out for another month. By that time I figure we won't have no trouble sellin' 'em in Richmond."

"You're right about that, Buford." Clay nodded. "But we give the Richmond Grays first shot. Bob and Lonnie and the rest of the boys would sure like some good ham and bacon this winter."

Buford showed them the finer points of the hogs; then they all went back to the cabin for dinner. As they sat down at the table, Clay looked around and smiled. "I remember the first time I ever sat down at this table." He looked at Melora, who was going around the table pouring buttermilk into cups and glasses. "It was the first time I got to sit up and eat after Irons brought me here when I was so sick. Bet you don't remember what I ate, Melora."

"Mush and some dumplings."

Clay stared at her. "How in blazes can you remember that? You weren't more than seven or eight."

"I was six," Melora said, then sat down beside her father. "Mister Clay, please ask the blessing." She waited until he was through, then said to Rena, "Your father gave me my first book. I still have it, along with all the others."

The meal was fine, and afterward Clay talked for an hour with Buford, mostly about plans for next year's crop of corn and pigs. Melora enlisted Rena's help in cleaning up, and finally it was time for the Rocklins to go. Clay had only a moment alone with Melora while the children ganged up around Rena, begging her to come back and bring more books and candy.

"I miss Jeremiah," Clay said simply. "I think he was the best man I ever knew."

"I think we all loved him. He was so kind!"

Clay hesitated, then said, "I wish he had lived, Melora. I would like to see you with your own family, your own home."

She smiled. "I know, Clay. But I can't help but wonder if I could have made him happy. Jeremiah knew I was fond of him, but he also knew he could never have all of me." Her green eyes met his squarely. "He knew I loved you."

Clay nodded. She spoke so directly, so

honestly! "I wish things were different, Melora."

"I know that. It's all right, Clay. God knows our hearts, and He will help us to do what is right."

And then Rena was there, and the two mounted and left the homestead. Rena talked most of the way home, explaining how she was going to get some new books and take them to Melora and the children.

Clay said little until they pulled up and dismounted. "Let's go see how your grandfather is," he suggested.

They found Thomas Rocklin out in the scuppernong arbor watching a flock of sparrows fight over the crumbs he threw them. "When a man's good for nothing but feeding a bunch of dumb birds, it's pretty bad, isn't it, Clay?"

"How do you feel today?"

"Well — I feel more like I do now than I did before I felt like this." Thomas laughed at the puzzled expression on Rena's face. "Figure that out, girl." He looked bad to Clay — his face was pale and his tall frame shrunken. Clay knew his father had a bad stomach, and the doctors could find no definite cause. Now Thomas smiled up at his son. "Sit down and tell me the news.

When do you have to go back to the regiment?"

"In four days," Clay said. "Let me tell you about my pigs. . . ." In the midst of his story, the sound of wheels on the bricks came to them. Clay paused briefly, glancing up to see his wife, Ellen, in her wheelchair. Clay nodded at her, said hello, then kept on with his story.

Ellen sat there listening and then, to the shock of the three across from her, cried out, "I knew you'd been to see that woman! I knew it! And to take your own daughter with you on your nasty business!"

Clay and Thomas stood up, both of them trying to speak.

"Ellen, it was just a visit — ," Clay began, but Ellen flew into a rage, cursing him.

"Rena," Clay said sharply, "go to the house. Your mother's not well."

Rena, who had turned quite pale, ran at once to the house. As she fled, she heard her mother screaming obscenities and her father asking her to listen to reason. She ran upstairs and threw herself on the bed, burying her face in a pillow. She began to weep, her body torn with great sobs. After a time, she heard her door open and looked up quickly to see her grandmother, who came to her at once.

Susanna Rocklin sat on the edge of the bed and took the girl into her arms, holding her tightly, stroking her hair. "I wish you hadn't heard that, Rena."

"I hate her!" Rena sobbed. "She's so mean to Daddy!"

"You must not hate her, child. She's all mixed up inside. Has been for a long time. I know it's hard, but you must not let hate get a hold on you. That would only hurt you . . . and none of us — not your grandfather, nor I, nor your father — could stand that!" Susanna waited until the girl's sobs ceased, then held her at arm's length. "Ellen is a difficult person, Rena, but she is your mother. Promise me you'll let Jesus love her through you. It's the only way any of us can love those who misuse us."

Rena wiped the tears that still streamed down her cheeks. "How can I do that, Grandmother?"

"I'll try to tell you. . . ." And the two sat there, the older woman speaking quietly, Rena listening intently.

Outside in the grape arbor, Thomas shook his head, grateful that Ellen had finally wheeled herself off. "I'm proud of you, son," he said, looking at Clay. "Not many men would hang around and take the kind of punishment that woman hands out."

Thomas reached out to do something he couldn't have done at one time, something that only the grace of God in his life and in Clay's life made possible: He put his arm around Clay's shoulder and said, "You're a fine son to me. I couldn't have had better!"

Inside, Ellen sat in her room, watching the two men from her window. Her mind was filled with rage, and she muttered, "That woman — she won't have him! I'll see to that!" She wheeled herself around, got some paper from her desk, and began scribbling furiously. When the letter was finished, she put it into an envelope, sealed it carefully with wax, then made her way to the front porch.

A tall young black was working on the yard, and he looked up when he heard his named called. Dropping his spade, he went to the porch and removed his hat. "Yas, Miz Rocklin?"

"Highboy, take this letter into Richmond. Take it to the Crescent Hotel and give it to the man at the desk." She handed him a coin. "That's for you, but this is nobody's business but mine, you understand?"

"Yas, Miz Rocklin. I do it right now, but you hafta tell Miz Susanna why I didn't finish —"

"Go on! Take one of the saddle horses!"

Ellen watched as the tall slave hurried to the stable, then came out five minutes later. She kept her eyes on him until he disappeared, then smiled cruelly.

"We'll see about Miss Melora Yancy!" There was a wild light in her eyes, and she talked to herself as she wheeled away, muttering and laughing in a disturbing way.

Chapter 20
A Dangerous Assignment

The letter came in an innocent-looking envelope, addressed simply to Miss Frankie Aimes, Hartsworth, Richmond, Virginia.

As soon as Paul handed it to her, saying, "Letter for you, Frankie," a stab of fear shot through her.

She took the envelope and remarked casually, "Wonder who it could be from?" She broke the wax seal, pulled out a single sheet of paper, and read it quickly:

My dear niece,

I have just come from your home, and my brother informed me that you are now in Virginia working as a photographer. Needless to say, this came as quite a surprise to me. As you know, I have been in England for the last eighteen months, traveling extensively, so I did not get the news that you had left home.

I will be passing through Lake City, a

408

small town in Virginia, on May 20. Unfortunately I cannot spare the time to get to Hartsworth, or even to meet you in Richmond. If, however, you could come to Lake City, we could have a short visit, and I would like that very much. We have been out of touch, and if we could have just a brief time together, we could get caught up on all the news. I will be staying at the Elite Hotel and hope that you can find the time to come.

Oh yes, my friend Allan will be with me, and he asks me to give you his encouragement to come. He remembers you with affection, and I know you would like to see him again.

Your loving uncle,
James Miller

"My friend Allan," Frankie thought quickly. *That's Allan Pinkerton. I'll have to go!*

She looked up at Paul, who was reading a letter of his own. "It's from my Uncle James," she said. "My father's brother. He's going to be passing through Lake City, and he'd like for me to come and see him."

"Lake City? Well, that's not far. When will he be there?"

"On the twentieth. That's the day after tomorrow."

Paul was interested, for Frankie had never spoken of her family. "Would you like to go?"

"Oh yes. I've always liked Uncle James. He's a businessman and travels a lot, but it would be nice, if you can spare me."

Bristol shrugged. "I'm not sure it'd be good for you to ride a horse that far. Might not be good for that wound. I'll drive you over in the big carriage."

"Oh no!" Frankie spoke impulsively. "I can drive a buggy."

Bristol was surprised at her adamant refusal. "I don't mind, Frankie."

"I know, but . . ." She thought desperately, then blurted out, "I — I don't think Miss Luci would like it." She saw Paul's jaw harden and knew that he was going to be stubborn. "And she's right, I think," she said quickly. "It's one thing for us to travel together to get pictures, but this is personal. I think it would be better for me to go alone."

Paul seemed about to argue; then he sighed. "You're right, of course. I'll have one of the stable hands drive you. Or, if you insist, you can go alone if you're sure you're up to it."

"Oh, I'd enjoy the drive, Paul!" Relief ran through Frankie, and she said lightly,

410

"Look, I can hold my arm up now so easy!" She held up her right hand triumphantly. "See? It's almost as good as new."

Bristol was pleased. "Just do me a favor and don't ever get shot again, Frankie. It's too hard on an old man's nerves." He smiled at her. "I'll pay your salary before we leave, and maybe toss in a bonus for a job well done."

"Oh, don't do that!" Frankie protested. She was wearing a pair of beechnut-dyed men's trousers and a long-sleeved cotton shirt partly covered by a brown vest buttoned halfway up. Bristol noticed that she'd gained back the weight she had lost while recovering from her wound, and from the color in her cheeks, no one would have suspected that she had been ill.

She felt his eyes on her and reddened slightly, saying, "Well, I'll only be gone overnight."

"When you get back, we'll go to Richmond. My parents have been invited to some sort of party at Colonel Chesnut's. They want you to go with us."

"That would be nice, Paul. I'll look forward to it."

All that afternoon and through most of the night, Frankie thought about the summons from Tyler. When she finally left early on the morning of the twentieth, it was with a mixture of relief and apprehension. She drove the team easily, glad to discover that her wound was no problem. She was also glad to discover that Marianne had been right when she had assured her the scars were small and would grow less noticeable with the passage of time.

Frankie stopped twice for a drink of cool water, then at noon pulled over under the shade of some large hickory trees beside a small creek. She watered the horses and ate the lunch that Blossom had packed for her — sandwiches, boiled eggs, and sweet rolls. The food made her drowsy, and when she leaned back against one of the huge trunks and closed her eyes, the humming of bees and the warm air put her to sleep. Waking with a start, she looked at the sun, noting with relief that she hadn't slept too long.

Guess I'm not fully recovered yet, she thought, stretching and yawning. *Can't remember the last time I had to take naps in the middle of the day!*

Shadows were growing long as she pulled into Lake City. She put the buggy up at the livery stable, instructing the stubby hostler to grain the horses well. She was glad that the streets were mostly unoccupied and the stores were closing up — no one would be around to notice or remember her. But when she entered the hotel lobby, she found the same thin man who'd rented her a room before behind the desk.

He watched with interest as she came up to the desk. "Hello. Back again, I see."

"Yes. I need a room just for tonight."

"Take 216," he said, and as Frankie signed her name, she was struck with apprehension. *It's bad that he remembers me. We should have used another place,* she thought. But she took the small suitcase she'd packed and went to the room, which was a carbon copy of the last one she'd had, right down to the bed, dresser, and one straight chair. It took only a few moments to unpack her things and place them in the drawer of the shaky dresser. She removed her vest and shirt and sluiced away the dust from the road, then put them back on. There was nothing to do for the next hour but sit in the chair beside the window and watch the street below.

Finally it was time for the meeting, so she lit the lamp, turned it down low, and left the room. The restaurant was fairly busy, but there was no sign of Tyler or Pinkerton. Frankie smiled when she spotted a large hand-printed sign over the back wall next to the kitchen door: IF YOU DON'T LIKE

OUR GRUB, DON'T EAT HERE! She moved to a table, and when the waitress said, "We got buffalo fish and pork chops," she chose the fish. The wait for her food was long, and she was tempted to ask if they had to go to the lake and catch the fish, but she refrained. No sense in saying something that the waitress probably would remember her for.

She drank buttermilk while she waited, watching the patrons carefully. None of them looked like spies . . . but then she shook her head. *How would I know what a spy looks like?*

Finally her meal came, and though the fish was greasy, it was flaky and crisp. Taking a bite, she found she was very hungry and so finished all on her plate, including some turnip greens that had been added. The waitress came to ask if she wanted some blackberry pie, and she sampled that, too, along with something that was called "coffee" but was actually made from ground and roasted acorns. Still, it was hot and black, and glancing back at the sign, Frankie smiled and drank half of the bitter liquid.

Finally she rose and paid the bill, then left the restaurant. She had thought Tyler and Pinkerton would be there by now. For a woman, there was nothing at all to do in town to pass time — not for a young unescorted single woman, anyway. A man could go into one of the three bars to drink and gamble, but Frankie knew that if she even walked down the street, she would be noticed — just what she didn't want. So with a sigh she mounted the stairs and entered her room. Turning up the lamp, she pulled the chair close to it and began to read the Bible that Sol Levy had given her.

The evening was warm, and there was little breeze coming through the open window — although mosquitoes and flies had no trouble finding their way in. Frankie ignored the pests, reading steadily. She was fascinated by the Bible, amazed at how it spoke to her. Before and after her conversion, she had tried to read the scripture but had given up in despair. It wasn't until Marianne had taught her how to begin, and she'd become caught up in the gospels — especially the Gospel of John — that she'd found she could enjoy reading the Bible.

"The Spirit of God will teach you, Frankie," Marianne had said. *"You couldn't understand the Bible before you were saved because only those who are born of the Spirit can understand and accept what is written there. Those who are lost have nothing in them to help them understand, but when you were saved,*

God put His Spirit in you. And the Spirit acts as a kind of interpreter for us. Pray as you read, and you'll find that God will speak to you and help you understand His words."

That had happened, and as Frankie read on, she was made more and more aware that the Christian life was basically knowing Jesus. Other things were important, but the joy in her came from the absolute certainty that somehow Jesus Christ was *in* her. She never heard voices, but there was a strong sense that she was not alone — and that was a wonderful thing!

Finally she grew sleepy and put the Bible down, then stretched out on the bed and drifted off to sleep. She came awake instantly when a faint knocking came at her door. Coming off the bed, she went to the door. "Who is it?"

"Your uncle James."

Frankie unlocked the door, and at once Tyler stepped inside. He was wearing the same suit she'd seen him wear before, and he still carried the cane, though he seemed not to need it. The yellow lamplight fell on him, and he was smiling. "I'm glad to see you, Frankie," he said quietly.

Frankie answered his smile and put her hand out. When he took it eagerly, she said, "I'm glad to see you, too, Tyler. Come and sit down." She saw that his limp was very slight as he moved. "You're walking better all the time."

"Oh yes, but not enough to march with a full pack." He sat down on the chair, and she came to sit on the bed. "Now how are you? Does the wound trouble you?"

"No, it's almost well. If it had been a little lower, I don't think I'd be here."

"I was worried sick when I didn't hear from you for so long!" Tyler blurted out. "When I got your letter, of course, you were out of danger, but it made me feel so helpless, knowing you'd been through that and all I'd done was sit around here! I almost came to Hartsworth to see how you were."

"That would have been a mistake."

"Sure, but when a fellow's not thinking straight, he's apt to make mistakes." He studied her carefully, then nodded his approval. "You look good. Now tell me all about it."

Frankie told the story. When she finished, Tyler said, "Sounds like Paul Bristol is a handy sort of fellow to have around, especially when you get shot." He asked with a rather casual air, "How do you two get along?"

"Why, well enough, I suppose."

Tyler shifted a little, seeming to hunt for

words. "Well, he's kind of a different man than most of the Rocklins, I guess. He always seemed caught up in things the rest of us didn't really understand, his art and all. We always wondered why he never joined the war or married."

"He's engaged to a young woman now. Luci DeSpain."

"Is that right? I hadn't heard that it was official. What's she like?"

"Very rich and beautiful."

Tyler grinned suddenly. "Better than marrying a girl who's poor and ugly!"

"You idiot!" Frankie laughed. She found herself very much at ease with Tyler, and for half an hour they talked, mostly about Tyler's family. Finally he said, "Well, I guess you were pretty shocked to get my letter."

"Yes. Especially the part about Pinkerton being here. Where is he?"

"Actually, he's not coming." Tyler shrugged. "It would be pretty dangerous, of course. But an agent came this morning with a set of instructions straight from him. Right now he's with McClellan and the Army of the Potomac."

"What does he want us to do?"

"If you'll turn your back, I'll fish it out and read it to you. I'm carrying it under my clothes."

Frankie turned her head away, amused. As he struggled to get the packet from beneath his shirt, she said, "You weren't so modest when I was nursing you."

"I didn't have any choice. Ah, here it is." She turned back to him and saw him pulling a paper from an oilcloth pouch. He began to read, and Frankie listened to the message carefully. It outlined a highly complicated plan that called for the two of them to gather detailed information on the location and strength of Confederate troops and to pass it along to couriers. There were signs and countersigns and all sorts of precautions involved, and Frankie lost track of most of it. When Tyler finished, he replaced the paper in the pouch, saying, "Sounds like he wants more than we can deliver."

"It's so *complicated,* Tyler!" Frankie protested. "If just one part of it goes wrong, the whole thing will break down."

"I know it," Tyler answered gloomily. "This kind of thing is an obsession with Pinkerton, I think. He gets too clever and thinks that if a plan is complicated enough, it'll confuse the Rebels. Trouble is, this thing is so blasted complicated that it confuses *me*!" He sighed heavily, then added, "Well, what do you think?"

Frankie sat there trying to think, but she was aware that her heart was not in any of this. From the first she had agreed to help Tyler, but now that she had met the Bristols and the Rocklins of Virginia, she felt a sharp twinge of guilt at the thought of her task. Heavily she said, "I wish it were over, Tyler. I — I can't help thinking of how fine the Bristols are, and the Rocklins, too." She saw him prepare to argue, but she was familiar with all the arguments, so she spoke up quickly. "Oh, I'll do it, if it can be done."

Tyler was relieved and began speaking rapidly. "Here's what's happening. McClellan got slowed up at Yorktown, Virginia. Joe Johnston fooled him pretty bad — made him think he had about five times as many troops as he really had. But now McClellan is headed for Richmond." He frowned, shaking his head. "The trouble is, Stonewall Jackson is somewhere in the Shenandoah Valley. There are three Federal armies there under Shields, Banks, and Fremont, so they should be able to handle him, but McClellan is counting on the three Federal armies to help take Richmond."

"Why, one army couldn't beat *three,* could it, Tyler?"

"Well, they *shouldn't,* but Jackson is a fox! Anyway, McClellan is headed up the peninsula for Richmond. Now, the Rebels know he's coming, and they'll throw every man they have into the battle to stop him. What we have to do is pinpoint *where* Joe Johnston puts his forces. If McClellan knows that, he'll win. Now, I know Pinkerton's got some agents there, but none of them will be as free to move around as you."

Frankie remembered the reports that Paul had given her of his sessions with the president and some of his advisers. "I'm not so sure that we'll be going to the battle, Tyler. The president didn't like some of the pictures we made — of the dead and wounded. And the advisers were dead set against letting Paul go back."

"But — if you can't move around, our whole operation is busted."

Secretly Frankie hoped Paul *would* be taken off the job, but felt there was little real chance of that. For all the advisers' complaints and objections, President Davis still seemed in favor of the photographs. "Well, I'll do what I can. But you can bet on one thing: McClellan may not know where the Rebels are, but they'll sure know where *he* is!"

"Sure! Every farmer and hunter in the country will be feeding the Union position to General Johnston. That's why we need to get McClellan the information he needs. Without it, he'll be fighting blind."

"Tyler, how will I get the information to you? I can't get away to come here."

"No, you can't. That's why I'm coming to Richmond."

"You can't do that!" Frankie blinked with surprise, then shook her head. "They'll be watching strangers like a hawk, Tyler; you know that."

"I won't have anything in writing." Tyler's eyes were bright, as if he welcomed the danger — as indeed he did! He felt that he had failed by not being in the active service, and throwing himself into a dangerous mission helped him to feel better. It was foolish, but it was the way he felt.

Now he laughed at the expression on Frankie's face. "Think of it this way: If a fellow's born to be hanged, he'll never get drowned, will he?"

Frankie shook her head, a dread rising in her. "It's too dangerous. Nobody will be watching me, but you can bet that the minute you start moving around, you'll get stopped. Last week they caught a spy in Richmond. They searched him and didn't find a thing, until one of the officers made him take off his shoes. He had secret papers for the Union there. They . . . they hung him from a lamppost!" She shivered and pleaded with him. "We'll have to think of a better way."

But argue as she would, Tyler would not budge. Finally he said, "Look, this isn't as dangerous as charging the Rebs with a bayonet. We won't put anything in writing unless we have to, and we'll do it in the order forms, like we discussed with Pinkerton."

Frankie sat there, unhappy and afraid. "I'm thinking of your mother and your father," she said quietly. "If something happened to you —"

"Sure, I know, Frankie, but I've got to do it." He leaned over and took her hand, and when she lifted her head, he smiled. "I like it when you worry about me."

Frankie bit her lip, then said quietly, "I do worry about you."

Her hand was warm in his, and he held it tighter. "I feel very strongly about you, Frankie. I guess I owe my life to you and Sol Levy. Makes me feel that somehow we were meant to be a part of each other's lives." He stood up, and when she rose, he kept his grip. "Now don't jump out of your skin," he said in a cautious, serious tone, "but I'm going to give you a very mild, innocent little kiss."

Frankie smiled, amused at his careful manner. "Well, stop talking and do it, then."

Tyler stared at her, speechless, then leaned forward and kissed her lightly. Shaking his head, he marveled, "What happened to the girl who almost took my head off last time I tried that?"

Frankie moved away from him to look out the window. The yellow lanterns that dotted the night glowed like fireflies, and she watched as a young man and woman walked along the plank walk, holding hands.

She turned back to face Tyler, a brightness in her eyes and a look of expectancy on her lips as she said, "I didn't tell you all that happened at Shiloh. Sit down, and let me tell you the best thing of all!"

Tyler sat down, and for the next fifteen minutes Frankie told him of her new discovery — how she'd found a new peace and freedom and joy. She spoke simply, with no trace of the slight pride that new converts sometimes manifest. When she spoke of Jesus, he noticed it was with the same sort of happiness and contentment she might have used in talking about any dear friend.

She smiled at him now. "Ever since that moment, I've been . . . oh, I don't know how to say it." She looked down at her hands, thinking how best to explain. Finally she shook her head. "It can't be said in words, I guess. But all my life I've felt alone and cut off, somehow. Now I feel like I'm — complete."

Tyler considered her, his broad face filled with something like envy. He'd seen this in his parents and in the Steeles enough to know that it was real. "But . . . what does becoming a Christian have to do with kissing?"

Frankie flushed. "I . . . think all my life, Tyler, I've been trying to be something I wasn't. I told you how my father wanted boys and never had them, except for one son who wasn't what he wanted? Well, I guess I tried to be the boy he really wanted. And I guess I became afraid to let anyone in, to trust anyone to see who I really am. Especially any man." Her face clouded for a moment. "Seemed like anytime I tried to care about a man, or to let them know how I was feeling, deep inside . . . I just got hurt. But now" — she looked at him, and the light in her eyes was wonderful — "since I met the Lord, I don't feel the same." She thought about it, then said, "Marianne helped me a lot with it. She says —"

When she broke off, Tyler demanded, "What did she say?"

"Oh, it was nothing." Frankie flushed and

then smiled shyly. "She just said that the first time she saw me, she knew there was a — a beautiful woman inside, trying to get out."

"Well, she was right!" Tyler said and reached for her, his eyes bright.

Frankie put her hands out, laughing. "None of that now, Tyler Rocklin! I still need time to get used to this change in me, and you're just going to have to behave yourself until I do." She picked up his cane, handed it to him, then pushed him toward the door. "Now where will I contact you in Richmond?"

He allowed her to hustle him out, turning to give her a grin. "Look for me at a little hotel named the Arlington. One of the agents said nobody would be paying much attention to it. Pretty bad place, I guess, but you can send for me there. I'll still be James Miller."

"I'll get word to you as soon as I have something, Tyler. Now you go on —"

He paused and took her hand for a moment, then lifted it to his lips. He pressed a gentle kiss against it, then closed her fingers around the warm spot he'd left in her palm. His eyes twinkled at her as he said, "There! You can just keep that safe until you let me give you a real one." His smile grew serious then, and he added, "And you can keep yourself safe, too." With that, he was on his way.

She stood for a moment, a thoughtful look on her face, then sighed. She realized that she had allowed Tyler to think that she was more interested in him than was the case. *He's such a fine man,* she thought. *But there won't ever be anything between us but friendship. I'll have to be careful . . . no more kisses. And somehow I'll have to make sure he knows what my real feelings are. It would be terrible to hurt him!*

Frankie closed the door slowly, then walked to the mirror and stared at her face. She pulled off her vest, turned sideways, and fluffed out her curly hair. Then she suddenly laughed at herself, saying aloud, "You're just a farm girl, at best, Frankie Aimes! Put on all the dresses you like; you're still rough cut and more tomboy than girl." She suddenly thought of Luci De-Spain's delicate beauty, then looked at the reflection of her own rough hands and strong limbs — and for no reason that she could discern, a heaviness came over her. "You may be a woman," she said, meeting the eyes of her reflection, "but you'll never be a beauty." She turned from the mirror in disgust.

Later, after she had put on her nightshirt and was in bed, reading, she happened on a scripture that seemed to leap out at her, as many of them had been doing lately. She read it aloud slowly: " 'Behold, thou art fair, my love; behold, thou art fair; thou hast doves' eyes.' "

The words were from a book in the Bible she'd never read before: Song of Solomon. *What a strange thing to say in the Bible!* she thought as she read the next few verses.

Behold, thou art fair, my beloved, yea, pleasant: also our bed is green. . . . I am the rose of Sharon, and the lily of the valleys.

"Oh, that's nice!" she whispered, and then she read the next line and could not believe what she was reading:

As the lily among thorns, so is my love among the daughters.

Frankie blinked, and her hands trembled so that she could not see the print. *"As the lily among thorns . . . ,"* she thought. *Not one of the thorns, like I've always thought I was, but a lily among thorns!* She had no idea what the theological meaning was, but the words charmed her: *As the lily among thorns . . . the rose of Sharon . . . thou art fair.*

For a long time she read, confused but entranced by the rich imagery of the language. It was like nothing she'd ever read, and the sensuous quality of some of the lines brought a flush to her cheeks.

Why, it's like a love letter! she thought. Many of the passages spoke of physical love, while others seemed to be more about spiritual love. She read avidly, and remembering how Marianne had instructed her to ask God to help her understand His Word, she did just that.

Finally her eyes grew tired, and she read one final passage from chapter 5. It seemed to be a question asked by a group of young women.

What is thy beloved more than another beloved, O thou fairest among women? what is thy beloved more than another beloved, that thou dost so charge us?

Frankie thought about the question, wondering who the beloved of the young woman was. Then she read the young woman's answer to the question.

My beloved is white and ruddy, the chiefest among ten thousand.

His head is as the most fine gold, his locks are bushy, and black as a raven.

His eyes are as the eyes of doves by the rivers of waters, washed with milk, and fitly set.

His cheeks are as a bed of spices, as sweet flowers: his lips like lilies, dropping sweet smelling myrrh.

His hands are as gold rings set with the beryl: his belly is as bright ivory overlaid with sapphires.

His legs are as pillars of marble, set upon sockets of fine gold: his countenance is as Lebanon, excellent as the cedars.

Frankie was caught up in the description. Though she wasn't at all certain of the meaning, she was filled with wonder at the magnificence of the language. Suddenly the image of a strong face flitted through her mind. Quickly she shut her eyes and tried to force it away . . . but it remained there, blue eyes glowing warmly. She started to close the Bible, but before she did, her eyes fell on the last verse: "His mouth is most sweet: yea, he is altogether lovely. This is my beloved, and this is my friend, O daughters of Jerusalem!"

Abruptly she shut the Bible and blew out the lamp. But even as she lay in the bed with her eyes shut tight, the face she'd seen lingered . . . and she seemed to hear a voice she knew well, saying softly, "Behold, you are fair, my love."

CHAPTER 21
NO MERCY

As McClellan probed forward with his army of more than one hundred thousand men, every Southern eye was turned toward the blue-clad host. Clay Rocklin and his two sons, Lowell and Dent, returned to their unit, the Richmond Grays. There they were placed in the first of the three lines of troops that ringed Richmond. General Joseph Johnston and President Davis for once agreed on tactics, and they bled the other areas dry, shifting every available man to the Richmond theater.

The entire country was rampant with rumors, and at Gracefield, the Rocklins were more on edge than most. The men had left with their regiment; and Paul and Frankie were gone, as well, having been given new assignments by President Davis — assignments that sent them ever closer to the front lines. As though that wasn't enough to worry about, another problem had grown so severe that neither Thomas nor Susanna knew what to do.

Ever since Ellen had been sentenced to a wheelchair, she had grown more and more acrimonious and difficult. She demanded attention, flying into fits of weeping when she didn't get her way or fits of rage when she was crossed. During Clay's leave, she had done all she could to make life terrible for him. After he returned to the front, she poured out her bitterness on anyone who had the misfortune to come near her.

The slaves dreaded her, for she cursed them and even struck them when they came within reach. But they had the advantage of living in their cabins in the slave quarters rather than in the Big House. In that place, there was no escape from the woman's mindless rages.

David, Denton's twin brother, was far more easygoing than his twin and could put up with Ellen's impossible demands with a patience that astonished Thomas, David's grandfather. One day, when Ellen had cursed David and struck at him wildly, he merely said, "Mother, I'll take you for a ride after a while."

Later, when David had come to sit with his grandfather in the grape arbor, Thomas said, "David, Dent would have gone crazy if he'd had to put up with your mother. Yet you never seem to lose your temper with her."

David considered the remark, then said, "Mother's the most miserable person I know, Grandfather. She's cooped up in a helpless body. Seems to me that would be terrible for anyone, but it's worse for her because she has no resources, no good things to concentrate on. She doesn't like her husband or her family, but what's worse is she doesn't like herself. I think that's why she's done the things she has. She's always felt inferior, and I guess she always sought out the kind of company that matched that bad opinion she had of herself."

Thomas stared at his tall grandson, something akin to awe in his eyes. "You think deeper than the rest of us, David," he said. "Most Rocklin men shoot from the hip, usually without thinking, but you're always looking and watching and thinking about things. And you're right about your mother, but I'm afraid to think of what's going to happen if she doesn't accept her situation."

"She probably won't. If it were Grandmother, it would be one thing, because Grandmother has God. But Mother has only herself, and she hates herself. I figure that's why she's always screaming at everyone. She hates what she's been, and she's helpless to do anything about it. So when she screams at me or hits me, I know it's all really meant for herself. And if it helps her to feel better for a while, well, I can handle it." He lowered his voice, casting a look at Rena, who was in the yard playing with Buck, her huge, formidable deerhound. "Mother is the type who could take her own life, you know."

Thomas started, then, after a moment, nodded slowly. "Yes, I think she could. Her mind's getting worse, isn't it?"

"Every day she slips a little." David's face grew sad. "If she doesn't find peace, she'll lose her mind completely, I'm afraid."

"She was happy for a while after you fixed the buggy for her." The buggy had been Ellen's one diversion. David had taken an old rig and had a carpenter work on it, fixing it so that Ellen could be placed into it. Then David had found an old horse incapable of more than a fast walk to hitch to it, and given the rig to Ellen. It took a strong man to pick her up from her chair and place her in the cut-down seat, but once there, she could take short drives alone.

"Yes, but it didn't last long, did it? Now Mother says the rides just remind her of all she's lost."

As the two sat there talking quietly, Ellen was in her room. Located on the first floor, the room had been the master bedroom, used by Thomas and Susanna until Ellen's accident. When they had given it up and moved upstairs, Ellen had not so much as said a word of thanks. She simply complained constantly about things she didn't like about the room. Now she wheeled herself to the window and glared balefully at the two men and Rena.

"They're talking about me . . . I know them!" she muttered angrily. For a short time she watched, then had to move, to do something. David's analysis — *"She has no resources"* — had been highly accurate. Ellen had never been a reader. If she had loved books as her daughter, Rena, did, she might have been able to use them to fight off the terrible boredom that crushed her. Nor did she sew or quilt or do any of the fine needlework that most Southern women took pride in. She had no interest in the plantation, either. Gracefield was a source of income to her, a place where she could go when she got tired of Richmond society. But she knew nothing about the operation of the place — and could not have cared less that this was the case.

This, then, was the root of the problem:

Ellen Rocklin had nothing to do. If Susanna had been put in the wheelchair, she would have run Gracefield from it. She would have been busy with her family, her home, her Bible, her church — being confined to a wheelchair would have been an irritation, but no more than that. But Ellen was basically an empty woman who had filled that emptiness with the wrong things — men and alcohol — and now that those fillers were no longer available, the days became a torment. She roamed the house and the grounds, restless as a caged animal, ready to strike at anyone who came close to her.

Turning from the window, she shoved herself across the room and pulled open a drawer in the cherry dresser. The drawer was stuffed with papers and mementos, which she yanked out, scattering them over the floor. Rummaging through the drawer, she found a single piece of gray paper with a few words scrawled in a rough hand: *Will meet you Wednesday in the arbor at midnight. Don't have nobody with you!!*

There was no signature, and Ellen stared at it fixedly, then tore the paper to shreds and tossed the fragments into the drawer. Wheeling around, she left the room and, passing one of the maids, snapped waspishly, "Bessie! Go clean up my room! It looks like a pigsty!"

She spent the day moving over the grounds on the brick paths, going to the kitchen to complain about the food. Dinner passed, then supper, and the house grew quiet as the family went to bed about nine o'clock. Ellen's nerves grew tighter as she waited impatiently for midnight. At eleven thirty she left her room, moving across the pine floor slowly. The family bedrooms were all upstairs, so there was little danger of waking anyone. However, sometimes the house servants were on the lower floor. Of course, they usually were in bed by now.

That seemed to be the case, for Ellen saw no one as she carefully opened the kitchen door and wheeled herself outside. She left the house and wheeled herself as quietly as possible toward the scuppernong arbor. The wheels of her chair clattered on the brick, and once she stopped, holding her breath, thinking that she had heard something. But as she listened, the only sounds around her were the chirping of crickets and the hoarse cry of a bullfrog from the pond.

Though the arbor was next to the house, no one could see inside the thick covering of vines, nor could they hear a conversation. It was for this reason that she had sent a message to Clyde Donner to meet her at this spot. She pulled inside the arbor, stopped, and waited.

Thoughts ran through her mind, sometimes flashing and sharp, sometimes random and without logical pattern. She was aware that she was not thinking in normal patterns and, in rare moments of lucidity, feared she was losing her mind. But this was not a lucid moment. Rather, as she sat in the warm darkness, she thought of Melora Yancy — and hatred washed over her like a red tide. There had been a time when she had believed Clay and Melora had done nothing wrong, but lately a fixation had come to her. . . . She'd been having dreams in which Clay left her and went to the younger woman.

Of course, Ellen no longer felt any love for her husband — if, indeed, she ever had. She had known when they were married that young Clay was in love with Melanie Benton, who was now married to Gideon, Clay's cousin. Ellen knew Clay had married her only because she had tricked him into it, yet she laid the blame for the unhappiness of her marriage at Melanie's feet. The years had passed, and Clay had long since resolved his feelings for Melanie . . . but now there was Melora. And when Ellen thought back to the past, the acid of old memories bringing aching bitterness, she often could not distinguish between Melanie's face and Melora's. In her mind, they had become one. And all of her hatred was focused on that mixed image of the two women she believed wanted to steal her husband from her.

Ellen shivered. She knew time had become vague and indistinct to her, that she often wandered in her mind between the past and the present — and it frightened her greatly. Sometimes she wept in terror, tears running down her cheeks, and wondered how she had come to such a terrible fate. Now, though, as she sat there in the darkness, there were no tears, for the thought of Clay and Melora filled her poor twisted soul, leaving room for nothing but a cold fury.

The sound of a horse coming down the road startled her from her bitter thoughts. The animal stopped, and there was a long silence; then she heard faint footfalls and a hoarse whisper. "Anybody here?"

"Come into the arbor, Clyde," Ellen whispered urgently. A sense of exultation came to her. He was here! Now she could do it! "Don't worry; everybody's in bed. Come closer so I can see you."

She peered at the short, stubby figure of the man who advanced. He wore a black hat low on his forehead, but the moonlight was bright enough for her to recognize him. Donner was a gambler who was not good at his trade and so had turned to robbery — and worse — to offset his losses. He had a lantern jaw and a pair of smallish blue eyes. Ellen had known him for a long time — for a brief time they had even been lovers — then Donner had been sent to jail for theft. This was the first she had seen him since he had gotten out of prison.

A crafty man, Donner looked around, alert as any animal. "Don't like to come like this, Ellen," he said. "What you want?" He holstered a revolver he'd been holding at the ready and came closer. "You must be hard up to send for me!"

Ellen had always been able to handle Donner by playing on his addiction to lust, but that was before her accident. Now she knew her only tool was money. She narrowed her eyes and spoke softly. "Clyde, I want somebody hurt — bad."

Donner's pale eyes glinted with a sly expression. "That mean you want 'em dead?"

"Yes!" Ellen almost choked on the word, then forced herself to smile. "You're a sharp fellow. I always said that."

"No, you always said I wasn't very bright,"

Donner answered. "Who you want shot? Your husband?"

Ellen's head snapped back. "Clay? Of course not!"

Donner shrugged, his mouth holding a slack smile. "When a woman loses her man, she usually wants him killed."

"Who says I've lost him?" Ellen's eyes glinted with a wild expression, and she grasped the arms of her chair, her back arching in a vain effort to rise.

"Well, you ain't no good to him no more, are you? Man wants a good, strong woman, not a cripple."

Blinding lights seemed to go off inside Ellen's head, and a sharp metallic taste came to her mouth. What went through her mind were not thoughts — they were not orderly enough for that — but waves of hatred so strong they seemed to scald the inside of her skull. But for all that, she still retained enough craftiness not to lash out at Donner. He was her only hope of getting at Melora, and she would take no chances on alienating him. She waited until the storm inside her head subsided, then said, "That's none of your business, Clyde. Clay's a man, and men are weak. No, I want you to kill the woman who's trying to take him from me."

"Sure, the Yancy woman." Donner grinned when he saw Ellen flinch, then shrugged his heavy shoulders. "No secret 'bout that, I reckon. Especially as you told it all over Richmond 'fore you got shot."

Ellen closed her lips firmly for a moment, then took a deep breath. "All right, it's her. I'll give you two hundred dollars to kill her."

"Two hundred dollars?" Donner gave her an insulted look, then turned to go. When she called out to him, he stopped and faced her impatiently. "In the first place, I ain't killin' no woman. I got my standards, Ellen, and unless I *got* to do it, I ain't shootin' no female! And in the second place, even if I was to do the job, it'd cost a lot more than two hundred dollars!"

"I'll give you more!" Ellen whispered. "Five hundred!"

"You ain't *got* five hundred," Donner snapped. "This place is having a hard time like all the other cotton plantations. They're all mortgaged to the hilt. You couldn't raise five hundred dollars hard money to save your life! And Rocklin ain't lettin' you handle no money, is he, now?" Donner sneered at the woman, enjoying himself. Watching her squirm was little enough revenge for the many times she had taunted and humiliated him — and for the way she'd refused to see him after he got out of prison.

He grinned at her, sharklike in the pale moonlight. "Look, honey, you had your good times; now let that husband of yours have his! So long!" And then he was gone, having disappeared into the darkness.

Ellen sat there, struck dumb with the rebuff. For a long time she stayed in the arbor, her mind rolling with images that flashed and seemed to go on endlessly. Finally she lifted her head and blinked several times. "I don't need you, Clyde! I don't need anybody!" she whispered.

Her journey back into the house was uneventful, but instead of turning to go to her room, she turned the opposite direction. The double doors that led into the study gave her a problem, but she managed to open them. Moonlight fell through the tall windows on the east of the room, and she slowly rolled to the huge rolltop desk where Thomas Rocklin did his work. Carefully she opened a lower drawer, reached down, and pulled out the pistol that lay inside. She put the gun in her lap, fingering it almost lovingly, then closed the drawer and left the room.

When she was safely inside her bedroom, she moved to turn up the lamp on the table, then examined the weapon. It was not a large gun — much smaller than the .44 that Clay kept. Thomas had bought it for use against prowlers and had tried to teach Susanna to use it, but to no avail. "I'll trust the good Lord and not a pistol!" Susanna had said firmly.

Ellen knew little about guns, but she could see that the chambers in the cylinder were loaded. She pulled the hammer back and spun the cylinder as she had seen Thomas do, then put both hands on the handle and aimed the gun at a picture of Jefferson Davis on the wall. She squeezed the trigger very slightly, felt it move, and released it at once.

A strange smile came to her lips, and she rolled her chair to the dresser. The right drawer, which she kept locked, was stuffed with old letters. Once when she had raged at the servants, accusing them of spying on her and picking at her things, David had installed the lock himself, removing it from an old chest in the attic. She carefully unlocked the drawer, moved the letters to the front, then put the gun down and covered it with the letters. Locking the drawer, she moved to the table and picked up a piece of paper and a goose-quill pen. Dipping the pen into the inkwell, she began to write slowly:

Miss Yancy,

You will be shocked to receive this letter from me, I'm sure. We have not been friends, of course. In fact, I must confess that I have hated you for years. Undoubtedly you have heard of my misfortune. I am confined to a wheelchair, and will be for the rest of my life. When one is in this condition, there is a lot of time to think, and I have been thinking about my husband a great deal.

He assures me that there is nothing more than friendship between you two. I have found that hard to believe, but I would like to trust Clay. He is all I have left now, and if I could really know that he is faithful, I could bear my infirmity much better.

I need to hear the truth from you. My mind is not clear on many things, but you are, from what others tell me, an honest woman. If I could only talk to you, I'm sure I could look into your eyes and see the truth! It would mean so much to me.

I do not think it would be wise for you to come to Gracefield. And I can't come to your house. I am able, however, to drive a buggy. I have no right to ask this, and you will probably refuse, but if I drove out toward your place some afternoon, could you give me just a few minutes? I am sending this letter by a trusted slave, one who will tell nothing. If you would see me, give him the message, and I will be on the old plank road by the deserted sawmill at dusk tomorrow. You know the spot. It is close to Gracefield and far from your home, I am afraid, but I cannot make long journeys. Just tell the slave that the answer is yes if you will come, and please burn this letter!

Please come!
Ellen Rocklin

When she had signed her name, she sprinkled fine sand over the letter, sifted it, then dropped the sand into a wastebasket. She put the letter into an envelope, heated a small cylinder of red wax, and carefully sealed the flap. Then she sat back in her chair, trembling.

It was done.

She went to bed, managing the transfer from chair to bed with difficulty, then waited for sleep. *I'll give Highboy ten dollars to take the letter, and I'll tell him he'll be sold down the river if he ever tells anyone about it.*

The sun looked weak and tired as it dropped over the top of the hill, pale and obscure from its labor of heating the earth — or so it seemed to Melora as she rode along the abandoned plank road. She had thought of little else but Ellen Rocklin's letter since receiving it. She had been startled when a tall black man had stepped out from behind a tree as she was on her way to the hog pen.

"Miz Rocklin, she said give you dis and not let nobody see me," he had said.

Melora had read the letter quickly and knew that she had no choice. "Tell Mrs. Rocklin the answer is yes," she said. The tall slave had nodded, then disappeared at once into the woods.

Over and over Melora had read the letter but had said nothing to her father. Today, acting as casual as she could manage, she had said, "I'm going to the store, Pa. I'll be a little late coming back, so don't worry."

Buford was accustomed to Melora's wanderings and said only, "Bring back some blackstrap, daughter. We ate the last yesterday."

Dressed in men's overalls so that she could ride astride, Melora had made it a point to go to Hardee's Store and pick up some blackstrap. Then she had headed north. Now as her mare trotted toward the spot Ellen had named, Melora thought of the strangeness of what she was doing. In the last few months, she and Rena had grown close. The young girl had often shared facts about her mother with Melora, and she well knew that Ellen was not only physically infirm but failing in her mind.

She's a pitiful thing, Melora thought as she turned off the main road. For the rest of the journey, she tried to think of some way to speak to Ellen so that her innocence — and Clay's — would be evident.

The old plank road had once been used for passage to a sawmill, but the mill had been abandoned for years, so only hunters and fishermen used it any longer. The surrounding terrain was rough, broken by deep little valleys and sharply rising ridges. The road snaked around the high places, skirting abrupt drop-offs, and as Melora rounded a sharp bend, she saw in the fading light a woman seated in a small buggy. The rig was on a narrow road — so narrow that there was only room enough for the buggy. To the left was the steep wall of a bluff. To the right, a sharp drop-off. It would take careful driving to thread the dangerous spot.

As Melora rode up, she was greeted at once.

"So you did come!" A smile appeared on Ellen's lips.

"I told your slave I'd be here." Melora slipped off the horse and dropped the reins. The horse was trained to stand and made no move as Melora went to stand beneath Ellen.

"I'm glad you asked me to come, Mrs. Rocklin," Melora said quietly. "I've wanted to talk to you for a long time."

"And I've wanted to see you, too." Ellen's smile appeared to be fixed on her lips. She had slept not at all since receiving Melora's reply, and now she had a headache, fierce and raging — the kind that often came when her mind grew too active. "Did you tell anyone you were coming to meet me?"

"No. I didn't think it was necessary."

"Ah, good! Well now, tell me about you and Clay." The pain in Ellen's head came sharply, causing her eyes to blink, but her pleasure at finding the woman before her made her endure it. "Tell me there's nothing between you!"

"We have been good friends for many years," Melora began, trying to speak as clearly as she could. She was troubled by the expression on Ellen's face, the fixed

450

smile and the wide-staring eyes with the bright glitter. However, she spoke clearly and without hurry. She felt a great pity for Ellen, knowing that the woman had nothing to sustain her in her great trial. She thought of Rena and Clay and prayed that somehow her words would be able to persuade Ellen that she had nothing to be jealous about.

Finally, when she had spoken as well as she could, she concluded, "Your husband is an honorable man, Mrs. Rocklin. Even if I wanted to take him, he'd never leave you."

Ellen had listened, saying nothing. Now she nodded and whispered, "You're very beautiful, Melanie. . . . You always were."

Startled, Melora looked at the woman. "I'm Melora, Mrs. Rocklin."

And then Ellen laughed, a wild, crazy laugh that seemed to resound around them.

She's insane! Melora thought with a jolt.

"Oh, you don't need to lie, Melanie," Ellen said with a nod. And then she lifted the revolver, which she'd been holding on her lap. She smiled at the look of shock on the young woman's face. "I've wanted to kill you for years," she said almost pleasantly. "Ever since you took Clay away from me."

Melora knew she was in terrible danger but allowed no fear to show in her face. "Mrs. Rocklin, you're not well. Put the gun

451

down. . . . I'll take you home."

"Take me home? Oh, you're clever! And they'll lock me up in the crazy house in Richmond?" Again the wild laugh, and then the smile faded and the glitter in Ellen Rocklin's eyes grew brilliant as she began to scream. "You'll never have him! He's mine, do you hear! You can't take him — !"

She lifted the revolver and fired.

Melora felt a burning sensation on the left side of her neck as the bullet grazed her, but had no time to do more than throw up her hand in a futile gesture. Ellen's horse, startled by the sudden explosion, suddenly reared, which threw the crippled woman back against the seat. As she fell, she pulled the trigger again, but this time the bullet struck the horse a raking blow on the side of her rump. Instantly the mare went wild, uttering a shrill scream and lunging forward, blind with fear.

The buggy flew into the rocky side of the bluff and then careened wildly toward the other side of the road. Melora spun around in time to see the buggy wheels drop off the sheer edge and hear Ellen's scream: "Oh my God! No!" Then the buggy flipped over, and Melora watched with horror as Ellen was thrown from the buggy into the sharp outcroppings of stone. She hit on her neck and shoulders and then went rolling down the bluff, legs flopping loosely.

Melora ran to the edge, scrambled over the side, and plunged down the jagged edges until she came to the limp body. Ellen was lying on her face, motionless. When Melora rolled her over, she saw no terrible wounds. Ellen's face was bruised, and blood oozed from a slight cut on her left temple, and she was unconscious. Melora checked to be sure the woman was breathing, then gently laid her back down and climbed up the slope. The buggy was gone, pulled away from the edge and dragged around the bend by the crazed mare, but Melora's horse was standing nearby, his eyes fixed on her.

Got to get help! I can't carry Ellen back up the slope!

Melora started to run toward her horse, then spotted the revolver lying near the edge of the cliff. She picked it up, stuck it in the pocket of her overalls, then mounted quickly and drove the roan at a hard run. She kept the pace up until she arrived at the road that led to Gracefield. By the time she pulled up in front of the mansion, the horse was white with lather. Melora fell off the mare, stumbled, and saw David come running out of the house.

"Melora!" he cried out, coming to her at

once. "What happened?" His eyes widened when he saw the blood on her neck, which had soaked into the neckline of her dress. "You're bleeding!" he said in concern.

Melora shook her head. "It's just a scratch," she gasped. "But your mother . . . sh–she's had a terrible accident!"

Thomas and Susanna had come out of the house, and they listened with grim expressions as Melora went on. "She was on the plank road. . . . She asked me to meet her there." She hesitated slightly, then said hurriedly, "The buggy went off a cliff. I'm afraid she's badly hurt."

At once David wheeled and began yelling orders. "Highboy! Hitch up the light wagon! Lucy, bring some blankets from the house! And tell Chester to ride like the devil to get Doc Slavins!"

Melora stood there, a tragic light in her eyes, and although no one asked, she knew she had to share what had happened. Susanna ordered the slaves to bring water and salve for Melora's neck as Melora briefly told David and his grandparents about the note and the meeting — not mentioning the gun until David had run to ready a buggy.

Thomas watched grimly as Susanna quickly cleaned and bandaged the place where Ellen's bullet had grazed Melora's neck. Melora told them the rest of the story as quickly as she could, then said, "I'll go back with David. I don't think anyone except you two needs to know that she tried to shoot me." She pulled the gun out of her pocket and handed it to Thomas. "She didn't know what she was doing."

Thomas looked at the weapon. "She must have taken it from my desk." He shook his head. "But you're right, my dear. Nothing to be gained by telling Clay or any of the children."

Ten minutes later Melora was on the seat of the wagon, with David beside her and two strong field hands following on mules. "She wanted to talk to me alone, David. She was so determined! The . . . horse bolted, and when the buggy went over, she was thrown clear."

David gave the young woman a strange look, and she knew that he was not sure of her story. But he did say, "She's a very confused woman, Melora. And she's had a lot of trouble."

Ellen was alive when the men brought her back up the slope. Melora rode in the back with her, cradling the injured woman's head while David drove as carefully as he could over the rough road. When they got back to the house, all was ready, and Ellen was put in her own bed. She remained unconscious through it all, even when Dr. Slavins came and examined her.

"How is she, Doctor?" David asked when Slavins came out into the hall.

"I can't say. She's in some sort of coma." He studied David's face and decided to add, "I'm afraid she's in poor shape, David. Her condition was bad enough before this incident. And . . . she may never wake up. But on the other hand, we mustn't give up hope."

David dropped his head, unable to respond. After a few moments of silence, he lifted his eyes. "Thank you, Doctor. I'll send for Dad right away."

"Might be best. And have Lowell and Dent come, too, if possible."

Melora would not stay — she feared it would distress Ellen greatly should she awaken and find her there — so Thomas sent her home in a carriage. As she left, he said painfully, "You're a generous woman, Miss Yancy. God bless you for what you tried to do."

Melora could do no more than nod. All the way home she thought about the poor broken woman who lay like a stone in the deep feather bed at Gracefield . . . and could only cry out silently, *Oh God! Help her!*

CHAPTER 22
BEFORE THE BATTLE

General George McClellan glared across the table at the short form of Allan Pinkerton, anger in his stern eyes.

"You've failed in your assignment, Mr. Pinkerton," McClellan stated bluntly. "You inform me that the rebels have over 150,000 troops, but you can't tell me *where* they are. I can't blindly commit this army to a battle!"

Allan Pinkerton clamped down his lips on the short cigar between his teeth. His nerves were on edge, but he kept them under firm control. "My agents are doing their best, General, but two things are against them. First, the security in Rebel territory around Richmond is very tight — so tight that I've lost four of my most trusted men, all hanged as spies. Second, the troops are being shifted around so fast that information that was good yesterday is worthless today."

McClellan took a deep breath, then shook his head. "I know it's difficult, but I've *got* to have at least a general idea of where Johnston's troops are concentrated. Can't you go yourself?"

"Yes, I intend to. Our best agents haven't reported in. I'm going to go find them myself. They're right on the inside, General, and if they haven't been caught, they should have all we need to know. I'll leave now, and if things go well, I should be back within three days with the information you need to make the attack."

"Make it as fast as you can, Mr. Pinkerton," McClellan said, a worried look on his drawn face. "I've got my forces split in two parts by the Chickahominy River, one corps on the north bank, the other four to the south. If the Rebels attack before I can pull the army together, we'll be in serious trouble."

He said a brief good-bye to Pinkerton, then returned to a study of his map. He was a careful, patient man and knew how to train and move an army, but something had gone wrong with his plan. Three things, in fact.

First, McDowell's corps, which had been promised to him, had been kept in Washington. Stonewall Jackson's spectacular success in the Valley, where he had defeated three Federal armies, had so alarmed Lincoln that he had kept McDowell's troops to protect the capital. And although McClellan didn't know it, Jackson's small army was even now back at Richmond under Lee's command.

The second disadvantage that McClellan faced was the fact that General Joseph Johnston had been wounded at the Battle of Fair Oaks, and General Robert E. Lee was now in command of the army. If McClellan had known what this actually meant, he would have gone back to Washington at once, for Lee was the most aggressive general in the war, on either side. Johnston was great at retreat, but Lee had the fighting instinct that only a few great generals have had. That, combined with the man's knowledge of tactics, made him the most dangerous opponent the North ever faced.

The third obstacle was the weather. The rains had come with a vengeance, taking out bridges, flooding the bottomlands, and sweeping away the corduroy roads. The entire country was a bog, and the two parts of McClellan's armies were helplessly separated by a sea of mud. The longer he stared at the map, the more worried the general grew. Finally he said aloud, "If Pinkerton doesn't get me the position of the Rebel Army, we will be defeated!"

■ ■ ■ ■

Even as General McClellan was studying his maps and trying desperately to make some sort of a plan, General Robert E. Lee was meeting with his staff with much the same intention. The difference was that Lee had accurate information on the position of the Union army. Initially he had gotten tips from farmers who had ridden in daily to give information about troop movements. He had followed this up by sending General Jeb Stuart on a scouting mission. Stuart, a brigadier at twenty-nine, was square-built, of average height, and had china blue eyes, a bushy cinnamon beard, and flamboyant tastes in clothing. Generally, he wore thigh-high boots, a yellow sash, elbow-length gauntlets, a red-lined cape, and a soft hat with the brim pinned up on one side by a gold star supporting a foot-long ostrich plume. In addition, he had a strong thirst for exploits.

When Lee ordered Stuart to scout the location of the Federals, the flashy general had taken his twelve hundred cavalrymen and, in three days, had ridden around McClellan's entire Federal Army. He had returned to a hero's reception, having lost only one man — and having brought back 170 prisoners, along with three hundred horses and mules. But more important than prisoners or mules was the information Stuart brought back, which pinpointed McClellan's army. He drew the enemy's locations out on a map, then handed it to General Lee, saying, "There it is, sir, Little Mac and his Bluebellies!"

Lee studied the map carefully, knowing that he would have to act soon. There was no way he could use his small force of fewer than eighty thousand men to drive one hundred thousand well-entrenched soldiers away from Richmond. He had but two choices: to retreat, thus abandoning Richmond, or to strike before his opponent got rolling. But he saw at once that he would have to take a tremendous gamble: He would have to pull most of his army away from the larger Union corps, leaving only a small force south of the Chickahominy to stand against the Federals. Then he would strike Major General Fitz John Porter's corps on the flank beyond the Chickahominy. This would enable him to seize McClellan's base at the White House. Once the Union commander was cut off from his supplies, he would be obliged to come out and fight on the ground of Lee's choosing.

So it was that at almost the same moment as McClellan was looking at his maps, General Robert E. Lee was presenting his own map to four men who would fight the battle. All four were young men, though they disguised the fact with beards. James Longstreet was the oldest at forty-one; Ambrose Powell (A. P.) Hill, at thirty-six, was the youngest. Daniel Harvey (D. H.) Hill was forty, and Stonewall Jackson thirty-eight. Twenty or so years earlier, all had attended West Point.

Now they gathered around a table, bending over to study the map, listening as Lee explained what had to be done. "Here is the plan, gentlemen," Lee said as he traced the part each would play in the battle:

"As you can see, I am leaving only Generals Magruder and Huger to hold McClellan's main force in place. General Jackson, you will bring your men down from the north, keeping General Stuart's cavalry on your left flank. The rest of you will cross the Chickahominy in sequence: General A. P. Hill first, then General D. H. Hill, and then you, General Longstreet. You will sweep the left bank of the river, clearing Porter's troops as far as New Bridge, where you will cross the river and strike the main Federal force from the rear."

The council broke up about nightfall, and the four generals went to their headquarters. Each of them had about the same thought: *If we can push Porter out of the way and hit McClellan from the rear, the Federals will run like rabbits for Washington — just as they did at Bull Run!*

Thus two mighty armies faced each other, each well aware that the next few days might bring an end to the Civil War. If McClellan could use his superior force to overwhelm Robert E. Lee's thin gray line and take Richmond, the South would be lost. But if Lee's plan worked and the armies of the North were whipped as they had been at Bull Run, McClellan would take them back to Washington — and the powerful Peace Party might well be able to force the president and Congress to simply let the South go its own way.

An air of destiny hovered over the rain-soaked fields outside of Richmond. Fate was about to move, to turn the course of the nation. The events of the next few days would determine the course of what some called the "War of Secession" and others called the "War of the Rebellion."

While mighty hosts were gathering for the onslaught of battle and the nation was holding its breath over the future of the entire country, life went on pretty much as always in the lives of common people. War and destiny, powerful as they might be, did not set aside everyday living.

War, with all its banners flying, might shake the earth with a mighty thunder of guns, but it did not feed the pigs and chickens. The earth still had to be broken for planting; weeds still waited to be chopped out of the rows of cotton. Work went on, and love went on. Robert E. Lee and George McClellan might grow weary studying maps, but to Tabitha, the slave woman bringing her first baby into the world in a small cabin at Gracefield, all the armies meant nothing. Her world was no larger than the pain that tore her apart as she lay writhing on the rope bed, aided by Susanna Rocklin and one of the black midwives.

Likewise, the blacksmith, Box, paid no heed to the wild rumors that the Yankees might come across the fields of Gracefield at any moment. At the age of seventy-one, he cared little for such things. Let the Yankees free black people; he would keep right on making horseshoes for Thomas Rocklin. Ten thousand men might die that day in battle, but for Box, that was not reality. For him, reality was the ten-pound sledge he lifted, and the shoe he was making for the mare, and the hot sparks that flew as he dropped the hammer against the iron. The mare was real; the horseshoe was tangible. And so he beat the red-hot metal skillfully, his world no larger than the curving piece of iron on the anvil.

As for those who lived inside the Big House at Gracefield, they found themselves feeling strangely out of place. They had grown up inside the big mansion, but childhood days seemed eons away now — memories that slipped in from time to time, flashing images of activities and gatherings. Memories summoned on this day by Ellen Rocklin, though she was silent and still in her bed.

By some miracle, despite the impending battle, Clay, Denton, and Lowell had all managed to get emergency leave. Colonel James Benton, who was Melanie's father, Gideon Rocklin's father-in-law, and Ellen Rocklin's uncle, had received the message about Ellen from David. Benton had then called Lieutenant Dent Rocklin into his tent at once, saying, "Denton, your mother has had an accident. I think it's serious."

Dent Rocklin's good looks had been spoiled by the slash of a saber at Bull Run.

One side of his face was as handsome as that of any man in the South, but the other side was marred by a scar that ran down his cheek, drawing one eye down in a seemingly sinister expression and marking the flesh with an angry, deep trench. But those who knew Dent Rocklin knew that his marred appearance was a poor reflection of the man, for he was good and honorable and did all he could to serve his country and his God.

Upon hearing of his mother's accident, Dent had stared at his commanding officer, listening as the older man gave what information he had. "You know we'll be fighting very soon," Benton said, compassion in his eyes. "But I think we have a few days, perhaps a week. Get your father and Lowell and go home. I've made out passes for all three of you."

Dent took the slips of paper. "Thank you, Colonel. This is handsome of you. We'll leave at once, and we'll be back as soon as . . . we find out something." He had left the tent and gone to find his father drilling some recruits. Drawing him off, he said quietly, "Mother's had an accident. You and Lowell and I are leaving as soon as I can get three horses."

The three of them had ridden their horses

almost into the ground on a flying trip to Gracefield. They had arrived at dusk and were greeted by Thomas, whose face was pale with fatigue. "Glad you all got here," he said, embracing each one.

"How is she?" Clay demanded as soon as they were in the foyer.

"Very bad. Come into the parlor and I'll tell you about it. Susanna is with her now, taking care of her needs. When she comes out, you can go in."

Thomas had explained the accident carefully, leaving out only the matter of the gun. He noted that when Melora's name was mentioned, Clay's eyes sprung wide, and the two boys showed surprise. He ended by saying, "The horse got spooked, Melora said, and Ellen lost control. She was thrown down a steep slope, and Melora rode here and got David at once. He brought Ellen home, but she hasn't come out of the coma."

At that moment Susanna came into the room. She embraced Clay at once, then her two grandsons. "You can come in now," she said quietly. She led the way, and when the men were inside the room, the three of them stared down at the woman in the bed.

"She . . . doesn't look bad," Dent whispered. "I was afraid. . . ."

When he halted his speech, Susanna spoke up. "Dr. Slavins can't find any bones broken, and she wasn't cut up much by the fall." She hesitated slightly. "What he fears is that somehow the bullet that they couldn't get out got pushed closer to the spine."

"She hasn't spoken at all?" Clay asked.

"Not a word, son. And she hasn't moved a muscle. I . . . think what Dr. Slavins fears is that she's completely paralyzed."

The three tall men stood around the bed, helplessly looking down at the wife and mother who had given none of them happiness — and yet the sight of her still, white face made each man forget the misery she had brought to him. Finally they turned and left the room, going back to the parlor. Rena came to throw herself in Clay's arms, her eyes swollen with weeping. She clung to him fiercely for a few moments, then moved away, whispering, "I'm glad you're here, Daddy!"

And so the long vigil began. Servants crept by, whispering. Meals were set out that no one wanted. Dr. Slavins came and went, unable to give them the reassurance they craved. Short conversations would start, only to quickly break off. And long silences stretched on while the family sat around, silences interrupted only when someone would rise and go outside to walk aimlessly around the grounds.

The next morning the Bristols and Franklins came, along with other friends and close neighbors. Rachel and Amy Franklin and Marianne and Claude Bristol gave what comfort they could, which was woefully little. Finally Claude said to his brother-in-law, "Thomas, we've got to go to Richmond. I hate to leave you alone at a time like this —"

"Go on, Claude," Thomas said at once. "Ellen may live for a few days or a month, or she may survive, after all. You can't wait around here all that time. Now what's going on in Richmond?"

Bristol shrugged, a cynical look coming into his face. "A fancy dress ball — if you can believe it. With the world about to fall around our ears, we're going to a dance!" He shook his head, then spoke in a lower tone. "We're only going because of Frankie. You know what happened to her at the last ball — coming out in that horrible dress and everyone laughing at her! Well, Marianne's determined to set that right. We're going to buy the girl a fine gown and get her hair all fixed, you know." He shrugged, saying, "Just between you and me, Tom, Marianne is convinced it was Luci DeSpain

470

who engineered the whole mess last time, and she's going to see to it that Frankie gets another chance if it costs every dime we've got. I swear, my wife has latched onto that girl like she's some long-lost daughter just returned to her."

Thomas nodded. "Well, women do get the strangest notions sometimes, and we sure don't do ourselves a service by fighting them. Now you go on. I'll let you know if there's any change." He said good-bye to Bristol, then went to speak with his wife. When he informed her of the Bristols' mission, he was surprised at her reaction.

"Good!" she snapped, her eyes sharp. "Paul Bristol is blind as a bat! That DeSpain girl will make him miserable!"

"Why, I didn't know you felt like that, Susanna!" Thomas stared at her, then came up with a smile. "I guess I'm pretty blind about things like that myself." He suddenly put his arm around her, and a flash of the charm that had been his as a young man appeared. "I still remember when you were eighteen at the ball in Atlanta. You were the prettiest thing I'd ever seen!" He kissed her cheek and smiled. "You still are!"

"Oh, Tom!" Tears appeared in Susanna's eyes at the rare gesture, and the two of them clung together for a moment, thinking of the days long gone.

Early one evening, Paul pulled the wagon up in front of the Spotswood Hotel and for a moment sat there, so weary he dreaded the simple task of getting to the ground. He and Frankie had not stopped working for days except to camp.

Just before they had left on this assignment, Paul had agreed to meet his parents at the hotel so his mother could help Frankie get ready for the Richmond Ball. "I'm not leaving anything to chance this time," Marianne had told her son.

Now, glancing across the seat, he saw that Frankie was sound asleep, utterly exhausted. Reaching out, he gave her shoulder a slight shake. "Wake up. It's time to go to bed."

Frankie jerked as she came out of sleep, then looked around wildly. Then she saw the hotel and gave Paul a tired smile. "I must have dozed off."

"For two hours, but I don't blame you. I'd have gone to sleep myself if I hadn't had to drive the wagon." He nodded toward the hotel. "You go on in. My parents ought to be there, but even if they've gone out, they'll have gotten a room. Better take your things."

Frankie scrambled into the interior of the

wagon, threw some clothes into her old carpetbag, then emerged and climbed to the ground. "What about you?"

"I'm going to store these plates somewhere." He scratched his whiskery cheeks. "Then I'll get a bath and a shave."

"Will we be going back to take more pictures tomorrow?"

"No, not unless the battle starts." He hesitated. "I'm supposed to take Luci to a couple of things — a dress ball and a party at the Chesnuts to start with." He kicked the brake off, looking thoughtful for a moment. Then he seemed to shake his thoughts off and smiled down at her. "Go take some rest, Frankie. You deserve it!"

Frankie watched as he drove down the street; then she turned and entered the hotel. She felt more conspicuous than usual — the Spotswood was the most elegant hotel in Richmond, and her dirty, wrinkled clothing made her a draw for every eye. Trying to ignore the stares of those around her, she walked up to the desk. "Are Mr. and Mrs. Bristol here?"

The clerk, a short man with slick black hair and a fussy manner, turned to stare at her. "Why . . . ah, yes, I believe they are. May I . . . ah, help you?"

"Which room?" Frankie demanded, too

exhausted to get angry at his condescending tone.

"Ah . . . I believe the Bristols are in 306." He looked at a card, then back at her. "Are you . . . ah, Miss Frankie Aimes?"

"Yes."

"Then you're in . . . ah . . . room 308."

Frankie took the key, stared at the clerk, muttered, "Ah . . . thank you very much," then turned and marched up the stairs. She went first to the Bristols' room, but no one answered her knock. So she went to room 308, opened the door, stepped inside — and froze in a stunned silence. She stared at the room with awe, for she'd never seen such ornate furnishings and decor! She closed the door, then moved around, touching the fine cherry furniture carefully. As she fingered the fine sheets on the bed, fatigue hit her heavily. She took off her clothes, washed her face, then put on a nightshirt and fell into the bed, going to sleep at once.

She awoke when an insistent knock came at her door. Groggy with sleep, she grabbed at the old cotton robe she sometimes wore, then went to open the door. "Oh, Marianne!" she exclaimed. "Come on in. I was asleep."

Marianne gave Frankie a hug, then said, "I wanted to let you sleep. That son of mine has worn you out!" She stood there smiling at the young woman. "We saw him a few hours ago, and he told us what a hard time the two of you have had. He was worried about you, Frankie."

"Oh, I'm all right. Just a little tired."

"Well, if you think you're tired now, wait until *I* get through with you! Taking pictures may be tiring, but it's nothing compared to shopping, I can tell you! Now first we get some hot water up here to give you a bath, and then we're off."

"What are you talking about?" Frankie asked with bewilderment, still fuzzy from lack of sleep. But Marianne just took her in hand to such an extent that she didn't really *have* to think a great deal.

Before long, maids came to the room carrying copper teakettles filled with scalding water. Frankie was ordered into the bathtub; then she was scrubbed and soaped. Next she was fluffed and powdered to within an inch of her life and practically wedged into a dress and a pair of lightweight ladies' shoes. When she finally stood, her hair brushed and combed, for Marianne's inspection, she complained, "You're treating me like a big doll!"

The older woman came to take the girl's shoulders in her hands, gripping them gently. "I haven't had a daughter to dress for a ball since Marie was very young. And I want you to be the most beautiful girl at the ball. We are going to do it, aren't we?"

Nonplussed, Frankie stared at Marianne. Then a smile lit up her face. "I read a verse in the Bible that said, 'You are fair.' It . . . it made me feel so odd! Like . . . like a woman, Marianne!"

"Good!" Marianne nodded. "Now let's go get the most beautiful girl at the ball ready to turn Richmond upside down!"

CHAPTER 23
ACT OF FORGIVENESS

Clay had been sitting beside Ellen for two hours, staring out the window at the setting sun and at the slow-moving slaves who were cutting the green grass around the huge trees. From time to time the sound of their liquid voices drifted to him. Buck, Rena's huge dog, broke into a crescendo of barking as he chased a gray squirrel up a tree. *That dog has tried to catch a million squirrels — and never caught one. You'd think he'd learn!*

Rocklin closed his eyes, which were reddened from lack of sleep, and at once began to drift off. Soft sounds came to him from the rest of the house, and that, added to the heat of the room, caused him to nod off. He sat there dozing until a slight sound inside the room brought him awake.

His eyes flew open, and a quick glance outside told him it was late, for stars dotted the dark sky. With a sigh, he looked down: Ellen's eyelids were fluttering, and her lips were moving slightly.

Clay came out of the chair, caught her limp hand, and whispered, "Ellen! Ellen! Can you hear me?"

At first there was no response — in fact, he began to wonder if she had moved at all. Then slowly her eyes came open, and he cried out again. "Ellen! It's me, Clay." He leaned closer, noting that her eyes were clear but somewhat confused. "Can you hear me, Ellen?"

He held his breath, waiting — and then her lips moved! It was only a faint movement, and he put his ear next to her lips and strained to hear. Nothing . . . and yet, *something*! Clay said, "Try to say my name if you can hear me, Ellen."

Indistinctly he heard her speak, and it seemed to him that she whispered, "Clay!"

Clay lifted his head and began to speak to her as gently and reassuringly as he could. "Ellen, you had an accident." As he spoke, he watched her eyes and was certain she was understanding him. Finally he said, "Can you move at all? Can you move these fingers?" He lifted her hand and stared at the fingers, but there was no movement that he could discern. He held on to her hand, nodded, and smiled. "Don't worry; it'll come back." He reached out and touched her face, whispering, "I won't leave you, Ellen."

He sat there for a long time, watching her closely and speaking from time to time. Though he was encouraged by her ability to communicate, her deathly pallor and dull eyes filled him with a sense of foreboding. It would not be long.

Finally he laid her hand down, saying, "I'll go get the boys —," but he paused, for her eyelids were blinking rapidly, as if she wanted to speak. He bent closer, asking, "What is it, Ellen? What can I get you?" He stood there helplessly, then said, "I'm going to name some things. When I name what you want, blink twice. Blink twice now if you understand."

Her eyelids blinked twice, and Clay said, "Do you want water? No? Food?" He named the things that came to his mind, none of which she wanted. Finally he asked, "Is it someone you want to see? Yes!" He smiled encouragingly, then began to name the family: "Denton? David? Lowell?" but none of these brought a response. Finally he shook his head, saying, "I'll go down the alphabet. When I get to the first letter of the person's name, blink twice. Now, *A, B, C . . .*" And so it went with no response until he reached *M*. She blinked twice.

"*M?* Let me see, is it Marianne? No? Well, is it Mattie?" He named everyone he could think of, but the eyes remained still. "I can't think of anyone else — let me get Mother —"

But Ellen's eyes blinked furiously, and so he stopped. "You don't want me to go? Well, let me —" Clay halted abruptly, then looked at Ellen, surprise on his face. "Is it Melora?" At once Ellen's eyes blinked, and he could only stare at her. To be sure, he said, "You want to see Melora?" Her eyes closed twice, slowly and deliberately. "All right, I'll ride and get her. I'll go tell the boys." He hesitated, then leaned over and kissed her cheek.

It was the first caress he'd given her in years, and he felt strange. When he lifted his head, he saw two tears tracing their way down her pale cheeks. Taking out his handkerchief, he wiped them away, whispering, "It'll be all right, Ellen." Then he left the room, calling as soon he was outside: "Dent! David! Lowell!" When they came, he told them rapidly what had happened, adding, "She wants to see Melora. I'm going to get her. Go in with your mother, but remember that she can't do much, just blink once for no and twice for yes. Don't let her be alone, boys."

And then he was gone, running hard down the hall and out the door.

Clay pulled the buggy up in front of the Yancy cabin, leaped off the seat, and went to bang on the door. It was after midnight, and Yancy's voice came roughly: "Who's there? Stand away!"

"Buford! It's me, Clay Rocklin. Open the door!"

Yancy pulled the door open, his face registering his surprise and concern. "What's wrong, Clay?" Even as he spoke, Melora came into the room tying the belt of a robe. Clay looked at the two.

"It's Ellen. I think she's dying — and she's calling for you, Melora."

"I'll get dressed," she said at once and left the room.

"I'll need to change horses, Buford," Clay said, and hurriedly the two men left the cabin. By the time they had switched teams, Melora was ready and got into the buggy.

"I'll have her back when I can, Buford," Clay said, leaping into the seat beside Melora and whipping up the team.

Yancy waved as they left and yelled, "Hope she's better, Clay. Don't spare them horses!"

As the buggy bounced along at top speed,

Clay told Melora of Ellen's condition. "I don't think she can live long," he concluded.

"We must pray," Melora said, and they both did so, silently, all the way back to Gracefield. When they arrived, Clay jumped down, ran around, and reached up to pluck Melora up and set her on the ground. He held her arm as they hurried up the steps, where the door was opened by his father. "How is she?" Clay asked.

"No better, I'm afraid. She keeps dropping off into some sort of coma. You'd better hurry —"

Clay and Melora went at once to Ellen's room, where they found Marianne and Clay's children. As he approached the bed, Clay heard his mother say, "Come, let's give them some time alone." He was vaguely aware of their departure as he bent over, saying, "Ellen." When her eyes opened slowly, he said, "Here's Melora."

Melora came at once to the other side of the bed and took Ellen's hand. "Mrs. Rocklin, can I do anything for you?" She watched as the sick woman's eyes seemed to strain and her lips moved slightly. Melora leaned close, her ear almost touching Ellen's lips. The sick woman was making some sound, trying to talk, but it was vague and indistinct. But Melora finally made out the word.

" 'Forgive'? Is that it, Mrs. Rocklin?" Ellen blinked twice. "You want me to forgive you?" Melora again received the sign. "Oh yes!" she whispered. "I forgive you with all my heart!" She saw Ellen's lips try to move again, leaned close to listen, and thought she understood. "I forgive you everything, Mrs. Rocklin, not just for what happened at the mill, but for all the things in the past. I can forgive you because God has given me a special love for you!"

Ellen was listening, they saw, and at Melora's words, tears gathered in the woman's eyes. Clay gently wiped them away, and Ellen fixed her eyes on him.

"She wants you to forgive her, I think," Melora whispered.

Clay had long ago gotten all bitterness against his wife out of the way — or so he had thought. But now as she looked at him, he realized that he had not been complete in his forgiveness. He bent his head, took her hand, and held it firmly. He put his hand on her cheek and said, "I forgive you, Ellen — for everything. But you must forgive me, too. I treated you and the children terribly. I forgive you. Can you forgive me?"

As Clay and Melora watched, the eyes that had for so long been filled with hate and bitterness grew soft. She blinked twice, and Clay said thickly, "Thank you, Ellen!"

He and Melora sat beside the dying woman, both aware that she was passing from the world. After a few moments, Melora said, "Mrs. Rocklin, I've forgiven you, and so has your husband, but you need the forgiveness that comes from heaven. May I tell you how to get forgiveness from God?"

Clay watched as Melora sat there, her face filled with compassion, speaking of the love of God for sinners. She spoke softly yet with certainty of Jesus — how He had come to save sinners, how He loved all who had sinned and had paid on the cross for their sins. Ellen's eyes were fixed on the young woman, and time and again Clay had to wipe away the tears that ran down his wife's pale cheeks.

Finally Melora said, "I know you can't speak, Mrs. Rocklin, but God knows your heart. I feel He is speaking to your heart now. Jesus wants to come in and make you pure. Would you like for Him to do that?"

Clay hadn't realized he was holding his breath until Ellen blinked twice, and then he let out a sigh of great gladness.

Melora smiled brightly. "Oh, Mrs. Rocklin! I knew you would! Let me pray with you, and as I pray, you pray, too. The words aren't as important as people might think. Jesus died to save you, and He's been waiting for years to hear you call on Him! Now let's ask Him to save you."

As Clay bowed his head and prayed for his wife, his cheeks were damp with tears. Neither he nor Melora could pray eloquently, but both pleaded with God to hear Ellen. When Clay finally opened his eyes, he saw a look in his wife's eyes that he had never seen before. For the first time in her life, Ellen Rocklin's eyes glowed with peace.

Melora began to praise God, for it was clear a miracle had taken place. She and Clay sat with the dying woman for a long time, and finally they rose and called the family. When the others had gathered in the room, Clay told them of Ellen's coming into the kingdom, and there was great rejoicing, for Ellen had been the last member of the family to become a Christian.

Ellen died at sunrise, surrounded by her family. Just as the first rays of the crimson sun broke through the window and fell on her face, she opened her eyes. She looked at Clay, then shifted her gaze from face to face: Denton, David, Lowell, Rena, Susanna, and Thomas. And then Melora.

Clay leaned forward to brush his wife's

hair back from her forehead. "Are you happy, Ellen?"

She looked at him, blinked twice, and then looked toward the sunrise. She seemed to watch the golden bars of light that fell across the room, lighting the faces around her. Then, slowly, she looked again at each face, ending with Clay. He took her in his arms, held her gently. She watched him with eyes that suddenly were filled with love.

Then her eyes closed . . . her breast rose and fell . . . and it was over.

Carefully Clay laid his wife's still form back on the bed and arranged her hair around her forehead. Then he rose and went to his children. "Your mother has gone to be with the Lord."

Melora moved across the room, pausing at the doorway to cast one glance at the family surrounding the bed, embracing each other. Rena's face was pressed against her father's chest, and Clay's sons held him from each side. As Thomas and Susanna moved to be included, Melora left the room. Closing the door, she went outside and looked at the rising sun, tears coming to her eyes as she stood under the sky.

She had never felt so alone. She was a strong woman, but now she felt weak. How long she stood there, fighting back the awful loneliness, she never knew. But then she felt a hand on her shoulder, a hard but gentle hand — and peace came to her, the loneliness fleeing as she turned.

CHAPTER 24
FRANKIE'S DRESS

Once again Paul Bristol practically turned Richmond upside down seeking a place to store his precious wet plates, but to no avail. Richmond was crowded to the walls, and there was no room anywhere to store the plates safely. Finally in despair Paul drove to Hartsworth and put them carefully in his laboratory. Exhausted, he went to his room and fell into bed, sleeping that night and half the next day. When he managed to pull himself out of bed, he remembered the ball in Richmond. Groaning, he stumbled to the washbasin, shaved, then dug out his best suit and put it on.

When he arrived at the DeSpain home, Luci gave him a cold greeting. "You missed the party last night at the Chesnuts," she said, turning her cheek to take his kiss.

"I'm sorry, Luci," Paul muttered. "But I wouldn't have been good company. Frankie and I haven't slept a full night for two weeks. I believe we've taken a picture of every soldier in the Army of Northern Virginia, and of every ditch and fortification in this state!" He was tired and irritable, and when Luci only frowned, he said shortly, "If you don't want to go to the ball, I'll understand."

"Not go!" she exclaimed in astonishment. "What in the world are you talking about, Paul? We've *got* to go to the ball!"

"Well, let's do it, then," he said brusquely, and they left the house and rode along the streets of Richmond. They arrived at the Auction Hall, where the ball was to be held, and they had to wait while gowned ladies and handsomely dressed gentlemen disembarked from carriages and entered the brightly lit structure.

Once inside, they found themselves greeted by friends of Luci, most of whom Paul had met briefly but didn't really know. Luci had grown up in Richmond at the top of the social ladder and was swarmed by a group of young people at once. Glancing around, Paul noted that most of the young men wore gray uniforms. He felt as out of place as a sparrow at a convention of peacocks.

Luci made the situation no better by apologizing over and over for Paul, explaining that he was doing important work and couldn't serve in the army. Once, when she made this explanation to a captain of artillery, Paul said in exasperation, "I'm too old and decrepit to be a soldier, Luci, and the captain doesn't give a bean why I'm not in uniform — do you, Captain?"

The young man was too embarrassed to answer. Luci, on the other hand, was furious — and had plenty to say. When she got Paul alone, she rounded on him and said between clenched teeth, "I don't understand you, Paul; I declare, I don't! You've got to tell people *something*! People look down on every man who isn't in uniform!"

"Well, let them look down, Luci," Paul said wearily. "I'm not going to be wearing a uniform, so we'll just have to live with their looks. But stop apologizing for me, will you?"

They moved to the dance floor and danced the first dance in stony silence. Then Paul surrendered her to a tall young lieutenant named Dale Phillips. "Luci and I are old beaux, you know, Mr. Bristol," Phillips warned him lightly. "I fell in love with her when I was sixteen years old. Better keep an eye on me — I might give you trouble."

Paul liked the young man's direct approach. "All's fair in love and war, Lieutenant," he said with a smile. "If you tamper with her affection, it'll be pistols for two and whiskey for one!" But Phillips could tell by his tone of voice that he wasn't serious, though Luci frowned at her fiancé's seemingly light manner.

Paul turned and made his way to the edge of the dance floor, then heard his name being called. Turning, he saw his mother motioning to him. Going to her, he said, "I heard about Ellen's accident when I got home. How is she?"

"Not well." Marianne frowned. "Claude and I wanted to stay with Tom and Susanna, but we'd agreed to come to this ball. We'll go there after we leave here tonight."

"I'll go by Gracefield, too." Paul looked around the room. "Where's Father . . . and Frankie?"

"Claude's talking with some of the officers in the dining room. I don't think Frankie's come down yet."

Paul frowned. "I hope you got a decent dress for her, Mother." The thought of the last ball came to him, and he shook his head, adding, "And maybe you could keep her from putting on too much makeup."

"Oh, I think the dress will do," Marianne said offhandedly, a twinkle in her eyes. "Why don't you meet her when she comes in so she doesn't have to face the room alone?"

"All right." He looked out over the dance floor to where Luci was gliding across the floor, smiling up into the lieutenant's face. "Luci is happy now," he said without expression. "She doesn't have to feel embarrassed anymore by being with a man who isn't in uniform."

"Isn't that the Phillips boy?" Marianne asked suddenly. "He was engaged to Luci once — or almost engaged — I forget which. But everyone was sure they'd wind up together. He comes from a very wealthy family."

Paul watched the pair for a moment, then shook his head. "Maybe I can get a job as a doorman or something. If a uniform is what she wants, I guess I ought to get one for her."

"Don't be silly! People love one another for what they are, not for what they wear!"

"I suppose." The dance ended, and Paul started to move toward Luci, but before he made two steps, she was claimed by a blond major of the cavalry. Paul gave his mother a caustic smile. "Can't compete with the glamour of the cavalry." He moved away and went at once to the dining room, where a group of men were seated around a table, talking and smoking cigars. Paul took a seat beside his father, listening as the men discussed the only subject of importance: when the fighting would begin, and whether or not Lee could win over McClellan's numbers.

Quickly he grew tired of the talk and whispered, "I'd better go check on Luci."

The room was brightly lit by the chandeliers, and the dance floor was a colorful mosaic of red, green, and yellow dresses glittering under the lights. The men's red and yellow sashes made a brilliant counterpoint to the women's outfits, giving the whole room a festive air.

As Paul entered, he saw that Luci was dancing with Phillips. He waited to feel some jealousy . . . but none came. As he moved through the crowd, he was thoughtful and even puzzled about that. *Shouldn't I care that she's dancing with an old flame? When I was twenty, I'd have called a fellow out for just talking too long with a woman I wanted, but now . . . I don't even care.*

He found a place against the wall and was leaning against it when his mother came to him. "Paul, you've got to do something about Frankie!"

He came away from the wall with a start, looking around the room quickly. "Frankie?

493

What's wrong with her?"

"She's afraid to come into the ballroom. I guess the memory of the last time was too much for her."

Paul didn't even hesitate — a fact that Marianne noted with a barely concealed smile. "Where is she?" he asked firmly. "I'll go get her."

"She's sitting outside in one of those little alcoves. Go out through that door over there, and you'll see a pair of french doors that lead to sort of a tiny garden. Go talk to her, Paul, but for heaven's sake, don't be rough!"

"Rough? What's that supposed to mean?" Paul asked in astonishment.

Marianne put her hand on her son's cheek and held it there. "You always think of her as a sort of tough young hooligan because of the way she's been. But she doesn't need firm handling tonight. She's out there alone and terrified, and she needs a man to treat her gently and to tell her she's attractive. Will you do that, son?"

"Why, certainly, Mother! I must say, you make me out to be quite an insensitive character!" With a sniff he turned and made his way through the crowd, passing outside the main ballroom and entering an empty gallery. He spotted the french doors at once, and as he moved toward them, he thought of his mother's admonition. Setting his jaw, he resolved to do his best with the girl. *We've gotten to be good friends — ought not to be too hard,* he concluded as he stepped outside. His eyes were accustomed to the glare of the lights, and for a moment he stood there, unable to see.

"Frankie?" He spoke quietly. "Are you out here?"

"Yes."

Paul turned to his right and saw her standing beside a large white pillar. He stepped closer, but she stood in the shadow of the pillar, so that all he could see was a shadowy image. "I came to get you," he said quickly. "Let's go inside."

"No. I'm not going in there."

Frankie had been delighted with her time with Marianne Bristol. The two of them had visited every shop in Richmond, or so it seemed. Frankie saw how much it pleased the older woman to look at the dresses, and though she herself was not convinced that she could be made into any sort of beauty, she had enjoyed the shopping. But that afternoon as Marianne had helped her get ready for the ball, her newfound confidence had begun to wane. By the time the music was beginning and she was dressed, she wanted nothing so much as to turn and flee the whole thing!

Still, she had managed to come from the hotel with the Bristols, but the moment she had stepped out of the carriage, she had felt a blind panic. With a muffled excuse, she had escaped to the ladies' dressing room. Marianne had found her there and coaxed her as far as the gallery — but that was when Frankie's courage failed. She had dodged out the french doors, telling Marianne, "You go on. I'm going to stay here!"

Now as Paul stood before her, tall and handsome in his dark suit, his shirt's pure white ruffles gleaming in the moonlight that flooded the garden, she felt herself trembling.

Paul stepped closer and took her arm. "You can't stay out here," he said lightly. "Come on, now, let me see your new dress."

"I don't want to!"

At the stubborn tone of her voice, Paul wanted to pull her out of the shadows, but he remembered his mother's warning to treat her gently. He stood there, trying to think of a way to win her confidence, but nothing came. Finally he said, "Well, I'll tell you what, Frankie, I'm not having a very good time inside, myself."

"You're not?"

"No. Luci only likes to dance with men in uniform, which leaves me out."

"She — she shouldn't do that!"

"Oh, I guess I can see why she'd like the young fellows in their bright new buttons and sashes. A girl likes romance, doesn't she?"

"You look fine! You're romantic enough for —" She suddenly broke off.

Paul laughed. "For what? For you, Frankie? Well, I'm glad to hear that, because I've got an idea." He looked around at the flagstone terrace, which was illuminated by the silver rays of the moon and the amber beams of light that came through the french doors. Then he looked back at her, smiling in a winning way. "This is going to be *our* dance floor, just yours and mine." He looked very young to Frankie at that moment, and she caught her breath when he held his hands out to her. "I think that's a waltz, isn't it? Will you join me, Miss Aimes?"

Bristol looked so fine, and there was such a kind expression on his face, that the fear that had frozen Frankie began to leave. If he had pressured her, she would have resisted, run away. But he just stood there, smiling that gentle smile and holding his hands out to her.

Frankie took a quick breath and then put her hands in his. His fingers closed around hers with a gentle yet firm pressure. He held them, seeming to enjoy the simple act. She felt the strength that was in him, and for once took pleasure in the knowledge that she was weaker. She stood there in the shadows for a long moment, the music floating on the warm air . . . and then she stepped into the gleaming moonlight.

Paul took one look, and his face changed abruptly.

Frankie saw the change at once and shook her head, fighting to hold back the tears of mortification that sprang to her eyes. "You don't like the dress, do you?" she asked softly. She tried to pull her hands away, but he held her fast, his eyes wide as he studied her. He had hoped for some sort of *acceptable* dress — one that would not embarrass the girl — and for some sort of hairstyle and makeup that would not subject her to ridicule. But what stood before him was far more than any of that. What stood before him was an absolute vision.

The dress was a light blue — with just enough green to catch the emerald of Frankie's eyes — and trimmed with silver. Its simple lines fitted Frankie snugly at the waist and bosom, then fell to her feet in graceful folds, setting off but not flaunting her trim figure. For a moment, Paul stared at her wordlessly, finding it impossible to reconcile the youthful and womanly curves he now saw with the girl in baggy clothes to which he'd grown accustomed.

Her hair was arranged in curls that framed her square face, and even in the poor light, he could see the reddish tint that gave such life to her tresses. Somehow the short hair seemed very feminine, for the curls were delicate and moved lightly as she turned her head.

And her face looked so — so *different*! Paul took in the wide eyes and the long, thick lashes that lent the girl an air of mystery. Her cheeks were smooth, and though she had always had a beautiful complexion, now he admired the alabaster sheen of the fine skin on her face and neck. He would not have known her lips, either, for they were soft and full — as though she were waiting to be kissed.

Waiting to be — *!* Paul drew in his breath sharply, startled by the thought, then suddenly noticed that Frankie was trembling. He met her eyes and was shocked to see tears there. With a sinking heart he realized he hadn't responded to her question. He spoke quickly, with a throat that had inexplicably gone dry, making his words hoarse. "Frankie, I — I don't know what to say!"

"It's all right, Paul," she answered huskily. "You don't have to —"

But he broke in as though she hadn't spoken, his voice hushed with wonder. "You look absolutely beautiful!" She lifted her head abruptly, her eyes filled with surprise, and he quickly went on. "I expected you to look presentable enough, of course. I knew Mother would see to that . . . but I never thought to find you so changed!"

"Changed, Paul?"

"Why, didn't you look in the mirror?" Paul demanded. "And it's not just the dress, Frankie — it's *everything*!"

Frankie's lips trembled, and she stared at him, trying hard to believe what she was hearing. "If you like me — the way I look . . . then I don't care what the others think," she whispered.

As if from far off, Paul noticed the music was playing. He smiled down into her eyes. "Our dance?"

Frankie felt him gently pull her into his embrace, and timidly she put her hand on his shoulder. The touch of his hand on her back sent a strange sensation through her as he began to move to the sounds of the waltz. She found herself following him, and as they went around the flagstone terrace, wheeling and turning, she was suddenly aware of what it meant to follow a man's lead. Somehow she *knew* exactly what he would do next, where he would step, which way he would turn. It came to her through the touch of his hand on her back, perhaps, or maybe in the way he held her hand in a tight clasp. No matter how it happened, Frankie Aimes found herself sweeping across the terrace effortlessly and with a grace she had not known was in her, held secure in the arms of Paul Bristol.

As for Bristol, he was speechless. The woman he held in his arms . . . this could *not* be the same boyish figure he'd seen every day for weeks! And yet it was! He had known many women, but none had the innocence and youthful beauty of this one. Perhaps it was the faint trace of awkwardness that set her apart, for the women he'd known had been polished — too much so. Or maybe it was the scent that Frankie wore, a faint fragrance that filled his senses and that somehow made the girl seem even more fragile and feminine.

Fragile! He'd always thought of Frankie as tough, but now he realized that what he'd been seeing was only the image she'd chosen to show the world. She was innocent and vulnerable, and that realization brought a warm rush of sudden protectiveness to him. She seemed very young, and as he looked into her eyes, he found himself feeling younger, too.

Around and around they went, until the music finally stopped. Slowly, almost regretfully, they came to a halt. Paul bowed and she curtsied. Then Paul said with a wicked grin, "I believe the next dance is mine?" he asked.

"Let me look at my program, sir," Frankie responded pertly. She took the small card that Marianne had given her, looked down at the blank lines, pursed her lips — *A most delightful habit, indeed!* Paul thought — and said, "I do think I can spare just *one* dance, Mr. Bristol!"

They danced the next three dances. But Paul eventually realized he could keep her away no longer and said, "Should we go inside? Give the young fellows a shot at the prettiest girl at the ball?"

When she only shook her head and said, "No, please — let's stay out here!" a great gladness filled him, and he swept her back into his arms.

They danced several more times, and finally a very slow set began. "Time for a rest, Miss Aimes," Paul said. He drew her close, and they moved slowly around the terrace. The music was soft, and as they moved in rhythm to its beat, Frankie slowly moved closer — not purposely, but in a natural manner. Paul was acutely conscious of the firm curves of her body as they moved. If it had been any other young woman, he would have known that he was being teased on purpose, but as he looked down into Frankie's face, he saw that the smile on her face was contented and innocent — almost as though she were unaware of her partner.

They moved more slowly as the music died. With a sigh, she looked up and said, "The dance is over —," but broke off as their eyes met. There was a still moment that caught at both of them. Paul knew in that moment that he had never seen anything lovelier than Frankie's face and nothing had ever filled him with such a sense of wonder as her wide and trusting eyes. Slowly he pulled her closer. "My mother told me to do something, Frankie."

"What was it?"

"She said, 'Be gentle with Frankie, and tell her she's the most beautiful girl at the ball.' " His arms tightened around her, and she rested her cheek against his chest, looking up at him. His eyes roamed her face, and he whispered, "You *are* beautiful, Frankie!" And then, without haste, he lowered his head and put his lips on hers.

Frankie could have moved her head aside, but she did not. When his lips touched hers, she waited to feel the fear and disgust that had filled her when Alvin Buck had kissed her — but this time, she felt only a sense of trust . . . and joy. Paul's arms drew her tighter, and she surrendered to his embrace, for the first time in her life knowing the richness of womanhood without shame.

As for Bristol, he found that there was a gentleness in him that he had never felt for any woman. Frankie was soft and yielding, her lips fresh and innocent. He wanted to go on holding her, to never let her out of his arms or his life, for she stirred him as no woman ever had.

At last he pulled his head back and said huskily, "Frankie, you are the sweetest young woman in the world —"

At that moment the french doors swung open, and Luci DeSpain's voice snapped across the terrace. "Well, Paul, are you quite finished?"

Frankie stepped back, her face flushed, and Paul said hurriedly, "Now, Luci, don't be upset —," but that was as far as he got.

Luci could have borne it if Paul had been

chasing any other girl — any girl, at least, of *class*. But her voice was icy as she cut him off. "Paul, I've seen this coming for some time. Well, you've got what you want now, so I won't stand in your way. Here!" She pulled off the ring he'd given her and thrust it at him, then turned and stalked away, her back straight.

Paul stared at the ring, then looked up at Frankie. He saw the humiliation on her face and said quickly, "This isn't your doing, Frankie. It's been coming for some time. Don't let it upset you."

But it had upset her, and she whispered, "Will you take me to the hotel?"

"Of course. Let me tell my parents and get your coat."

It was a difficult ride, for Paul was aware of how hurt the young woman was. She kept her face averted, refusing to speak. When they got to the hotel, he started to get out, but she said, "Please . . . don't come in. I — just want to be alone."

"Frankie —"

"Please! I–I'll see you in the morning, if you want."

"Well, all right, but tomorrow things will look better."

"Good night, Paul," she murmured and ran into the hotel without looking back. She unlocked her door and stepped inside, then closed it and threw herself on the bed and wept, muffling her sobs by pressing her face into the covers. She didn't know how long she lay there, but after some time she sat up and held her arms across her breasts. Catching her reflection in the mirror on the wall opposite the bed, she noted with disgust that her hair was in disarray and her eyes were red and swollen.

But that was not the worst of it. Somehow . . . she felt ashamed, but did not know why. Could it be that her feelings when Paul had kissed her were shameful? Had she been wrong to kiss him back? She had no experience in such things — only the few kisses Tyler had given her, and they didn't compare in any way to what she had shared with Paul — so she just sat there until a dullness set in. Listlessly she undressed, throwing the dress across a chair with revulsion. A fine nightgown lay across the bed — a gift from Marianne — but she reached out for her familiar old nightshirt and pulled it on. Then she put out the light, slipped under the covers, and lay there in the darkness.

Images of Paul came again and again. She remembered each step of every dance, and she remembered the laughter and the sight of his face. How young he had looked tonight! And how happy! She closed her eyes and could feel his arms around her and his lips against hers — and then all broke into disarray when she remembered Luci bursting into the little world that she had found so wonderful.

Finally she dozed off, but her sleep was fitful and filled with restless dreams. When a sharp knock sounded on her door, she sat bolt upright. The knock came again, followed by two more.

Tyler! That knock was the sign they had agreed on! She came out of the bed, slipped into her robe, and opened the door. Her friend stood there wearing an old black coat and a shapeless hat that she'd never seen before. His face was pale, his mouth a mere slit.

"Tyler! What is it?" she whispered.

He stepped into the room, saying in terse tones, "Get dressed, Frankie! Quickly!"

She saw that he was tense as a wire and said, "Turn your back." While she dressed in her old clothing, she asked, "What's happened?"

"They're onto me — and you, too, I think."

"Tyler! How could they be?"

"A double agent," he said grimly. He related how he'd been on the move, getting what information he could about troop locations, but he'd been betrayed by a man named Henson, a Confederate spy who had managed to get into Pinkerton's service. "I gave him the slip, but he'll have everyone in the country on the lookout for me! We've got to get back through the lines — and it's going to be tricky."

Dressed and ready, Frankie came to put her hand on his arm. "What are we going to do?"

"Pinkerton's waiting for us at a place called Miller's Crossing. It's pretty safe, if we can get to it. I've got two fast horses, and one of our agents is going to guide us through the backcountry. Are you ready?"

"No. I — have to write a letter."

"There's no time for that!"

"You go on, then!" Frankie blazed at him. "I'll get out on my own!"

Tyler stared at her; then a weary smile broke across his face. "Write your letter. I'll wait."

Frankie found a pen and paper and sat down at the small desk in the room. She wrote steadily for ten minutes, then put down the pen, folded the letter, and put it in an envelope. She wrote the name *Paul Bristol* across the front of the envelope, then put it faceup on the table. "Let me throw my things in a bag, and I'm ready."

Five nerve-wracking hours later, she and Tyler stood at dawn in a small room, facing Allan Pinkerton. They had given him the positions of the Confederate Army, and when they were finished, Pinkerton said, "Good! I'll get this to General McClellan." He half turned, then wheeled back to say with a small smile, "You two have done well. But don't show your faces in Richmond! Go back to Washington. I'll send for you when I get back."

"Not for me, Mr. Pinkerton," Frankie said, looking him in the eyes. "Remember what you promised."

Pinkerton nodded at once. "Then take with you our thanks, Frankie. You've served well." He glanced at the young man, asking sharply, "You'll see that she gets back safely?"

"Yes, sir, I will!"

Pinkerton left, and Tyler stood there, suddenly very tired. "Well, it's over. I wonder if what we did was worth it all?"

Frankie stared at him, her lips trembling. "I hope so, Tyler — but how much would that have to be to make up for betraying people who love you?"

Tyler looked at her sharply. "People who love you . . . or people you love?"

Frankie felt a blush color her cheeks, but her gaze didn't waver. Reading his answer in her eyes, Tyler looked stricken.

"But — what about *us*, Frankie?"

Her eyes softened, and she reached out to touch his arm lightly. "Tyler, I admire you so much . . . but there could never be anything more between us than friendship. There is only one man for me, Tyler —" Her voice cracked. "And I doubt he will ever want to see me again. I — I don't know what's ahead for me, but whatever it is, I'll have to face it on my own."

He started to protest, but she halted him by holding up her hand. His eyes searched her face, and the pain he saw reflected there struck him deeply. He lowered his eyes to the floor, struggling with a sense of defeat.

Frankie wanted to comfort him, but she knew instinctively that the greatest kindness she could show her friend was to walk away. She turned and left the room, not pausing as she walked down the hallway and out the door of the building. She mounted her horse and spurred it into a run, and Tyler had to hurry to mount and catch up. Behind them the rumble of distant cannon fire sounded, and the dark horizon flickered with tiny spurts of flame.

Frankie rode on, her eyes half blinded

with tears. She said nothing to Tyler as they rode away from the sound of the guns, and he knew that Frankie Aimes was not the same girl who had ridden out of Washington a few months earlier.

CHAPTER 25
"YOU'RE A WOMAN!"

Always when the harvest had come, Silas Aimes had been aware that the most certain factor in the process would be Frankie and the work she did.

Now as the last August sun seemed to drag itself over the inverted gray circle of the sky, it was harvesttime. But Aimes was aware that this harvest was to be different. Unless, of course, Frankie came to herself!

He chopped wood steadily, each movement precise and machinelike, and was troubled by thought. Usually he performed routine tasks without much thought, but since Frankie had come back, he had been shaken from his routine in several ways.

Aimes didn't like changes. He'd been heard to say, "There've been a lot of changes since I was a young man, and I've been against every one of them!" His splitting maul struck the round cylinder, and the two pieces fell neatly to the ground. He picked up one, split it, and then grabbed the other.

Frankie used to do some of the wood splitting. He straightened up and turned his eyes toward the house, and a frown creased his brow. *What'd she come back for if she didn't want to work?*

And yet he knew that wasn't quite right. From the minute she'd come back three weeks ago, she had worked — but not in the old way. She'd dressed differently, acted differently. Aimes snorted. *Wears a dress all the time — spends all day cooking and working inside the house!*

He piled his arms high with the split wood, walked to the house, and entered the kitchen. Dumping the sticks inside the wood box, he turned to Frankie and the two girls who were standing over the stove. "What you three up to?"

"I'm teaching them to make candy," Frankie said. She was wearing a simple brown dress, and somehow it bothered Silas. She looked so — so *womanly* in it. He'd never thought of her as a woman, not particularly. Now the very way she held the bowl and stirred it with a wooden spoon — why, she didn't seem at all like a boy, not anymore.

"Need some more wood split," Aimes said, and he cast a watchful eye to see the effect his speech had on Frankie.

"I'll tell Monroe to do it when he comes in." Les Monroe was the teenage neighbor who had come to take up the slack that Frankie had left. Silas had assumed that he could let the boy go and save the cost of his wages now that she was home, but it hadn't turned out that way. He stared at Frankie, half tempted to tell her that she wasn't too good to split a little wood — but for some reason he decided not to. He turned and stalked out of the kitchen.

Frankie knew what was on her father's mind but had never made an issue of it. When she'd come back, she had needed the solitude of the farm. It had taken awhile, but slowly she had lost the tense look around her lips. Now she had grown more peaceful and relaxed, though she was still unwilling to speak of what she'd done while away from the farm. A fact that caused the two younger Aimes girls no end of curiosity — or frustration, for Frankie wouldn't answer even one of their constant questions.

Timothy knew her best and so asked no questions at all. Not at first. He saw that she was on edge and carefully gave her his attention when she needed it and let her alone when she required that. On her first day back, she had told him about becoming a Christian, and he'd been filled with joy and relief. He'd known the time would come for Frankie to find God, and he was grateful it had finally happened. But as for the other things that troubled her . . . well, he would just wait until she was ready to talk about it.

He knew, of course, that some great change had taken place in her. Not just because she now shunned men's work, seeking instead the work usually done by women. No, it went much deeper than that, and Timothy, for all his isolation, was very insightful. *She's met a man somewhere,* he decided very soon. *And I'd guess he let her down.*

Frankie had known they were all puzzled by her behavior but could not bear to speak of Paul or of her work for Pinkerton. She tried to block it all out of her mind, filling her days with teaching the girls the simple skills, keeping house, and reading book after book.

That worked very well during the days, but the nights were long, and nothing seemed to stop the memories from trooping in the moment she closed her eyes. Then there were the dreams — full of images of Tyler and Pinkerton . . . and Paul. Many mornings she rose looking more worn out than when she'd gone to bed, and she knew Timothy watched her with concern — and prayed for her constantly.

As the days passed, though, she began to grow calmer — the monotony of the life was good for her — and she slowly became more talkative.

"What's wrong with her, anyway?" Silas asked Timothy once. "She's acting mighty strange."

"I don't know about that, Pa," Timothy said, shrugging. "I think she's acting *right* for the first time."

Silas had glared at him, frustrated by what he sensed was criticism. He'd had his own thoughts of the thing and was a man who hated to admit he was wrong. "She was happy enough until she run off," he grunted. "Wisht she'd never of done it!"

Finally Silas Aimes gave up. *She ain't never gonna be no good to me except as a cook.* When he came to that conclusion, the tension that had surrounded him passed, and he found himself strangely content with his family. The food was better, the house was well kept, and the work got done outside. He was vaguely relieved, feeling that he had successfully solved a problem.

One Friday evening they were all sitting down to an early supper when they heard the sound of a horse outside. Silas looked at Timothy. "Who kin that be?" he asked, and when a knock sounded, he got up and went to the door. Opening it, he found himself facing a tall, well-dressed man who looked to be in his thirties.

"I'm looking for the Aimes place," he said.

Frankie was standing at the stove, taking out biscuits. She turned out of curiosity to see who was at the door and, at the sound of the voice, dropped the pan of biscuits. Timothy rose and picked them up, but when he started to tease Frankie, he stopped abruptly, for her face was pale and she was trembling.

Silas Aimes had turned around at the sound of the biscuit tin hitting the floor, and he, too, noted that Frankie was upset. At once he turned back to the man, his eyes narrowing. "I'm Silas Aimes," he said gruffly. "Who are you?"

Paul Bristol looked over the man's shoulder, aware that this obviously was the father of the clan. When his eyes met Frankie's startled stare, he smiled.

"Well? Answer me!" Aimes demanded. "Who are you? What've you come here for?"

Still holding Frankie's gaze, Bristol drawled, "Well, Mr. Aimes, who am I? I'm the man who's going to be your son-in-law.

As for what I came for . . ." He paused, then stepped past Aimes and went right across the room to stand in front of Frankie. "I've come for you," he said quietly.

A dead silence fell on the room, and then Timothy said, "Well, I'm your future brother-in-law. My name's Timothy." He put out a thin hand and smiled. "Welcome to the family."

Paul returned the smile, immediately liking this young man. He took Timothy's hand, then turned and said, "Mr. Aimes, I've come to ask for your daughter in marriage. I love her." He glanced at Frankie sideways, grinning. "And I think she loves me."

"Well, if you don't beat all — !" Silas Aimes burst out. "You come in here, a total stranger, and want to take my daughter? Get out!"

Paul did not seem disturbed by the old man's anger. He turned to Frankie and asked, "Will you come for a walk with me, Frankie?"

Frankie's hands were trembling, a fact she tried to hide by snatching off her apron. "Yes, but not for long!" She led the way out of the kitchen, not even noticing her blustering father, and Bristol closed the door behind them.

"Is he really gonna marry Sister?" Jane asked, her eyes large as silver dollars.

"I'd say he's a man who's used to getting his own way," Timothy answered with a grin. "Better get used to it, Pa. She's gonna rare a bit, but you can be sure she'll have him."

Outside Frankie had walked rapidly until she came to a large oak, then turned and began, indeed, to "rare" at Paul.

"You must think you're really something," she said coldly. "Marry you! Whatever gave you such an idea —"

Paul took off his hat and let it fall to the ground. When she had first disappeared, leaving only that cursed note, he'd had a bad time of it. He'd had to struggle through feelings of betrayal and anger — he'd even wanted to hunt her down and make her pay for what she'd done. A spy! He could scarcely believe it. But since it had been there, written in her own hand, he'd had to believe it. Then, after too many sleepless nights had made him almost impossible to live with, his mother had taken him aside for a talk. It hadn't taken long for the real source of his pain to come out: He couldn't bear losing Frankie. He could live without a lot of things, but he'd discovered that he couldn't stand the thought of life without her! He knew from her note why she had worked for Pinkerton — and he knew they would need to really talk things out someday — but right now, none of that mattered. All that was important was that he loved her — and he wasn't returning home without her.

He paid no heed to her protests. He simply waited until she ran down, then said simply, "Frankie, I had to come. I've told other women I loved them, but now I know it wasn't so. I wish I'd never said those words before, because I want to say them for the first time to you."

Frankie grew very still, her eyes searching his face. He stepped forward and took her face gently between his hands. When her eyes opened very wide, he whispered, "Never be afraid of me, Frankie. I'd cut my arms off before I'd hurt you." He lowered his head and kissed first her forehead, then her cheeks. "You must know that I love you, Frankie." His breath fanned her face gently as he spoke. "And I'm not leaving here without you." She shivered and closed her eyes, and he kissed her eyelids. "So you'd better agree to marry me, because I don't think your father and I would do so well living in the same house for too long." She gave a half laugh, half sob, and he covered her mouth with his, kissing her gently. She went completely still for a few moments, then, with a soft cry, threw her arms around him and held him fiercely.

His arms went around her possessively, and he smiled as she said in a muffled voice, "I — thought I'd lost you!"

Reaching down, he lifted her face. "You're never going to lose me — never!"

"I prayed that God would help you understand, that you wouldn't hate me. . . ." Her voice trailed off.

"Well, you gave Him a pretty tough assignment, at least at first. But you and God had a pretty effective tool in my mother. She helped set me straight one day." He smiled at the memory of their conversation.

"Paul Bristol," she had finally said, *"if you don't go after that girl and bring her back, then I'll know I've raised a complete fool!"*

He looked into Frankie's eyes and went on. "She helped me see what mattered most to me, and so I came here to claim it . . . to claim you. So you might just as well marry me, Miss Aimes, because I'll be hanged if I'm going to live without you!"

Then he kissed her, letting the fierce emotions he'd been holding back spill out — and she kissed him back with equal fervor. They clung to each other, and finally Bristol said, "I'm too old for you, I haven't got any money, and have absolutely no prospects. Will you marry me?"

Laughter bubbled up in Frankie, and her eyes twinkled merrily as she cried out, "Yes!" He held her tight against his chest, and she snuggled close, feeling safe, protected, and cherished.

After a few precious moments, they started back to the cabin, but Paul kept Frankie nestled close against his side as they walked. She glanced up at him and asked about his people. "They all hate me, don't they?"

"They don't have anything to hate you for." Surprise showed on her face, and he shrugged. "Only my parents and I read your note. We didn't see any reason to tell anyone else about it. The authorities did suspect Tyler, and after talking to the hotel clerk, they believed he had an accomplice. But no one had any idea it was you. We were questioned about Tyler, seeing as we are family, but we could tell them quite honestly we didn't know what he'd been doing or where he had gone." He looked down at her, smiling tenderly. "It was wise of you not to write anything about him in your note. So nobody knows about your involvement except Mother, Father, and myself. My parents won't say anything, because they understand . . . and because they happen to love you. They know you only did what you had to. And they want you to come home."

She laughed ruefully, and her eyes were green in the sunlight. "All the spying I did — and it didn't do a bit of good! General Lee whipped the socks off Little Mac! I might as well have stayed at home!"

"I'm glad you didn't," Paul said. He stopped and drew her close again. "You and I are different from most others, my love. Neither of us believe in the war. But I do believe that when it's over, we may be able to help bring healing — to both sides."

"What will we do until then?" Frankie asked. She looked up at him, and he smiled down at her.

"You're a woman, Frankie," Bristol said. "You'll be that, and I'll be the man who loves you." He kissed her gently. "That's good enough for me. Is it enough for you?"

With a contented sigh, Frankie leaned against him. "Oh yes, Paul, it's enough!"

ABOUT THE AUTHOR

Award-winning, bestselling author, **Gilbert Morris** is well known for penning numerous Christian novels for adults and children since 1984 with 6.5 million books in print. He is probably best known for the forty-book House of Winslow series, and his *Edge of Honor* was a 2001 Christy Award winner. He lives with his wife in Gulf Shores, Alabama.

The employees of Thorndike Press hope you have enjoyed this Large Print book. All our Thorndike, Wheeler, and Kennebec Large Print titles are designed for easy reading, and all our books are made to last. Other Thorndike Press Large Print books are available at your library, through selected bookstores, or directly from us.

For information about titles, please call:
  (800) 223-1244

or visit our Web site at:
  http://gale.cengage.com/thorndike

To share your comments, please write:
  Publisher
  Thorndike Press
  10 Water St., Suite 310
  Waterville, ME 04901